THE DEATH OF PERRY MANY PAWS

Deborah Benjamin

2013

The Death of Perry Many Paws. Copyright©Deborah Benjamin, 2013
All rights reserved

ISBN-10: 1494252597
ISBN-13: 9781494252595

Author photograph: Mark Benjamin
Cover design and illustration: Marie Buckley

To my parents, Patricia and Richard Bessey, who brought me up in a world where everything had a funny side and laughter was always preferable to tears. I miss you every day.

Acknowledgments

The following people have all contributed to making this book happen. Without their support I'd still be convinced that solving a murder is easier than creating a book.

My husband, Mark, for giving me time and space to write and for gently prodding me to keep moving when I got discouraged.

My readers and editors: Richard Benjamin, Melinda Ginter and Kathy Johncox.

Yes Richard, women do really talk like that.

Mindy, I have no idea how the fire in Tamsen's library is always ready to be lit.

Kathy, thank you for hacking through the jungle of self-publishing and then being a good friend and coming back to lead me through.

My cover artist, Marie Buckley, who took a vague idea and turned it into reality.

My world revolves around six people. Without your daily love and support I'd be lost. Mark, Richard, Daniel, Mindy, Mama and Ope, I love you.

To: Timothy Fletcher, Editor

From: Tamsen Mack

Re: Draft of the opening page of Perry Many Paws Book #6

Date: September 1

Tim-

I want to go in a different direction for the sixth Perry Many Paws book. What do you think of this as a start?

Tamsen

Perry Many Paws stretched his six furry legs and tried to touch the top of his cave with his six chubby paws. He was hungry but he was happy to see the sun shining into the mouth of his cave. He rubbed his fat tummy and wiggled his back against the stone floor. Then he rolled over to his feet. It was a happy new day for exploring and adventure!

Perry stood at the opening to his cave and looked out. Suddenly Perry realized he wasn't happy any more. Something was wrong with this day. He scratched each side of his head with his two front paws and rubbed his tummy with his two middle paws. Why wasn't he happy? Then he remembered. Squeaky Squirrel and Friendly Frog were gone. He needed to find some new friends.

Tamsen-

New friends? Are you insane? Absolutely not. The kids love Squeaky Squirrel and Friendly Frog. Don't mess with a good thing. Keep to the formula.

Tim

Chapter One

"**D**oes anyone else hate Perry Many Paws as much as I do?" I asked, grabbing the last chocolate cannoli and pacing around my library. I turned to the three other members of our Women of a Certain Age group, otherwise known as WOACA—Grace, Syra and Diane. Bing, Syra's brother and our official pastry chef, ignored my familiar lament as he laid more pastries on the plate.

"All I know is that perimenopause is costing me a fortune in home pregnancy kits. These irregular periods are terrifying," Diane said. "The doctor said this perimenopause stage can last for years. Sometimes I'm totally regular and other times I ..."

"I'm talking about my character, Perry Many Paws, not your missed periods," I said.

"Oh, well, him. We're trying to be supportive of what you're going through with your editor, Tamsen, but it's hard to empathize with someone who actually has a career," Diane said softly. Diane never raised her voice or got angry. She was the most serene person I knew. The only aspect of Diane that was not serene was her hair, which sprang up all over her head like a Chia Pet on steroids.

I agreed that I'd been pretty lucky with my writing and sank into the only remaining seat—my daughter Abbey's beanbag chair. Hopefully someone would remember to help me out of it before they left or I'd be stranded here indefinitely. The library of my rambling 19th century house was one of my favorite rooms and the beanbag chair didn't really blend with the décor. But it was Abbey's favorite chair and, even with her away at college, I couldn't bear to move it.

"I can't believe you and your editor, Tim whatever, can't come to some agreement," Syra said, stretching toward Bing's dessert platter and helping herself. Syra had recently had a double mastectomy and was undergoing radiation treatments. She was suffering from hot flashes and other symptoms of menopause. We'd gotten used to her removing layers of clothing and fanning herself with whatever was available. Bing was devoted to her and dedicated to fattening her up and getting her back to her high-energy self. Bing rarely left their house but he always baked for WOACA and seemed content to help us stuff ourselves with pastry and listen to us bemoan the perils of middle age. Bing didn't really have a life.

I heard the back door open and the clicking of toenails as my dog Mycroft, the world's most lethargic bloodhound, slowly sauntered past the library door. He was followed by my husband, Cam, who poked his head in the door, saw that the weekly meeting of WOACA was still in session, and quickly disappeared after giving me a cross-eyed grin. I grinned back. There is really nothing cuter than a fifty year-old redhead with freckles, especially when you are still madly in love with him after twenty-five years of marriage.

"To be honest, Tamsen, I think you should either piss or get off the pot. If you don't want to write anymore, then just quit." Grace Trenary Kelly licked the cannoli filling off her fingers and slumped her Rubenesque body deeper into the sofa cushions. "Good cannolis, Bing."

WOACA is our forum for dissent against middle age but not against each other, and we all sat and stared for several seconds, absorbing the change in the emotional atmosphere. Grace was one of my dearest friends and she was rarely cross with anyone, especially me. Only her stepson, Ryan, could make her so surly.

"What's Ryan done now?" I asked.

Grace slumped even deeper into the cushions until her legs stuck out straight in front of her and she seemed in danger of sliding onto the floor like a hunk of dough off a well-greased cookie sheet.

"I have no idea why I got married in the first place. Hugh and I were happy dating. We did it successfully for eight years. I don't think people are meant to marry for the first time when they're almost fifty years old. What's the point?"

We were hard pressed to reassure her, as we all had the same thought when she and Hugh decided to get married two years ago. They seemed to have a perfect relationship. But then Hugh's ex-wife had died in a car accident and his son, Ryan, had come to live with him fulltime. Hugh started pushing for marriage shortly after Ryan moved in and Grace had caved.

I was beginning to get a headache, feeling my own creative frustrations, worried about Grace's marital woes, concerned about Syra's health and anticipating Diane's quiet, controlled rant about her elderly parents and her teenage children. Diane was the poster woman for the sandwich generation.

In addition to the conflicts with my editor, I had been suffering from empty nest syndrome since Abbey, my only child, had left for college in Boston the previous month. I wasn't able to wallow in it too much, though, because Cam was even more upset and lonely than I was. I spent a lot of time reassuring him that Abbey was doing what we raised her to do and we were good parents. Being a woman of a certain age had its difficulties. In many ways it had been easier being a teenager—hormones, angst and all.

I was jarred out of my self-indulgent reverie by the sound of purring. We had long ago learned not to look around on the floor for a cat, as it was the ringtone of Diane's phone. Since no one in her family could go for long without calling her, we had become oblivious to the sound. She ratted around in her purse trying to find the phone.

"Hello …" As was the custom, Diane would just murmur and nod for most of the call. No one in her family seemed to understand the art of conversation but they were well-versed in the practice of venting.

"Both keys? Well, they must have one at the front desk. Or the housekeeping people can … No, I don't have an extra key. Just go to the front desk … Yes, I'm sure it happens all the time. No one is going to move you to the dementia wing. No, sorry, I don't know what *gourmet* macaroni and cheese is. Okay. Bye."

"Your mom?" Syra asked. "How are they settling into their new apartment?"

"They love it at Bugg Hill but they haven't gotten used to taking a key with them when they leave their apartment. My mom is in constant fear of letting anyone know they forgot something, or that they're confused. She thinks they'll haul her screaming and fighting to the dementia wing. Oh, and they're having *gourmet* macaroni and cheese for dinner," Diane informed us. I was sure that tomorrow would start with a phone call from her mom telling her exactly what made macaroni and cheese gourmet when served at the Bugg Hill Senior Living Home.

Diane didn't seem too worried about her parents, so I started in again about my career frustrations. "Is it unreasonable for me to want to do something else with my characters? After all, I'm the author. I created Perry Many Paws. If I want Perry to have new friends or to do something different I have the right, don't I?"

Everyone nodded and murmured various levels of agreement.

"My editor doesn't like any kind of change. With him, everything is so formulaic. If it worked in books one through five then we need to do the same thing in book six. Well, what if I don't *want* to do the same thing in book six? If Dr. Seuss had my editor he would have followed *The Cat in the Hat* with *The Pig in the Wig* and *The Frog in the Fog*. We would've been deprived of *Green Eggs and Ham* ..."

"Exactly. What kind of world would that be?" Grace chimed in.

Diane leaned toward me timidly. "But Perry Many Paws and his friends are so successful, why ..."

"Now you sound like my editor!"

"Maybe you could use the same characters but have them do something a little different," Diane suggested. "What if you change the location of their next adventure? Take them out of the woods and away from Perry's cave and have them go to a lake or the mountains or something. Would that make you feel more fulfilled as a writer?"

"No. I want to do something completely different with Perry. Give him some new friends, for instance. Whatever made me give him friends with names like Squeaky Squirrel and Friendly Frog? Squirrels don't squeak and even if they did, squeaking is an annoying sound, not an endearing one. And Friendly Frog is so bland. If he has to be friendly all the time he's impossible to work with in an interesting way. I hate Squeaky and Friendly. I want some edgier characters."

Diane shook her head. "I don't think children's books are supposed to have edgy characters."

"How about Promiscuous Pig and Horny Owl?" Grace suggested. "Having a slutty pig and a randy owl to work with should give you a little more leeway in your story lines."

"Now, Grace ..." Diane admonished, but I burst into laughter. This was the Grace I knew and loved.

"That's exactly what I need, Grace. I wish my editor understood as well as you do."

"Well," Grace pulled herself into a more upright position on the couch. "Now that we've resolved Tamsen's crisis, maybe we can work on the fact that my marriage is falling apart and my stepson hates me and the feeling may be mutual."

"What happened?" I asked.

"For starters, you all know he hates me. I understand that his life's been totally uprooted in the past two years since his mother died and he moved in fulltime with Hugh. Then I moved in shortly after, but that was two years ago. Shouldn't things be better now?"

"So what has he done now?" I asked. I was sure there was more to this than just the same old "he hates me" complaint.

"Last night he told Hugh that he didn't want to have friends come over to the house because he was embarrassed ..."

Diane shook her head, her hair continuing to vibrate for several seconds after she stopped. "That doesn't make any sense. You and Hugh have a beautiful house with ..."

"It's not the house that embarrasses him, Diane, it's me. He told Hugh that he was embarrassed to have friends over because I was so fat ..."

"And Hugh *told* you he said that?" Bing burst out. He jumped up and squeezed onto the couch with Grace, hugging her. If anyone could commiserate with Grace it would be Bing. Grace was 5'7" and carried her weight well; Bing was about 5'1" and built in a perfect circle.

Grace hugged him back. "I was witness to the whole thing. Hugh was outraged and completely lost it. He and Ryan followed each other around the house screaming and threatening each other. I was afraid they were going to get in a fist fight and we were going to end up featured on some horrible reality show."

"I hate those shows," Bing said.

"It was so ugly. I've never lived like that before. My family was always so quiet. I pretty much hate my life right now. I loved being Grace Trenary but I hate being Grace Kelly."

Diane nodded. "I just want a minute to myself. I hate my cell phone."

"I just want my body to feel normal again. I hate feeling sore and tired all the time," Syra added.

"I want Abbey to move back home and I want the freedom to write what I want to write," I chimed in. "I hate Perry Many Paws. I wish I could kill him."

***

I was lying in bed thinking about what it would be like to wish I hadn't gotten married, when the man who made me glad I was married came to bed.

"I was just texting with Abbey," he said. "Is there some reason no one actually *talks* on the phone anymore? It takes ten times longer to have a conversation by text, but when I tell Abbey I'll call, she says she likes texting better."

I snuggled into the crook of his arm. "That's because she can do other things while you text," I explained. "The last time we talked by text she was able to put her laundry in the dryer and was writing an anthropology paper on the Bog Man. It's the younger generation multitasking with more efficiency than we ever imagined."

Cam rubbed my back and nuzzled my neck. "Regardless, I would like my daughter's full attention at least once in a while. I'm going to call her tomorrow and have a real conversation with an immediate response rather than asking a question and waiting until she changes her sheets before she replies."

"I'd be thrilled to think she was even changing her sheets. Please don't interrupt that."

"You know what I mean …"

I rolled over on top of him. "Do you know what I mean?"

Cam laughed and pulled me close. "I sure hope so."

I completely forgot to ask him if he was glad he'd married me. Anyway, I already had the answer.

Chapter Two

I'm not being modest when I say that I live in the ugliest house in Birdsey Falls. The house was built in the 1880s by Roger Behrends, Cam's great-grandfather. Unfortunately, Roger Behrends, aka Birdsey Falls' own "Robber Baron," as he was nicknamed, had more money and ego than taste. He designed the house himself based on castles he had visited during an extended stay in England in the early 1860s, successfully avoiding the "unpleasantness" of the Civil War. He hurried back to the United States in 1865 at the conclusion of the war to take advantage of the post-war cleanup—financial cleanup. He made his fortune in the South and then settled up north in Birdsey Falls, and built this monstrous house.

If he'd kept to a single design, the house might have been more pleasing to look at. Instead, he created a sprawling Victorian style house and added what he considered improvements, making it ostentatious—his intent—and ugly as sin—probably not his intent. I'm quite attached to the house and while I know it's ugly I have grown to love it. The library and the solarium are my favorite rooms. The library is dark paneled with a high ceiling. There is a massive fireplace on one wall, and tall long windows that stretch from ceiling to floor on the opposite wall. The other two walls are ceiling to floor dark cherry built-in bookcases. There's even a secret passage behind one of the bookcases that contains a narrow staircase that leads to the master bedroom. I sometimes make use of it running back and forth on the perilous staircase to exchange a book late in the night when the hot flashes hit and I can't sleep.

Roger the Robber Baron outlived each of his three wives and most of his eleven children. When he died, he left the house to Alden Behrends, his only surviving son, apparently forgetting that he also had three living daughters. Growing up among numerous brothers and sisters, Alden had a more realistic view of his place in the world and, thankfully, more aesthetic taste. He had the enormous Arc de Triomphe, the stone lions and the six story watchtower at the entrance to the property removed and replaced with beautiful wrought iron gates. He took the monstrous ballroom and divided it into several cozy family-sized rooms, including a train room for his three children, Alden Jr., Franklin and Claudia. He also added the solarium, a perfectly proportioned circular room with walls made up of windows that look out on the gardens.

The solarium is the one true beauty in this rambling hodgepodge of a house. You walk down a dark, paneled hallway lined with portraits of Behrends that seem to extend back to the days of cave painting. This dreary passageway leads you to a breathtaking sight that can actually bring tears to your eyes as you enter the room flooded with light and color. It's the feeling you get when you go from the cacophony of a crowded restaurant to the silence of a church. You are physically, spiritually, mentally and emotionally lighter, as if you are walking into the presence of a great spirit. You cannot be unhappy in this room. Entering my solarium is the closest you'll get to "walking into the light" and still be alive to tell about it.

You are instantly enveloped by a rainbow of colors streaming through all the windows. It's like you're in a Monet garden, with the light and the windows giving the outside flowers the foggy and unfocused look of an Impressionistic painting. On various delicate antique tables around the room are enormous vases of flowers from the garden, echoing the outdoor vista with an added dimension of color and fragrance. It is my spot of heaven on earth and I wish that its architect had been allowed to tackle the rest of the house.

Cam's mother, Claudia, inherited the house when her father died. Her brother Alden Jr., a Princeton graduate, had died at Pearl Harbor. Her brother Franklin, the imaginative and creative one, had also shown a great deal of promise. He had started getting "strange" during his mid-teens and eventually drifted into a hermit-like existence, never marrying and preferring to live in the old gardener's cottage on the Behrends property. So Alden Sr. had left the house to Claudia along with money in trust for Franklin, enough to take care of him for the rest of his life. Perhaps by leaving the house to his only daughter, Alden Sr. felt he was making amends to his three sisters who were ignored in his father's will. My guess is that wherever they were, they agreed it was way too little, much too late.

I remember the first time I saw The Castle, as it was affectionately or derisively called, depending on your viewpoint. I had just graduated from college with a degree in English and had answered an ad for a summer job.

Wanted for the summer: College graduate with good organizational skills, a sense of direction, no allergies and a love of books needed to catalog extensive family library. Ability to tell a first-edition Charles Dickens from a Harlequin Romance preferred.

They also offered room and board and a weekly salary that worked out to a dollar over minimum wage for a forty-hour week, more money than I had ever made in my life. I immediately sent a letter and resume to C. Mack, address The Castle in Birdsey Falls. I was hired, sight unseen.

The day I arrived, a petite, well-dressed woman answered the door and introduced herself as Claudia Behrends Mack. I assumed she was the C. Mack of the ad and therefore would have a good sense of humor. I soon discovered that she wasn't and she didn't.

"You must be the girl we hired from the advertisement."

I nodded my head and introduced myself as she looked me up and down, neither approving nor disapproving, just *looking*. Eventually she opened the front door all the way and I entered.

"I don't usually answer the door myself but it's Beatrix's day off. When Beatrix isn't here my son answers the door but he appears to have gone off also." She looked around the two-story foyer as if this son of hers might suddenly appear. I stared at the chandelier that hovered like a giant blimp over my head and moved a few feet to the left.

"You may leave your luggage in the foyer and I'll show you around after you tidy up."

I hoped that 'tidy up' was a euphemism for going to the bathroom because I really was about as tidy as I could get. I could tell I was already a huge disappointment to her and wondered what it was she was expecting. I was everything outlined in the ad, including having no allergies and a good sense of direction. "I had no problem finding the house," I said, to drive this point home.

Claudia proceeded to show me the first floor of the house. She informed me who all her relatives were, taking time with each portrait, staring at it like she had never seen it before, touching the faces affectionately and cocking her head and smiling.

"This is my father, Alden Behrends, Sr." She touched the frame of a stern-looking man who appeared to be a cross between a basset hound and a rabbit. "Wasn't he handsome?"

"Oh, definitely," I said, crossing my toes, my fingers and my eyes.

"And this is a family painting of my parents and my two brothers and me. I'm the one sitting on my mother's lap in the lacy dress." She lightly caressed the child in the dress. "This is me." Was she one of those rare people with such a dry sense of humor that you had to pay close attention to know they were being funny? "The boys standing on each side of the chairs are my brothers." I glanced at her again. No, she was totally serious. Now I wasn't sure if she was simpleminded or if she thought I was.

"The two adults are your parents," I said.

"Of course," she answered, unimpressed.

After that we saw a painting of Claudia and her two brothers as adults. She was still the one in the dress. There were three paintings of Roger Behrends with each of his three wives. Roger was a dapper-looking fellow with a twinkle in his eye that didn't fade from one decade or wife to another. I mentioned to Claudia that I thought Roger was a very handsome and interesting looking man and she stared at me like I had said I ate cat litter for the fiber. She obviously had some as yet undiscovered affliction that made her unable to distinguish a handsome man from a homely one. Therefore I was rather intrigued to meet her son when she described him as "not as good looking as my father." I couldn't imagine that anyone could be less good looking than a man who resembled the offspring of a rabbit and a basset hound.

I had settled in my room, which was large, light-filled and lovely. A sense of curiosity and obligation sent me to the library to begin poking around and making a plan for getting all the books in order. Claudia hadn't bothered to show me the library but had pointed it out in passing so I knew where it was. She had gone to her room for her pre-dinner nap and I was left on my own. The library door was still closed so I tentatively knocked and, hearing no response, pushed open the door.

I could only stand in the doorway and stare. The structural beauty of the room was totally overshadowed by disarray and clutter. Books were piled like columns all over the floor, some tilting so precariously that the landing of a fly could send them tumbling. Since the floor was already littered with books, no one would notice if another couple dozen were added to the mess. Half the bookshelves were empty and spiders had built complex condominiums in all the open spaces. The sunlight forcing its way through the windows illuminated the clouds of dust that filled the air and attached to every surface in the room. As I stared, mesmerized by the floating particles, I thought I could distinguish actual human shapes floating around the room, landing on the books and then launching themselves back into the air to swirl up to the ceiling two stories over my head. I looked at the landing that ran around the second floor of the library and thought I saw ethereal beings lined up peering over the railing at me. Suddenly the leather chair next to the fireplace seemed to be occupied by a pipe-smoking rabbit-faced man who stared at me with disinterest. The dust continued to swirl and the rabbit-faced man reshaped and floated up to join the others at the railing. I wanted to scream. I needed to sneeze.

"My father was not a tidy man," a voice boomed behind me, causing me to both scream and sneeze at the same time. I turned around so abruptly that I lost my footing and had to grab onto the door frame to keep from falling. Standing there with his hands in his pockets and grinning was one of the most interesting men I had ever seen. He was well over six feet tall and built like a swimmer, broad across the shoulders but lean everywhere else. His hair was a flaming red that Lucille Ball would have envied, and he wore it long. It gently curled and waved around his head like a red halo. His face was so covered with freckles that it looked like he had just returned from a beach holiday and had applied sunscreen haphazardly with a squirt gun. His eyes were an emerald green and, oddly enough, surrounded by thick black lashes that any woman would die for. His smile was warm and lit up his whole face. He wasn't much older than me but the crinkles around his eyes indicated that he smiled a lot and found life to be amusing. He stuck out his hand. "I'm Cam Mack. You must be Tamsen Darby. Welcome."

I got my balance and shook his hand, smiling at his infectious grin. He gestured toward the library. "You can see why we need help."

I nodded. "What happened in here?"

"Nothing. This is the way it always is. This is how my father liked to work. He died six months ago and we just closed the door. I finally convinced my mother that we needed to do something in here to protect the books and see if there are any papers or other things we should be taking care of. My mother doesn't do manual labor and I didn't want to do it by myself." His attention wandered off me and to the disastrous library.

"I'm sorry about your father. I can see why it would be difficult for you to do this alone."

He tore his eyes away from the room and returned them to me. "I try to get home most weekends but I'm in grad school in Boston and some weekends I just can't make it. It'll be good for my mom to have someone else living in the house with her in addition to getting this room sorted out. I'm glad you're here."

I suddenly felt, for the first time, that I was glad to be there.

The summer turned out to be life changing. I rarely saw Claudia and sincerely doubted that she felt any comfort by having my presence in her house. Her older brother, Franklin, who lived in a small gardener's cottage on the property, came over several times a week and did the heavy lifting and cleaning for me. Although probably not much more than sixty, he seemed twenty years older. He shuffled when he walked and seemed like a man burdened with aching joints. Yet he was able to move the furniture around easily and climb up on the ladder to wash and clean without any problem. One day I came in and he was on the top of a ladder cleaning the chandelier and looked like a young man, totally engaged in what he was doing, almost enjoying himself. When he saw me, he darted back into his shell and aged twenty years. We rarely spoke. I was grateful for his help so respected his privacy.

While he was busy cleaning, I was able to do the more challenging work of cataloging the books.

There was one day, early in the summer, when we had a one-sided conversation. It was the first time he came over to help me. Claudia had brought him in, introduced him and left. We had stared at each other for several seconds and then he had made a growl-like sound and banged his hand on the desk, causing dust to fly all over the room and papers and books to tumble to the floor.

"Room should never be allowed to look like this," he muttered under his breath as he picked up the books and laid them gently back on the desk. "My father would be disgusted by what that man did to this room. This is what happens when you let someone other than a Behrends run the house. Never understood what Claudia saw in that Mack guy. Married beneath her. Claudia deserved better. Glad he's gone."

I later asked Cam about his strange uncle and he had shook his head and smiled. "He's always been an odd one. I know he disliked my father and felt my mom had married beneath her but I think Franklin felt that anyone who wasn't a Behrends would have been beneath my mother. I know both she and Franklin tried to convince my father to change his name from Mack to Behrends so the name wouldn't die out. My father indulged my mom in many ways but he held firm on retaining his name."

My favorite days were the ones when Cam was there and we would work side by side, chatting. I learned that he had a sister, Cassandra, who was six years older. He seemed to be comfortable with the fact that he was an accident. He stated matter-of-factly that his mother had lost interest in the whole mothering thing by the time he was born and, once he had outgrown his nanny, had spent most of his childhood with his dad or the family housekeeper, Mrs. Knapp. I found out that "going to grad school in Boston" really meant attending Harvard for his MBA. In high school, he had balked at attending a private boarding school like Cassandra and had been happy in the local high school, where he was editor of the newspaper, played baseball and had been voted most likely to be a politician. For someone brought up in a locally wealthy and prominent family, he seemed more like Huck Finn than privileged rich kid. He said it was because when he was born, his mother had taken one look at him, pronounced him very un-Behrends-like, and resumed directing all her attention to his sister. This seemed to suit him fine. By the end of the summer I realized that being as un-Behrends-like as possible was the better path in life.

As the library got whipped into shape, Cam and I spent more and more time away from the house taking walks, having picnics, going to the movies and eventually going to Boston for the weekend for some privacy. It was the best summer of my life and when Cam proposed in August I said yes, never more sure of anything in my life. I knew I would have Claudia and Franklin and Cassandra to contend with, but it was worth it to spend the rest of my life with this funny, adventurous, kind and gentle man. In the middle of a glorious cherry-paneled room with towers of beautiful books, lacey cobwebs and ethereal dust, I had found my soul mate.

Chapter Three

It was several days after our WOACA meeting and Cam remained frustrated in his attempts to talk to Abbey. The first time he called she was in the library and couldn't talk. The next time she was out to dinner with friends and could only talk a minute. Then she was on the subway and didn't have good reception. She promised that she would be able to talk to us tonight.

Abbey had always been a daddy's girl, and her departure to college had hit Cam hard. Although she had my features, she had Cam's red hair and freckles and they had always been a striking pair who attracted attention wherever they went. They had bonded the minute Abbey was born and Cam deeply felt her absence. He had left for work this morning in a good mood anticipating the opportunity to have a real conversation with her tonight.

My phone rang and I was disappointed to see that it was my mother-in-law calling. If Claudia wanted to talk to you, she wouldn't give up until she had accomplished her mission, even if it meant leaving her luxurious senior living apartment, hopping in her Cadillac and driving over here. Then I would have to listen to the list of all the things we hadn't done with the house that we should have, and all the things we had done to the house that we shouldn't have. If Dorothy

Parker hadn't beaten me to it, I would have coined the phrase "what fresh hell is this" whenever I saw Claudia's caller ID on my phone.

"Tamsen, dear, you answered the phone yourself. How delightful." The conversation always started this way, as if Cam and I had a house full of servants who took care of these mundane tasks for us.

"Claudia, how are you?" I popped a can of diet soda and settled into the kitchen chair, resigned to get through the conversation as painlessly as possible.

"I'm doing very well, dear. I haven't heard from you or Christian for a while so I thought I'd better call to make sure you were both all right." His mother was the only person who called Cam by his given name.

"We're fine," I assured her.

"Oh, just too busy to call. I understand." Her tone made it clear that she didn't understand at all. Did she think all fifty-year-old men called their mothers every day? Probably.

"I won't keep you but I wondered if you would mind going to the cottage to check on Franklin. I don't suppose you've talked to him lately?" A couple of generations ago families kept their oddball members hidden away from society in their attics. We kept ours in the gardener's cottage.

"No, Claudia. The last time I went to the cottage to take him some lasagna he refused to answer the door and just stared at me through the window. We peek in on him frequently but we haven't actually talked to him or been let into the cottage for months. We do what we can."

Claudia sighed. "I know he is a bit odd but he answers the phone when I call, at least most of the time. I've been calling since yesterday and ... I was wondering if you could wander over to the cottage and check on him."

I reluctantly agreed to check on Franklin and call her back. I also ended up agreeing to bake a pie for her Ladies Guild flower show next week and to "man" the refreshment table for two hours. It occurred to me that Claudia really didn't need to get in touch with her brother at all, and it was just a ruse to get me to volunteer my dubious baking skills and precious time.

I didn't really mind taking the walk to Franklin's cottage as long as I wasn't expected to try to converse with him. Cam and I generally took a walk out there most evenings, peeked in his window, waved at him and nodded as he scowled at us and, on occasion, threw a dinner roll, a magazine, or a finger at us.

The four-room gardener's cottage was at the farthest end of the property from our house, not visible until you were almost at its front door. I meandered through the back garden, which was drooping and looking tired now that it was October. The gold and red leaves would all be down soon and we would move into that ugly stage of naked trees and withered flowers. I loved the fall but hated the post-fall season. From the garden I moved into the woods, watching my footing on the tree roots camouflaged by fallen leaves, looking and listening for the last of the birds. The squirrels chased each other playfully, their claws scratching on the rough bark, the boughs of the trees creaking as they landed and swayed before leaping to the next. They definitely were *not* squeaking.

It would have been a perfect day to have my trusted dog by my side as I swished my way through the leaves and felt the chilly air on my face, but Mycroft was taking one of his series of naps and could not be budged for a walk under any circumstances. We could barely push him out the door to do his business and even then he went as close to the house as we would let him. He was the only housebound bloodhound I'd ever heard of. It suddenly struck me that he was the canine version of Uncle Franklin minus the ability to throw things at us.

All too soon I arrived at the faded, mustard-colored cottage. It was badly in need of a paint job but we were afraid to submit a stranger to the vagaries of Uncle Franklin. Cam had been planning to paint it himself but it was always at the bottom of his to-do list. We knew the shabbiness of the cottage didn't bother Franklin because he hadn't been outside to look at the cottage for years. It probably looked pretty good the last time he'd seen it. We could keep up the pretense a little longer.

As usual, the place looked deserted. There was no sign that anyone lived here. There was no mailbox—what little mail he received came to our house. We had arranged to have the newspaper delivered to him daily but I wasn't sure he even read it. Cam had picked up the garbage the day before last and Franklin hadn't put any bags out since then. He rarely turned his lights on until late in the evening and although he never closed his curtains, there was never any movement visible. I had no idea what he did during the day. Probably just sat and stared out the window.

I took my usual route around the cottage looking in the windows, prepared to give my wave and get his hollow-eyed stare in return. I looked in the kitchen window first as that is usually where we find him during the day, sitting at the kitchen table. Franklin wasn't there and the room was cleaned up, which was odd. I expected to see breakfast dishes piled on the counter next to the sink. Franklin did his dishes once a day, so his breakfast and lunch dishes accumulated in a pile on the counter until after dinner. But the kitchen was clean, like it looked before he went to bed. Franklin was an incredibly odd man but he was also obsessively routinized. The apparently small inconsistency of the clean counter made me uneasy. I hesitated and thought of returning home. I wished Cam were with me.

I reluctantly moved to the front of the cottage to peek in the living room window. Nothing. Franklin spent very little time in this room, as far as we knew. I don't think we had ever seen him in here. When we check on him he is usually in the kitchen or in an incredibly messy room that we have termed his study. I stepped across the front stoop and peeked in the study window.

Franklin sat in his favorite chair, facing the window, scowling at me. It was exactly what I expected to see. The letter opener plunged into his neck was a surprise.

Chapter Four

The next week was a blur. Cam handled all the arrangements. Abbey came home the day of the funeral and then went back to school. I don't even remember talking to her although Cam assures me I did. Grace and Hugh, Syra, Diane and her husband, Scott, attended the funeral. Bing didn't, but he supplied us with enough baked goods to open our own bakery. I went through the motions, but didn't feel like I was really in my body. I'm not sure where I was, but it wasn't in the present.

I talked to the police numerous times, but I have no idea what I said. I tried to talk to Cam about what it was like finding Franklin, but I didn't have the words to express what I was feeling. I didn't attend the weekly meeting of WOACA at Diane's house, even though I needed their comfort and support more than ever. Oddly, it was my mother-in-law and her friend, Sybil Bright, who eventually got me out of my shocked funk and back into reality. It was the one-week anniversary of Franklin's death ... murder. I was sitting at my kitchen table drinking a diet soda and staring out the window when Claudia and Sybil appeared at my back door. I don't believe I'd ever seen Claudia at the back door before.

I let them in and Claudia marched into the kitchen, poured herself a cup of coffee left over from Cam's breakfast, and sat across from me like she still lived here. I gave Sybil a help-yourself wave and she poured herself a cup and joined us at the table. Claudia sipped and dabbed at her eyes with a delicate embroidered handkerchief. As usual, Sybil took charge.

"Cam is worried about you, Tamsen. You need to pull yourself together and move on," she announced as she ripped up several pink sugar substitute packets and shook them into her coffee. "I know you were the one to find poor Franklin, and I know that is distressing, but you have to put it behind you and get back to normal life. Claudia's getting back to her life, and it's time you did, too."

My whole body felt like lead, and not only was it hard to raise my head to look at her, it was too much trouble to answer her. Fortunately that didn't matter. Sybil rambled on.

"The police have no idea what happened in that cottage. There was no sign of a fight or even of another person being there. There certainly was no motive to murder poor Franklin. Although he was a wealthy man on paper, he didn't have anything of value in the cottage. And he certainly hadn't made any enemies sitting in that cottage for sixty-plus years. I don't think anyone outside the family even remembered he existed. You know what I think?"

Claudia clutched her handkerchief to her chest and interrupted.

"It's difficult to say this about my own brother, but I think it was suicide ..."

"What?" I wasn't even sure it was my voice because I hadn't heard it for a while so I tried it again. "What? I saw him! There's no way ..."

"Tamsen dear, I know the thought of suicide by a Behrends is difficult to accept but ..."

"Claudia, what is difficult to accept is that someone would kill himself by shoving a letter opener into his own throat."

I had to take several deep breaths after saying it because that image is the brick wall I hadn't been able to get past—the scowling old man sitting in a chair staring at me through the window with a blade sticking out of his neck like some horror house prop. Even though I hadn't gone inside, I could smell the gamey metallic aroma of blood mingled with stale old-man smell.

"There is no way someone could do that to himself." I started to feel nauseous and wondered what the proper Claudia would think if I threw up diet soda and breakfast M&Ms all over the table while she was drinking her coffee.

"But Franklin wasn't normal," Sybil needlessly reminded me. "Who knows what was going on in his head? Claudia and I certainly ceased to understand him ages ago. His actions would not be the same as yours or mine."

I pressed my thumb against my inner wrist, something that I had read in a magazine to counter nausea. "What do the police think of your suicide idea?"

Claudia would never do anything as uncouth as roll her eyes but she did flick them up and down a little. "They didn't seem to take the suicide idea very seriously. But then, after not finding a motive or signs of an intruder and no sign of anything missing or disturbed, they may change their minds. It takes them a while to open their minds to other options."

"It may take them quite a long time to open their minds to *that* idea," I said. "I wouldn't hold your breath."

"I don't plan to, dear. In my heart I know what happened and that is all that matters. Now, I have something I would like you to do ..."

It suddenly occurred to me that I had neither made a pie nor manned the refreshment booth at the flower show last week. I apologized. Claudia nodded, graciously accepting my apology.

"I didn't go to the flower show this year and no one expected anyone in our family to do anything about it so don't worry. The Ladies Guild grants some leeway in obligations when there is a death in the family, especially one as spectacular as ours. What I have in mind is something totally different."

Sybil got up and poured herself the dregs of the coffee and then got me a diet soda out of the refrigerator, possibly fortifying me for what her friend had to say. Claudia calmly waited until I popped the tab and took a drink.

"Tamsen, dear, I feel you would be the perfect person to go through all the papers and books in Franklin's cottage. Sybil keeps offering to do it, but I need her by my side."

One thing I can say about my mother-in-law is that she is way too classy to flinch when someone spews diet soda across the table and into her coffee. She merely moved the cup away, took a napkin and wiped off her hands.

"I don't really want to go back over there, ever ..." I protested.

"It really is asking a lot of Tamsen," Sybil agreed. "Why not let me do it. I don't mind at all."

"Nonsense, Tamsen. You did such an adequate job that summer when you organized our library and there is so much less involved in cleaning out Franklin's place. You and Cam can have any books that might be valuable or of interest. Most of the stuff in there can be donated to Goodwill. But I think it's important to have someone in the family sort through it all. Cam is much too busy. And I can't bear to be without Sybil right now."

By the time they left, I had traded not baking a pie and manning a refreshment booth for clearing out the house of a murdered man.

Chapter Five

I am not a brave person. The last brave thing I did was to give birth. And let's face it, I really didn't have a choice. For my latest foray into the world of the courageous, I decided to ramp up my fortifications and take Grace, Diane and Syra with me. I would have brought Bing, too, but he was semi-agoraphobic and would only venture out across the street to my house. Straight back and forth across the street and nothing more. So Syra left him at home to bake us something as a reward for what we were about to do and we took off, armed with garbage bags, water bottles, cookies and cleaning supplies.

Syra sensed my dread of returning to the crime scene and tried to distract me by asking about my ongoing battle with my editor over Perry Many Paws and his friends.

"He's rejected two of my opening chapters so far. He won't let Perry find any new friends. He won't let me temporarily lose Squeaky and Friendly. He won't let me move Perry to some exotic location and he won't let me involve Perry Many Paws in anything that even whiffs of mischievousness. Oh, and Grace, he did not like your name change suggestions. Promiscuous Pig and Horny Owl are definitely out. My hands are tied."

Grace tramped behind us, struggling to keep up and balance her water bottle and box of garbage bags. "I need a walking stick. Isn't there a way to drive to this cottage?"

"Actually, there is," I yelled back, holding aside a tree bough until Syra caught up with me. "But you still have to walk in from where you park the car, and that trail is grown over because it's never used."

"It's got to be shorter than this," Grace swatted at some imaginary bit of nature that she felt touching her face.

"It's shorter but you'd need a machete to get through. We're almost there."

"Will there be anything, you know, disgusting?" Diane asked, stepping gingerly over a fallen branch, flicking away bits of leaves that fell onto her white twin set sweaters.

"Don't worry. It won't be like an episode of "CSI". The police gave us the okay to have professional cleaners come in to get all the, uh, traces of disgusting stuff. We just need to sort through Franklin's personal stuff. Most of it we'll probably throw away, but there might be something we can salvage for Goodwill."

We came to the clearing by the cottage and I stopped dead in my tracks. Like dutiful attendants, Syra and Diane smacked into my back. Grace was able to stop before adding to the domino effect. Syra gave me a gentle shove. "Nothing to be afraid of. There are no ghosts," she reassured me. This elicited an indignant sniff from Grace, who firmly believed that not only were there ghosts, or spirits as she called them, but she could see and communicate with them under the right circumstances.

From the outside, the cottage looked better than when I had last been here. It was as if the removal of the scowling old man and the subsequent cleaning up inside had affected the whole aura of the place. Maybe this task wouldn't be so bad after all.

"My sneakers are all dirty," Diane said, apropos of nothing. We all ignored her and made our way to the front door. Just as my hand touched the knob, Diane's phone began to purr and we all screamed and clutched at each other, stumbling off the porch and moving back towards the woods.

"Hi Kara, what's going on? (pause) No, I can't bring you another pair of gym shorts. What's wrong with the ones you took this morning? (longer pause) Well that's what happens if you take them out of the dryer before they're dry. (longest pause) Then you'll just have to take them to the locker room and hold them under the hand dryer." Diane snapped her phone shut and starred at us. "Why am I the only one on the porch? Aren't we going inside?" She opened up the cottage door and marched in.

Light was flooding through the windows and the place smelled strongly of lemon. While the others set their bags on the kitchen table, I went ahead and peeked in the study, trying not to recall the last time I'd looked in there. The rug was gone. The floor was clean. It wasn't scary at all.

"It's all cleaned up. It's fine," I said to my reinforcements.

"Okay," Syra replied. "Tell us what you want us to do."

Grace had flopped in the kitchen chair and was already into her water bottle. It was the same chair Franklin sat in to eat his meals, but I didn't mention it. Maybe she would get a spiritual vibe from it.

Diane volunteered to do the kitchen. "I love poking through kitchen stuff and there may be some pots or bowls or things the boys could use, if you don't mind." Her twin sons, Kevin and Keith, were juniors at Clarkson University and had moved off campus this fall to their own apartment.

I nodded. "Take anything you think they might want. It will save them a trip to Goodwill. Syra, do you mind going through the bedroom? Most of Franklin's clothes probably aren't in good enough shape for Goodwill, but you might find something that is. You can dump the rest in the garbage bags. Same with bed linens and towels. Just throw them out."

Syra saluted, grabbed a box of garbage bags and headed to the bedroom. Grace joined me in the study and for about five minutes we just circled it and stared, not knowing where to start. The shelves were jammed with books; some left open for what may have been years. The floor was stacked with newspapers and magazines, toppling over and encrusted with spider webs and who knows what else. There were stains on the hardwood floor that were probably spilled juice or beer or whiskey that had never been wiped up but had been left to become part of the patina of the wood. Not a look I recommend.

"I wonder why the cleaning people didn't dust off the bookshelves or the piles on the floor." Grace kicked at the newspapers and leaped back as a cloud of dirt ascended into the air.

"They were only hired to clean up the, um, mess from the crime scene. They weren't supposed to thoroughly clean the cottage."

"Oh well, I wish these newspapers weren't so dirty. I'd really like to look at them." Grace owned a bookstore, so any reading material was fascinating to her.

"Help yourself," I offered, "but you may want to put something over your mouth and nose. I'm going to attack the bookshelves and see if there's anything I can rescue. Some of these books look really old and intriguing."

We pulled our hair back with rubber bands. We found moderately clean dish towels in the kitchen and tied them around our faces to keep out the dust. We looked like the James brothers pulling a bank job.

"It's good to see you back to normal," Grace commented as she tentatively poked and kicked at the stacks of magazines. "Weird things have been happening and I missed having you to talk to."

"Yeah, I've been in a daze since finding Uncle Franklin. Shock, I guess. I hardly remember anything from the past week. That's probably a good thing." I pulled a beautiful leather-bound Dickens, *Pickwick Papers*, from the shelves and dusted it off with my shirt. "Look at this!! It's gorgeous." Grace reached out for the book and lovingly opened it and looked through the pages.

"Real leather. This is how all books should be made. Of course most people wouldn't be able to afford them and I certainly couldn't afford to stock them in my shop, but it's perfect."

"It's like a work of art." I took the book back and laid it gently on the table. "This definitely goes back to the house." My hands lingered on the leather a while longer. "Grace, you said weird things have been happening. What weird things?"

Grace sat down in the chair next to the table and pushed her cloth off her face. "I'm not sure what it means but I know I'm not imagining things …"

"What things?"

"Diane has been flirting with that policeman investigating the murder."

"Huh?"

"Not only is she all coy and flirty around him, she talks about him incessantly. She's even called him a couple of times, supposedly about something stupid she forgot to tell him in her interview. Tamsen, she's obsessed with this guy. It's like a teenage crush."

"Does her husband know?"

"I assume Scott doesn't. I mean, you don't go home and tell your husband you have a crush on some other guy who, on top of everything, has to be at least fifteen years younger than you."

I was mystified. "This is so unlike Diane. I can't picture her flirting with anyone— including Scott." By now I had lost interest in the promise of treasures in the bookcase and sat down close to Grace so we could talk quietly. "Have you said anything to her about it?"

"I did mention, jokingly, that she seemed to be flirting with the guy, but she brushed me off and said I was imagining things. I pointed out that she talked about him a lot and she actually got angry with me. She implied that because things were shaky for me at home, I was imagining romantic intrigue where there wasn't any."

"It's not like her to snap at you, or at anyone. She's always so calm and ..."

"I *know*. That's what's so scary. She's like another person. One I don't much like, either."

"Grace, she probably felt you had her cornered, so she lashed out. She's not an unkind person."

"I know, but still ..."

"I wonder if she and Scott are having problems."

"I have no idea but I'm starting to feel like we're in some twilight zone world where nothing quite works anymore. It's very unsettling."

There wasn't more to say so we got back to work. If you're a reader and a lover of books, you'll understand how even under less-than-hygienic conditions, a person can become totally absorbed in the process of opening and perusing book after book after book, totally losing track of the time. Grace was in the same state of printed word euphoria as she sorted and read through newspapers and magazines. We were finally jolted out of our concentration by the announcement that cold water and cookies were being served in the kitchen. As I removed my ad hoc mask, I glimpsed a framed photo lying on the floor under Franklin's desk. I grabbed it and joined the others in the kitchen.

Diane and Syra had obviously been hard at work. The bedroom had been stripped of curtains and bed clothes, and the closets, dresser drawers and kitchen cupboards had been cleaned out. The refrigerator was defrosting and all contents were in bags labeled "trash" or "Goodwill". All Grace and I had been doing was reading. Luckily, reading in the study had been a very dirty activity so at least we *looked* as if we'd been hard at work.

We sat at the kitchen table and ripped into the cookies like a pack of starving wolves. We polished them off and followed them up with candy bar chasers supplied by Grace, who was rumored to own stock in Hershey. Diane had found a set of Corelle Old Town Blue dishes that she thought would be perfect for Keith and Kevin's new apartment. She had also salvaged a cheese grater that looked like it had never been used—probably true, because I couldn't picture Franklin grating cheese any more than I could picture him changing his sheets.

Syra had found a couple of pairs of jeans that had hardly been worn and some underwear and socks still in their original packages. These had gone into the Goodwill bag. She hadn't had time to finish clearing out the bedroom closet and announced there were still a few creepy-looking bags, old clothes on hangers and shoes in there.

My findings had been a bit more positive. "I found an annotated Sherlock Holmes that I'm definitely going to keep," I announced. "And there's a complete set of Edgar Allan Poe as well as Jack London's *Call of the Wild*, *White Fang* and *Sea Wolf*. These are first editions, published between 1903 and 1906! I'm taking them up to the house to put in the library there, unless Claudia wants them."

"It's good that something from here can be taken out and used," Diane said. "Otherwise it seems like a pretty sad way to have lived, surrounded by stuff that other people feel is garbage once you're gone."

"Did you find anything interesting, Grace?" Syra asked.

Grace nodded her head. "Very. Worth saving? Probably not. He had years and years of *National Geographic* magazines."

"Claudia gave him a subscription every Christmas," I confirmed.

"And piles of paperbacks in very poor shape. We should toss them."

"What about the newspapers? Were there more than just that one pile in the corner?"

"That's all I could find. Now here's something odd: at first they looked like a bunch of random newspapers going back seventy some years. But when I began to sort through them, I realized there was only one newspaper for each year and that it was the newspaper from the same day each year, April 1."

Syra laughed. "He saved the newspaper from April Fool's Day each year? What was the point?"

"I've no idea. But they were in order all the way back to 1938. Over seventy years of newspapers from April Fool's Day." Grace got up from the table. "Do I dare use the bathroom? I've had four bottles of water."

"Sure, I already used it and it's clean. I even unwrapped a new roll of toilet paper. There's no soap or towels though because I threw the towels away. You definitely wouldn't have wanted to use them. I'm sorry I even had to touch them," Syra said.

Diane tidied up the dregs of our unhealthy feast. "How are we going to get all this trash out of here?"

"I think that's a job for Cam, a truck and a machete. We'll just leave all the trash in the house for now. Cam will help get all the books up to the house, too. I don't think we want to do it one trip at a time walking through the woods."

Grace returned from the bathroom, wiping her hands on her jeans. "I think we should keep the newspapers."

"Why?" Diane asked. "I thought the point was to get rid of anything that wasn't usable. Old newspapers definitely fall into that category."

"It's just such a strange thing," Grace said. "Over seventy newspapers from April 1? It can't hurt to hold on to them for a while. I'd like to see if there are any articles about my bookstore in them."

"Fine with me," I agreed, "as long as you store them at your house, not mine."

I had set the old photo on the table when I sat down to eat. I suddenly remembered it and picked it up to study more closely. Five children—two boys and three girls—posed casually on a large lawn near a grouping of trees. They wore light jackets and the trees were starting to bud, so it must have been in the spring. It must have been a dry day because one of the boys and the older girl sat cross-legged on the ground, which was awkward for the girl as she wore a skirt. The other boy stood in the middle with two younger girls on either side. The two boys and the seated girl looked to be around the same age, older than the other two girls. I wiped it off with my paper towel and passed it around the table.

There was much oohing and aahing over how cute the little girls looked in their old-fashioned ruffled dresses. Both the boys were declared very handsome, especially the one standing with an impish grin on his face. We agreed that the girl sitting on the ground, dressed in a plainer dress than the little girls and wearing what looked like sturdy boots, must have been a bit of a handful, while the two little girls, her sisters maybe, looked like perfect little ladies, five going on forty. They must have been important to Franklin because it was the only photo we had found in his house.

Chapter Six

That evening Cam spent most of his time on the phone with Abbey trying to fix her computer in the most inefficient way possible—miles apart. But he had a good time. It felt like when she lived at home and the two of them puzzled over the vagaries of technology together. I told him about the trip to the cottage and what we found there, but he wasn't that interested. Once you've found a dead body, there isn't really much you can report that doesn't seem dull by comparison. I thought more about the newspapers and the photo and by morning had come to the conclusion that I would need to drive out to Chez Claudia to discuss our findings with her. I needed to report on the books and see what she wanted to do with them. Maybe she would have some insight into the odd newspaper collection and who the children in the picture were.

Claudia now lives in a gracious senior living complex. When she first moved out of the Behrends castle after Cam and I were married, she and Sybil had traveled and cruised around the world for several years, stopping by briefly between trips. She had been happy traveling until Abbey was born and then she wanted to be close by, and permanently returned to Birdsey Falls. I had been petrified that she would want to move back into the house with us and "help" with the baby—a fear that made Cam laugh out loud. He was right, of course.

She returned to town and moved into a cottage affiliated with the senior living complex. It was a spacious two-bedroom bungalow with a large yard and she was able to hire someone to maintain a garden so she could enjoy the flowers she loved.

Once she turned seventy, she had moved out of the cottage and into the independent apartment complex. Here she enjoyed restaurant-style meals, massages, swimming, lectures, fitness sessions, crafting and group excursions. She had a spacious apartment with a large bedroom, a den and a living room large enough to accommodate her grand piano. The kitchen was small but she rarely used it for anything other than coffee making or an occasional meal when she didn't feel up to going to either the large formal dining room or the coffee shop. Over the years she had built up a large network of friends and was always busy. I called after breakfast to make sure she would be there and not in the midst of some activity when I arrived.

Walking into the Ashland Belle Senior Living Complex always makes me feel like Scarlett O'Hara. I want to swish my long skirts as I cross the meticulously maintained lawn and walk across the columned front porch. I feel like I should curtsey to the white-haired colonels and their ladies rocking on the porch, sipping their mint juleps and discussing the frivolous social gossip of the day. I can see why after decades of living in the ugly Behrends castle, Claudia had chosen the perfectly proportioned beauty of Ashland Belle. There were winding walkways lined with delicate tables and chairs for outside tea time. The plush lawn gently sloped down to a man-made pond where you could sit in a gazebo and gaze at the surrounding gardens, water fountains and statuary. If you felt restless, you could walk along the path around the pond and feed the ducks. It was a spiritually replenishing place. It was no wonder that every year dozens of people were married on these grounds, much to the delight of the senior citizens. It was the kind of place you felt you had to dress up to come visit, so instead of jeans I had on my gray wool slacks and a blazer. I knew Claudia and her friends would be sporting their family pearls, diamonds and whatnot and dressed in their Sunday best no matter what day of the week it was.

Claudia had assured me she would be in, so I headed right up to her apartment on the second floor. I took the winding staircase rather than the elevator to retain my Scarlett O'Hara persona as long as possible. The hall carpet always looked new and the halls wound gently so you didn't have the feeling you were in a long institutional corridor. The handrail was discreetly built into the wall so it looked like wainscoting. Oil paintings and water colors, many done by the residents, hung on the walls, and antique tables with fresh flowers and comfortable chairs were placed at each alcove where the hallway curved. Each person's apartment had a brass doorknocker and a gold name plate. Very classy. I probably should have worn a dress.

Claudia had on a long mauve plaid wool skirt, mauve cashmere sweater, pearls and bare feet. She graciously ushered me in and went to get me coffee, which she knows I don't drink. I only drink water and diet soda, but she refuses to believe it, so always gives me coffee, which I thank her for and never drink.

"Here's your coffee, dear. I hope this is the way you like it," she said as she handed me the Royal Winton chintz cup and saucer. "Do you find it more difficult to find bras now that your figure is becoming more matronly?"

I instinctively glanced down at my chest. "No, not really," I replied as if this was a perfectly normal question. "Thank you for the coffee, Claudia." I set the coffee down on the end table where it would remain until I left. I heard a noise coming from the kitchen. "Is someone here?" I asked.

My mind began to race with visions of Claudia entertaining a paramour when I had called and the two of them not being able to break the bonds of passion in time for him to disappear before my arrival twenty minutes later. Although always a beautiful woman, Claudia had not, to the best of my knowledge, been romantically involved with anyone since Cam's father died. Maybe she had had a long-time lover Cam and I had never known about, or even a series of them flitting in and out of her life, being tossed away after they became boring. Perhaps this was why she had been so happy to give Cam and me the house when we had gotten married. She needed privacy to indulge all her romantic escapes and still retain her dignified Matron of Birdsey Falls persona. I began to get that same feeling of dread I had experienced walking around the gardener's cottage the day I discovered Uncle Franklin.

Sybil Bright entered the room, wiping her hands on a dish towel. I breathed a sigh of relief. Of course, it would be Sybil. Sybil was a childhood friend of Claudia's and they had made a pact that when they were old ladies they would live together. Sybil lived across the hall and she and Claudia were inseparable. Sybil had had many careers besides having been married at least four times. She'd lived in New York City when she was in her twenties and once had a bit part in a Broadway play. Sybil didn't just dress, she wore costumes. Today she wore a jade and teal sari, which looked good with her flaming red hair. She had her full theater makeup on, the pancake foundation competing with the wrinkles in an effort to emerge. I had to control myself not to stare. I was so distracted by Sybil that I actually took a sip of my coffee. Claudia gave me a triumphant look as if that proved I really did like coffee and had previously perversely refused to drink hers.

I gave Claudia a list of the books that I had found at the cottage that I thought we should keep. The first-edition Jack Londons had been her father's and I thought she might want them. She didn't and agreed that they should all go into the library at The Castle. She also agreed with letting Diane's sons have the kitchen items she had selected. She didn't seem to want anything from her brother's cottage.

Other than the books, there really wasn't much in the cottage worth keeping, but I thought she might want something as a memento. I was wrong. As I handed her the old framed photograph from Franklin's desk, she did perk up.

"Oh, Sybil, look at this!" She and Sybil were seated next to each other on the couch so all she had to do was lean over and show it to her. "I can't believe Franklin still had this photo. It was such a long time ago."

I moved over to the couch and perched on the arm. "Who are these children? Neither Cam or I could identify anyone."

Claudia rubbed her hand back and forth over the image as if conjuring up the memory of that long ago day when the five children had stopped their play long enough to reluctantly pose for some camera enthusiast.

"The tall boy standing in the middle is Franklin ..." Claudia's voice broke. I stared at the handsome boy with the big smile. It was impossible to see the man Franklin had become in this vigorous laughing teenager. Claudia caressingly pointed to each person in the photo.

"Standing to his right is Sybil and I'm on his left. The girl sitting on the ground is Hetty Foster and the boy next to her is Edmund Close. Hetty, Edmund and Franklin were quite the adventurous trio. Remember how they used to try to drag us into their games, Sybil?"

"Of course. Hetty was a real tomboy, which Claudia and I were not, so nothing they did appealed to us. There were a lot of games where they dressed up as pirates and hid things in the woods for each other to find with a treasure map," Sybil said.

"Franklin used to spend hours making those maps. Hours and hours."

"And other times they were soldiers fighting the American Revolution and Hetty would run around with a lantern screaming, 'One if by land. Two if by sea.' And the boys would come rushing out of the woods with guns and sabers and fight with the trees. It all seemed pretty silly to us but they always had a good time. I think they were in the middle of making a new pirate adventure when this picture was taken. Remember, Claudia?"

Claudia nodded, her eyes still glued to the picture. "Yes. I remember Franklin was always up late into the night making maps and my dad would scold him about going to bed. When he was interested in something, he would totally immerse himself in it. He was a very focused and creative boy."

"What happened to him?" I asked. We all had accepted Franklin for the recluse that he was and never really thought about the fact that he had once been a normal, energetic boy. To me Franklin was always the old man I saw through the window. "What changed him, Claudia?"

"I have no idea. I was so young and ..." Claudia began.

"When you're six, your whole world revolves around your toys and your playmates. Older siblings and their friends are annoyances," Sybil added. "When Franklin was with Edmund and Hetty they were all especially annoying. I think Claudia and I were too ladylike for them."

"Franklin just seemed to fade away into himself until he was totally gone. I don't think anyone ever knew why. I just don't know," Claudia sighed wistfully. The three of us sat silently looking at the photo in Claudia's hands.

"You should keep this picture, Claudia. Everything in his cottage is more yours than it is Cam's or mine. And are you sure you don't want any of the books?"

"No, I'd rather they go in the library at the house. That's where they belong." She looked at the photo again and then returned it to me.

"Was there anything you found at the house besides the books and kitchen things?" she asked.

"There were bed linens and clothes, a pile of newspapers ..."

"Those should be thrown out."

"Probably, but there was something curious about the newspapers."

Sybil clapped her hands gleefully. "I love anything curious! What was it?"

"They were all dated April 1. There was only one paper for every year since 1938 and each paper was the April 1 edition. Any idea why?"

"That date has no significance that I can think of other than the obvious. And Franklin was hardly interested in April Fool's Day ..." Claudia replied.

Sybil cut in. "Maybe not now, dear, but he certainly was as a boy. Remember all the tricks he used to pull on us? He had a great sense of humor and could be quite inventive in his pranks."

I pictured the shell of a man who had stared out the window at me for twenty-five years and never even acknowledged my presence. A prankster? It seemed impossible. Hearing what he had been like as a boy made his life even sadder and more difficult to understand. Maybe modern medicine could have helped him lead a more normal life. As far as I knew he hadn't been to a doctor since Cam and I were married. At the bottom of all this was the most obvious question. Who would want to kill a man who was a recluse and hadn't spoken to anyone but his sister in decades? The only valuable things he had owned were those first-edition books, and they hadn't been touched. Nothing in the cottage had been touched. It appeared totally random and senseless and, most of all, motiveless.

Sybil had gotten Claudia laughing about some April Fool's joke Franklin, Edmund and Hetty had pulled on them when they were young girls. I got the impression that it was one of those things that is funnier in retrospect than it was when it happened. As they were reminiscing, something interesting occurred to me. I waited until there was a break in their conversation.

"Did you say the girl in the photo was named Hetty Foster?" I asked.

Sybil nodded, wiping away tears of laughter with her sleeve. "Yes. Her real name was Henrietta but everyone called her Hetty. She always seemed more boy than girl to me."

"Very unladylike," Claudia chimed in. "I don't know why her parents didn't get her in hand …"

"She came from a good family, although her parents traveled a lot as I recall …"

"You expect boys to be able to run wild but certainly not a young lady. I don't think she ever even took piano or voice lessons."

I wasn't sure this was really such a major faux pas in parenting, but let it go. It wasn't Hetty's lack of social polish I was interested in. "You said her last name was Foster. Was she related to Syra and Bing?"

"Hetty was certainly related to Syra and Bing although I'm sure they never mention her. Hetty was their mother." It took me a full minute to absorb this information.

"But her last name was Foster and their last name is Foster …"

"Exactly. That is why I'm sure they never mention her. She wasn't married when either Syra or Bing was born. I told you she was a wild and very unladylike girl," Claudia informed me.

"No one else we knew had children out of wedlock. Shocking, really," Sybil added.

It was true that neither Syra nor Bing talked about their parents but I assumed it was because they were dead. They didn't seem like people who would be ashamed of having an unwed mother. They were both in their late forties. Surely this wasn't still a sore point with them.

"And obviously they have different fathers," Sybil added. "Syra is tall and shaped like an ironing board, like her mother. Heaven knows what Bing's father must have looked like. It's hard to imagine someone built like Hetty having a passionate affair with a man who came up to her shoulders and was built like an overweight penguin."

"Well, Hetty was different from other girls and I suppose there is no accounting for taste when one's baser instincts rule one's life," Claudia proclaimed in her best high society voice. It was times like this that I especially didn't like her.

"What can you expect from a girl who never had piano or voice lessons?" I said. In a sad commentary on my inability to successfully express sarcasm, both Claudia and Sybil nodded in agreement.

Sybil reached over and patted my hand, "You are so right, dear."

"Did you know, Tamsen, that both Syra and Bing were named after exits on the New York State Thruway? I don't know if that is where they were conceived or where they were born." Claudia informed me.

I didn't really care about where or how they were conceived but very interested in the origin of their names. "What exits were they named after?"

"Syracuse and Binghamton. I believe those are their actual given names. Ridiculous names for children. For all we know, Hetty had all kinds of children and the only way she can remember who their fathers are is by naming them after the town they were conceived in."

I remembered a trip Cam and I had taken with Abbey to see the Corning Museum of Glass in Corning, New York. Nearby was a town named Painted Post and another named Horseheads. Thank goodness neither Syra nor Bing had been born there.

I thought Cam and I were pretty imaginative when we had named Abbey. I would never have told my mother-in-law that we had gotten the name from Glastonbury Abbey in Somerset, England. And I certainly would never tell her that her granddaughter had been conceived in the historic George and Pilgrims Hotel in Glastonbury on our sixth wedding anniversary after a shared bottle of French wine. Some things are best kept to oneself.

Shania Twain started singing from my purse and I started digging for my phone, knowing it was Grace. She is a big fan of Shania. I let all my friends pick their own ring tones—that way when I can't find my phone before the ringing stops, I at least know whose call I missed.

As soon as I said hello, Grace said. "Tamsen, you have got to get over here. I found something, something awful. I need for you to see this. I don't know what to do. I don't know what it means ..." She began sobbing and I couldn't understand what she was saying. Grace wasn't much of a crier, so hearing her sob was disturbing. I told her I was on my way. I took a hasty leave of Claudia and Sybil, yanking on my jacket and telling them Grace needed me.

"Who *was* that singing," Sybil asked Claudia as I let the door shut behind me.

Chapter Seven

Legally it should have taken me twice that long but I made the drive to Grace's house in ten minutes. Her front door was open and I walked in, calling her name.

"In Ryan's bedroom," she yelled back and I ran up two flights of stairs to the attic, where Hugh had made Ryan a private sanctuary away from the rest of the house. I could barely breathe by the time I reached the top. I needed to get more exercise. I was only forty-seven, for heaven's sake. Grace emerged from Ryan's bedroom and grabbed my arm, pulling me into the room.

There was a pile of books by the unmade bed, a few car-related magazines scattered on the bureau, several action movie posters haphazardly taped to the walls, and some damp towels draped over the open closet door. I flashed back to my bedroom when I was fifteen and the chaos that had ruled in my mini kingdom; this wasn't bad at all. While I surveyed the room, Grace moved nervously to the closet door.

"In here," she whispered, which really freaked me out. I hate the sound of whispering, especially when my nerves are already on edge. She pointed at the floor.

On the closet floor lay a pile of clothes. Grace bent down and gingerly picked up a gray t-shirt that looked like a red pen had exploded all over it. She dangled it in front of my face for a few seconds and then threw it back on the closet floor as if it was burning her fingers.

"It's blood," she pronounced.

I flashed back to the image of Franklin, sitting in his chair, staring at me, the blood covering his shirt and puddled on the rug beneath him. "Oh Grace, you can't possibly be thinking that Ryan ..."

"Of course that's what I'm thinking," she shrieked. "What else could I be thinking? He's been acting stranger than ever the last couple of weeks and this t-shirt has been wadded up in the closet until it's all stiff. How did it get like this? It couldn't be Ryan's blood. There's too much. If he bled this much we would've known. He would've needed a doctor. Oh God, Tamsen ..." Grace collapsed on Ryan's bed, sobbing into her hands. I bent down and picked up the shirt and looked at it more closely. It did look like dried blood. And it was spattered all over the shirt as if it had spurted out ...

"What the hell are you doing in my room?"

I hadn't seen Ryan for a while and was amazed at how much he had grown in that short time. Suddenly he didn't seem like the skinny awkward boy I remembered. He was taller and heavier and, right now, with his hands on his hips and his face white with anger, very threatening. I dropped the t-shirt and moved over to Grace.

"What are you two doing in my room?" He turned to Grace. His hatred filled the room and made it difficult to breathe. "I don't go in your room and wave your gigantic underpants around, do I? What right do you have to come in here with your friends and look at my stuff? What the hell kind of person are you? Get out. Now."

"Wait just a minute, young man. You can't ..." My voice trailed off. There was no way I could deal with so much negative emotion. I'd only make things worse for Grace. I reached down and tugged at her hand.

Still glaring at us, Ryan slowly moved away from the doorway and Grace and I silently hurried out. We were both terrified of this angry outraged young man that neither of us really knew. We stumbled down the stairs.

As we stood in the living room, she looked me in the eye. "I don't want to stay here. I need to get out," she sniffed, fighting back the tears. "I'm afraid Tamsen. Look how much he hates me. I'm afraid of that t-shirt and what it means. Please, help me pack. I'm going to stay at the bookstore."

"Grace, you can't stay at the bookstore. You have to come home with me. We have loads of room and you shouldn't be alone. We'll sort it all out."

She enveloped me in a huge hug worthy of Perry Many Paws and we hastily packed her suitcase and headed out into the autumn sun, the sound of angry pacing over our heads.

Chapter Eight

I sat on a stool at the kitchen counter downing diet soda and watching Cam prepare our dinner. There was salad and lasagna, one of Cam's specialties, in the oven, and garlic bread sticks ready to dip into an oil, pepper and rosemary mixture. Oh, and there was chocolate cake for dessert. Ice cream, too.

I'd told Cam about our adventure in Ryan's bedroom several times in several ways by now and he kept assuring me that there must be some reasonable explanation.

"It could be some kind of initiation," Cam suggested, pulling the lasagna out of the oven to set before we cut it. "Teenage boys can get into some really weird stuff."

"Did you get into weird stuff when you were fifteen?" I asked.

"Dinner's almost ready," he said.

"You're avoiding my question." I gave him a gentle punch in the rear end. "I promise I won't tell Claudia."

"Well, I don't recall any blood being involved, but we did go through a period of dares as part of an initiation into a club when I was a freshman in high school. Just stupid stuff. I hope this lasagna is firm enough." He stuck his finger into the hot pan and then jerked it away.

"Don't put your finger in the lasagna, especially when it's just come out of the oven. What kind of stupid stuff?"

He ran his finger under the cold water and pretended that he had to delve deeply into his memory to recall some of the stupid things he'd done when he was fifteen.

"Mmm. Let me think. It was a long time ago …"

"A mere thirty-five years, sweetheart."

"I seem to remember having to steal a pair of my sister's underpants to add to the collection …"

"Ryan mentioned underpants, too. What is it with you guys and women's underpants?"

"Oh, girls' underpants are very important in the life of a fifteen-year-old boy. Didn't you ever read *Portnoy's Complaint?*"

"Gross. Don't talk about that before dinner," I admonished. "I don't remember my friends and I ever talking about or being interested in boys' underwear. Did you say you had a *collection* of underpants?"

"Not me, personally. The guys, the club, had a collection and to join the club you had to add to it. The sexier the underwear the more status you had. I was lucky because I had an older sister. Some of the guys had to resort to stealing their mom's underwear which was decidedly *not* sexy."

"Did Cassandra know you filched her underpants?"

"Naw. She had so many clothes she never missed them." Cam took the wine and wine glasses into the dining room and I followed him with the salad. As I headed up the stairs to get Grace, I thought of one more question.

"What did you end up doing with this awesome lingerie collection?"

"The same thing you do with all precious treasure. We buried it."

Grace and I both react to stress the same way—we eat. Cam had to be very flattered by the amount of lasagna we consumed as the three of us kept rehashing the scene in Ryan's bedroom and all the possible meanings of the bloody shirt. Cam held strongly to the belief it was some kind of initiation. Although Grace and

I were disturbed by the thought of an initiation that resulted in so much blood, we were reassured by thinking that it was the blood of an animal rather than a human—either Ryan's own blood or Uncle Franklin's.

"But if it was animal blood, why wouldn't he just tell me?" Grace questioned.

"Because that would have brought a whole new set of questions and, when you're fifteen, you hate answering questions," Cam explained. "Where did all the lasagna go? Should I have made more?"

"No, it's fine, dear. All he had to say was, 'it's animal blood' ..."

"But would you two have left it at that? It probably never occurred to him that you would think it was human blood, especially a murder victim's. All he saw was two middle-aged women poking around in his private stuff. I don't think he was angry about what you found as much as he felt violated by you both snooping in his room. Remember how closely Abbey guarded the sanctity of her bedroom? I really should've made two batches of lasagna but we used to feed all three of us and have enough for leftovers before ..."

"Stop fussing about the lasagna, Cam. There's plenty."

"Ryan's been out late at night. Maybe there *is* some kind of club or something. Hugh's been arguing with him about being out late on school nights. He's supposed to be in by nine but the last month or so he's been coming in at ten or later ..." Grace said.

"See, sounds like a group of fifteen-year-olds spreading their wings, breaking curfew and misbehaving in typical fifteen-year-old-guy ways," Cam reassured her. "They may be doing stupid things that we don't really understand but I sincerely doubt murder is one of them."

"And what would be the motive?" I asked. "Ryan didn't even know Franklin. He may not have even known there was anyone else living on our property. Nothing was stolen. Even if Ryan and his friends had been snooping around and ran into Franklin there was no reason for them to feel threatened."

"But maybe Franklin felt threatened by them," Grace suggested. Cam shook his head.

"Even if he had, he had no means to seriously scare them into thinking they needed to defend themselves. At the most he would have cursed at them. Probably he would've just ignored them ..."

"What if they started heckling him? Would he have fought back then?" I asked.

"Fought back with what? He didn't have a weapon. The police didn't find anything in the cottage disturbed or any signs that someone had broken in or seriously caused a threat to his well-being. There's just no motive."

"That's the whole problem. There's no reason for anyone to hurt Franklin. He was a harmless old man who had no contact with the outside world. It all seems so random ..."

"That's what's so scary as far as Ryan is concerned," Grace interrupted. "If there's no motive and no reason for someone to murder Franklin, it just makes it seem more likely that it was a horrible accident, a prank or a dare gone tragically wrong. It's easy to see a fifteen-year-old, especially one as hostile and unhappy as Ryan, being involved in something like that."

"Well, if that's the case," Cam said solemnly, "we have a two-victim crime."

With that sad thought we cleared the dinner dishes and moved into the library for coffee and dessert. I find nothing more comforting than sitting by a fire in a room filled with books, a dog snoozing at my feet and a huge hunk of chocolate cake and two scoops of ice cream by my side. Although snuggling in bed with Cam on a stormy night runs a close second. In an attempt to move the conversation off Ryan,

I told them about the trip to Claudia's and the identification of all the children in the old picture.

Grace picked up the photo and looked at it again. "I can't believe this girl is Syra's and Bing's mother. Neither of them have ever mentioned having roots in Birdsey Falls."

"I know. I thought they just happened to move here ages ago. They never said they were coming home."

"Maybe they weren't coming home," Cam suggested. "Maybe they'd never been here before. It sounds like their mother may have taken off from Birdsey Falls when she was a young girl and worked her way down the New York State Thruway ..."

"Cam, that's so rude. We have no idea what happened to their mother."

"True. But my point is I doubt Syra and Bing ever lived here. I certainly don't remember them growing up, do you, Grace?"

"No."

"Maybe their mother talked about where she grew up and they decided, as adults, to check it out and ended up staying. When did they move across the street, Tamsen? Do you remember?" Cam asked.

"Yes. Thirteen years ago when Abbey was just going to kindergarten. I remember because I was glad a woman my age was moving in across the street. Someone to visit with while Abbey was in school. And I was hoping she would have children, maybe a playmate for Abbey. Both she and Bing were in their thirties."

Grace set the photo down and put her feet up on the ottoman. "Do you remember where they came from? Why they came here?"

I was finding it very difficult to enjoy the relaxation of the fire in the fireplace while wracking my brain for information going back more than a decade. "No. We probably talked about it when I first met them but I don't remember. I remember Syra telling me about Bing's agoraphobic tendencies and how I had felt honored that he would wander over to our house and visit even if he never went anywhere else. But we became friends and they just were Syra and Bing and I accepted them at face value. I know Syra went to college and Bing didn't, I do remember that discussion."

"No talks about childhood or where they came from?" Cam asked.

"Not that I remember. I never felt they were being secretive, though. It just seems like it never came up or, if it did, it was so normal it went in one ear and out the other. Nothing suspicious. Can you think of anything, Grace?"

Grace shook her head. "I'm too enmeshed in my own problems to remember anything not directly connected to Ryan, Hugh and the whole mess that is my life."

We all sat silently looking at the fire and thinking our own thoughts. Mycroft was the only one able to sleep without a care in the world. A dog's life looked pretty good right now. When the doorbell rang Cam went to let Hugh in. After a brief greeting and the offer of coffee and cake, Cam and I excused ourselves and left Hugh and Grace alone to discuss their problems. I heard the front door close around 2:00 a.m.

Chapter Nine

I repeat— I'm not a brave person, and the horror of finding Uncle Franklin coupled with the ugly scene in Ryan's bedroom had not been conducive to making me bolder. One more incident and I would join Bing in the world of agoraphobia. He certainly seemed happy enough staying in his house and baking all day. When he needed some outside stimulation he wandered over to our house and brought us baked goods. If he was desperate for company he joined the weekly WOACA meeting and listened to discussions on menopause, hot flashes, empty nests, marital woes and teenager frustrations, to name a few.

We didn't really know a lot about Bing. Syra insisted that Bing was really just a happy, simple guy who loved to stay in the house and bake and occasionally socialize with the few people he felt comfortable with. He was compassionate, a good listener, never seemed troubled or unhappy, except in empathy, and he certainly was an excellent pastry chef. He and Cam were friendly but Bing was much more comfortable around women and didn't have any male friends. Syra said that since his only real interest was baking, it was difficult for him to find a common ground with other men. I frequently envied him his uncomplicated and serene world.

Unfortunately my world was more complicated and chaotic than ever before. Between the murder, Grace's marital problems and her fears about Ryan, Cam's empty-nest anxiety, Diane's caregiver issues and possible affair and Syra's breast cancer recovery woes, I continued to float around in post-traumatic stress and tried to be supportive, although I was clueless about what to do. I felt over-whelmed. If I hadn't wanted to see Grace in the morning I would have just stayed in bed, preferably with the covers over my head.

Grace didn't talk much at breakfast. She was tired and depressed and I didn't want to press her for details of her talk with Hugh last night. She left claiming she had to get to the bookstore and open it because her manager had a doctor's appointment. Cam was mumbling about an email that he'd sent Abbey yesterday that she hadn't answered yet and I had to remind him, for the hundredth time, that she had a life of her own and that's exactly what we wanted her to have.

I lingered at the kitchen table, picking at the coffee cake and drink-ing another diet soda. I popped a vitamin and a calcium chew and felt virtuous. After absentmindedly rinsing off the breakfast dishes, but not going so far as to actually wash them, I wandered upstairs and made my bed then flopped on it. I debated whether to unmake it and get back in, versus the effort of having to remake the bed once I finally got out. What would Cam think if he came home and I was still in bed? He was able to get up and go to work every day despite having a murdered uncle and an empty-nest. Grace was able to work at the bookstore all day despite having marital problems and a possibly rabid stepson. My mother-in-law's brother had been murdered and she was still able to get dressed in her cashmere and pearls and play bridge.

I closed my eyes and thought about a conversation Grace and I had had many years ago. I'd been upset with Claudia about something she'd done that I perceived as especially selfish and self-centered. Grace tried to soothe me by telling me that the world was full of old souls going through their last incarnations as well as new souls who were experiencing life for maybe only the fifth or sixth time. She felt that Claudia stood out as a new soul. Even though she was chronologically older than us in this lifetime, her soul was actually much younger. Claudia had an immature soul's view of the world—that people fell into classes, that there was only one right way of living, that intolerance was a sign of good breeding, that appearance was important and that judging others harshly elevated you. The world revolved around you and your needs and your desires. The young souls are so in love with themselves that they are unable to love anyone else. The young souls were the first ones into the Titanic's life boats; the old souls stayed on board and played "Nearer My God to Thee". I tried to remember this when dealing with Claudia so I could be patient.

I opened my eyes and stared at the ceiling. I knew I should be writing and revising the outline of my next Perry Many Paws book, so I could keep Tim, my editor, off my back. Cam had convinced me that I should honor my contract with at least one more Perry book adhering to the successful format. Then I could branch off to another creative endeavor far removed from Perry and his friends. I knew he was right but I didn't want to just bang out a book to honor my contract. I wanted to be excited about the story and to write it with the usual enthusiasm I had when the writing muse struck. Right now I was totally blocked and couldn't think of a single adventure for Perry other than possibly solving the murder of Squeaky Squirrel, found surrounded by her winter nuts with a letter opener in her neck. I knew better than to even mention that to my editor. Until this murder was solved and my family's and friends' lives were back on the right track, I wouldn't be able to write anything fit for a child to read.

I went into the bathroom and decided to brush my teeth until I could think of something useful to do. If I lost all the enamel on my teeth I would have no one to blame but my indecisive self. Then I came up with a plan. I would return to Franklin's cottage and remove some of the more valuable books. Cam hadn't gotten around to scything through the brush so he could get his truck in to take anything out, so it was all just sitting in there. It probably didn't matter but bringing a few of the books home, as many as I could comfortably carry, would be something more positive than lying on my bed. Plus I needed the exercise.

I also wanted to talk to Syra to find out more about her mother. Syra never mentioned her parents and now that I had seen her mother's picture and knew she was a childhood friend and fellow adventurer of Franklin's, I was curious to know more. Deciding to accommodate my current I'm-not-a-very-brave-person persona with my I'm-curious-about-things-that-are-none-of-my-business trait, I called Syra and asked if she would go with me to the cottage to pick up the books. Being a good friend, she agreed.

October is my favorite month. October creates her perfect weather by borrowing the dying summer warmth of September and combining it with the exhilarating chill of November. Today the weather was leaning more toward a November chill so Syra and I quickly walked to the cottage, not wasting any breath talking. The cottage was just as we had left it two days ago, which was an enormous relief. I had no wish for any more surprises. I turned the heat on as soon as we entered and Syra and I headed for the study to pick out the books we wanted to take back to the house.

"This place could be really cozy if it were redecorated. It's small but just right for one person," Syra mused as she pulled down books, stared at them and then reshelved them. "It's very picturesque. It would feel good to sit out here in a winter storm, and feel like you were all alone in the world even though you knew civilization was just a short walk away. What are you and Cam going to do with it now?"

"If I can't get rid of the haunted feeling and my last vision of Uncle Franklin, I'd just as soon tear it down," I said. "Besides, we have so much unused space in the house that we don't need to put guests out in the woods."

Syra starting taking the first-edition Jack London books off the shelves and piling them on a small table. "I'm sure you want to get these books out of here as soon as you can. I think they should have first priority."

I nodded. I'd meant to take them with me when we were cleaning last time but had gotten involved with the photo. I took *The Call of the Wild* and began to page through it. The pages and the bindings had the feel of old friends that had been visited many times. The lack of dust indicated that Franklin had read them recently and I wondered for the millionth time about the man who'd lived alone, re-reading favorite books and avoiding all human contact. Had he been retreating from a world he found too loud and confusing? Or was he hiding from something or someone? And had the person he'd been hiding from all these years finally found him? What had Franklin done that had driven someone to murder? Whatever it was, it had to have happened a long time ago because he hadn't left the cottage or the property for decades. Decades is a long time to hold a grudge, to let it simmer and stew until it boils over in a murderous rage. It was impossible for me to match the man I'd known with any youthful indiscretion that would have resulted in murder seventy years later. From what Claudia and Sybil had said, he'd seemed like a normal kid with a good imagination, a joy of the outdoors and a keen sense of adventure that he shared with his friends. What had happened?

I dug back into my purse and pulled out the photo of the five children and laid it on the desk.

"Is this the same picture you found when we were cleaning out the cottage on Saturday?" Syra asked as she picked it up and casually looked at it. I watched her face for a sign of recognition but she set it down without registering any emotion at all. "It's funny to think of kids running around in those outfits, isn't it? They seem so well dressed for playing outside compared to what kids wear now. They're like miniature adults."

"Maybe today's kids would be better behaved if they dressed like little adults," I suggested. "I took the photo to Claudia and she was able to identify everyone in it. She actually remembered the day it was taken."

"No kidding? That's great. Who are the little people? Is one Franklin?" Syra handed the picture to me and leaned closer, munching on a cookie from the supply Bing had given her for our outing.

I pointed to the handsome boy with the big smile. "Believe it or not, this is Franklin. Claudia said he would've been around fifteen when this was taken. The two little girls are Claudia and her friend Sybil ..."

"You've got to be kidding! That sweet little thing is Claudia? She looks so innocent and precious, even lovable. And Sybil is adorable. Who are the other two older kids?"

"The boy is named Edmund Close and he was a good friend of Franklin's." I pointed at the seated girl and watched Syra's face. "This is Hetty Foster, also a friend of Franklin."

Syra set her cookie down and slowly took the picture out of my hands bringing it up close to her face. She stared at it for a full minute. Her expression didn't change at all. Then she handed the picture back to me. She continued munching on her cookie.

"That little girl looks like a handful, doesn't she? So different than the prissiness of Claudia and Sybil. I wonder what became of her."

What became of her? I wanted to yell, *she's your mother*, that's what became of her. Did she really not know that was her mother? If she did know it was her mother, why not say something? The more I watched her, the more I was convinced that she had no idea that the tomboyish girl in the picture was her mother. Should I tell her?

She began to talk about her latest doctor appointment and the new series of exercises she had started since last time we spoke. She was totally normal and comfortably talking while I was fidgeting all over the place. If she weren't so wrapped up in her new exercise plans she would have noticed that I was inattentive and agitated. But she didn't notice and the longer she talked about her physical limitations and how she was planning to overcome them, the less courageous I became until the thought of confronting her about her mother seemed totally out of the question. I let the perfect moment pass.

Chapter Ten

Since Cam and Grace were both working all day, it only seemed right that I make dinner. I wasn't enthusiastic about doing it but was driven by guilt and a sense of fairness. I make an excellent beef stew and it's a good comfort meal that is perfect on a chilly fall evening. I really should have started the stew in the morning and let it simmer all day but it was one of those dishes you could hurry along by parboiling the slow cooking vegetables and cutting the potatoes into smaller chunks. I could have it ready by six o'clock and bake up a batch of baking powder biscuits, too. We could have leftover chocolate cake and ice cream from last night for dessert. A person never tired of chocolate cake and ice cream. I didn't have any salad ingredients so I thawed some frozen strawberries and mixed them into yogurt, sprinkling a little granola on top for a side dish. That stretched my culinary skills about as far as they could stretch without breaking.

I had half an hour before anyone came home so I took my knitting into the library, lit the fire in the fireplace and settled into my leather chair to knit and think. Knitting is a very relaxing pastime as long as you are knitting something you are familiar with and you don't have to count stitches. I was making a large tote bag that I would eventually felt by boiling and agitating the wool. Right now, pre-felting, it was huge, almost like an afghan lying across my lap, and it was cozy to work on when it was cold. I felt calm for the first time all day. Occasionally I held it up, trying to picture how small it would get after felting and trying to figure out when I should stop knitting. The last one I'd made had been three feet tall before I felted it and was strong enough to carry a six-pack of soda, a couple of books, my purse and other miscellaneous things I threw in. It was so strong I could fill it until I could barely pick it up and hoist it on my shoulder and it still hung tough. As long as you didn't throw a set of steak knives in there it could carry anything.

The thought of steak knives slicing through the felted wool pushed my thoughts back to Uncle Franklin. It was probably easier to shove a sharp letter opener into an old man's body than through felted wool. Now that was a pleasant thought. I wondered if I'd ever be able to go longer than thirty minutes without thinking about his murder. If there was resolution, if I could understand who and why, it would be easier to have closure and move on. Right now it was a huge gaping unresolved mystery, like a pond of quicksand that was beginning to suck my friends in. Ryan's bloody shirt. Syra's mysterious mother. Cam's family. Like Alice I was becoming curiouser and curiouser.

I thought about calling Diane to see if she mentioned anything about the policeman and whether she seemed as obsessed with him as Grace thought she was. Diane was a very stable person but she was also stretched thin dealing with her parents and five children, three of them still at home. I could see how a woman could become sucked dry by her family and need something special just for herself. What I couldn't see was someone like Diane, whose life revolved around her family, jeopardizing their welfare for an affair. You don't devote yourself to something and then turn around and risk losing it all to get some relief. I could see her taking a vacation by herself or with her friends. Or maybe taking a college class. Or Tai Chi. Possibly horseback riding. But not an affair. That was not how Diane dealt with life.

I heard Cam and Grace in the front hall commenting on the great smell coming from the kitchen. Those of us with dubious culinary skills have to savor our praise when we can. When I felt they had peaked in their olfactory compliments, I went to greet them, hoping tonight's dinner would be more serene than last night's.

Cam had had a lot of interesting adventures at work. He was a good storyteller and even incidents that were only mildly amusing seemed more exciting when he told them. Grace actually laughed and seemed to enjoy herself. By dessert, Cam's one-man show was starting to wind down and over coffee and chocolate cake we lapsed into more serious issues. I told Grace and Cam about my trip to the cottage with Syra and how I had shown her the photo and gotten no reaction from her.

"Since Syra never talks about her parents or her childhood, we have no idea if she and her mother are still in contact or whether she's even still alive. Maybe Syra hasn't seen her for so long that she is just sort of a vague memory," Grace suggested. She accepted a second piece of chocolate cake but refused another scoop of ice cream. "It could be that she never saw a picture of her mother as a young girl. I'm not sure I would recognize photos of my parents as kids. Maybe Bing would have a different reaction."

"He's younger than Syra so if she doesn't recognize her mother then he isn't going to," I reminded her.

"Still, it couldn't hurt to try. What other choice do we have? I'd be interested in asking Claudia more about the kids in the photo and what became of them and if she knows what happened to Hetty Foster. We know what happened to Claudia, Franklin and Sybil. But what about that Edward person?" Grace asked.

"Edmund. Edmund Close. No idea what happened to him. Are there any Closes around here? Do either of you remember any family named Close when you were growing up?" I asked Cam and Grace. They were both Birdsey Falls natives whereas I was the outsider who had only lived here for twenty-five years.

Cam refilled his and Grace's coffee cups and sat back down. "There was a guy named Close in high school, wasn't there, Grace? He had a strange first name."

Grace shook her head.

"I remember him because we were in a couple of gym classes together. He never hung out with anyone that I can remember. Sort of a loner. His last name was definitely Close though. I remember that. Maybe he was the son of this Edmund Close."

"Let's get out your high school yearbooks and check him out," I suggested. "Maybe there were other Closes in other grades that you didn't know about ..."

"I didn't even know about the Close who was in my own class ..." Grace interjected.

"Maybe they were all reclusive."

"And maybe they are no relation to Edmund Close. Just because they have the last name doesn't mean they were related," Cam reminded us. "Also, I have no idea where my high school yearbooks are. It may take me a while to track them down."

"Let me look for mine first, Cam; my house is much smaller than yours ..." Grace's voice trailed off as she remembered that she wasn't exactly living at her house right now.

Cam picked up on Grace's discomfort before I did. "Come to think of it, I'm sure mine are in my old bedroom someplace. Let me check in there. It's easier than you going home to look for yours, Grace."

"Yeah, you should see his old bedroom. His mother left it like a shrine with all his old posters on the walls and clothes in the closet.

It's kind of creepy but also an interesting look back into the teen-aged Cam. Now Abbey expects us to do the same with her room. In a few generations we will have a museum of social history here with examples of bedrooms from teenagers of several generations."

"That's actually not a bad idea for a museum. I'd enjoy walking down a hallway with an example of a bedroom from several generations of fifteen-year-olds. Do you have your dad's bedroom from when he was a teenager?" Grace asked.

"No, the shrine starts with Cassandra's and my rooms and continues with Abbey's. When my grandchild gets his or her bedroom enshrined we'll be ready to open the museum up for viewing. I think we need at least three generations to make it interesting," Cam laughed.

Grace began clearing the dishes but I shooed her back to her seat and took over rinsing and putting the dishes into the dishwasher. Cam waved the coffee pot around inquisitively and when Grace declined, poured the rest of the coffee into his cup.

Mellowed by chocolate, we headed into the library to once again join Mycroft lounging by the fire. I started thinking about Cam's and my future in this huge old house. If I got to the point that I couldn't get up and down the stairs, I think I would move my bedroom into the library. I could easily live in just this room, the kitchen and the solarium and be happy. I didn't picture Cam and I ever leaving our home but who could predict how we would feel about the house if one of us were gone. Sometimes you just know it's time to move on.

"What did you and Hugh decide to do about the situation with Ryan's bloody shirt?" Cam asked. "Did Ryan have a good explanation for it?"

"He had an explanation but it wasn't a good one," Grace said. "He claimed he and some friends found a deer lying on the side of the road. He went over to have a closer look and got blood on his shirt."

"Sounds made up. And why hide the shirt in his closet?" I asked.

"He said he didn't know how to get the blood out so was going to look it up on the Internet and try to clean it. Neither Hugh nor I are very happy with the story but, no matter how much Hugh pushed him, he wouldn't change it. Eventually they both got mad and stormed off."

"What happened to the shirt?" Cam asked.

"Hugh took it. That really made Ryan angry. He's definitely been acting strange, but then he's always strange if you ask me. Even Hugh seems to feel he's stranger than usual. Hugh asked Ryan to show him the deer but Ryan refused on the grounds that having to show his dad the deer meant his dad didn't believe him. Which is true. We don't believe him."

"But Ryan wasn't hurt, right? The blood couldn't be his?"

"We aren't even sure of that. He doesn't have any cuts or signs of injury that we can see. That's one of the reasons Hugh took the shirt. He wants to find out if it's human blood or animal blood."

"How's he going to do that?" Cam asked. "He's an antiques dealer, not a CSI tech."

"He has a friend who's a biology professor at the college. He's going to ask him to analyze it. It certainly would make us both feel better to know it's animal blood rather than Ryan's or some other kid's."

The three of us sat in comfortable silence for a while. This was a peaceful room meant for reading and contemplation. I think my blood pressure dropped significantly whenever I stepped into the library. It was impossible to be upset or agitated in here.

"Oh my God!" Cam exclaimed, obviously not feeling as mellow as I was. "We've got to be the three most stupid people in the world!" He pounded his fist several times on the leather armrest, jumped out of his chair and began pacing back and forth in front of the fireplace. "Stupid. Stupid. Stupid."

"What is it?" Grace and I asked in unison.

"We've been so stupid …"

"Okay Cam, we have the stupid part down. *What* have we been so stupid about?" I demanded.

Cam rushed back to his chair, flopped back in his seat and moved to the edge of the cushion, putting his elbows on his open knees as he leaned closer to Grace and I seated on the couch.

"Okay, Tamsen, imagine this. Grace brings you a picture of a group of young kids. You honestly do not recognize any of them. She tells you their names—John Smith, Rosie Jones, Abbey Mack ..."

I could feel all the blood rush from my head. Grace's eyes opened so wide I thought they were in danger of popping out. Of course. It was so obvious. Syra didn't necessarily need to recognize anyone in the photograph, but she should have recognized the name "Hetty Foster." At the very least wouldn't she have said, "That girl has the same name as my mom"? She may not have thought it actually was her mother but anyone would have mentioned the coincidence. But Syra hadn't said a thing. She'd acted like she'd never heard the name Hetty Foster before. Ryan wasn't the only person who was hiding something.

Chapter Eleven

It had been twelve days since Uncle Franklin's murder. Diane had hosted WOACA on the interim Tuesday but I hadn't gone, since I was still in my shocked stupor stage. We all agreed it was time to get back to normal life and an afternoon meeting at my house seemed a good place to start. Bing had brought one' of the group's favorite treats—pecan sticky buns. Bing didn't skimp on the pecans, and you didn't need to ration out the sticky sweet topping because it was all over the place. Even with the abundance of sugar and nuts, they were surprisingly non-filling and we were all able to eat at least two; some of us three. Bing also was considerate enough to bring a tub of wet wipes and we were passing those around and scrubbing our hands and faces when what had been a sunny fall day suddenly turned overcast and windy. Without saying a word, we all grabbed the remaining sticky buns, the coffee pot and our knitting, and moved to the library. I lit the fire and we all resettled ourselves. The sudden output of physical energy apparently made everyone hungry so the sticky buns made their third trip around the circle and everyone freshened up their coffee.

Diane was telling us funny stories about Keith and Kevin and their adventures at college. I usually enjoyed hearing about their exploits now that Abbey was also in college. The Keith and Kevin stories involved a lot of partying and late nights and near misses with campus police. I couldn't really identify with that sort of behavior because I knew Abbey spent most her time in the library studying or with her girlfriends eating popcorn and watching old black-and-white movies in their pajamas. I was pretty sure Abbey had no idea there even were campus police.

While Diane was telling some tale about climbing on the roof of some building and hanging another school's mascot, my eyes and my mind began to wander. Eventually both landed with a jolt on Diane, who was removing her cardigan and displaying quite a bit of flesh in her V-neck sweater underneath. Diane always wears twin sets; she must have one in every color. They are always the same, a cardigan with a short-sleeved crew-neck sweater underneath. Sometimes, in the dead of winter she will wear a turtleneck. Never a V-neck. Diane had bought a new sweater, one that showed cleavage. I glanced over at Grace, who was also staring at Diane. Slowly she drew her eyes away and turned her head to me. Our eyes locked. Without saying a word, the following conversation took place:

Did you see Diane's sweater?

Of course, how could I miss it?

I can't believe no one else is noticing.

I can't believe Diane has that much cleavage.

She must have bought some new underwear when she bought the sweater.

Why is she wasting it on us?

I told you she was having an affair.

You may be right. What should we do?

I have no idea.

Grace and I turned our attention back to Diane's story, which was just winding up with one of the twins falling off the roof but luckily being so drunk that the fall didn't hurt him. Everyone without college-age children thought it was hysterical. I was starting to feel nauseated. I'm not sure if it was the idea that being drunk and falling off roofs was widely accepted as normal college behavior, or the realization that

Diane might very well be having an affair that was the culprit. Or maybe it was the four sticky buns. Diane took one look at my bilious countenance and immediately turned the conversation over to me.

"I'm sorry for monopolizing the whole meeting with stories of Keith and Kevin," she apologized. "I know you want to talk about Perry and I'm anxious to hear how negotiations are going with your editor." Everyone murmured agreement that it was time for a report on the latest on my book, so I roused myself with a slug of diet soda and reported.

"I've sent several drafts of new story beginnings and outlines and Tim has rejected them all. He's really being adamant about keeping with the formula. I've lost all enthusiasm for the project ..."

"Isn't that going to get you into trouble? Don't you need to deliver something on a deadline?" Syra asked.

"Tim's being lenient because of the situation with Uncle Franklin. He thinks I'm not myself because I discovered the body. He's right about that, although wrong about that being the reason I'm having trouble writing. But I'll let him keep thinking along those lines as long as it gives me time."

"But is time going to solve anything?" Grace asked. "I don't think time is going to change your mind and it doesn't seem like it will change Tim's, either."

"You're right, but I just don't want to think about it right now or write anymore, so it gives me time to forget about it temporarily."

"I'll just think about it another day— that's what my mom used to call the Scarlett O'Hara solution," Bing chimed in. "I do it all the time and it usually works."

Like they had been pulled by a strong magnetic force, Grace's and my eyes met. Bing went on to tell a story illustrating how the Scarlett O'Hara approach worked, while Grace and I both mouthed the word, "mother?" and carried on our own wordless conversation:

Bing does remember his mother.

That means she was there when they were growing up.

That also means they must know her name.

So that means Syra was lying when she didn't know who Hetty Foster was.

I think we should show the picture to Bing.

I agree. But how can we do it without Syra knowing?

I have no idea.

I had a throbbing headache from having telepathic conversations with Grace. Now Grace was giving me the emphatic "look over there" eye signals and I glanced quickly at Syra. Perched at the edge of her chair, she had started fidgeting when Bing mentioned their mother. The sweater sleeve she was knitting was becoming shorter and shorter as she rhythmically pulled out stitches and stared at her brother, willing him to stop talking. Their telepathy was apparently not as well honed as mine and Grace's because Bing just kept chatting away.

Suddenly Syra threw her knitting on the floor and yelled out, "What is the deal with that sweater, Diane? Why are you showing so much boob?"

Well, that was certainly a conversation stopper.

Diane's head jerked from Bing to Syra and her hand flew up to her chest. Oh dear, this is it. The whole affair accusation is going to be out in the open in a minute and, although I longed to know what was going on with Diane and the cop, I definitely didn't want to know it under these circumstances. Diane continued to stare at Syra and tears streaked down Syra's face.

"I don't see why you have to dress like that now," she sniffed. "You know my situation."

"Oh God, Syra. I'm so sorry. I didn't mean anything …"

"Then why do you have to dress like that now when you have never showed off your body before. I feel like you are flaunting your figure when I …"

Everyone jumped to Diane's defense, assuring Syra that Diane didn't mean anything by her outfit, that we all knew Diane better than that, that we all were more sensitive than that, that we all were more caring. Syra burst into tears. Diane burst into tears. Bing burst into tears. Even Mycroft began to whimper. I started counting my breathing, the exercise I use to bring me into the current moment. Then realized I didn't want to be in the current moment and switched to my serenity scene to take me away from the current moment. I had almost escaped when Grace jumped up and announced, "Syra, it has nothing to do with you. Diane's having an affair with the policeman and is wearing sexy clothes for him!"

Conversation stopper number two.

I was immediately wrenched out of my imaginary walk through the garden and back into reality. "Jesus, Grace," was all I could say.

"Well, we all know something is going on," Grace said. "I mean, well, don't we?"

Bing shook his head. "I don't."

"Oh Bing, you're clueless," Grace countered. "The rest of us couldn't help but notice Diane flirting with the cop and then talking about him all the time. It's obvious something is going on ..."

"Nothing is going on!" Diane denied, face flushed with anger. "What's wrong with you? You're supposed to be my friends. You all think this? Why is everyone against me?"

"No one's against you, Diane," I assured her. "It's because we care about you that we're worried you might be getting into something that ..."

"I just told you nothing is going on! I don't want to talk about it anymore." She took a deep breath. "I have a new sweater. So what? Since when can't we buy something new, and a little different? Why does this suddenly have to escalate into me being insensitive of Syra because she had a mastectomy or me having an affair? Can't I just buy something new without it having to *mean* something?" She grabbed her cardigan and yanked it back on. "If you want to talk about some-thing suspicious, why don't we talk about why Grace is living with Tamsen and why Ryan was at the police station yesterday talking to Donny."

"Who said Ryan was at the police station? Why didn't I know that?" Grace was back on her feet, looking around the room as if for the answer. Mycroft lumbered to his feet and began to sniff around. Awesome bloodhound.

Diane slapped her hand over her mouth so hard I was sure it would leave a red mark. "Oh my God. I wasn't supposed to say anything."

"Well you have to say something now!" Grace looked like she was going to grab Diane by her new V-neck top and shake her. Syra and I both jumped up and ushered Grace back to her chair, patting her comfortingly on her back. For some reason, Bing continued to just sit there and cry.

"It's just that Donny told me ..."

"Who the hell is Donny? Oh yeah, that must be your boyfriend ..." Grace rolled her eyes.

"He's not my boyfriend! Do you want to hear or not, Grace? If you were living at home you'd know, because Hugh was at the police station with Ryan all afternoon yesterday. Do you even know what's going on in your own family? Do you even care?"

"Of course I care!" Grace grabbed a pillow and began to sob into it. "It's just so hard being a family. I don't know how to do it." I put my arm around Grace and hugged her and said soothing nothings until she calmed down. Syra blew her nose on a napkin and stuffed it in her purse. Diane had stopped crying and was just mad now, glaring at all of us. Mycroft's sniffing expedition had ended in Bing's crotch and Bing was absentmindedly petting the old hound while the tears continued to stream down his face.

"Diane, can you tell us what this Donny guy said? I assume he's the policeman you are, uh, acquainted with." I continued to pat Grace's back while questioning Diane.

"Well, I'm not supposed to say anything. I lost my temper and it spurted out. But I guess it's OK to tell because if Grace had been home she would have known ..."

I shook my head. "Please don't start that again, Diane."

"OK. OK. All I know is that Ryan and Hugh went to the police station, on their own, and brought in a shirt of Ryan's. It had human blood on it ..."

"Oh God ..." Grace groaned.

"I don't know what they talked about but they were there all afternoon and then they went home. That's all I know."

"No one was arrested?" I asked.

"No, they just talked."

"See Grace, it's not as bad as it sounded," I tried to console her. "And it's good that Ryan and Hugh went there on their own rather than having someone come pick them up for questioning. They are trying to do the right thing so it means there is a good reason for the blood, something that has nothing to do with Uncle Franklin."

Diane cleared her throat. "Well, it is good that they went down there on their own with the shirt ... but ... well ..."

"What?" I snapped.

"It was Franklin Behrends' blood all over the shirt."

Grace screamed and Bing burst into tears.

This was definitely the worst WOACA meeting we'd ever had.

***

Dinner was quite subdued that evening. After the meeting broke up, Grace starting calling both Hugh and Ryan and couldn't reach them.

She'd driven over to the house but no one was home. In frustration she'd left phone messages and a note at her house and returned here in time for dinner. I hadn't been grocery shopping in recent memory and even Cam, the most creative of cooks, was unable to produce a dinner out of what was sitting in our near-empty cupboards. We ordered in pizza and wings. I was starving. I didn't need to take a test in a woman's magazine to know I was an emotional eater. I'd had a brief conversation with Cam and filled him in on the disastrous WOACA meeting. We agreed not to bring up either Ryan or Hugh unless Grace did. Cam had found all his high school yearbooks so he had those at the table and we flipped through them, constantly wiping our hands on napkins between bites of pizza and page turning. While Cam was fervently looking for the boy named Close, Grace and I were checking out hairdos and making fun of the pictures of Cam.

"All these kids look so happy in these pictures," Grace sighed. "I don't remember seeing Ryan smile since his mother died. I've been a terrible stepmother."

"He hasn't really given you a chance," Cam said. "He's been in a depressed and hostile mood since you and Hugh married. It's not you. Maybe the three of you could go for family counseling."

"We should. I just hope we aren't doing it in a jail cell."

"Here he is! I found him pictured in the French Club photo. See?" Cam handed the book around and pointed at a skinny, sullen boy who could give Ryan some competition for most unhappy teenager. "His name is Sylvester. Sylvester Close."

"He looks so sad," I commented. "What was he like?"

"I can't remember much about him at all except that he wasn't a whiz in gym class. If your name was Sylvester you wouldn't be very happy either. What were his parents thinking?"

"Maybe it was his father's name," Grace offered. "But if it was, that leaves out the possibility that he's Edmund Close's son.

I continued flipping through the yearbook I'd been assigned and suddenly noticed something, "Uh, Cam ..."

"Yeah?"

"If you look at the back of the yearbook, there's an index for each person. It lists their school activities and the pages they appear on in the book. It's faster than looking at each page and reading each name ..."

"Damn. Why didn't I notice that? OK. Everyone check their indexes to see if there are any other Closes listed."

We all dutifully flipped to the back of the books and checked the indexes. The only Close any of us found was Sylvester. The French Club had been his only activity all through high school and he appeared in the club group picture and his class picture and nothing else.

"Was he voted most likely to do anything other than speak French?" I asked. "Who has his senior yearbook?"

"I have the senior year. Let's see ... oh look how cute Cam's senior picture is! 'Most likely to be Secretary of State'. Quite an honor, Cam," Grace said. "Here's Sylvester Close. Still not smiling. Maybe he didn't have any teeth. 'Most likely to bury us all.' Yikes. That's a little foreboding."

"Most likely to bury us all? Oh my God, did they think he was some kind of serial killer?" I asked. "That is truly creepy. I think we need to find out what happened to him. Do you think he's still in town? Do you think he had actually already killed someone by the time he graduated high school?" Cam took the book from Grace and looked at it. Grace and I shuddered and grabbed the last two chicken wings.

"Uh, Tamsen ..."

"Yes, dear ..."

"If you continue looking in the back of the book you'll see ads from well wishers ..."

"So?"

Cam pushed the book toward me and pointed to an ad on the last page:

Best wishes to the class of 1976 from the Close Funeral Home

For some reason we all thought this was hysterical and were still laughing when all the dishes were cleared from the table and Grace's phone rang. She excused herself and went into the living room to answer it. Cam and I rinsed dishes and loaded the dishwasher. After we had finished, I remembered that all the dishes in there were clean and I had forgotten to unload it. We ran it anyway. Cam filled three bowls with chocolate macadamia nut ice cream and we headed for the library and waited for Grace to join us. She looked tired but smiled gratefully when I handed her the dish. We let her eat a couple bites in peace and then couldn't stand it anymore.

"Was that Hugh? What's going on?"

Grace nodded and put down her bowl. Her spoon fell to the floor and no one noticed except Mycroft who reached out a paw and pulled the spoon to his mouth. "That was Hugh. They're home now and saw my note and got all my phone messages. He apologized for not telling me what was going on but Ryan made him promise not to until they got home. It was part of the agreement that persuaded him to go to the station and talk to Officer Donny."

"Diane's friend."

"I think so."

"So what precipitated this trip to the station in the first place?" Cam asked. "I'm assuming the shirt started the whole thing …"

"Exactly, and things snowballed from there. Hugh took the shirt in to the University to have it tested by his friend in the Biology Department. That guy reported to Hugh that it was human blood and

Hugh freaked out. Between Hugh and Ryan there is a lot of freaking out that goes on ..."

"Hereditary. How we react to stress is both a result of nature and of nurture ..."

"Cam, please. Let Grace finish."

"Sorry."

"Anyway, Hugh freaked and went to Ryan, who also freaked, so they screamed at each other for what was probably hours without me there to interfere and play referee. The gist of all the screaming was that Ryan agreed to go to the police and explain the blood on his shirt ..."

"Did he tell Hugh it was Franklin's?" I asked.

"Eventually. Hugh said he came up with several lies on his way to the truth but Hugh can be unrelenting and finally broke him down and he confessed it was Franklin's."

"But he didn't—" I couldn't finish the sentence.

"No. He didn't confess to killing him. He swears he didn't and Hugh believes him."

"It's a good sign they didn't keep him at the station. This Officer Donny must believe him also," Cam added.

"So what's his story?" I asked. "How did he get Franklin's blood on his shirt?"

"Well, here's where it gets weird," Grace said. "He and some friends had been spying on Franklin for several weeks. One of the boys happened to notice Franklin in his cottage one night as he was cutting across your property to go home ..."

"I bet it was Jason Willetts," Cam interrupted. "I've noticed him cutting through our yard many times when he's out walking his dog. It gets Mycroft all agitated. I've also heard that he's had a couple run-ins with the police. Not the kind of kid I'd want my son to hang out with."

"Yeah, I think that was the same name Hugh said. Jason some-body. Well Jason apparently had been checking Franklin out as he went past ..."

I nodded. "Franklin never closed his curtains and with the light on he was easy to see."

"For some reason this Jason kid found Franklin amusing and told Ryan and this other friend named Mike. They decided to spy on him at night when they had nothing better to do. So several nights in a row they sat in the woods and watched Franklin through the window, each night daring each other to move a little closer."

"Typical," Cam muttered.

"They eventually got to the point where they were sneaking right up to the cottage and peeking in the windows ..."

"They were probably scaring poor Uncle Franklin to death," Cam said.

"No. They swore Franklin never saw them. I don't think they were tormenting him. Ryan said Franklin never once noticed they were out there."

"So how did the blood get on Ryan's shirt?" I asked. Somewhere in the story Ryan had to have gotten into the house.

"This is the part of the story that had to be dragged out of Ryan. Apparently they finally got up the nerve to try the back door, the one that leads into the kitchen, and began daring each other to go into the house and see how far they could get. On Mike's night, he'd opened the door and stepped into the kitchen then heard Franklin moving around in his study and bolted out the door. On the second night, Jason's night, Jason went through the kitchen and waved at the guys through the living room window and then high tailed it out of there."

I shook my head. "Girls don't do stupid things like this. I can't imagine Abbey and her friends being this stupid." Cam gave me his wide-eyed "don't change the subject now" look and I dropped it.

"Then it came to Ryan's night to go into the house," Grace continued. "He had to do one better than Jason so he said he planned to go into the doorway of the study where Franklin sat every night and wave at the guys from a spot where Franklin couldn't see him. The boys hid outside the study window. Ryan went in and waved at the guys as planned. Franklin's back was to Ryan and he was facing the window but the other two boys were far enough back that he couldn't see them in the dark if he looked out, which they said he never did."

"So where did the blood come from?" I asked.

"I'm getting there. Franklin was alive the night Ryan went into the study for his dare. It was the next night that the trouble took place. After Ryan's trip into the study, no one could think of anything more daring that any of them were willing to do. Ryan said that up until the last minute the dare had been for someone to go into the house and use the bathroom and then sneak out, minus the flushing. Then when Franklin went in the bathroom he would wonder if he forgot to flush. Pretty juvenile ..."

"It's starting to sound like harassment to me," I told her.

"I didn't say it was nice of them. They were obviously being jerks, even Ryan knows that. Jason and Mike didn't want to do the bathroom stunt, but Ryan was feeling pretty daring and superior after getting into the study the night before, so he volunteered to go into the house again even though it wasn't his turn. But he decided to go one step further. There was a photo on a table behind Franklin ..."

"Oh jeez. This sounds bad ..."

"... so Ryan decided he would sneak in behind Franklin and take the photo. He walked into the room and waved at his friends and kept walking closer and closer to Franklin to gain more status. At some point he started to notice that Franklin wasn't moving and one thing led to another and he ended up catching Franklin's body as it began to slide out of the chair ..."

"Thus getting covered in blood."

"Right. He straightened the body and then took off. He was covered with blood so he took his shirt off, wadded it up, and threw it in the bottom of his closet. The other boys were petrified and they all agreed to keep quiet because they were afraid people would think they killed him. End of story."

"And Hugh believes him?" I asked.

"Yes, absolutely. And I do, too," Grace answered. "Ryan's messed up in a lot of ways but he isn't a murderer and he had no reason ..."

"Unless it was a dare that got out of hand," Cam said. "I don't mean to argue with you, Grace, but what if everything is true except that Ryan *did* try to get the photo and Franklin caught him and they struggled and Ryan stabbed him in self defense?"

Grace emphatically shook her head. "That definitely couldn't have happened. I'll never believe Ryan killed Franklin, even by mistake."

I could tell Cam wasn't convinced but he didn't want to upset Grace. He fell into his own thoughts, and Grace and I discussed what would happen to Ryan next (we had no idea), what we could do to help (we had no idea) and who might have actually killed Franklin (we had no idea). After talking to Hugh, Grace had agreed to go home the next day and be there while the three of them tried to work through this latest Ryan escapade. Grace knew she could always come back to The Castle if she needed to, and having that to fall back on made it easier for her to go home and give it another try. I was glad she and Hugh were working things out but I would really miss her company for dinners and evenings in the library. Our house really needed a third person.

Chapter Twelve

When I said this house needed a third person, I meant I was missing Abbey and now missing Grace—people to eat with and talk to. I was not referring to the company of spectral beings.

Grace is a staunch believer in the presence of spirits. She firmly embraces the idea that those who have crossed over are still nearby and within reach if we need them. There's no fear in her belief but, rather, comfort. I can understand where Grace is coming from. She and her sister, Sarah, lost their parents when they were in high school. Both parents were killed in a collision with a truck on an icy February evening. Grace and Sarah moved in with their grandparents and, when her grandfather died, Grace inherited Trenary Booksellers, her grandfather's bookstore. She still ran and operated the bookstore and Hugh rented the antiques store next door, which is how they met.

Grace claims to have talked to her parents and her grandparents many times since they died; she says this has brought her great inner peace. Syra and Diane think she's nuts. I'm not so sure. I've had a few incidents where I swear a guardian angel or benevolent spirit has intervened to help me out. Grace insists that the rest of us are always so busy and harried that we don't spend enough quiet time listening and paying attention to the world around us; we aren't receptive to the quiet voices of those who want to help and guide us. Since Abbey went to college I've had a lot more time on my own and my mind has been freer and quieter. I'm doing more listening, more introspective thinking, more experiencing of nature and complete silence, and because of this I am starting to believe that Grace is right. What is better proof of life after death than the presence of loving spirits who have passed before us, living in another dimension and offering their advice and protection. It's a lovely idea, and the older I get the more sense it makes.

I was feeling melancholy the first night without Grace in the house. It was the same way I felt every time Abbey left to return to college. The house had seemed full and now it seemed too quiet. Even Mycroft was more sullen and that's saying a lot for a bloodhound. Cam admitted that the house seemed too empty, but I knew he was referring to Abbey's absence and not Grace's.

No matter what kind of sleeper you were prior to motherhood, you instantly become a light sleeper once you give birth. In contrast, Cam is a very deep sleeper. Nature is all about balance. I was having trouble sleeping and was dozing fitfully. I woke up and looked at the clock, 3:23 a.m. Good. I'd slept forty uninterrupted minutes. I made a quick trip to the bathroom then hurried back to bed to snuggle up to Cam to get warm. I was nuzzling his shoulder and trying to wedge myself into the spooning position, which is difficult when one of the spooners is comatose. Then I heard it. At first I thought it was my imagination. Then I heard it again. A definite bumping noise. And it was coming from directly below us, from the library. Mycroft started to howl, a soft, almost whining sound.

"Cam! Wake up." I untangled myself from Cam and the covers and sat up, shaking his shoulder.

"Wha …?"

"Mycroft is howling. Listen."

Cam opened one eye and reached for me. "Are you trying to say you want to have sex?"

I stared at him. "What the hell are you talking about?"

"You said Mycroft was howling. I thought that was code for having sex. Remember how he always howled …"

I shook him. More than vigorously. His head flopped back and forth.

"I don't speak in code. Listen to me! Mycroft's sleeping in the library and he's howling and I heard a noise down there …"

"I really need coffee, sweetheart, if you want to get up this early and talk …"

"Oh for God's sake, Cam, wake up!"

"I'm trying …"

"Cam, there's a burglar in the library!"

Cam bolted upright and jumped out of bed. "A burglar in the library! Why didn't you say so? Call 911. I'm going down …"

"I'm coming with you."

"You stay here. It's not safe …"

"No! You can't go alone. There's safety in numbers." I grabbed his arm. "Wait a minute. Stop! Let's go down the secret passage. We'll surprise them, maybe see who they are so we can give the police a description …"

"The police should be here soon, don't you think?"

"Ahh. No one called them!" I grabbed the phone and dialed 911, gave them the abbreviated version, and then hung up even though they told me to stay on the line.

To use the secret passage that goes directly from our bedroom to the library, you have to go into our walk-in closet, move the clothes aside and lift a latch on the far wall. We didn't dare turn on any lights—in retrospect, I have no idea why—so we bumbled around in the closet, got hung up in the clothes, tripped over the shoes on the floor, felt frantically all over the wall searching for the latch, and eventually got the door open. The staircase leading to the library is a very tight circular one and, again, we were determined not to turn on the light. Cam went first and I hung onto the belt of his robe, in case he fell, and followed carefully, holding the railing with my other hand.

"Will the door squeak when I open it?" Cam whispered. He whispered so quietly that all I could hear was 'hiss hiss door hiss hiss open?"

"Yes," I whispered back. Cam stood there indecisively, so I nudged him. "Open it!"

"I can't if it's going to squeak. It'll give us away."

"Jesus. Just open the door and be quiet about it."

"But …"

I couldn't take it anymore so I reached past him and pushed the door open just a crack.

"It didn't squeak at all …"

"No one said it would. Are you even half-awake?"

The door in the library is behind a bookcase, the usual revolving bookcase like you see in the movies. There wasn't a light on in the library or else even the most clueless burglar would notice a library bookcase that swung open enough to allow two people to look out from behind it. The only greeting we received was from Mycroft who lumbered over and began sniffing at us and pawing at the bookcase. There was no other sound.

"I don't think there's anyone here. Hand me the flashlight," Cam whispered. Of course I didn't have one. I ignored him. He must have caught on because he didn't mention it again. "I'm going in. You wait here."

"No!"

"No, you don't want me to go in …?"

"No, no I don't want to wait here!"

Just as we began to inch ourselves into the room, Mycroft raced out and began howling in the front hall, his toenails doing a tap dance on the marble floor. We both hesitated, not wanting to expose ourselves to the burglar if Mycroft had gotten his scent in the hall. We were still at the point where we could pull the bookcase closed and stay hidden in the wall if we had to. Suddenly there was pounding at the door and Mycroft started barking in earnest. One of us screamed and the other one swore, but I'm not sure who did what. Then it dawned on us that the police had arrived and we bolted out of the passage to the front door to let them in.

What followed was the usual police procedural. In summary, there was no sign of a break-in at either the front or back doors. None of the windows had been tampered with. Nothing was missing. Nothing was disturbed. I was waiting for them to tell us it had to be an inside job, which pretty much made Mycroft the culprit as Cam and I could alibi each other. An hour later they were gone and we were wide awake. Cam started a fire. I made him some coffee and grabbed a diet soda, caffeine-free, for myself. I also brought in a package of cookies and a doggy treat. The three of us sat around the fire munching and staring and trying to figure out what had happened. Cam reached over and squeezed my hand.

"You were incredibly brave, sweetheart."

I squeezed back, "So were you, once you woke up."

"Yeah, my emergency response time could use some work. Coming in through the passage was a good idea. If someone had actually been in here, we would've been really exposed coming in the regular door."

I pulled my hand away. "What do you mean *if* someone had been here? Don't you believe anyone broke in?"

"Well, no one was here and nothing was disturbed ..."

"Cam, I heard something down here. Mycroft was howling. You know he would never do that if he were alone."

"He might've had a bad dream."

"I heard something, someone. I know I did. Someone was in here. I'm sure of it."

"What would they have been doing in here? How did they get in? I don't think we should worry about something that may not even have ..."

"Maybe they were in here during the day and just hid until we went to sleep ..."

"Oh, that's reassuring."

"Well, the house is so big we could have dozens of people hiding in here and never know it."

"We could install heat sensors in all the unused rooms so an alarm would go off if entire families were hiding on the third floor," Cam suggested, a tad too sarcastically.

"Be serious, Cam."

"I'm being as serious as I can be when I never heard a thing, never saw a thing and neither did the police. They're professionals, and if there were signs of a break-in they would find them. They were here for over an hour going all over the house and didn't find anything suspicious. The fact that Mycroft howled, rare as that is, doesn't mean someone broke in. You should be glad no one was here. It seems to me that 'false alarm' is the best conclusion we could hope for." He put his arm around my shoulder. "You aren't disappointed that there wasn't a break-in, are you? If so, we need to add some adventure to our lives."

"What I'm disappointed about is that no one believes me when I say someone was in here. Oh, forget it. Let's see if we can go back to sleep."

We agreed that we would go up the main staircase and close up the passage. As we left the library, Mycroft pushed himself to his feet and started after us. Mycroft always slept in the library at night and in the solarium during the day. He was physically unable to make it up the stairs anymore. As we reached the bottom of the staircase Cam knelt down and gave Mycroft a good ear rub.

"Time for you to go back to bed, boy. We'll see you in the morning." He gave him a hug and tried to head him back toward the library. Uncharacteristically, Mycroft refused to budge and continued to paw at the bottom stair and sniff around.

"I think he's all discombobulated. I wish we could take him upstairs with us," I said as I reached over and rubbed his head. "Poor little guy has no idea what's going on."

"Well, that makes three of us. I guess we can just let him wander around down here for a while if he's restless. He'll eventually work his way back to the library." We each gave Mycroft a good night hug and headed up the stairs. When we reached the top I turned around to see if he had headed back to the library. He was right where we left him, standing at the bottom of the stairs staring up at us. Only this time he held something white in his teeth. It looked like cloth.

Cam and I scampered down the stairs and removed it.

"It's all wet and drooly," I said. "What is it?"

Cam held it up and shook it out. It wasn't really white, more of a creamy yellow, and it was quite beautiful, with lacy edges. "It's a lady's handkerchief. Where would that have come from?"

"It looks pretty old. Part of it is starting to unravel. There's something sewn on it," I said. "Look. There's an embroidered monogram in the corner."

"I think it's an 'S' and a 'D.' No, wait, it's a 'B.' An 'S' and a 'B.' Oh Jesus," Cam said as he sat down with a thud and let the handkerchief drift to the floor. I picked it up and stared at it. Then I stared at him.

"What's wrong?"

The same husband who had told me that he didn't hear a burglar and didn't see a burglar so therefore there was no burglar blurted out, "Sylvie's back. We're being haunted!"

Chapter Thirteen

Not surprisingly, I overslept. It was after nine. I reached over for Cam but of course he wasn't there. He had gone to work. Cam is the Director of the Birdsey Bugg Foundation, one of the oldest and least known charitable foundations in the country. The foundation was started in the early 1800s by Horatio Birdsey and Adolphous Bugg. Both men were very well off and were able to leave money to their heirs in addition to starting the foundation to benefit the people of Birdsey Falls. The current President of the foundation, and Cam's direct boss, was Wilhelmina Bugg. I smiled remembering when Abbey used to tell everyone that her daddy's job was to give people money.

With Abbey on my mind, I closed my eyes for a few precious seconds more when I heard a scraping sound over my head. Oh no. Last night the noise had been under me and today it was above me. And Cam wasn't here to explore it with me. I wasn't nearly so brave when he wasn't here. I lay there hoping it had been my imagination, but then I heard it again. Scraping followed by a rubbing sound, something heavy being pulled across the floor. I stared at the ceiling. What room is directly above us? We don't use the third floor except for guests so it has to be one of the guest rooms. Without at least one diet soda in the morning I can't think. Granted my house is enormous but I should have a general floor plan in my head. Above me is ... ah, Cassandra's old room! It was one of the shrine bedrooms in the house, kept exactly as Cassandra had left it when she moved out. She didn't even use it when she stayed with us, instead preferring one of the larger guest rooms with a queen-sized bed. No one used that room, so why was there noise in there?

"Shit!" someone bellowed.

Cam! I would recognize that swearing anywhere. I grabbed my robe and ran to the bottom of the stairs.

"What are you doing up there? Why are you home?" I saw his rear end scooting across the third-floor landing as he dragged a box across the floor.

"Hey," he called from his upside down position. "Sorry to wake you but I cut my finger on this stupid box."

"Why aren't you at work?"

"I took today off. I wanted to be sure you were okay after last night and didn't want to leave you alone in the house. I'm bringing this thing down. Watch out in case I drop it."

He proceeded to lug the box down both flights of stairs and into the dining room, plopping it on the dining room table. I got a diet soda out of the fridge and noticed that Cam had already consumed half a pot of coffee. "I wish Bing were here with those sticky buns," I said.

"If you toast some bagels I'll fish through this box and find what I want to show you," he offered.

"Deal." I thawed two bagels in the microwave and then put them in the toaster. "What is that box, anyway?"

"It's stuff from Cassandra's first couple of years of college."

"Why do we want to look at that?" I peered over his shoulder and saw a bunch of notebooks, postcards, photos and a beanie. "Is there a photo of you and Meggie whatever …?"

"Meggie Smalls? No. I doubt Cassandra kept photos of me and my prom date but Cassandra was fascinated with the Sylvie story …"

"Sylvie? The ghost who left the handkerchief in our house last night?"

"Yes. Cassandra wrote a story about her in college. I remember reading it and it was pretty good. Rather than have me tell you the story I thought you should read what Cassandra wrote. Look! Here it is. I already ate once this morning so why don't I read it to you while you eat?" Cam said.

"Read away and don't leave out a single word."

"You remember that Roger Behrends lived in New Orleans after the Civil War …"

"Right, after he returned from England where he hid out during the war so he wouldn't have to fight," I said.

"Yeah, he was a good businessman but not much of a fighter …"

"If you can call carpet bagging in the post-Civil War South 'good business practice,'" I protested through a mouth of cranberry bagel.

"It *was* good business, in the sense it was profitable. Not good business in the moral sense. I agree. When Roger was living in New Orleans he fell in love with Sylvie Darcantel, a beautiful French girl …"

"Where's her portrait? I've seen all the Behrends portraits and, no offense, there wasn't a single beautiful girl among them."

"You need to let me read the story before you can ask the questions."

"Sorry. Go ahead."

Cam opened the folder and began to read.

Sylvie's Story

Roger Behrends was the handsome son of Bascom Behrends, a very successful businessman in Birdsey Falls. He turned twenty-one in 1861 and decided to visit relatives in Devonshire, England. Once the Civil War broke out, he decided it was best to remain in England until things were settled. He went into business with his English cousin, Wilton Behrends, and moved to London. There he remained until

1865, making money and studying the architecture of the stately homes and castles of England. He returned home determined to build a castle for himself but found the town and surrounding area economically depressed after the war. When he discovered that there was easy money to be made in the Reconstruction South he packed up and moved south to add to his fortune.

While doing business in New Orleans, Roger met Sylvie Darcantel, a black-haired beauty with deep blue eyes and skin as white as marble. This was the late 1860s and New Orleans was a colorful and mysterious city, populated by Creoles, French, Haitians, Indians, Gypsies, freed slaves and plantation owners. Lots of hustle and bustle, lots of wheeling and dealing, lots of money to be made and lost, and lots of exotic and interesting people to meet. All this was very different from Birdsey Falls. Roger certainly had never met anyone there who was as enchanting and exciting as Sylvie Darcantel. He fell madly in love with her and she with him.

Sylvie came from a prosperous family but they had lost everything in the Civil War. They were now living with her great aunt, who had a small house in the French Quarter. The four Darcantels and her great aunt and uncle were all crammed into this little house and barely getting by, but when they went out they wore their best clothes and paraded around the city as if they were still prosperous. When Roger met Sylvie he assumed her family still had money. She certainly led him to think so. She would have him pick her up in front of one of the mansions in the Garden District. She pretended she lived there but the truth was that she and her mother worked there as seamstresses for the Bettencourt women, the ladies of the house. At the end of the work day, if Roger were coming to pick her up, she would change into one of her beautiful dresses left over from when the family was wealthy, and meet him at the front door of the house, leaving the door open enough so he could see how ornate and well appointed it was. But she never let him inside.

Sylvie told him that her parents did not approve of him because he was a Northerner, and the truth was that they probably wouldn't have approved of him had they ever known about him. Sylvie kept her secrets and lived in her own little world where she was still the daughter of a wealthy man living in a beautiful home in the richest part of the city. Roger was enchanted with her and believed everything she told him, as it fit in with his dreams, too. Before long he asked her to marry him and she agreed. She also told him they would have to elope because her parents would not allow her to marry him. By now Roger had made a lot of money in New Orleans and was anxious to return to Birdsey Falls, build his castle and get on with his life. Eloping and moving north seemed like the ideal plan. He and Sylvie spent many evenings together talking about the house they would build, the grandest and richest house in all of Birdsey Falls.

Sylvie didn't have money but, a skilled seamstress, she had made herself dozens of beautiful dresses. She now began making her own trousseau and led Roger to believe that she was shopping in all the best shops in New Orleans and going to all the most stylish dressmakers. Instead she was taking her old dresses and updating them with pieces of lace and velvet she had left over from sewing for the Bettencourt women. She would sneak scraps and sometimes full yards of material from the sewing room and take them home to the French Quarter, where she would sit up late into the night making nightgowns and lingerie. Everything she made was beautifully crafted.

All was going well until Roger's ego intervened. He decided that if he met Sylvie's father he could impress him with his old family money and charm him with his business acumen and dashing personality. He was sure Sylvie's father would recognize and appreciate a man like himself, prosperous, smart and cunning, a man who knew his way around. He decided to call at the Darcantel house, unannounced.

Of course, nothing was what he expected. The butler answering the door insisted that the house was owned by a family named Bettencourt, not Darcantel. When Roger kept insisting that Sylvie Darcantel lived there, the butler informed him that Sylvie and her mother worked there but lived in the French Quarter, and gave Roger the address. Roger rushed to the address in the French Quarter and banged on the door, demanding to see Sylvie. The door was answered by her younger brother, Alain, who explained that Sylvie was at work. Roger forced the boy into telling him that the Darcantel family was impoverished and the father's prosperous pre-war business was now owned by carpet bagging Northerners.

Roger staggered away from the little house in shock.. He loved Sylvie but his ego was bigger than his heart and the love quickly plunged into anger and then hate. He left the French Quarter and returned to his lodgings and his business, vowing never to see Sylvie again.

It was several days before the butler at the Bettencourt house mentioned to Sylvie the man who had come to call on her, mistaking the Bettencourt house for hers. Between that and Alain's report of Roger's visit, she knew she'd been exposed. She felt remorse but was sure that the love she and Roger shared would overcome her deception and they could still get married and move to Birdsey Falls to the castle of her dreams that Roger had promised to build her. When it looked like Roger was no longer coming to call on her, she assumed he was angry but felt she could charm him back to her. She turned for help to an old Creole woman, the cook at the Bettencourt house. Sylvie knew that this woman made potions and charms and had helped many young women who secretly came to the back door of the house for her help. The woman agreed to make her a potion to get Roger back and Sylvie faithfully used it, to no avail. By this time it was dawning on her that *since Roger hadn't even bothered to confront her and let her explain why she had lied, perhaps he didn't love her as much as he had professed. But what finally turned her heart from burning love to seething hatred was an announcement in the* New Orleans Daily Picayune*: Roger Behrends had married Martha Littlefield and they were planning to make their home in Birdsey Falls once Mr. Behrends had completed his business in New Orleans.*

Sylvie went back to the old Creole woman. This time she didn't want a love potion, she wanted revenge. She wanted voodoo. The nature of the curse that was put on Roger Behrends was never known. These things are secret. But Martha never made it to Birdsey Falls to live in the house that Roger had originally planned to build for Sylvie. While in New Orleans, Martha quickly became pregnant and was not able to travel. Shortly after having her portrait painted with her baby, she died. Roger immediately returned to Birdsey Falls and married Evelyn Dudgeon and, when she died after giving him several children, Genevieve Alden. Roger led a fairly normal life, but on October 2 of every year of Roger's lifetime, the last day Sylvie ever saw him, a black cat appeared in the garden of the Behrends castle in Birdsey Falls and a white handkerchief, supposedly from Sylvie's trousseau, appeared somewhere in the house. It had the initials "SB" on it for Sylvie Behrends, a name she never got to use.

I handed the story back to Cam. "Poor Sylvie. I feel so bad for her sitting up late at night sewing her trousseau and being in love with such a jerk. I wonder what happened to her."

Cam shrugged his shoulders. "Since no one knew about her romance with Roger, her reputation was still intact so she probably met some nice man and was able to use all her new clothes on her honeymoon with him."

"Perhaps his last name started with a 'B' so as not to waste all the monogrammed handkerchiefs and who knows what else."

"Yeah, she deserved that," Cam agreed. "It is a sad story. I wonder if …"

"Cam! I just realized something!" I grabbed the story from him and flipped to the last page. "Here's the last paragraph. Listen to this. 'Roger led a fairly normal life, but on October 2 of every year of Roger's lifetime, the last day Sylvie ever saw him, a black cat appeared in the garden of the Behrends castle in Birdsey Falls and a white handkerchief, supposedly from Sylvie's trousseau, appeared somewhere in the house. It had the initials "SB" on it for Sylvie Behrends, a name she never got to use.' Well, what do you think?"

"Um. It's not October 2, so the handkerchief shouldn't have appeared in the house?"

"No, it's not October 2, but that's not what I mean."

"Okay, but …?" Cam cocked his head like Mycroft does when he is listening to you, only somehow it wasn't nearly as cute.

"October 2. That's the day Roger Behrends was haunted. One day each year …" I reminded him.

"Go on."

"Uncle Franklin had a stack of newspapers in his cottage, one for April 1 each year. One paper for the same day each year and …"

"But it's a different day. Same pattern but …"

"What day was Uncle Franklin murdered?" I prompted.

"Jesus. It was October 2."

Chapter Fourteen

I had forgotten that I'd promised Diane to go to lunch at Bugg Hill with her parents. I persuaded Cam to go into work since I wasn't going to be home alone and then quickly showered and dressed. Bugg Hill was no Ashland Belle, so although I thought I should at least be clean, I didn't feel I needed to dress up.

As if I didn't have enough on my mind already, when I looked at the calendar to confirm the lunch date I also noticed that my period was ten days late. I'm forty-seven and I've heard that people in the perimenopause stage, sort of the training time before actual menopause, will miss periods. This hadn't happened to me. So far I was extremely regular and had missed a period only once in my entire life and I had Abbey to show for it. Could I be pregnant? Maybe I had complained about empty nest too much the last two months and *someone* had misinterpreted and thought I needed a replacement child. I looked at myself in the mirror. I did look a little pale and tired. But I'd had a pretty rough night. I pushed at my jelly stomach. I had been three months pregnant with Abbey before my stomach had even started to round out the tiniest bit. I had a good six-month pregnancy look going already and, at most, I could only be about three weeks pregnant. What would I look like by nine months? Oh, God, why was I thinking like this? I didn't want to have a baby. Cam might, but his fifty-year-old body didn't have to carry it. Between the break-in last night and worrying about my period, I was in a very low mood by the time Diane arrived to pick me up.

I didn't have to make much small talk because she spent the whole ride over to Bugg Hill on the phone with various children. Kara, her eighth grader, called from the nurse's office at school to say she had a headache. Diane gave the nurse permission to give her an aspirin and send her back to class. Immediately after Kara's call, Kristen, her sixth grader, called to ask if she could walk home instead of taking the bus because the boys on the bus were too stupid and noisy. Diane reminded her that they lived five miles from the school, so walking seemed like a bad idea. She would have to tough it out on the bus. Then Kevin called from college to report he might be getting a "D" in math and wanted to drop the course. Diane told him it was only October so he had plenty of time to get his grades up and, if he was planning to be an engineer, dropping math was a really bad idea and failing it was even worse. I was just beginning to think that if I heard the phone purr one more time I might grab it and throw it out the window. I had missed my period. These children had no concept of what real problems were.

The entrance to the Bugg Hill Senior Living Home is a hand-painted sign with an arrow. Unlike Ashland Belle, there were no cottages here or magnificent plantation-style building. Bugg Hill was just one two-story building that snaked around a large lawn with a minimum of landscaping. Diane's parents were waiting for us in the modest lobby.

"From the look on my dad's face I'd say they are having gourmet mac and cheese today," Diane whispered as we greeted them both with hugs.

"Mac and cheese today, girls! You're in for a treat. It's *gourmet* mac and cheese, so be prepared!" Ted, her father, announced. Ted was so average, I was surprised his wife could even identify him in a crowd. He was average height, average weight, thinning hair that was average for someone in his seventies. His features were even. Even his wrinkles were symmetrical. He had absolutely no distinguishing features at all.

Ted linked his arm in mine and escorted me to the dining room. Ashland Belle has tablecloths, chandeliers and brocade upholstered chairs in their dining room. The dining room at Bugg Hill was card tables and chairs and fluorescent lights overhead.

"Tonight there's a big bridge championship in here. Things might get a little ugly," Thelma warned us. Like her husband, Diane's mom was fairly plain looking, but she did have one distinguishing feature: a nose that was about three times larger than it should have been for her thin face. It was so large it seemed in danger of falling off every time she moved her head. I sometimes wondered how her parents even kissed. Oddly enough, Diane was very attractive. There's no accounting for DNA.

"I heard the most interesting thing on the news today," Thelma announced as we seated ourselves around the table. "On a farm some-place chickens were dying and they couldn't figure out why. Eventually they discovered that the chickens were being scared to death ..."

"How could someone scare chickens to death, mom?"

"That's the second most interesting part. They were being scared to death by low-flying air balloons that launched out of the fields by the farm ..."

"And the first *most* interesting part?" I had to ask.

"When the chickens were scared they would run around uncontrol-lably and eventually run smack into some solid surface. The unhatched eggs inside them would explode and they would die of periodontal disease!"

"Mom, periodontal disease has to do with gums and we all know chickens don't have gums."

"Oh, it's something like that ... ah, I remember, peritonitis. That's what it was. Peritonitis."

"Where did you hear such a thing?" Diane asked.

"Paul Harvey Jr. news on the radio this morning."

Ted nodded, forking a mound of mac and cheese into his mouth. "We listen to Paul Harvey Jr. every day. He has all the interesting news, doesn't he, honey?"

"You betcha, honeybunch!"

Diane then proceeded to give a quick rundown on what each of her five children were up to. In addition to the twins in college and Kara and Kristen, she had a son Kaleb, who was a junior in high school. I was just musing on whether Kaleb might know Grace's stepson Ryan when Thelma grabbed my wrist just as I was about to take a drink of water. The water splashed into my mac and cheese. She didn't seem to notice.

"Tamsen. I can't believe we're going on and on like this about family without first offering our condolences on the loss of your uncle. I'm so sorry."

I patted her hand. "That's OK, Thelma. I was in a daze at the funeral but I did see you and Ted there and I appreciate that you came …"

"Oh, but we had to. For you, of course, because we've all been friends since you and Diane were young mothers, but we also had to come for Claudia."

"I didn't realize you and Claudia were friends."

"Oh, not what you would call friends exactly. We didn't really hang out with her, did we, Ted?"

Ted shook his head and started sneaking mac and cheese off Thelma's plate. She unclenched my wrist to slap his. "You've had enough. Don't be a pig! Now what was I saying. Oh, Ted and I grew up with Claudia and her brothers but we didn't run in the same social circles. But Franklin always seemed like a nice boy, didn't he, Ted?"

"Yup. He wasn't a jerk like some of his rich friends. He was always nice to everyone whether they were in his set or not. Good guy. Don't know what happened to him, though ..."

"Shush, Ted. We don't need to talk about that."

"No, wait. I'd like to hear about Franklin and how he changed," I insisted. "Claudia is always so vague about it. Do you know anything about what happened to him?"

"No, we don't really know for a fact, now do we, Ted?"

Ted shook his head and eyed Diane's plate. She pushed it over to him and he dug in. The man was insatiable when it came to gourmet mac and cheese.

"Do you have any idea at all about what happened to him?" It had never occurred to me that Thelma and Ted might know something about Uncle Franklin. They were about the same age as Claudia, and they did all grow up in Birdsey Falls, but I had never pictured them as acquaintances.

"I remember he liked to make maps and organize treasure hunts. He was really good at it. He would let everyone play and divide us into groups. Remember, Ted? You used to play, too."

Ted nodded. "Yup, it was a good time. He was a real smart fella. Good organizer, too. Would have been good in the military or some-place that needed organizers. I liked him. He was always decent to me."

"He was real artistic, too. Remember, Ted? Those maps he drew were real fancy ..."

"Yeah, real fancy maps. They looked like something from a book. Nice guy. Real nice guy."

Nice guy. Good artist. Excellent organizer. Well-liked. These did not seem to be the ingredients for a breakdown. Diane's phone rang and she excused herself and stepped outside the dining room. Ted quickly pushed her plate back to her place when Thelma wasn't looking. He smiled and winked at me and began to look around to see what the waitress was bringing for dessert. He caught her eye and she came by with a tray of tapioca pudding and Rice Krispie treats and handed one out for each of us. I passed mine over to Ted and he smiled and gave me another wink.

"Do you remember when Franklin changed, Thelma?" I asked.

"Well, I know he never went to college like the rest of his friends. Ted and I didn't go to college either but we weren't expected to. Ted's family had the grocery store so he naturally went to work there after high school and no one in my family ever went to college so I never even thought about going. Of course, we wanted Diane to go and I always wished that maybe I had gone, too, when I was her age. But after high school I was anxious to get a job so Ted and I could work a year or so and get married. Which is what we did …"

"Never regretted a minute of it, either."

Thelma started eating her Rice Krispie treat and looking around the dining room to see who was there. "Look Ted, there's Muriel Wilson. I haven't seen her for a while. I heard she got stuck in her bathtub and they had to call the EMTs to get her out. I wonder if she was hurt."

"Maybe just embarrassed," Ted suggested. "A woman her size should have a walk-in shower, not a tub. Can't imagine what the water displacement must be when Muriel hoists herself into the tub." I could tell Bugg Hill was a hotbed of gossip and getting stuck in your tub and having EMTs get you out had to be a story that lived on for a long time.

"You know, her uncle Ernie was real famous for finding a dead body once. Just stumbled across it in the woods while he was out walking his dog. Imagine that," Thelma said.

"Most bodies are discovered by either early morning dog walkers or joggers. If you avoid either activity you should be safe from running across something awful like that. Whose body was it?" Ted asked.

"No idea. That's as far into the story as she's ever gotten. Just announces her uncle Ernie found a body and then someone goes on to something else. Sometimes it's hard to finish a thought here because …"

"What's that Gladys woman done to her hair?" Ted interrupted, speaking quite loudly and actually pointing at her. Luckily Diane was just re-entering the dining room so it looked like her father was pointing at her. Thelma reached up and yanked his arm down.

"Don't point! I think they put too much conditioner or something in her hair because it's lying all flat on her head."

"But what about that weird color? Conditioner causes that? Don't we have conditioner in our shower? I'm not using that. Don't you use it, either. I don't want you to look like that!" Ted's arm started to come back up and Thelma slapped it back down.

"Thelma, you were saying something about Franklin and not going to college like his friends," I said, attempting to get her back on track. Although I was kind of curious as to what caused Gladys' hair to be that strange greenish color.

"Oh, yes. Franklin …"

"Nice guy. Real nice guy …"

"He was sick or something. Remember, Ted? He wasn't at school for the longest time."

"I think he had that kissing disease. What's it called?" Ted asked Diane.

"Mono, Dad. Kevin had it, remember?"

"Yup. I told Kevin it was the kissing disease. He liked that! Maybe that's what Franklin had. He was out of school for several months as I recall. But that isn't why he didn't go to college. It was a couple years before graduation that he was sick."

"Weren't you and Franklin on the basketball team together?"

"Yup. Now I remember. He must have had that mono our freshman year cause I remember he was out most of the spring and then couldn't play in the fall because he wasn't cleared by the doctor and was way behind in school. We needed him, too. Big loss to the team. As a matter of fact, he never played on the team again after that. I guess maybe he was always sickly."

"Were there any more treasure hunts or things like that?" I asked. Maybe I could start to narrow in on when Franklin started having emotional issues and then delve deeper. Claudia didn't seem to remember much other than what she personally had been doing and Sybil wasn't much better.

"We sort of outgrew the treasure hunt thing. But come to think of it, it might have been around that time. Without Franklin to organize them and make the maps and stuff we sort of drifted away from treasure hunting and on to other things. I don't remember doing any more treasure hunts after he came back to school. It was a long time ago."

"I know. And I appreciate anything you can tell me. I've always been curious about Franklin and now that he's dead ..."

"Murdered!" Thelma whispered loudly enough for everyone in the dining room to hear her and turn to look at us.

"Shush, mom!"

"I wasn't loud."

"Yes you were. People are staring," Diane scolded.

"Tamsen, do you think his murder had to do with the mono?" Ted questioned. "I've never heard of mono leading to murder."

Thelma got into the swing of things. "You know, if mono is a kissing disease then that means he had to be kissing someone and maybe they got sick, too, and wanted revenge."

"It may have taken all this time for them to track him down."

"That makes no sense, Ted. He's always lived in Birdsey Falls. You can track anyone down here in about ten minutes."

"True." That seemed to slow the conversation down.

Diane was beginning to look at me with the we-need-to-get-out-of-here look. "It's getting time for your naps."

Ted snapped his fingers. "I got it. Maybe the girl he gave mono to eventually married someone and they found out that Franklin had given her mono so the husband came to Birdsey Falls and killed Franklin for revenge."

"Wait! Maybe the husband found out and got jealous and deserted his wife so she got mad and killed Franklin for revenge for ruining her marriage, her only chance at happiness."

"Mom! The 'girl' would have to be in her eighties now. I don't picture an eighty year old woman stabbing Franklin because he gave her mono in high school."

"But her husband might," Ted offered.

I sincerely wished I had never brought it up. The next thing you knew they would be claiming Gladys of the green hair was the spurned wife and her hair was flat due to being a murderess. I stood up.

"Thelma, Ted, thank you so much for lunch. It's really been fun but I have to get going."

Diane grabbed her jacket. There were hugs and kisses all around and promises to get together again soon. When we left Ted was trying to attract the waitress's eye for another round of Rice Krispie treats and Thelma was sitting with her head in her hands staring at Gladys' green hair.

On the way home, I had planned to discuss Diane's relationship with Donny the cop and tell her about the excitement at our house last night. I wondered if word of the alleged break-in had gotten to Diane via Donny and what was being said. The drive from Bugg Hill to my house is not a long one so I would have to talk like a radio car ad disclaimer to fit this all in. In the end I opted for what was foremost on my mind.

"Sorry about that crazy lunch," Diane said as we climbed into her car. "Sometimes my folks get a little carried away."

I waved her apology away and fastened my seat belt. "Are you kidding? I love your folks. They're a lot of fun and so unpretentious. I'd rather have them for in-laws than Claudia any day."

"They are kind of cute, aren't they?" Diane laughed.

"Have you ever missed your period, Diane?"

"Of course, five times!"

"No, no. I mean since you've been in your forties. Sort of preparing for menopause or something. Do you know anything about that?"

"Sure. My ob-gyn told me I was in the midst of perimenopause when I had my last physical. He said it was the natural part of aging that signaled the end of my reproductive years. Frankly I was amazed that my reproductive years were finally going to end. Missed periods are a part of that. I've missed a few off and on the last two years. I can't wait until they stop altogether."

"I missed my period and that's never happened to me before. I'm not sure if its peri-menopause or if I'm pregnant."

"You could call your doctor but the first time that happened to me, and I told the receptionist my age, she suggested I take a home pregnancy test rather than come into the office because I probably wasn't pregnant. And I wasn't, thank God. It's happened a couple times since then and I've never been pregnant. I don't think I'll even bother taking the test the next time. We're getting old, Tamsen."

"At the risk of sounding like I'm in high school, I don't even dare go buy a home pregnancy test kit. I mean, most of the cashiers in the grocery store and the drug store are either people we grew up with or friends of Abbey's. I'd be so embarrassed."

Diane nodded her head vigorously. "I know. I know. The first time I went into the drug store to get the kit I got in line and noticed the cashier was a classmate of Kevin's and Keith's. I moved to another line and saw that the cashier was a woman I'd been on the PTA with, a horrible gossip. I ended up just leaving the kit there and walking out."

"So how did you finally get one?"

"Scott happened to be in Boston on business for a couple days. I asked him to buy me one there, where no one knew who we were."

"He didn't mind?"

"He wasn't too thrilled but after we found out I wasn't pregnant he was so relieved that he forgave me for the embarrassment of purchasing the kit. When it happened again, about six months later, the doctor told me this could go on for several years. Remember this summer when Scott and I went to New York for the weekend to see 'Spamalot'?"

"Yes."

"I bought six kits while we were there. That way we wouldn't have to agonize about buying them anymore."

"Do you have any left?"

***

It was only a home pregnancy test but I felt like I was carrying a concealed weapon in my purse as Diane turned onto my street. I was thinking about who I'd least like to run into right now and had just decided it was definitely Claudia when Diane swung into my driveway and announced, "Oh, look. Your mother-in-law's here."

As soon as Diane had given me the pregnancy test kit, I had wanted to use it right then. She offered me her bathroom but I wanted to be alone when I got the results. I had no idea how I would react, either way, and I wanted to be alone or with Cam. I certainly couldn't excuse myself and do the test when Claudia was there. Every single time Claudia pops in on us unannounced I say that *this* is the worst possible time for her to show up. But right now I believe she had outdone herself and this truly was the worst possible time for a visit.

I found her sitting in the solarium drinking a Bloody Mary and turning all my plants around. She gave me a little wave when I entered. "You need to keep rotating your plants, dear, so different sides face the windows. It's how the plants exercise, first all moving one way toward the sun and then moving the other. Plants need to exercise."

"I've never seen an overweight plant."

"Exactly right, dear. We could learn a lot from them." Since Claudia had never participated in any kind of exercise, much less one that would cause her to break a sweat, I knew she was referring to me and the ten, well maybe fifteen, pounds that I needed to lose. If were pregnant I could flaunt my extra weight in her face. But having a late-in-life baby to annoy your mother-in-law was probably frowned upon in most responsible parenting circles. I checked to make sure my purse was firmly zipped and set it down before joining her. She held up her drink.

"You didn't have any coffee on," she said making it sound both like an accusation and an excuse to be drinking.

"Making a pot of coffee is probably no harder than making a Bloody Mary," I countered. She turned and blessed me with a dazzling smile. "You may be right, dear." Yeah, that would be the day. She gestured me into the room and sat in one of the brightly upholstered wingback chairs, crossing her trim ankles and gently smoothing her wool skirt over her knees. I sighed and sat down in the chair across from her, lured into her web until she was ready to release me.

"I hear that you were a bit confused last night and panicked and called the police."

"Really it was Cam who first thought of calling 911."

"He does like to humor you, I know. Sometimes it is so difficult to deal with hysteria."

"I wasn't hysterical."

Conversing with Claudia was like fencing. Cam was adept at putting a stop to it by interjecting his boyish charm and defending me while at the same time not irritating his mother. I was lucky. Although Claudia thought she had Cam wrapped around her finger, he saw through her.

"We never had a break-in while I lived here," she announced proudly.

"How fortunate for you. These are different times, Claudia." I claim temporary insanity regarding my next comment. "You never had a murder when you lived here, either." Well, that hit home. She set her drink down and her eyes filled with tears. I'm such an insensitive clod. I blame it on hormones. I reached out to her although I didn't actually touch her.

"I'm sorry, Claudia. That was insensitive."

"Poor Franklin," she sniffed. She reached in her purse and brought out a lacy handkerchief and wiped her eyes. I wondered if I should tell her about Sylvie's handkerchief. The Birdsey Falls rumor mill hadn't circulated that information yet unless Cam went around the office today telling everyone that a ghost had left a hanky in his house last night.

"That's a lovely handkerchief. No one uses such lovely things anymore. Now it's all paper and people leave them all over the place. A tasteful cotton handkerchief is so much classier." I most likely would have rambled on like this for another five minutes but Claudia reasserted herself.

"It's linen, not cotton, and not very absorbent." She folded the handkerchief and returned it to her purse.

"Do you want a tissue?"

"No. I'm fine now."

"I'm sorry."

"Stop apologizing."

117

As Claudia and I sat staring at each other, neither of us knowing what to say next, Mycroft stretched where he was lying across the room in a patch of sun, and made a rude sound. Claudia didn't move a muscle.

"So, I had lunch with Thelma and Ted Harrington today," I said. "Do you remember them?"

"Of course. They live at Bugg Hill, don't they?"

"Yes. It's quite nice out there although nothing compared to Ashland Belle," I offered as a sort of peace token.

"The Harringtons would never be able to afford Ashland Belle. I don't think they ever did more than scrape by their entire lives. But then, their parents did the same. The pattern just repeats itself."

"Diane has done well, so maybe the pattern is broken now."

"Diane did what women are supposed to do, marry well and have babies. As I recall, Scott is from the Kinney family in Rutland. His grandfather was a judge and his father started the law firm he works for. Diane married well."

Faint praise for one of my best friends. I wondered what Cam would say if, when he came through the front door tonight, I announced, "I'm pregnant and I slapped your mother."

Instead I said, "The Harringtons were at Franklin's funeral and had good memories of him."

"I talked to them at the funeral and sent a note afterward thanking them for coming and for the flowers they sent."

"Ted remembers doing treasure hunts with Franklin and playing basketball with him."

"Franklin was *quite* athletic but he was more interested in reading and drawing maps and making puzzles. My other brother, Alden, who was killed at Pearl Harbor, was interested in history and politics and wanted to be governor one day. Being killed at Pearl Harbor destroyed those plans. Franklin was less outgoing." Her voice trailed off.

Now that was an understatement.

"Ted mentioned Franklin being sick and having to drop the basketball team. Do you remember that?"

"Franklin was in delicate health as a teenager. It sort of came on him suddenly and he never seemed to get back to his former self."

"Ted and Thelma thought he might have had mononucleosis. Is that true?"

"I was only six when he first got ill so it's hard to remember. He missed a lot of school. I was jealous. I recall I pitched several temper tantrums about the unfairness of the situation."

Gee, imagine that.

"It seems odd that a bout of mono would lead to his eventual withdrawal."

Claudia straightened her skirt and took a sip of her drink. "Tamsen, does it really matter now?"

"Maybe not. But I can't understand why someone would kill Franklin. Discovering why he became a recluse seems like a good place to start."

"It's not your job to determine who killed him. Let the police handle it. I doubt that we'll ever know."

"And doesn't that bother you?" I asked.

"Knowing who did it and why will not bring him back."

"But don't you want someone to pay for his murder? We can't have a society where people just go around killing people and there are no consequences."

"I'm not advocating that. But sometimes we have to admit that there are things we may never know and may never understand. Why Franklin became a recluse and why he was murdered may be two of those things. We have to learn to accept certain things in life."

I wasn't willing to do that.

"Was there a reason you stopped by today, Claudia? Did you need something?" I asked.

Claudia finished her drink and I swear she looked suspiciously at my purse as she rose and walked to the door. "No reason. I just thought you might have something to tell me."

It was as if she had X-ray vision.

Cam called to say he was coming home early and I was at the front door to greet him when he got out of the car. I opened the front door and yelled to him, "I'm not pregnant and I didn't slap your mother!"

He looked up at me and grinned. "Fantastic! What's for dinner?"

Chapter Fifteen

I bet most people haven't explored every nook and cranny of their own home. No matter how small your house is—and I'm not trying to sound like Claudia comparing house sizes—but you probably haven't looked at every inch of it. In my case, there were entire sections of my house that I hadn't explored. I've set foot in every room at one time or another, but not really explored the unused rooms or the old things that have been left behind by previous generations of Behrends. Cam and I often talk about taking one room at a time and weeding out all the useless junk, but we haven't gotten there yet.

Grace admits there are papers and cartons her grandfather stored in the basement of her bookstore that she's never looked at. Diane has bags of clothes that friends have given her for the kids that she hasn't sorted yet. Syra buys books at a much faster rate than she can read them. Even Bing hasn't looked at all the recipes in his dozens of cookbooks. If we didn't have something to finally get to what would we have to strive for? The more things we have that need our attention, the more time we buy ourselves in this lifetime to get it all done. So, at the risk of shortening my time on earth, I decided to poke around in the attic and see if I could find anything of Franklin's that might give me a clue to who he was and who wanted him dead. I felt that the answer to his murder was who he had been, rather than who he had become, and therefore, going through his cottage again was not going to tell me anything new.

Last night had been peaceful and restful in comparison to the previous one. I hadn't made anything for dinner so we ordered in pizza and wings, again. I told Cam about my lunch with Diane's parents, the visit from his mother and my pregnancy scare. He was suitably interested in the lunch, a little surprised by his mother for just showing up and absolutely astounded at the pregnancy scare. We weren't stupid. We used birth control. Cam offered to double up on the birth control and we got hysterical imagining him wrestling with that precaution during a moment of passion. I'd been thinking that we should just stop having sex until after menopause but then I changed my mind and decided to just stock up on pregnancy tests as Diane had done. We'd eventually get through this perimenopause stuff.

There'd been no more odd noises in the night and no more mysterious handkerchiefs. Cam had put the one Mycroft had found in the drawer of the Chippendale table in the front hallway. I checked after breakfast and it was still there. I'd had a dream where the "SB" handkerchief was floating around our house at night spying on us and reporting back to Claudia's *linen* handkerchief. If Sylvie's handkerchief had been out during the night it had safely made it back to its drawer and looked like it was settled in. Feeling confident that all was well, I decided to tackle the attic, where the really old stuff was stored.

I put a scarf over my head to avoid having to wash my hair after I was done in the attic. I had just washed it last night and the more often I washed it the faster the semi-permanent hair color washed out. I hated coloring my hair so liked to put it off as long as possible. I put on old clothes, collected a broom, a flashlight, a duster, wet wipes, a huge garbage bag for junk, a smaller garbage bag for treasures, a spiral notebook and pen, a mini-cooler with four diet sodas, my cell phone, a bottle of water and a rag (in case something was so filthy dusting alone didn't reveal what it was), a bottle of glass cleaner, a shoebox for small keepsakes, some bandages, a pair of rubber gloves, a candy bar and my camera. I put most of this stuff in an old backpack Abbey had used in high school. All I needed was a walking stick and I'd be all set.

Mycroft desperately wanted to come with me but he could no longer make it up the stairs to our bedroom on the second floor, much less up two more flights to the attic. I actually attempted to pick him up to see if I could carry him up three flights of stairs but couldn't even get him an inch off the floor. I gave him some doggie treats and a big kiss and asked him to stand guard and keep Claudia out while I was gone. Only I didn't call her that. And Mycroft knew who I meant.

Our attic is huge. There are several rooms and then rooms within rooms. There are stairs leading up a few feet and then stairs leading down. The one thing I really needed was a map because it was very possible I could get lost in here and not find my way out again. I should have left Cam a note telling him where I was in case I couldn't get cell phone reception this far from civilization. I should have brought more than one candy bar.

The attic isn't a total wasteland. There are lights and I switched one on when I opened the door. The naked bulbs were so dirty that the light was almost imperceptible but I figured I could dust them as I went and that would light the way. I had the flashlight in case I ran into an area of burned-out light bulbs. I should have brought light bulbs, too. I grabbed my notebook and made a note for my next trip.

Room one was like a large entrance hall. I cleaned off the bulb and swung my broom at the cobwebs. Not much here. I picked up a broken pair of scissors, a couple of dusty yellowed magazines, some plastic spoons and forks, three old soda bottles, several empty but still gross mouse traps and threw them all in my large garbage bag. There was one door across the little entrance way so I opened that and reached for another light switch. I found it and three dull bulbs lit up, displaying a long narrow room with windows along the right side and three more doors leading who knows where on the left. I labeled this as room two. I was making a map.

I made my way over to the first window and gave it a shot of glass cleaner in a failed attempt to let some light in. I needed a pail of soapy water for this task. After three more shots I was able to get one window pane clean enough to look out. I could see our bedraggled gardens and the path to Franklin's cottage. The attic windows that looked out over the front of the house must be through the three doors on the other side of the room. I cleaned off the first light bulb and set my garbage bag and backpack on the nearest chair, an old Victorian-style thing with a very faded gold velvet seat and some stuffing coming out of one of the arms. Why did people keep such things? Perhaps the chairs were valuable. I would ask Grace's husband, Hugh, who was an antiques dealer. I took a picture of it and wrote a reminder in my spiral notebook. There were a lot of lamps lying around, a few of them Tiffany style. I doubted they were authentic but I grouped them all together and posed them for a sort of lamp family photo. Hugh might be able to sell some of them in his shop.

I had to decide what my focus was going to be, scouting for antiques or looking for information about Franklin. I needed to find papers or trunks of old clothes and pictures. Personal items. Insights to Franklin were not going to be found in old chairs or lamps. A fast walk through the long, narrow room revealed that it was all discarded parlor and dining room furniture. It all seemed pretty impersonal. I made a note to come back sometime and take more photos for Hugh or, better yet, get him up here to look around. I swung around and faced the three doors trying to decide which one to tackle first. I felt like I was on a rerun of "Let's Make A Deal" trying to decide what was behind door one, door two and door three. In the end I opted for the most systematic approach and pushed open door one.

Room number three via door one, opened up to expose one of the windows that looked out at the front of the house. It was rectangular with the door at one end and the window at the other. I was thinking that if the other two doors opened to rooms identical to this, the attic would have made a good apartment with an entrance hall, the long living room and then three nicely sized bedrooms. Of course we would have to have a family of at least fifteen members before we would have to resort to making the attic an apartment for anyone.

Not for the first time I wondered if Cam and I should have done something more with this house and all the space. What it would have been I don't know. But we had really neglected all but the rooms we had used. Suddenly I had the urge to clean out every room in the house, inventory all the furniture and things, get rid of what we didn't want and make the house our own rather than living in a house borrowed from Cam's ancestors. I sat down on the nearest hard surface and began writing furiously in my notebook. I felt the urge to get a huge flag with Cam's and my names on it and plunge it into the attic floor declaring this to be *our* house and not Claudia's or Alden Sr.'s or Roger's. It was the Mack family house, not the Behrends. And only good-looking people were going to have their portraits on my walls.

After several pages of notes, I pulled myself back to my task and began to look around room three for something that might have been Franklin's. More old furniture, mostly chairs. Not even a drawer to peek into. I needed to move on.

Door two opened to a room which was, as I had suspected, identical in shape and size to the room next door. So now I jotted down room four via door two out of room one in my notebook and looked around. More chairs. Dining room chairs, upholstered chairs, footstools. I marked the room as "miscellaneous seating", and opened door three. Same room architecturally as the others but this one held some dressers and desks. I set my supplies down and randomly opened dresser drawers. Empty for the most part, although I did find a few interesting old buttons and put them in my shoe box. I got out a couple of wet wipes and cleaned off my face and hands, opened a can of diet soda and sat at one of the desks. I systematically pulled out the drawers and tentatively reached in to see if there was anything in them. I wish I knew whose desk this was because I didn't really want to waste a lot of time looking for hidden drawers and messages in an old desk of Alden's or Claudia's, not that that might not be interesting at a future time. I let my mind wander into a scenario where I would find an old diary of Claudia's that would expose her adoption by the Behrends family, the child of an under-aged prostitute and the Behrends' milkman. I could hold it over her head and threaten her with it whenever she was being especially annoying. But there was nothing in the desk at all. Apparently the Behrendses really cleaned out their things before they brought them into the attic.

I carried all my things back into the long narrow room and headed to the end of the room, looking for more doors. I found one at the farthest end of the room. It opened to a small set of six stairs, so I climbed them and pushed open yet another door. Whereas the other rooms had been rectangular, this one was more of a trapezoid with zigzags in the walls. There were three windows to my right and two to the left. The lights worked and the windows were less dirty. This room wasn't as well organized as the previous ones; this was promising. Maybe it meant furniture had been hastily shoved into these rooms and not cleaned out for proper storage. I labeled a new page in my notebook as "room six, zigzag room". I took a picture from the door of the room, as I had in all the other rooms. If we ever decided to have a party where we wanted a dozen velvet chairs with the stuffing coming out, I would know right where to find them.

I performed my wet wipes ritual and opened another can of diet soda and the candy bar. I knew all this drinking would catch up with me eventually and I dreaded having to go back downstairs to use the bathroom in the middle of my explorations. I surveyed the room to see what item had the most possibilities. A trunk! I hadn't opened any of those yet, and despite visions of scurrying mice, I knelt down by the trunk nearest me and pushed open the top. It was empty.

"Oh, come on!" I yelled in annoyance. Either the mice had eaten everything in the attic or else there were no mice because there was nothing to gnaw at. "What's wrong with you people?" I really did dislike each and every one of the Behrendses. What kind of a stupid name was that anyway? It was probably an old Native American name that meant 'runs with ass showing'. Claudia had tried to persuade us to saddle Abbey with Behrends as a middle name. I had been horrified and Cam had held strong. Abbey's middle name was Elizabeth, after my mother. Suddenly I missed Abbey so much my chest began to hurt and I started to cry. I pulled out my cell phone and dialed her number. It was the middle of the morning and she was probably in class with her phone off, but at least I could leave her a message.

"Hi Mom! What's up?" She sounded so cheerful and full of life and I wished she were home and helping me look for clues in the attic.

"Hi Abs. Nothing's up. I just miss you and wanted to hear your voice. What're you doing?"

"Walking to Anthropology class."

"Still studying the Bog Man?"

"No, we're learning how to lay out an archeological dig on a grid. It's like making a map."

"Hey, that's what I'm doing, too!"

"You're making a map? Why?"

"I'm up in the attic, making a map of all the rooms up here and what's in them. I know it sounds stupid but …"

"No, it sounds like fun! I wish I were there. Save some of it for Thanksgiving and I'll help you. I bet Dad would like doing that, too. Oh, gotta go. I'm the last one to class. Good luck hunting. Love you!"

I sat and cried for a few minutes. There is no greater reward in life than happy, well-adjusted children. None.

Time for another round of wet wipes. Should have brought tissues. Which reminded me of the handkerchief, which put me back on track and I moved over to another trunk. Next to the trunk was a perfectly proportioned pyramid of rolled-up socks. It was a work of art and I carefully skirted past it so I wouldn't knock it over.

I carefully laid a pair of dusty skates on the floor so I could open another trunk. I was almost hoping for mice at this point because it would mean there was actually something inside it. Abbey must have brought me luck because there were no mice but there were some boxes and papers and clothes. Yippee! Something to paw through at last.

Hats. Lots of hats. Some with wrinkled veils; some with crushed crepe flowers. I lifted them out and put them on the floor. Would Hugh want these? I'm sure someone would buy vintage hats. I picked up a small wooden box and shook it. It rattled. I opened it up and there were about twenty coins in it. They were foreign coins, probably souvenirs from someone's trip. I put them in the pile for Hugh. If he didn't want them he might know a coin dealer who would. The next wooden box held marbles. They were beautiful and I wish I had some sunlight to hold them up to. These would look good downstairs in a glass jar on one of the shelves in the library. Or maybe in the solarium where the direct light could hit them and flash the colors all over the room. I pushed some clothes out of the way and found two more boxes. One was empty but the wood was pretty with an inlaid design on the top that was striking. I set that with the box of marbles to take downstairs. The second box rattled seductively and I opened it with childlike anticipation. It was full of teeth. Ugh. Someone must have kept all their baby teeth. Or else this was the Tooth Fairy's depository. I would have to ask Claudia if they had the Tooth Fairy when she was growing up. My hand waivered over which pile to put these in. I decided to put them back in the trunk.

Next to the trunk was an old desk that looked promising. One of the drawers was jammed, exposing some yellowed papers. I gave the drawer a vigorous tug and it flew out of the desk and onto the floor, barely missing my toes. I gathered up the papers and sat down to thumb through them. They were Franklin's school papers. Finally I'd found something that I could say for sure belonged to Franklin. I read through several dull essays on American history. It sounded as if they had been copied from a text book. Tucked in among the school papers was a scrap of paper folded in half. I opened it up and read:

There are some secrets which do not permit themselves to be told—mysteries which will not suffer themselves to be revealed. Now and then, alas, the conscience of man takes up a burden so heavy in horror that it can be thrown down only into the grave.

—Edgar Allan Poe, "The Man of the Crowd," 1840

Disturbing. I turned the paper over but there was nothing else written on it. I reread it several times, caught up in the poetry of the words as well as their creepiness. I was suddenly very tired and no longer interested in exploring the attic. I added the piece of paper to my other "to go" items and worked my way back through the attic and down the stairs. I dumped everything on my bedroom floor and then went to take a shower. I even washed my hair.

Chapter Sixteen

I love Grace's bookstore. Trenary Booksellers is where Grace and I first met many years ago and forged a deep friendship based on mutual love of all kinds of books. She'd gone all out when my first Perry Many Paws book had been published and featured it in her shop window and in her monthly advertisements and, eventually, on her website. The bookstore had a huge bay window where a mannequin family lived. Her grandfather had purchased his first mannequin a year after he'd opened the bookshop in 1940. She was a perfectly proportioned size 8, with thick auburn hair and full red lips. Grace's grandfather had named her Willoughby and she'd taken up residence in the store. He'd enjoyed posing Willoughby in different parts of the bookshop, one week browsing in the children's books and another in the mysteries. During World War II, Willoughby had acquired a square-jawed, black-haired husband and the young couple had assumed their current residence in the display window. Eventually husband William had donned a uniform and been banished to the storeroom until V-J Day, when he triumphantly returned home to the arms of the lovely Willoughby.

During the 1950s, mannequin children James and Melissa had joined Willoughby's family, dutifully reading the current and classic children's books, always in proper seasonal attire. Her grandfather had never been particularly creative in his displays, content to merely change the calendar to the current month and put sweaters or short sleeves on the mannequins as the season dictated. When Grace had come to live with him after her parents died, she'd taken over dressing and posing the mannequins, and shopping for vintage clothing for real Victorian Christmas celebrations. Trenary's window family began to drift from one era to another based on the holiday and the clothes available. She'd always changed the display at least once a month and Grace and Willoughby's family had been featured in the *Birdsey Falls Gazette* on an annual basis. The mannequins were Perry Many Paw's biggest fans and were the first to read the newest book while keeping the older ones on their bookshelf, prominently displayed. I loved gazing in the window and looking at all the interesting details Grace included in her tableaus. Willoughby and her family drew you in and, like the old friends they were, I always needed to visit with them a few minutes before I went into the store.

I'd actually walked into town, something I rarely did any longer. It was over a mile and I never seemed to want to take the time to walk it when I could drive. But today, buoyed by the negative pregnancy test and resolving, once again, to lose that fifteen pounds that refused to budge, I decided a good walk was just what I needed. It was chilly but not the biting chill that would come in another month or so. There was a refreshing nip in the air rather than that dagger of icy cold that rips through every layer of your clothes and numbs you before you even get down your driveway. It might be the last good walking day of autumn and I wanted to take advantage of it. Oddly enough, instead of getting warmer, the longer I walked, I began to get colder and colder and pulled gloves and a scarf out of my bag and put them on. Maybe this wasn't the last good day of autumn but the preview of winter.

For this visit I did have an agenda. I was anxious to tell Grace about the break-in, the handkerchief and the significance of the October 2 date. I knew she would take the Sylvie story seriously, maybe even help me to do some research on voodoo. I also wanted to know what was going on with Ryan and how things were between her and Hugh. I'd copied down the poem I'd found in the desk in the attic, the desk I was pretty sure belonged to Franklin. I needed to know more about the Edgar Allan Poe short story it had come from and see if there was something in that story that might be a clue. Had Franklin just written down a random quote or had the entire Edgar Allan Poe story had some meaning for him? Was the bout of mono significant in Franklin's life? Had he even had mono or had it been something else, another disease or perhaps an emotional breakdown with a physical label to cover it up? I had a million loose ends but nothing to tie them together. Grace had a lot on her plate but being distracted might be good for her. And maybe she could help me out.

Today the mannequin Trenarys were getting ready for Halloween. The chairs were draped with costumes and the table held several intriguing masks as well as theatrical makeup and a wig. I stared for a while at the scene trying to decide what the costumes would eventually be and who would be wearing what. The clues were all there. Every October Grace held a contest to see who could figure out what the costumes would be. If you were correct on all four you received a free Halloween book. On the 30th Grace would dress the mannequins, using only the materials displayed in the window, and the suspense would end. I entered the store, relieved to be out of the cold.

The store was furnished in what Grace referred to as "substandard" antiques. These were things Hugh had found in people's attics or barns, items that were old and had a good warm look and feel about them but that were not really valuable. They gave the shop a cozy, homey feel that was perfect for shelves and shelves of books. The bookcases were not uniform, so your first impression walking in the door was that you walked into the room of an undisciplined book collector. The Victorian chairs placed throughout the store, the side tables with old lamps giving off a warm yellow glow, the faded rugs on the hardwood floor all added to the image of someone's personal cozy reading nook, although the store was really quite large. In the children's area there was an old library table with sawed off legs and small chairs around it. Colorful posters and an enormous stuffed giraffe added a sense of whimsical playfulness to the area. There was a brightly up-holstered love seat where Grace sat when she gave book readings for pre-schoolers on Wednesday mornings. Abbey and I had sat in that love seat many times, looking at books and trying to make a decision on a birthday gift for a friend, usually coming home with both a gift for the friend and a new book for Abbey. Books are my weakness and for me, a child asking for a book is equivalent to a child asking for a plate of vegetables. It's hard to say no.

The mystery nook featured a Victorian parlor that resembled the study of Sherlock Holmes. There was a violin on the table as well as a deerstalker cap, a cape and a pipe. I've often sat in here reading bits of books from new authors, trying to decide which author to collect next. I'm a lover of the mystery series and will not read one book until I have bought all the books in the series. Then, as the years go by I add to my collection as the new books come out, re-reading the entire series every four or five years. Claudia has often questioned why I would read the same series of books over and over again when there are so many books written that I'll never have time to get to. I've tried to explain that a good writer makes her characters so real you become friends with them when you read book after book of their exploits. I can't imagine leaving these friends and never returning. When I finish a series I love, I'm comforted by the fact that I can and will return to visit with them in a few years. I'm always looking for new authors but I never get rid of my favorites. Like a real friend, I forgive the characters their density at the beginning of the book when the clues, on the fourth reading, are now so obvious.

I stopped to say hi to Jenny, who was working the cash register. Jenny is an incredibly upbeat, personable young lady who knows very little about books. Grace's other employee is a man in his late fifties, Hiram, who had been the librarian in the rare book collection of a local university library and had had to retire early because of the unrelenting pressure of his job. He didn't care for people and could only do one thing at a time, but he knew everything there was to know about books and authors. You could tap into his vast resources of information faster than you could the Internet. He was also a skilled accountant and kept Grace's finances and book orders up to date. He worked in the back of the store and rarely ventured out of his little cubicle until everyone had gone home. Combining Jenny and Hiram, Grace had one excellent employee, and they had both worked there for several years.

Grace motioned me back to her office with two cans of diet soda, a lure she knew I could never resist. I also knew Grace kept a stash of candy bars back there. Right now I was more in need of a hot bowl of chili but chocolate was a passable substitute. While I unwrapped myself from all my layers of clothes, Grace sat down, popped open her drink and tossed several different candy bars on her desk. I reached for one, then remembered my plan to lose those fifteen pounds. I didn't want to negate everything that I had accomplished by my frosty walk, so I held off on the candy and just took the diet soda.

I wanted to immediately plunge into my list of troublesome thoughts and get Grace's take on everything. However, I realize that sometimes we get so involved in our own troubles and family issues we forget that other people are dealing with worries as well. Instead of launching into my own intriguing stories, I reached across the desk and squeezed Grace's arm. "How's everything going?" I asked.

"Oh, Tamsen, I'm such a horrible friend. You let me stay at your house and took care of me and then I left and you never heard from me again. It's just that I have so many problems that I can't think of anything else right now. I'm so sorry you had to drive way over here.

I decided not to tell her I had walked because it would only make her feel worse. "You're a wonderful friend and you know it. Besides, I've been as immersed in my life as you have in yours so let's call it even and catch up. First of all, what is the latest with Ryan?"

Grace broke her candy bar into little pieces and nibbled on them like a mouse. "He's a person of interest. He's not supposed to leave town and Hugh is responsible for making sure he's available for questioning again whenever the police want to talk to him. I thought maybe they were going to put one of those GPS things on his ankle to keep track of him, but as long as he doesn't do anything stupid, like disappear, they're trusting Hugh to keep him in line."

"What does he say about what happened?" I asked.

"Same old story: Franklin was dead when he found him, he knocked him over accidentally, tried to sit him back up and that's how he got blood on his shirt. He comes home from school and hides out in his room. I hardly ever see him. Hugh is convinced Ryan is telling the truth and we just have to wait it out until they find the real killer."

"But as far as I know, Ryan's bloody shirt is the only thing they have to go on," I said. "Oh, sorry. There may be more clues we just don't know about."

"No, you're right. Awful as it is, I don't think they have any other leads to follow up on other than Ryan. I wish there were an escaped lunatic or something who we could blame it on."

"Yeah, all the Birdsey Falls lunatics are out and functioning in society."

Grace smiled. "Have the police said anything else about the case to Cam?"

The police had originally been keeping both Claudia and Cam informed of their progress, but Claudia told them to communicate only with Cam. The whole thing was way too unsavory for a lady. He talked to them several times a week so that's why I knew they had nothing else to go on other than Ryan. I didn't want to keep rubbing that in though. "I know they haven't stopped looking. Other than that, I don't know what they are looking at."

"Other than Ryan, you mean."

"Besides Ryan. I'm sure they're still looking. Cam didn't get the feeling that they felt the case was solved because they found Ryan. After all, it's a good sign that they didn't arrest him. They must have some doubts. Someone must believe him."

We sat lost in our thoughts for several minutes. Sometimes, when your mind is so weighed down, the mere act of making conversation can be too much, like trying to pull a heavy wagon up a hill. With friends and loved ones, these aren't awkward silences that leave you mentally scrambling for something to say to fill the void. We each drew comfort from the other's presence and that was enough. Grace finally spoke.

"You know, I still have all those newspapers from Franklin's cottage. I'd planned to look through them but I haven't had a chance. Do you want them?"

"Are they here, at the store?" I tried to picture myself toting seventy newspapers on my walk back home. I wasn't even sure I could tote myself back and had been thinking of ways to get a ride.

"No, they're at the house. I'd like to look at them some day, just for historical interest. Maybe there would be some articles about the bookstore and my grandparents. Those would be great to have. And I'd love to put some of them in the window. Having an authentic copy of the *Birdsey Falls Gazette* lying on the couch or being read by one of the mannequins would be a nice touch. But right now I don't feel like I'll ever get around to looking at them."

"Sure, I can pick them up at the house or ask Cam to," I said. "You're welcome to use any of them you want. Right now I'd rather poke around in those old papers than work on my Perry book."

"Are you making any headway on that? Is your editor still being stubborn about not allowing the series to get edgier?"

"No headway. Cam has almost convinced me to keep on going with the series and then, if it's not fulfilling me creatively, to write something on the side. Changing the subject, you'll never guess what happened the other night."

I told her about the break-in and about Sylvie as well. Grace has a very expressive face, so telling her a story, even if it's only mildly interesting, is a treat. This story really got her facial muscles working and I could see why the children so loved her Wednesday morning book readings. When I finished the Sylvie story, I launched into the attic excursion story as well. Grace pulled a legal pad out of her desk drawer and began writing furiously. I leaned across the desk to see what she was doing. I couldn't make heads or tails out of it. I tried to turn the legal pad in my direction so I could read what she was writing. She yanked it back and started making columns and arrows all over the paper.

"What are you doing? What are all those arrows?"

She turned the pad around toward me and said breathlessly, "That break-in, the stuff in Franklin's old desk— and we have to go back to your attic and look for more—and even the Sylvie story, all add enough information not related to Ryan to make the case against him seem less plausible. We need to make a list of all the extraneous clues or whatever and then throw them at the police to show that the Ryan inquiry is only one of many possible ways they could go with this.

We can swear it wasn't Ryan who broke into your house because he is practically under house arrest when he gets home from school. Hugh is watching him every minute."

"But we don't know that the break-in had anything to do with Franklin's murder." I protested.

"You've never had a break-in before. Then suddenly you have one, three weeks after a murder. It stands to reason they're related."

"I suppose."

"What we need to do, Tamsen, is to gather all this information and put it in some kind of order, make a timeline. The police aren't going to take the time to do this so we have to do it for them. Maybe we can solve this."

"I can't see that happening …"

"… or at least show enough other possibilities that it won't look like an open-and-shut case against Ryan. There's so much going on that has absolutely nothing to do with Ryan, stuff that happened before he was even born. We need to really pick Claudia's brain …"

"Such a bad idea …"

"… and find out what sort of person Franklin really was. Then maybe we can find a motive for his murder. We have to do this for Ryan. And to save my marriage. I can't see how Hugh and I will ever come out of this intact if Ryan goes to jail for murder. I know deep down that he isn't a murderer. If he had it in him to kill someone, *I* would be the one who was dead and ..." Grace took a deep breath and leaned forward to continue.

I interrupted. "The boys were obviously up to some mischief at the cottage. Maybe a prank gone bad?"

"According to Ryan, the boys were sneaking into his house to see how far inside they could get without him seeing them. I can see how Franklin might have chased after them and fallen and fatally hit his head or something. But to end up with a letter opener in his neck? And he was seated in his chair, not chasing anyone. It just doesn't seem like a prank gone badly to me." Grace sat back in her chair.

"I know. I agree. I truly don't feel Ryan hurt Franklin on purpose. I suppose the letter opener in the neck would be hard to do by mistake ..." I laughed grimly.

"Obviously. There has to be another answer that probably has nothing to do with anyone we know. Someone out of Franklin's past or maybe a recent acquaintance."

"But he never went anywhere or ever talked to anyone," I protested.

"Anyone that you know of. What about the times you and Cam are away? Or even when you're home? Someone could be visiting Franklin in the cottage."

"I think we would know if someone was out there."

"You never knew Ryan and his friends were there, did you?" Grace asked.

"Well, no ..."

"So who knows who else might have come and gone when you weren't home, or even late at night? People could have been slipping in and out of the cottage all the time and, if they were trying to avoid being seen, you probably wouldn't have known."

"But why would they try to avoid being seen? We would've encouraged any guests or friendships Franklin might've had." Thinking of him sitting out there alone day after day made us feel guilty, but we could never get him to come to the house for dinner or to visit with us. We would have loved to know he had someone to talk to.

"Maybe they weren't friends," Grace said. "If he was being harassed by someone from his past, would he have told you?"

"Hardly. He never talked to us."

"Exactly. Who knew what was going on in that cottage. Maybe there was something he didn't want you to see."

"So the hermit act was just that, an act? He did that to keep us away from the cottage so he could do nefarious things out there? Like what? Operate a still? Grow pot? Run a prostitution ring? Launder money? We didn't see any signs of anything other than an old man living a simple existence," I said.

"Maybe the murderer got rid of all the signs that something was going on out there. Franklin was killed before he went to bed, after you and Cam would've checked up on him for the evening, so the murderer had all night to clean up. He knew no one else would be at the cottage. He had hours and hours. And the cottage is small. It wouldn't have taken long."

"I still can't envision what kind of secret activities Franklin would've had going on out there. It couldn't be anything that involved many people because we would've noticed that."

"That kills off the prostitution ring. I think Ryan and his friends might have noticed something like that when they were spying on him," Grace said. It was good to see her getting her sense of humor back.

"Definitely not a prostitution ring. And definitely not pot unless he was growing it in clay pots in his windows. The police would've noticed marijuana plants out there."

"Likewise a still. OK, enough stupid ideas. We need to get serious." Grace pulled the legal pad back and began making a list. "Tell me all the weird things you can think of connected to Franklin's murder. I already wrote down how he was a hermit."

"Put down that he was a normal kid until he was about fifteen."

"Ryan's age …"

"… and then he became more and more reclusive. Put down 'mono' with a question mark."

"OK. I'm putting down the piles of newspapers, one from each year, all the April 1 editions. We really need to look at those …"

"I'll do it," I agreed. "What about the photo of Hetty Foster and Syra not acknowledging her as her mother? That's very strange."

"Right. Got it. I still think we need to tackle Bing on that …"

"… when Syra isn't around."

"Yes. Show him the photo and get him to talk about his mother." Grace flipped over the sheet of paper and started a second one.

"Write down the break-in and put down handkerchief with a question mark. Also note that nothing was taken, therefore someone must have been looking for something that wasn't found."

"Like what?"

"No idea. And put a line for Sylvie. Not sure if that has to do with anything but it is an odd story and the handkerchief is creepy. Oh, and put down this quote." I added.

"Do you have it with you?" Grace wrote the word "quote" and then made a big box.

"Yes, I have a copy in my purse. I brought it to show Hiram to see if he knew anything about the story it was taken from."

"Okay. I'll make a copy of it and tape it in here," she said tapping the box with her pen. "What else?"

"We have to put in about Ryan and his friends and the shirt, don't you think?" I asked tentatively.

"Yeah, I guess so. What else?"

"Write down 'attic'. I want to see if there's more up there that might tell us about Franklin as a child." I hesitated and then took the plunge. "I guess you need to write Claudia's name and star that. She's our best source of information about Franklin's youth, even though she seems so self-absorbed that I'm not sure she was paying much attention. But who knows."

"Maybe she just doesn't remember things. She's getting old."

"Claudia remembers what she wants to. It's just that if it doesn't directly affect her, she doesn't think it's worth remembering. But we can try."

A knock at the back door made us both jump. There are two doors to Grace's office, one leading directly into the bookstore and the other leading to a hallway that attaches her store to Hugh's antiques shop next door. At one time these two stores were one but when Grace's grandfather bought the building, he divided the space and rented out the shop next door. He built a hallway between the two shops and that is where Grace had her office and a storage room for the bookstore and Hugh had his office and storage space behind his store. Grace was actually Hugh's landlord as well as the landlord for the two apartments on the second floor of the building.

The door opened and Hugh came into the office, obviously startled to see me sitting there. He's a large man, big-boned and carrying a lot of muscle and a lot of weight. Grace and I agreed that he would be an excellent representative of the Gentle Giant society, if there were such a thing. We smiled at each other and then he looked at Grace. I immediately knew that their marriage was not in as much trouble as Grace thought it was. I was embarrassed to witness the tenderness and love in his expression as he bent down to kiss the top of her head. She returned the same look to him.

"I should get going."

"No, no," they both protested. Hugh pulled up a chair and looked at the pad in front of Grace.

"Ah, interesting. I see what you two have been up to this morning." Hugh wiggled around and pulled a folded up sheet of paper from his back pocket. He spread it out on the table. It looked similar to ours.

"You two *are* soul mates," I said. They both smiled at me. "Are you sure you don't want me to leave?"

"Absolutely not," Hugh said. "I want to compare notes." Hugh wasn't as well informed as Grace and I but he had written a detailed timeline of Ryan's involvement. Grace added dates and times onto our sheet as well as some detailed descriptions of what Franklin had been doing each of the times the boys were there. It was obvious that there wasn't much going on at Franklin's cottage in the evenings other than reading, eating dinner, doing the dishes and snoozing in his chair. The boys had never seen another person remotely near the cottage or ever seen Franklin leave the cottage. There wasn't a TV out there, so his evenings were spent reading.

I pointed to Hugh's list. "What does this mean, 'read/w'?"

"Reading and writing. Ryan said Franklin was either reading in his chair or writing at his desk," Hugh explained.

"Writing what?" I'd never seen Franklin writing anything.

Hugh shrugged. "No idea. Ryan just said he was either reading or writing in the evenings. Sometimes they walked by early enough to see him sitting in the kitchen eating. Then he would do all the dishes and go into his study for the night. He read or wrote. That's it."

Grace and I looked at each other, both thinking the same thing. We hadn't found any sign in the cottage that indicated Franklin had written much of anything. No journal. No letters. No papers with his writing on them at all. Not even a list. Cam and I shopped for him and usually he asked for the same things each week. If he wanted anything different— and he rarely did— he told us. He never gave us a list or wrote us a note. So what was he writing? And where was it now?

There's only so much you can discuss when you don't know any-thing. We went around and around about Franklin and the writing and got nowhere. Hugh promised to question Ryan again to make sure he wasn't mistaken about it although I'm not sure what else it would be that Franklin was doing that would make it look as if he were writing. Drawing? That was even stranger. Coloring? Stranger still. Grace and Hugh were both interested in talking more about Ryan so I left to talk to Hiram about the Poe quote.

Hiram's work space is behind a bookcase of travel books that tow-ers about six feet high. On top of the bookcase are old boats—ferries, sailboats and pirate ships—as well as some old trains and a couple of World War I vintage planes. My favorite transportation piece is a hot-air balloon filled with waving dolls, one of whom holds a cat and is waving its paw. Cam and I have always talked of going up in a balloon someday. I stood there staring at the balloon and picturing Cam and me in there, Cam holding Mycroft and waving his paw to our friends on the ground.

It suddenly occurred to me that Perry Many Paws and his friends could take a hot-air balloon ride! The balloon would give an opportunity for lots of bright-colored illustrations, something that is often missing when you have a bear, a squirrel and a frog in every picture. Plus, flying over farms and towns and various other types of landscape could be educational. Yes, a balloon ride would be perfect and, I think, Tim would even agree to let the characters out of the forest and away from the cave for that. Suddenly a shadow appeared over my shoulder.

"Hiram! You startled me."

"Sorry." His eyes went left and right and then to somewhere over my shoulder while his hands fidgeted in his pockets. He was the thinnest man I knew. His skin was stretched so tightly over his face that it looked like it could tear if you dared to touch it. Which I didn't. It occurred to me that if he wanted a face lift he would be out of luck because his skin couldn't get any tighter than it was now. He wore a baggy suit, completely overdressed for his job, and it hung on him like it was still in his closet. He was literally a human clothes hanger.

"Well ..." He turned around to go back into his cubicle behind the bookcase. Whatever he'd planned to do when he came out and startled me had been forgotten in his desire to return to the safety of his space. I hope he hadn't been on his way to the bathroom.

"Wait. Can I ask you a question?

He stared at me warily. "What kind?"

"Literary."

"Of course." He bowed elegantly and ushered me into his work area. It always surprised me to see the laptop computer glowing on his desk. He looked like he spent his days with his head in a musty old book. He indicated that I was to sit in the bright blue velvet overstuffed chair while he sat back at his desk.

"Yes?"

I felt like I was with a psychiatrist. His eyes were a dark gray and matched his hair. He had a full head of hair that he didn't get cut very often so it tended to sort of fall every which way on his face. Either it was unmanageable or just unmanaged. He was clean shaven, which must have been an easy task considering how tight his skin was. Probably never had a razor nick in his life. His nose was rather long and pointy but then everything on his face looked pointy including his cheekbones and his chin.

"Yes?"

He was also very patient. "Hiram, I found a quote and I was wondering if you could help me with it."

"You want to know the author?"

"Well, I know it's from a short story by Edgar Allan Poe. But I'm not familiar with the story and I wonder if you could tell me anything about it. Here." I handed him the paper I had copied from Franklin's note.

> *There are some secrets which do not permit themselves to be told … mysteries which will not suffer themselves to be revealed. Now and then, alas, the conscience of man takes up a burden so heavy in horror that it can be thrown down only into the grave.*
>
> *Edgar Allan Poe, "The Man of the Crowd," 1840*

"Ah, this is an excerpt of the actual quote. One assumes the person who copied it was only quoting the part that pertained to them," Hiram said. He stared at my feet, waiting for me to speak.

"Um, yes, one assumes so."

"This story, "The Man of the Crowd," isn't one of Poe's best known. But it's a good story nevertheless. One of my favorites. It gives you a lot to think about." He handed me back my paper and looked over my shoulder. I was not too impressed. I knew the name of the story from which the quote was taken and I knew the author. It was written right under the quote. And I'd never heard of the short story so I knew it wasn't one of Poe's well-known ones.

"Can you tell me anything about the story? I've never read it."

"It was first published in 1840 in *Burton's Gentlemen's Magazine*. That was the last issue of that periodical although I'm sure the demise of the magazine was in no way related to Poe's story."

Perhaps if the magazine had been named in a way that invited women to read it, it might have survived longer.

"It also appeared simultaneously in a periodical named *Atkinson's Casket*."

Another catchy magazine title.

"Can you tell me what the story is about?" I asked.

"Of course."

There was a long moment of silence. I mentioned earlier that quiet times between friends and loved ones are comfortable and soothing. This was not one of those times. Hiram finally gather his thoughts.

"It's about a man who has been ill who sits in a coffee shop in London and watches the people passing by. We aren't sure what his illness is, medical or mental, but he has a lot of free time on his hands to just sit all day and people watch. He feels isolated and notices that each person in the crowd is just as isolated as he. One man catches his attention, an old man in ragged clothes. He decides to follow him. At some point the narrator thinks the old man may have a dagger under his coat but he never actually sees one. The old ragged man wanders through London all night and the narrator follows. The old man goes into the poor and desolate sections of the city and through the markets until he makes his way back into the center of London. At the end of the chase the exhausted narrator stands in front of the old man and the old man does not even notice him. The narrator surmises that the old man is guilty of some horrible haunting crime, although he has no idea what it was, and that this crime condemns the man to wander forever through the streets of London, trying to forget."

"It seems sort of inconclusive."

"Life is inconclusive. We all have to draw our own conclusions. It keeps you thinking."

"But this isn't life, Hiram. It's a short story. It should have a real ending."

"But all writing is about life, isn't it? Most things in life don't have neat conclusions."

Well, apparently he hadn't read any Perry Many Paws books because they all had clear conclusions with a lesson or two thrown in. It's hard to have a life lesson if no one understands how the book ends. I decided I had taken up enough of Hiram's time so I thanked him and popped my head into Grace's office to tell her goodbye. Hugh was still there so I just waved and left. I wondered how Grace would feel if I told her there were no conclusions in life; we were all condemned to just wander through and make assumptions and then die without any answers. Very unsatisfactory.

Chapter Seventeen

C am and I lingered over breakfast the next morning. It was Saturday and he had his day planned— a ten o'clock squash game with his friend John Sullivan, lunch at a sports bar followed by the local high school football game where John's son was making his debut as the back-up quarterback. I had the whole day to myself.

Abbey had called last night and asked if she could bring some friends home for Thanksgiving. One of the girls in her dorm was from California and wouldn't be making the trip home so close to Christmas. One of the guys in her Anthropology class ('no, he's *not* a boyfriend') was from New Zealand and wasn't going home again until summer. We encouraged her to invite them. Claudia and Sybil would be joining us, as well as Syra, Bing, Diane and her family, Grace, Hugh and Ryan. I made a mental note to reserve the services of the Birdsey Falls Dust Bunnies to come clean the house and the guest rooms right before each of the holidays. I kept Abbey's room and the guest room Grace had stayed in dusted and vacuumed, but the other rooms weren't spruced up until we knew people were going to use them. I didn't want to send either of Abbey's friends back to college with lungs coated in dust, not to mention a very low opinion of my housekeeping skills, however accurate it might be.

Abbey had asked if my brother Graham would be here again for Thanksgiving. He wasn't a regular for the holidays but popped in once in awhile, usually when he had a new book out and was traveling up and down the East Coast promoting it. Last Thanksgiving he'd been doing the rounds for his new book, *The Argosy of Narcissism,* which was out "in time for the holidays." Why anyone would buy this book for the holidays, or any time, was beyond me. In his latest book Graham proposed that bisexuality was neither a deviant nor a normal alternative to hetero- or homosexual relationships and was not actually driven from any kind of sexual need or desire at all. He claimed that the bisexual was really asexual in his or her libido and was an extreme narcissist who needed the adoration of both men and women to be satisfied emotionally. The sex act for the narcissist was just the affirmation of his or her desirability and meant nothing to him/her sexually.

This theory, including numerous examples of famous bisexuals and their intimate sex lives, were expounded at the Thanksgiving table last year. Graham is the ultimate pompous ass so the delivery alone was irritating notwithstanding the actual subject matter. Cam and Abbey both claim that Graham is the evil twin of Kelsey Grammer's character Frasier, without the humor, charm or humanity. I have to agree. Although it's hard to get in even a "please pass the cranberry sauce" when Graham is pontificating, somehow Grace was able to interject her personal theory of bisexuality, which was that bisexuals were actually very old souls who had lived many lives as both men and women and thus didn't feel confined to loving just one gender. It was a Thanksgiving dinner to remember and I understood Abbey's concern about it being repeated when she had friends here. Luckily for all of us, Graham was in England researching a new book, the subject of which I was blissfully unaware.

Cam was planning to stop at Grace's house on the way home and pick up Franklin's newspapers. I had hurried home after my trip to the bookstore yesterday and written down my ideas about the hot air balloon adventure for Perry and his friends. I decided to spend the morning working on my idea and then send an outline to Tim. After lunch, when I knew Syra was at her weekly breast cancer support group, I would wander over to see Bing and pump him for information about his mother.

Cam headed out about 9:30 and I worked on my outline, so fully immersed in it that I lost all track of time. It's a wonderful and a scary feeling, to be able to transport yourself so far into your own head, and so deeply into what you are writing, that you don't even realize time is passing and an hour flies by like a minute. It's like being drugged or hypnotized. Satisfied that I had something decent to send to Tim, I emailed him and then made myself a grilled cheese sandwich with a couple slices of bacon. I read the morning paper while I ate. The *Birdsey Falls Gazette* is not very large so the paper was read long before the sandwich was finished. I stared out the window while I ate the other half and tried to channel Uncle Franklin. This would all be much easier if his spirit would come to me and explain his death so I could pass it on to the police and we could all get back to our pre-murder routines. No amount of staring would bring his spirit to me, so I rinsed off my dishes, loaded the dishwasher and gave Bing a call. You can't just pop in on Bing when he is home alone because he simply will not answer the door. He won't answer the phone, either, but he will listen to your message and then, sometimes, call you back. Luckily I was among the select few who warranted a call back and we agreed that I would come over in a few minutes.

I put the photo of Hetty and the other kids in my bag before I went over. I hadn't decided how I would approach this whole thing but wanted to have the photo with me just in case. Bing was standing at the door when I got there, anxious to get me inside. I had barely gotten into the house before he closed the door and locked it. I could smell cinnamon and my stomach started anticipating something sweet and sticky to eat.

Bing ushered me into the kitchen, his favorite room. Syra claimed he did everything but sleep in there. Their house is small, and the kitchen not large enough for someone as devoted to baking as Bing. After they moved in they had a second kitchen built in the basement, and Bing did all his experimental cooking down there. This morning he had made a small batch of cinnamon rolls in the upstairs kitchen.

We sat at the table and Bing took the fragrant rolls out of the oven, scooped them on to a plate and slathered them with white frosting. They were so warm I could hear the raisins percolating under the frosting. If I'd been Mycroft I would have had a puddle of drool on the table in front of me.

"Yum." I inhaled the sweet smell and felt the warmth in my hand. This was heaven. My stomach completely forgot the grilled cheese sandwich and pleaded for me to start eating. I obliged. "These are perfect, Bing."

Bing gave my shoulder a squeeze and sat down. He's a very warm and affectionate person and I've often thought it must be difficult for him being afraid of people and yet having a need to connect. "Have as many as you want. I always make more than Syra and I can eat. It's very difficult for me to make pastries for just two people."

"And we're all the better for it, believe me. Fatter too." Bing did resemble the Pillsbury Doughboy and, if not for the fact I was about six inches taller than Bing, I probably would, too. Weight control is extra difficult if you're short. I wondered if Bing had always been round. I bet he was an incredibly pudgy and huggable baby.

I then invited Bing and Syra for Thanksgiving, pretending that was why I'd come over. We discussed my menu, which was always the same, and Bing agreed to make pies, which he always did. I wondered if not seeing anyone but Syra was more difficult for him since she'd had her mastectomy and radiation treatments. Bing is a nurturing person so I knew Syra received loving care, but who took care of Bing when she wasn't up to it? I resolved to try to invite him over to the house more often, even when there wasn't a WOACA meeting, so he could have someone to talk to other than Syra if he needed to.

"Abbey's bringing two friends home with her for Thanksgiving. Will that be all right with you?" I asked, knowing that he was very uncomfortable with strangers. "Claudia and Sybil will be there as usual and Diane's family, Grace, Hugh and Ryan, so there will mostly be people you know. Just two that you won't."

Bing rubbed his mouth with his napkin. "Just two new people?"

"Yes, friends of Abbey who live too far away to go home for Thanksgiving. One is from California and one from New Zealand. I'm sure they're very nice." I started licking frosting off my fingers— pointless—because I was only going to get them sticky again when I had my second cinnamon bun.

"I guess that's OK. I probably wouldn't need to talk to them very much. Maybe not at all."

"I can seat you at the other end of the table."

It suddenly occurred to me that I should invite Hiram for Thanksgiving and see how he and Bing hit it off. They both kept to themselves. They could sit next to each other, never speak and both be happy as clams.

"Will your brother be there this year?" Needless to say, Bing hadn't participated in the origin of bisexuality conversation last year, and had been outright horrified.

"No, Graham's in England," I assured him. Somehow I needed to get this conversation steered in the right direction without being too obvious. "These cinnamon buns are really good, Bing. I wish my mother had liked cooking and passed that love on to me. Was it your mom who taught you how to bake?" I was glad Grace wasn't here be- cause this was such a lame subject introduction that I knew we would have both burst out laughing.

153

"Yes, my mom was a great cook. She understood how hard it was for me to leave the house so I got to stay home and bake with her. I had to do some lessons, too, but mostly we cooked and ate. I didn't have to play with any of the kids. It was a wonderful childhood."

Wonderful childhoods are obviously in the eyes of the beholder. I was sure it wasn't even legal back then to not send your child to school. Was baking considered home schooling?

I plunged ahead, using my most subtle questioning techniques. "My mom's name is Elizabeth. She never really liked it. How about your mom? Did she like her name?" Oh my God this was painful. I was embarrassing myself. Luckily Bing was not the suspicious type.

"She never really said. Her name was Mary so I guess there's not much to dislike."

Mary? Didn't he even know his own mother's name? Claudia and Sybil had said Hetty Foster was Bing's and Syra's mother. It was a testament to my belief in Claudia's ability to always be right that I actually assumed she was more likely to know Bing's mother's name than he was.

"Her name was Mary? Mary Foster?"

"Well, it was Foster after she married my dad. Her maiden name was Willard."

"So when she was a young girl, say around fifteen, her name was Mary Willard, right?"

Bing narrowed his eyes and stared at me. "Yeah, she was Mary Willard until she married my dad. Is there something strange about that?"

He had no idea how very strange it was. "No, it isn't strange at all. It's just that for as long as I've been friends with you and Syra I've never heard much about your childhood or your parents. It's interesting. What was your dad's name?"

"Fulton."

Fulton Foster. Try saying that three times fast. This was making no sense at all. What had happened to Hetty Foster? Was Mary Willard the same person as Hetty Foster? And who the heck was Fulton? For the first time in my entire acquaintance with Claudia I wished she was here. She would get to the bottom of this fast.

"Are your parents still living?"

"No. My dad died when I was a baby. I don't remember him. My mom died the year before Syra and I moved here, around sixteen years ago I think. I still miss her but when I'm baking it's like she's in the kitchen with me. I can remember her telling me how much of each ingredient to use and explaining to me the right way to present different dishes to show them off. We used to talk the whole time we were cooking. I had so much fun."

"It sounds like you and your mom had a special relationship. You're very lucky. How about Syra? Were she and your mom close?"

"Just average, I guess. They fought a lot when Syra was a teenager but from what I've heard at WOACA, that was normal. Syra wasn't interested in doing anything in the kitchen. She was reading all the time and that annoyed my mom. She thought people should be doing things."

As an author I wanted to disagree. Reading *was* doing something, something very important. If more people did it I would have better job security.

"Does Syra remember her dad?" What I really wanted to ask was whether Fulton was Syra's dad also but I couldn't bring myself to be quite so crass.

"She was about three when he died so probably not very well. We don't talk about him. We talk about our mom sometimes but never our dad. Do you want another cinnamon bun?"

"I do but I really can't stuff another one in me. Thank you." Bing got up and wrapped up the buns to put them in the refrigerator. I went into summarization mode. So this Fulton Foster guy, who no one remembers, was both Bing and Syra's dad. Claudia was wrong on that. She swore they had different fathers. Also, it didn't sound like Bing's mother was either the dedicated tomboy or the thruway floozy that Sybil and Claudia made her out to be. I mean, she stayed home and baked all day. Maybe she was a reformed thruway floozy. Reformed by Fulton Foster, the man who lived long enough to father two children, then died before either of the children was old enough to remember him.

Bing was looking at me expectantly and too late I realize I should have accepted another cinnamon bun, because now I had no excuse to linger and continue to question him. I reluctantly got out of my chair, picked up my jacket and sauntered toward the front door.

"You and Syra have such unusual names, Bing. Your mother must have had a great imagination. Do you know how she came up with them?" I slipped my arms into my coat and fussed around getting my bag situated on my shoulder.

"Our real names are Syracuse and Binghamton. My parents went to Niagara Falls for their honeymoon and liked the names of these cities along the thruway so that's what they named us. I guess it's kind of imaginative."

"Yes, very imaginative. Thanks so much for the treats, Bing. Tell Syra I said hi."

I didn't want to interrupt Grace in case she was involved in family matters so I sent her a long email to tell her about my conversation with Bing. When Cam came home with a sack of Franklin's newspapers I went over the entire conversation again with him. Neither writing about it nor talking about it made it any clearer. Was it possible that Claudia was wrong about Hetty Foster? It seemed so unlikely and yet the other option was that Bing had no idea who his mother really was. That too seemed unlikely. Was there a third version that made more sense? I wondered what Syra would say if I asked her the same questions I asked Bing.

Cam had brought home sesame chicken, beef and broccoli, egg rolls and a mountain of rice. I'm ashamed to say my appetite was good and I ate my fair share. So much for the positive effects of the walk to the bookstore yesterday. I'd completely negated those ten times over with what I'd eaten today.

"I wish I'd asked Bing where his mother was from but every time he answered one of my questions I was so totally dumbfounded that I couldn't sort out the best question to ask next," I told Cam as I polished off the last egg roll.

"Well, Bing can be a little skittish. It sounds as if you did a good job getting as much information out of him as you did. I mean, you couldn't just come out and tell him Claudia said his mother had a different name and that she was a tramp, conceiving children at various cities on the NYS thruway, all the way from Albany to Buffalo." Cam pretended to scratch his leg but I knew he was really giving Mycroft pieces of beef under the table.

"When we look at those newspapers we can keep an eye out for Fulton Foster and Mary Willard as well as Hetty Foster and the other kids in the photo with Franklin. Maybe something will pop out at us and it will suddenly make sense."

"Maybe. Do you think Abbey and this New Zealand guy are just friends or is she just telling us that so we won't ask her a lot of questions?" Cam bent down and scratched his leg again.

"Do you need some calamine lotion for that leg? Abbey said they weren't romantically involved so I think we have to assume she's telling us the truth. There's no reason to mislead us. We haven't even met him."

"Mmm. Maybe. But we assumed my mom was telling us the truth about Bing and Syra's mother and then we assume Bing is telling us the truth about his own mother and where does that leave us? Two truths?"

"There can't be two truths but there can be two lies. Maybe neither is telling the truth."

"Why would my mom lie about it?"

"Maybe she isn't lying. Maybe she's wrong."

"I seriously doubt that. My mother is never wrong."

You can't imagine how proud Claudia would have been to hear her son testify to her inability to make a mistake. I, on the other hand, was just annoyed. Cam bent down to scratch his leg.

"For God's sake, put a dish down there for Mycroft and stop pretending you have to scratch your leg. It's childish. And speaking of childish, your declaration that your mother is never wrong reeks of playground bravado. The next thing you'll be telling me is that your dad can beat up my dad."

"Here Mycroft, mommy says you can have some dinner." Cam put some beef on a napkin and handed it down to Mycroft. He stopped and scratched his leg on the way up. "My leg really does itch, for your information. I was just killing two birds with one stone, scratching and providing nourishment."

"Your mother predicted that Abbey was going to be a boy. She was wrong about that."

"That was wishful thinking on her part. She wanted a boy so we could change his last name to Behrends and he could continue the family dynasty in Birdsey Falls." Cam stood up and began to clear the table and load the dishwasher.

"Your mother really does think the Behrendses are like the Kennedys, doesn't she. I mean how can anyone, including the Kennedys, have a family dynasty in Birdsey Falls?"

"The Behrendses have always been big fish in a little pond. I'm not sure my mom realizes just how little the pond actually is. She sees herself a certain way and nothing, including facts, will change that. It's harmless …"

"It's annoying."

"But harmless."

"Then you admit it's annoying."

"Mmm …"

"Cam, that isn't an answer."

"It's not annoying to me but I can see why it is to you. Mom is just mom and she's always been that way, so I accept her as she is. As Abbey says, grandma is a queen. Her parents treated her like a queen, her brothers treated her like a queen and when she grew up she married a man who treated her like a queen. Even her best friend treats her like a queen."

"She's delusional. And annoying."

Cam turned on the dishwasher then came over to rub my shoulders. He bent his head down and rubbed his nose against my neck.

"She created me."

I leaned back against his chest. "I can't fault her there although I think you are 99% your father and very little Claudia."

"I'm not delusional."

"No, but you can be annoying …"

"But not right now."

"No, not right now," I agreed.

"Let's go upstairs and see if I can continue to not be annoying up there."

That's why we never got a chance to look at the newspapers.

Chapter Eighteen

"**D**o you think it's too late to ask your mom and Sybil to dinner tonight?" I yelled to Cam as I stretched in the bed and then pulled the covers back up to my shoulders. I'd wait until the house heated up a bit before venturing out. Cam, toothbrush in mouth, popped his head out of the bathroom door.

"Wha ouu zay?"

"Don't drip toothpaste! Stick your hand under there. I said, is it too late to invite your mom for dinner tonight? Too short of notice?"

Cam continued to just stare at me, toothbrush hanging precariously out of his mouth, hand dutifully poised under his chin. Then he shook his head and went back into the bathroom. He re-emerged a minute later and perched on the side of the bed, reaching out to touch my forehead with his palm.

"Do you have a fever?"

I gently removed his hand and propped myself up on both of our pillows, resettling the covers primly across my chest. I didn't want him getting any ideas because I had a lot I wanted to accomplish today and I can be easily distracted when he puts on the charm.

"I realize that I rarely suggest having your mother come over here but today I …"

"… want to quiz her about Bing and Syra's mother and try to reconcile Bing's story with hers."

"Exactly. Can you call her?"

"What excuse can I use? We hardly ever invite her over here for dinner unless Abbey is home."

"Well, it's Sunday and they don't have a big dinner at Ashland Belle, just that fancy brunch. She might like a nice home-cooked meal."

"Who's going to cook?"

That might sound like fighting words but they actually made a lot of sense. I'm not much of a cook and when we have company Cam always does the cooking. He handles Thanksgiving and Christmas and birthday parties and any other kind of party we might have. So it was a legitimate question and I wasn't the least bit offended. I was actually relieved that he was considering he might have to cook it because that's exactly what I had in mind.

"You know how much she loves your paella. If you agree to make it, I'll go to the store and get the seafood and pick up something for dessert," I bargained. "Why don't you call her while I jump in the shower and then we can make a grocery list. We didn't have anything else planned for today and …"

"Football. I want to watch football, at least the one o'clock game."

"You still can. We'll invite her for 4:30-ish. And you know she won't stay long because she hates to drive when it's dark. And be sure to include Sybil in the invitation."

Cam reluctantly agreed. Usually it was me who was reluctantly agreeing to have her here. I would have preferred to get the information over the phone, but when she and Sybil were together they fed off each other; since they both knew Hetty, having them talk about her together would bring out more information and memories.

I ran to the store and bought the necessary supplies, grabbing a handful of candy bars to have on hand. I hate not having chocolate around when I get a craving. I also picked up two turkey subs for Cam and me to have for lunch, my contribution to kitchen duty for the day. He did the preliminary dinner prep while I put away groceries and then we went our separate ways with our subs, him to the family room to watch football and me to the attic to continue my exploration of Franklin's desk.

The mysterious caverns of the attic were less foreboding today. I'd been here recently and charted my route back to Franklin's desk. I hoped that having stumbled upon his desk I was also in the vicinity of other items that might have belonged to him. I knew I could never get Claudia up here—"I don't do stairs, dear," she'd say, "especially two flights," — but maybe I could find some things to bring down to show her that might jog her memory of Franklin's teenage years and what precipitated his "going strange."

I headed back to the desk and sat in the companion chair to eat my sub. What had I been thinking to bring food up here to this dusty, dingy place? I hadn't seen any critters up here yet, but if they were nearby this sub was going to bring them out, and then I wouldn't get anything done because I would run screaming back downstairs, never to return again. I hate rodents, love of Disney characters notwithstanding.

It was quiet and peaceful up here. I leaned back in the old swivel desk chair and looked around at the looming boxes and furniture surrounding me. How did they get all this stuff up here in the first place? Who had to carry it up those stairs, probably cursing all the way? Someone must have decided the furniture was out of style so it needed to be replaced but it was still serviceable so it couldn't be thrown away. Now, if it were in decent shape, it could be valuable. We might have a treasure trove of antiques up here gathering dust.

Treasure. That reminded me of the photo of the five children and Claudia's and Sybil's memories of Franklin making treasure maps for the kids to follow. Then the vision of a teenage Cam and his friends stealing ladies' underpants and burying them flashed by. In the future would archeologists uncover that stash of underwear and build some imaginary religious rite around its discovery? I wondered where they were buried and if they were still there. Would Cam remember? I'd have to ask him, although not at dinner in front of his mother.

Did Claudia consider herself a good mother? Did she care? She wasn't a very hands-on mother, more of a figurehead, like Queen Elizabeth. Removed and protected. She did her duties but preferred to delegate when she could. She was never in the battle of life; she stood on the sidelines and directed or else walked away and ignored the battle altogether. She was sad about Franklin's death but didn't seem to care why he had died or who had killed him. Everyone in Claudia's life had enabled her to live sheltered and protected in her fairy-tale world. Why was that? In many ways she was like a woman in a bubble, like Glinda floating to earth in the *Wizard of Oz*. Not for the first time it occurred to me that I did not like my mother-in-law. And not just because she was my mother-in-law and thus could interfere uncomfortably in my life. I would not have liked her if she were my next door neighbor, my doctor, my yoga instructor or my Avon Lady. I was bonded to her for the rest of my life because even when she died she would still be Cam's mother and he loved her. I suddenly felt like Marley's ghost with Claudia adding to the links of the chain she had thrown around me when Cam and I married. Link by link it got heavier and heavier and I had to drag her around with me for eternity.

Sybil, on the other hand, would have been a fun mother-in-law. She had a bit of a past that she loved to hint at, although I didn't think it was any more risqué than the fact that she'd had four husbands. She had done some acting so maybe had had a fling or two while she was in New York. She was overly dramatic but in an amusing way if you didn't take her too seriously, which no one did. And she had a good heart. Luckily for me, Claudia and Sybil were inseparable so whenever I had to see Claudia I could at least look forward to Sybil being there, too. Sybil was like the spoonful of sugar that helped the medicine go down.

I couldn't remember how far I had gotten in exploring Franklin's desk so I started at the top left and began to methodically open drawers and peer inside with my flashlight. I had brought gardening gloves but I was still reluctant to stick my hand in dark places and hope for the best. There was the usual debris of an abandoned desk, paper clips, scraps of blank paper, brittle rubber bands, a couple inch-long pencils, a few pennies and lots and lots of dust. Routine and boring. I pulled out my cell phone and called Cam.

"Yup?"

"Am I interrupting anything impor …"

"… wait. Wait. Come on. Come on. Come on. You got it. You got it. Shit! Wide right. How could he miss that? It was only 35 yards. I could have nailed that kick. I mean, look what they're paying him …"

"Cam!"

"What? You wouldn't believe what just happened. It was a thirty-five-yard field goal attempt, no wind, overcast, nothing but a straight kick and he missed it. Unbelievable!"

"Can you talk now or should I call back?" I asked. I didn't really want to hear a play by play of the football game.

"It's an Escalade commercial now, so go ahead."

"Is it the red Escalade? I love that car."

"No, it's a black one. Why are we talking about this? Aren't you in the attic? Are you OK?"

"I'm fine. I'm at Franklin's desk and I can't find anything. Since you're a guy, I wondered where guys might hide stuff in their desks. Any thoughts?"

"If I had something hidden in my desk I would make sure I took it out before I moved my desk to the attic. You know, the black Escalade is pretty good looking …"

"Not as good as the red. If I'm buying an Escalade I'm getting the red one. OK. I just thought you might have some ideas about hiding places."

"Sorry. If I think of something, I'll call you," he offered.

This would be easier if I knew what I was looking for. Maybe I should tackle some of the boxes. I'd shied away from those because they were so unappealing and I envisioned swarms of bats breaking free the minute I opened one. The boxes weren't taped shut so I picked up an old hockey stick and, from a distance, used it to pry open the top of the closed box. Once I had it wedged open I stood on a chair and slapped at the side of the box, allowing anything that might be living inside to come running out. Luckily I had no takers so I got off the chair, put on my gardening gloves and took the lid completely off.

The box was full of holey sweaters and dead moths. I didn't know if the sweaters were poison or if the moths had overeaten and died of the sin of gluttony. Either way, there wasn't much to see. I used the hockey stick to flip the sweaters back and forth in case there was anything else in the box, but that was it. I had just finished stirring up box number four with my trusted hockey stick when the phone rang. The ringtone was Bob Dylan's "Blowin' in the Wind" so I knew it was Cam.

"How are you doing up there?" he asked.

"Nothing so far," I said, "except dead moths, lots of them."

"Did you find any desk blotter or something like that?"

"No, why?"

"Because that's where I would hide things. Under my blotter. If Franklin had an old blotter up there, that would be a good place to look."

"OK. I'll look. Thanks for thinking about it during the game. Are you yelling at the television even though there's no one else there?"

"Of course. I wouldn't have to if they played better. Love you. Bye."

Commercial must be over. I scoured around for some kind of desk blotter but found nothing. It's only in movies that someone finds a secret compartment in a desk or letters taped on the bottom of drawers. If there were a contest judging items of interest in proportion to attic size I would definitely be the loser. I was the wide right kicker of attic discoveries. Except no one was paying me a lot of money to be any better at it than I was.

"Come on, Franklin," I said out loud, "give me a little help. There's a fifteen-year- old boy who's going to be in trouble if this isn't resolved. You must feel for the poor kid. Think about yourself at fifteen and how your life changed for the worse. Give me a clue." My voice sounded strange in the quiet of the attic. Franklin had never talked to me when he was alive so I wasn't sure why he should bother now that he was dead, but I was getting desperate. If I were in the middle of a mystery novel, I might suddenly get an indescribable urge to open a drawer or look behind a dresser, maybe even open a box that was situated under a pile of junk, a box that was barely discernible but beckoning me to check inside. I looked around for a cobweb-encrusted chest that would squeal horribly when I pulled it open for the first time in fifty years. Maybe a flicker of light through a crusty window that would land on a cracked mirror and reflect onto a key hidden in the crevice between the floor boards. I patiently waited. Nothing.

"You're really pissing me off, Franklin." I slammed my soda can onto his desk and then quickly looked in case the impact had caused a secret drawer to burst open. Nothing happened. This is why some murders were never solved. There should be a law that in mystery novels only half the books could end with an arrest and a resolution to the crime. Too much reading had gotten my hopes up that if I just looked hard enough I would be able to solve this murder, save Ryan from jail, get Grace's marriage back on track, resolve the parenting confusion for Bing and Syra and maybe bring Diane to her senses regarding the allure of policemen. In addition, when my mother-in-law saw how smart and resourceful I was, she would suddenly break out of her cloistered little world and become a warm and fuzzy friend. Bing would come out of his house and join the rush of humanity on the streets of Birdsey Falls. Syra would be forever cured of cancer. I would lose fifteen—no twenty— pounds. The police would reward me with a red Escalade and a gas card. All of this could be mine if only I were a character in a book.

I started wandering around, pulling open dresser drawers (Surprise! Nothing!), opening armoires (ditto), poking at old mattresses (new dust), and mumbling vaguely obscene phrases regarding past generations of the Behrends family. The best thing I found was a beautiful old quilt, handmade and carefully folded with layers of paper protecting it from the dust but still allowing the fibers to breathe. It was heavy so I knew it must be huge, and I didn't want to risk ruining it by opening it up in the middle of this dust jungle. It looked undamaged and I was thinking that it would look spectacular on the bed in the guest room. Even if there were some damage I could get it restored. It was a work of art and I wondered which Behrends had made it. Maybe Claudia would know. I decided that this was the best I was going to find today so I carefully carried it downstairs to show Cam and to get ready for the onslaught of Claudia at 4:30.

Dinner was delicious. If Cam and Bing joined forces they could have a very successful restaurant business. I mentioned this observation over coffee and dessert in the library, attempting to get the conversation directed to Syra and Bing. Claudia and Sybil had taken control of the conversation when they entered the front door and had been telling us tales of Ashland Belle residents for over an hour now. Ashland Belle was like the land of the lost: lost keys, lost teeth, lost walkers, lost wigs and lost residents. They needed a good bloodhound there. They could keep him busy day and night.

"There has never been a Behrends who owned a restaurant or any other kind of commercial establishment. I don't think it would suit Cam," Claudia replied as if I were seriously suggesting Cam and Bing go into business together. I wanted to roll my eyes but Cam really hates it when I do that in front of his mother. Tonight Claudia was dressed in a soft rose-colored cashmere sweater and skirt set, real pearls and several large, precious stone rings. She is a small woman so the rings looked like boiled eggs jammed onto toothpicks. I was surprised she didn't need Sybil to pick up her hands for her so she could reach for her coffee. Sybil was wearing some kind of shiny purple ensemble that defied description and seriously clashed with her now orange hair. Her jewelry was huge and abundant but obviously costume jewelry with lots of bright colors and various beads and stones and who knew what else pasted together.

"Besides, Bing could never own a restaurant because he won't come out of his house," Sybil added as she slapped another piece of carrot cake on her plate. "It's some psychological thing about never wanting to leave the womb or something. I saw it on Oprah. Some people are just born strange."

Now was my big chance. "I was over at Bing's yesterday and we were discussing how his mother taught him to cook. He said his mother's name was Mary …"

"Ridiculous. You misunderstood him," Claudia regally stated as if that were the end of the conversation.

"No, I didn't, Claudia. He very clearly said that his mother's name was Mary and mentioned that it was a plain name. He also said her maiden name was Willard and that his father, who died when he was a baby and who was also Syra's father, was named Fulton Foster."

Claudia gave me an exasperated sigh and Sybil just looked at me with her head cocked, like Mycroft does when he hears a high-pitched sound.

"It seems odd that Bing would lie about it," Cam said offering token support.

"He's obviously lying or else ill-informed. Let's not talk about those old days. It makes me too sad," Claudia decreed. Surprisingly, Sybil continued.

"I think he has all the right names but he has them all mixed up. Claudia, remember Hetty's *mother's* name was Mary …"

"It doesn't matter and is all so boring."

"And I think Hetty's father's *first* name was Willard. Mary and Willard Foster. Yes, that's it. And Hetty and Fulton …"

"Did you say Fulton?" I interrupted.

"Yes, Hetty's brother was named Fulton. So see, Bing has all the family names right; he just has the relationships wrong. He's not quite right you know," Sybil explained.

"But if he thought his father was Fulton Foster that means his father would have been Hetty's brother … Oh, God, you don't think …" Poor Syra and Bing.

"Incest? Of course not. There's never been any incest in Birdsey Falls," Claudia reassured us.

"He probably heard all the names and got them mixed up. If you ask Syra I'm sure she can straighten it out," Sybil added.

"And there's no possibility that Syra and Bing have the same father," Claudia pronounced. "I mean, just look at them. It's genetically impossible. What Bing believes is not necessarily the truth. And it doesn't matter now anyway so why do we have to keep talking about it?"

Because we spent the entire dinner talking about what you wanted to talk about, that's why. "What did Willard Foster do?"

"Business. He traveled for business and left the kids home a lot with a nanny, which is why Hetty ran around like a wild animal," Sybil explained.

"What did Fulton do? Was he older or younger?" I asked. I wasn't going to be satisfied until I could make a family tree and understand all these relationships.

"Fulton didn't do anything. He was a child. He went to school and did whatever little boys did." Sybil had taken over the conversation for both her and Claudia because Claudia was now staring out the window, totally disassociating herself. If she wasn't the one talking she at least expected the conversation to be *about* her.

"I think Tamsen means, why wasn't Fulton in the photo with the rest of the kids. Or was he a lot older or younger than the rest of you?" Cam chimed in. That was exactly what I meant so I couldn't fault him for attempting to explain what I was trying to say. I obviously needed the assistance.

Sybil glanced over at Claudia. "How old was Fulton?" Claudia ignored her. "I'd say Fulton was maybe a year or two older than I was, definitely younger than Hetty."

"So he would have been around eight when that photo was taken?" I asked.

"I suppose so."

"Why wasn't he in the photo?"

"Because he never played with us. I mean he wouldn't play with Claudia and me because we didn't play with boys and he was too young to play with Franklin and Edmund. Fifteen-year-olds don't want to play with eight-year-olds."

Claudia did the ladylike equivalent of rolling her eyes, which was to sigh loudly. "And he was crippled."

"Crippled?"

Sybil nodded her head. "Yes, now I remember. He had polio and had to wear leg braces. So he was inside the house a lot. I don't even remember what he looked like."

Maybe I could track him down and see if he remembered Franklin as a teenager. Sometimes people who are housebound are very keen observers. If I were an eight-year-old stuck in the house all day I would spend a lot of time at the window watching the other kids play. Claudia and Sybil may have been oblivious to what was going on but I bet an eight-year-old boy wouldn't be, especially if his sister was playing pirates with the older boys. "What happened to him? Does he still live around here?"

Claudia shook her head. "Hardly, dear."

"Well, where did he go? What happened to Fulton?"

"He disappeared."

No amount of probing would get any more information out of either Sybil or Claudia. Claudia announced she was half-ill just from being forced to think about those days and she had to go home immediately. Sybil, either out of respect or fear, agreed with Claudia that they should leave and even though I badgered them for information all the way out to the car neither would say another word.

Chapter Nineteen

I sent out email to all the WOACA members to let them know there was an agenda for our Tuesday evening meeting. We were going to divide up the pile of April 1 newspapers and see if we could figure out why Franklin had kept them. Cam had suggested having each person read a certain section of the paper so they would notice if something kept reoccurring that might be a clue to why they were collected.

Bing and Syra arrived first so Bing could set up his refreshments. He had made tortes—lemon, chocolate and pecan. I supplied various hot and cold drinks and by the time Grace and Diane arrived we were all settled in the library snacking and discussing a plan of attack for the papers. As is the way among friends, the ugliness of last week's WOACA meeting was forgotten and forgiven.

"I'd love to take the classifieds," Diane volunteered as soon as she realized what we were doing. "I can't wait to see the romantic notes people put in the paper in the '40s and '50s. The ones during the war will be especially poignant."

"I'll take the Daily Living section or whatever it was called back then," Bing offered. "I want to look at the old recipes. I may find something good."

"I'll switch back and forth with Bing on Daily Living," Syra volunteered. "While he is caught up in recipes I'll check the advice columns and things like that. Also the obituaries— which shouldn't be in a section entitled Daily Living, by the way."

"That leaves us with the first section and the local news, Grace. Which do you prefer?"

"I'll do the first section news. You take local," she suggested. "Oh, what about sports?"

"I'll give that one to Cam. That's what he was anxious to read, anyway." We would separate the papers by section and then gather them together again, so we would end up with seventy complete editions instead of two hundred different sections spread out all over the room. It would be neat and methodical.

I took the 1938 local news and settled into my leather chair, my feet propped up on the ottoman, a must for long-term reading. I found an interesting article on the new Clancy's hardware store opening. There was a photo of the original owner, Jim Clancy, and his grade-school-aged son, Tom. Tom was "old man Clancy" now and his grandson, Ron, had just taken over the day-to-day operations. Unlike the Behrendses, the Clancy's had a family dynasty with something to show for it other than a monstrous house. I wondered if the Clancys had been in Birdsey Falls back when Roger Behrends had built this house. Maybe they had owned a different hardware store then and the construction workers for the house had bought their tools there. I was just thinking about all the things in life it would be fun to research and learn about if one only had the time, when Grace yelled out.

"Here's something I never heard about. Listen.

The body of Raymond Mayberry Ketchum, the alleged victim of a kidnapping plot, was found early this morning in Camden Woods. Mr. Ketchum disappeared from his home the evening of March 30 on his way to a meeting of the Knights of Columbus. According to fellow Knights of Columbus member Duncan Martin, Mr. Ketchum never arrived at the Knights of Columbus Hall on Berkeley Street. It is assumed he left his house at 7:00 *p.m., as was his routine, to attend the 7:30 p.m. meeting, and then disappeared. On March 31 Dr. Fletcher Ketchum, brother of the victim, received a note demanding $10,000 for Ketchum's safe return. Cursory examination indicates that Mr. Raymond Ketchum died in the early hours of March 31 from a gunshot wound to his head. The police are not commenting on the alleged kidnapping or whether a ransom had been delivered.'"*

Grace passed the paper around and we all looked at the photo of Raymond Ketchum, a rather non-descript, middle-aged man, slightly balding and chinless.

"I wish we had all of the papers for April 1938. I'd love to read the rest of the story as it developed," Grace said. "I wonder why no one has ever heard of this story before."

"It was over seventy years ago …" I said.

"But it was a kidnapping. How many of those do we have?"

"*Alleged* kidnapping. We don't even know the rest of the story."

"I'm going to get on the Internet and check the back issues of the paper tomorrow. This is intriguing."

"But it probably has nothing do with Franklin's murder seventy years later. He was fifteen when this Ketchum guy was killed," I reminded her.

"True. But it's interesting. I'll move on," Grace reassured me. With Bing looking for old recipes, Syra reading old advice columns, and Diane lost in the love laments of seventy years ago, I was beginning to think that I'd need to go through all the papers again myself. Grace was my only hope to stay on target.

Diane was next to share important information. "Listen to this. I think I found a stalker. There's an ad in the personals in 1938 that reads,

You dropped your glove on Vincent Street. I sleep with it under my pillow. I'll be on Vincent between 2 and 3 on Thursday afternoon with your glove.'

"It's signed Frankie ..."

"That doesn't sound like something a fifteen-year-old would write," Syra offered.

"Wait. There's more. On April 1, 1939, there's an ad that reads, *'You dropped your scarf in front of Clancy's hardware. I sleep with it under my pillow. I'll be in front of Clancy's between 2 and 3 on Monday afternoon with your scarf.'*

"Also signed Frankie."

"OK. I'm officially creeped out by this guy ..." Grace shuddered.

"... and in 1940 there's this personal ad:

'You dropped your handkerchief on the steps of the library. I sleep with it under my pillow. I'll be in front of the library between 2 and 3 on Wednesday afternoon with your handkerchief.'

"Signed Frankie. Do you think it could be Franklin stalking women up and down the streets of Birdsey Falls?"

"I agree with Syra. It just doesn't sound like a fifteen-year-old to me," I protested. I didn't want Uncle Franklin to be a teenage stalker.

"Believe me, *none* of us knows what goes on in the head of a fifteen-year-old boy," Grace reminded us. "What we need is a man to tell us if this seems realistic for a teenager. Is Cam around? No offense, Bing."

"None taken," Bing mumbled, continuing to peruse the recipes from the 1940s.

"I'll show Cam the ads tonight. I don't want to have this whole thing come to a halt over one series of ads. Who knows what else we may find. Let's make a list of all the weird threads to follow but keep reading the papers."

"OK," Diane agreed. "But I'm going to keep looking for the Frankie ads and then go back and read the rest of the personals. I feel like I have a hot lead here."

Diane started grabbing all the personal ads from the 1940s and settled in with a notebook and pen balanced on the arm of her chair. At least she was taking it seriously even though it seemed like a nothing lead to me. Of course all I had found was the opening of Clancy's hardware store, so who was I to judge?

After a few minutes Diane yelled out, "In 1941 Frankie found an earring outside the entrance to the cemetery."

"Is he sleeping on it?" Bing asked.

"Yup."

In 1942 Frankie found another handkerchief, this time in the movie theater lobby. In 1943 he found a red and blue hair ornament outside Dr. Griffen's office, and in 1944 he found a bell-shaped brooch on the steps of the post office.

"Tamsen, do you think this ad series *could* be Franklin? It would explain why he kept the papers ..." Diane asked.

"Well, I never heard anyone refer to him as Frankie. And what's the deal with it always being the April 1 edition?"

"No one called him Frankie now, but what about when he was a young man?" Grace asked. "We should ask Claudia. Why don't you call her?"

"Now?"

"Just ask the question and then get off the phone; how hard can it be?" Syra stated. She had never had a mother-in-law so I forgave her her naiveté. I reluctantly dialed her number and hoped she wouldn't answer.

"Hello?"

"Hi, Claudia. It's Tamsen. I'm sorry to call so late ..."

"It's only 8:00 and ..."

"... but I was wondering if anyone ever called Franklin 'Frankie' when he was a teenager."

"Never. We were always called by our given names."

"OK. Thank you. Goodbye." I hung up. Let her puzzle about that one for a while. I reported back to the group that he was never known as Frankie and they countered with that being an even more persuasive reason why he would refer to himself as Frankie in the paper, so no family or friends would connect him with the ads.

"But even if Franklin did stalk women until they dropped something, that doesn't explain why someone would murder him," I protested.

"Maybe not. Probably not," Syra said. "But it does shed some more light on his apparent strangeness that Claudia said started when he was around fifteen. This would be an example of how he sort of went off kilter."

"Right," Diane agreed. "He got reclusive and started following women and picking up items they lost, put in creepy ads, maybe even met them and returned the items or just kept the things, who knows. It fits the elusive strangeness Claudia refers to."

"But what about a motive for murder?" I pleaded. "No one kills someone because they have a collection of women's personal items. It just doesn't make sense."

"It doesn't make sense if you insist the newspapers are going to show us why Franklin was murdered," Grace explained. "But we only hoped that the newspapers would be the major clue to his murder. That doesn't mean they're going to be. This series of ads, especially if it goes all the way to …"

"I just found 1945's ad and he found a hat left in the Methodist church on Bridge Street …"

"… the present explains why he kept the papers. If he went out at the end of March and didn't come home until someone dropped something and then put the ad in every April 1 it would explain why he kept all the papers. It was part of the fun, to see the ads. Who knows if he kept the stuff or actually returned it?"

"We didn't find it at the cottage so he probably didn't have it," Syra chimed in. "You may have to face the fact that the newspapers aren't going to give us a clue to anything other than the odd way Franklin's mind worked."

"In 1946 this Frankie character found an umbrella outside your grandfather's bookstore, Grace! That's exciting."

"Too bad we couldn't ask Willoughby and the other mannequins who exactly found the umbrella and whether they returned it," Grace laughed. "Then our mystery would be solved."

"There's a wonderful recipe for ambrosia in here. I want to copy this. Does anyone have a pen and paper?" Bing asked. Diane supplied him with both from her cavernous purse. "Diane, I think you should keep on reading and see what else you come up with. It's premature to decide this personal ad is the reason Franklin kept the papers and ignore all the other years and other news items."

I shot Bing a grateful look but he was already bent over, carefully copying his recipe. Bing is always like this; you think he isn't paying any attention but then he says something that indicates he has listened to everything and digested it. It occurred to me that Syra was acting completely normal so Bing clearly had not shared our conversation about their mother. Syra would be upset if she found out I was pumping Bing behind her back, especially if what he was telling me was not information she wanted to have to explain to me later. I knew I needed to get this story about Hetty straight because somehow I felt strongly, just as I did about the newspapers, that a clue to Franklin's murder rested in that photograph and those five children.

"In 1947 Frankie found a small change purse at the bus stop on Dunbarton Street. There isn't a bus stop there now, is there?" Diane asked.

"No." We all answered simultaneously. Quite frankly I was getting a little tired of this Frankie jerk and his fetish. This had been going on for ten years now. This guy had to get a grip.

"And in 1948 he found a necklace on a seat in the now non-existent Fox Theater …"

Grace rattled her section of the paper to get our attention. "I have an update on Raymond Ketchum's murder from the next year's paper, April 1, 1939. It has that same photo …"

"I doubt he was having anything more recent taken." Syra said.

"… and this statement:

'A year ago today, on April 1, 1938, the body of Raymond Ketchum of 623 Danrich Street was found in Camden Woods by Ernest Whitcomb, who was out walking his dog. Mr. Ketchum had been missing from approximately 7:30 on the night of March 30 when he was supposed to attend a Knights of Columbus meeting. Subsequently, Dr. Fletcher Ketchum, brother of the deceased, received a ransom demand of $10,000. According to Dr. Fletcher Ketchum that demand was met and the money placed in the specified location. The police were not contacted as demanded by the kidnappers. The money disappeared and Mr. Raymond Ketchum's body was discovered with a bullet hole to the head. Placed in Mr. Ketchum's shirt pocket was a crudely scribbled note that stated, "This is what happens when you don't pay." Dr. Fletcher Ketchum swears that the money was placed in the exact location specified. After a year-long investigation the police still do not have any suspects in Mr. Ketchum's murder.'

"And then listen to this from the following year, 1940. The headline is 'Melee in Camden Woods on Two-Year Anniversary'":

'On March 31, the two-year anniversary of the murder of Raymond Ketchum in Camden Woods, the area where his body was found was overrun with treasure seekers. A brochure distributed in Birdsey Falls and environs last week suggested that the missing $10,000 that was left as Mr. Ketchum's ransom was still in Camden Woods. Mr. Ketchum was murdered by a bullet to the head and left with a note indicating that he had died as the result of an unpaid ransom. Mr. Ketchum's brother, Fletcher, formerly of Bridge Street, stated that he had taken the money to the specified location in a timely fashion. Dr. Ketchum stated that a detailed map accompanied the ransom note and he had followed the map and obeyed the ransom note demands, including not contacting the police. Yet Mr. Raymond Ketchum was murdered and apparently the ransom was not retrieved by the kidnappers. The rather lurid brochure has suggested that the money is still in Camden Woods. Dr. Fletcher Ketchum has gone to the site where he left the money with the police numerous times in the last two years to show them the exact location. After a two-year investigation the police have come to the conclusion that the kidnappers did retrieve the ransom money and Raymond Ketchum was killed because he recognized his kidnappers. The inquiry into Mr. Ketchum's murder is proceeding along these lines.'

"What do you think that means, proceeding along these lines?"

"I would assume that they started looking at his acquaintances, people he would have recognized," Syra answered.

"That must have been uncomfortable for everyone in town," I mused. "After all, Birdsey Falls in 1940 was smaller than it is now, so if he got out in the community much, he probably would have at least recognized everyone in town even if he didn't know their names. Imagine. A whole town under suspicion of murder."

"I think the brother did it," Bing said, setting aside his recipe list. "There were no witnesses that he even took the money to the location. Plus, who could be easier to kidnap than your own sibling. I mean, all he would have to do is invent some emergency or something to lure him away on his walk to the Knights of Columbus meeting and there you have it. Syra could take me anywhere and I'd never question it ..."

"... other than the fact that you wouldn't leave the house so I'd have to take you somewhere in our own house ..." Syra pointed out.

"... which probably isn't kidnapping. OK. But let's say I was normal and I left the house like everyone else does. It would be easy to persuade me to go anywhere with you because you are my sister and I trust you."

"But that means the brother would have to want him dead and set up the whole kidnapping thing to cover up his murder. Why would he want him dead?" I asked. I couldn't figure out why someone wanted Franklin dead and now I was worrying about why someone wanted Raymond Ketchum dead. How many murders could I possibly solve? Most likely none.

"There could be a million reasons. We don't even know these people. All sorts of ugly things could be hidden in their relationship," Grace offered. "I'm sure the police looked at the brother carefully. The immediate family is the first to be suspected. They must not have found anything."

"Maybe I'll write a book about all the unsolved Birdsey Falls murders once I finish my current Perry book. This Ketchum guy and Uncle Franklin may just be the bookends for seventy years of unsolved murders in this town."

"I'm beginning to think you would write anything just to get out of the Perry Many Paws series," Grace said. "Although writing mysteries could be fun. Writing true crime would be too depressing. If I were going to write something I'd ..."

"Oh my God! Wait until you see this!" Syra yelled, shaking her paper at us. "Unbelievable. It's in the wedding announcements, photo and all. Listen. It's from April 1, 1949.

'Sybil Mary Bright and Frank Harvey Bowe were married today in the Methodist Church on Bridge Street in Birdsey Falls. The couple picked the date of April 1, not usually associated with romance, because they met a year ago when Miss Bright lost her necklace in the Fox Theater. Mr. Bowe found the necklace and placed an ad, on April 1, 1948, in the personals column of the Birdsey Falls Gazette. Miss Bright contacted him immediately and they were introduced when he returned her necklace. "It had to be fate," Mr. Bowe stated. "This sort of thing would never happen in a million years." The bride wore ..."'

"This has to be *our* Sybil. How many Sybil Brights could there be?" Grace asked.

"I'm already on it." I had grabbed my phone and punched in Claudia's number. "Hello, Claudia. Sorry to call so late. Did Sybil marry a guy name Frank Bowe? Thanks. Bye."

"What did she say?" Bing asked.

"I only gave her a chance to say 'yes' but that's all we needed to know. I can't believe Sybil married that creepy Frankie guy."

"It just goes to show that if you go fishing long enough ..." Syra said.

"Yeah, like eleven years ..." Grace laughed.

"... you catch a fish sooner or later."

"I still can't believe that creep was her first husband. Let's see the picture." I reached for the paper.

We passed the paper around and checked out the creepy Frankie, who didn't look too odd, and the beautiful young Sybil.

"She could have done better," was all Bing said.

"She must have thought so, too, because he was only husband number one. There were three more after him. Well, we solved the

Frankie ads. I'm glad it wasn't Uncle Franklin. He was creepy enough without adding stalker to his list of oddities," I said.

"The personals aren't going to be as much fun anymore," Diane sighed. "I'll go back to 1938 and see what I missed while skipping ahead to look for Frankie ads."

"I'm intrigued by this Ketchum murder story. Can you check the later papers and see if that's covered again, Grace?" Syra asked. "For my part, I don't think I'll find anything better than Sybil and Frankie's wedding."

"I just found an old classic recipe for bread pudding. I'll be experimenting with this and bring it to WOACA next Tuesday," Bing informed us.

"I've been looking and there is nothing in '41, '42 or '43 that I can see. It may have moved out of the first section and into the local news. Tamsen?"

"I'm looking. Yes, here it is in 1941. Headline: Three Years. No Arrests. No Money.

Raymond Mayberry Ketchum was kidnapped and held for ransom on March 31, 1938. His body was found in the Camden Woods on April 1 with a fatal gunshot wound to the head. A $10,000 ransom demand had been made to and paid by the victim's brother, Dr. Fletcher Ketchum. The money has not been recovered and there are no suspects in the kidnapping and murder of Raymond Ketchum.

According to Dr. Ketchum, the ransom drop was an old maple tree on the edge of Camden Woods. The $10,000 was in a leather bag and hidden in an animal burrow that ran under the tree. Dr. Ketchum stuffed the money in the hole then immediately left the area to wait at his brother's home for his safe return. When Raymond Ketchum had not returned by sunrise, Dr. Ketchum notified the police. Meanwhile, the police were already on their way to Camden Woods based on a call *from Ernest Whitcomb, who had discovered Raymond Ketchum's body while out walking his dog.*

There have been several lines of inquiry over the past three years. Originally it was thought that Dr. Ketchum had placed the money in the wrong location and that the kidnappers never found it. This theory has led to all kinds of rumors about the real location of the missing money and searches, both professional and amateur, of Camden Woods. The money has never been found.

Another line of inquiry was based on the fact that Dr. Ketchum kept exactly $10,000 in his home safe. The coincidence was duly noted by the police. Friends, business associates and acquaintances of the Ketchum family were questioned repeatedly. Dr. Ketchum claims no one but he and his brother knew he had exactly $10,000 in his safe. If that is true, the police theorize that Raymond Ketchum himself may have come up with that amount when questioned by the kidnappers. Ketchum may have convinced them this was as much as his brother could get his hands on without going to the bank and possibly alerting someone that something was amiss.

There have also been theories that Raymond Ketchum was in on the kidnapping and that, after having gotten the money, the kidnappers disposed of him, indicating that the money had not been received. There are no grounds for this supposition, as both the Ketchum brothers are well-to-do and not in need of money.

Dr. Ketchum was under surveillance for several months after his brother's death. The police concede that he was very cooperative but continued to cross-examine him throughout the year following his brother's murder. Dr. Ketchum has recently retired from his dental practice and moved out of state.

Three years later the police have no arrests, no money and no suspects. We do still have treasure seekers who tramp through Camden

Woods every spring poking in animal burrows, digging up patches of dirt, even climbing trees to look for holes where the money may still be waiting for someone to discover, a discovery that would still be three years too late to help poor Raymond Ketchum.'"

"I think we should go looking for the money," Bing suggested.

"How are you going to look for the money when you don't leave the house?" Syra asked.

"I was using the royal we, meaning all of you. But our house backs up on Camden Woods so I could watch out the window. I wonder how close to our backyard the infamous old maple tree is."

"I never thought of that," I said. "Camden Woods does run all the way behind the houses across the street. I wonder if the money drop or the location of the body was anywhere near here or over on the other side of the woods by the high school."

"The articles never mention the exact location of the money drop but that didn't keep people from looking for it. Somewhere someone must have a basic idea of where the money was supposed to be …"

"It's not going to be there now, Grace," Diane warned. "Everyone has already looked for it."

"I know, but I'm curious, that's all. It seems like Bing, Syra and Tamsen would be curious, too, as they live right near the woods."

"I'd like to solve Uncle Franklin's murder before we solve Raymond Ketchum's," I said.

"I don't want to solve his murder. I just want to be the one to find the money that has been missing for seventy years," Bing explained.

"Is that the royal 'I'?" Syra laughed.

"Well, yes. By me I mean all of you, of course."

Suddenly Raymond Ketchum's murder and lost ransom seemed so much more real than Franklin's death, and we lost focus. We began to wildly theorize while Grace continued to check each April 1 edition to see if the mystery was ever resolved. Our favorite theory was that

Raymond had set up the kidnapping himself to get back at his brother for some imagined wrong. He didn't really need the money so he was satisfied to clean out his brother's safe, be "released" and return to normal life, a semi-victim/hero for a few days and to let the associates that helped with the hoax have the money. But the kidnappers hadn't trusted him not to turn them in, so they killed him. Or maybe they wanted him to ask for more money and he wouldn't do it. It felt better to believe he was the cause of his own death since we didn't know any differently.

Grace, with Syra's help, did discover that the kidnapping murder was mentioned in every April 1 edition of the newspaper until 1963. In 1948, 1958 and 1963 the tenth, twentieth and twenty-fifth anniversaries of the event—there were long columns recapping facts and theorizing once again. In 1963 there had been a memorial for Raymond Ketchum that took place in Camden Woods, followed by a treasure hunt. Grace actually remembered going although she had no idea why she and her little sister were in the woods on a treasure hunt. Of course the $10,000 wasn't found, but enough other goodies had been placed in the woods so the thirty or so participants, mostly children, had each come away with something. It was the last hurrah for the Raymond Ketchum case. In subsequent years the event was occasionally mentioned, warranting just a paragraph in the "Remember When" column.

"I don't want Uncle Franklin to end up like Raymond Ketchum, with his murder never resolved and people just forgetting about it," I sighed, putting down my pile of local news sections.

"Even if he isn't arrested, Ryan will be like Fletcher Ketchum, with people thinking he was involved just because they never found the real murderer. I don't want Ryan to be the name that keeps appearing yearly in the Franklin Behrends Unsolved Murder column."

"I know. I know. Don't worry, Grace," I said reassuringly. "Now we have to decide if these newspapers were just the collection of an old man who was interested in the Raymond Ketchum murder because it happened when he was fifteen near where he lived, or whether there is something else appearing every April 1 in this paper that we haven't found yet."

"Oh, Sweet Jesus. Look at this!" Diane yelled out. She startled me so much I dropped my pecan tart sticky side down on the rug. I gave her a dirty look as I bent over and peered at it, trying to decide whether it was worth pulling the fibers off.

"Look at this. It's in the 1951 personal ads. I can't believe it. *You dropped your Elvis magazine in front of the high school. I sleep with it under my pillow. I'll be in front of the school between 2 and 3 on Thursday with your magazine.' Frankie.*"

It was nine o'clock. A borderline time to call Claudia, but I couldn't resist. "Hello Claudia, it's Tamsen. Did Sybil and that Frank guy who was her first husband get divorced in 1951? Really. OK. Thanks. Bye. Yes! Sybil and Frank were divorced in 1951 …"

"… and he went right back on the prowl using his old techniques …"

"… at the high school. That is so disgusting. I hope he got caught."

"Can I take all these personal ads home, Tamsen? I want to follow through on this guy. But I really need to get going. I promised Scott and Kaleb I'd be home to watch one of the Batman movies with them," Diane said as she gathered up the papers strewn all over the rug.

It was time to break up for the evening. Everyone left with various sections of the papers and I went up to bed to confess to Cam that I had called and hung up on his mother three times tonight. Mycroft remained in the library, licking pecan torte off the rug.

Chapter Twenty

On Wednesday, the day after our WOACA meeting, nothing went right. Cam had been miffed that I had called his mother all evening and then hung up as soon as she answered my question. I felt that in twenty-five years of marriage I had treated her much better than she treated me, so I should be allowed a little pay-back. We had mildly argued about that for a while and then gone to bed. This morning I had overslept, which meant Cam had intentionally been very quiet getting ready so as not to wake me. I felt that meant he didn't want to talk to me before he went to work. It was difficult for Cam to be quiet in the morning. He really had to work at it to not make a single sound. Very annoying.

When things aren't right between Cam and me, it bothers me way out of proportion to how it should. That's just the way I am. I have a small circle of loved ones and as long as everything is all right with them nothing else bothers me, but if the smallest thing isn't going right within my circle I'm all discombobulated until it's right. Cam had probably forgotten the whole thing by now and I was stewing. This annoyed me even more. In addition to this stewing, I finally got my period. Now, was this the period I was supposed to have before and it just arrived really late, or should I count it as the period it wasn't time for yet, arriving early? If I'm going through perimenopause I suppose I should keep track of things like this.

I stomped downstairs to have a diet soda and a bagel. Usually Cam left a bagel out to thaw but he hadn't this morning. More passive-aggressive behavior intended to annoy me. I coupled his name with some various swear words I'd been wanting to try out and liked the sound of it. It kept me entertained while I microwaved my bagel into submission and then toasted it, topping it off with a full half-inch of peanut butter. Screw losing fifteen or twenty pounds. I was going to eat what I wanted and get as fat as I wanted. *That* would show Cam. Bing had been kind enough to leave some tortes, so I polished off my bagel with a lemon torte chaser. Good to round out the protein with some vitamin C.

I wandered out of the kitchen trying to decide whether I wanted to start playing around with the idea I had for a new book, a non Perry Many Paws book. I'd been tossing the idea around since the night of the break-in, making a few odd notes here and there but I had yet to really work it through. Cam had put the "SB" monogrammed handkerchief in the Chippendale table. Since I was going to use that in my book, I decided to take it to my desk to use as inspiration. I opened the drawer and fished around but it was empty. I bent over and stuck my nose right in the drawer so I could see into all four corners but it was definitely empty. I wandered around the first floor systematically opening drawers and looking inside in case Cam had moved the handkerchief for some reason. After twenty minutes of diligent drawer searching I came up empty. No handkerchief. Perhaps Frankie had found it and was willing to return it to me after he finished sleeping on it.

I sent Cam a brief email asking him where the handkerchief was. As was fitting for my current state of mind I did not include any endearments or queries as to how his day was going. About ten minutes later he replied stating that he had not moved the handkerchief and that it was in the drawer of the table at the bottom of the stairs. I wrote back to reiterate that was where I had looked and it was empty. He wrote back to reiterate that he had not moved it and it was in the drawer of the table at the bottom of the stairs. There was only one thing to do.

I went to the table and yanked out the drawer. I got my camera and I took several photos from various angles. I then went back to my computer, downloaded the photos and sent them to Cam. No words, just the photos. All ten of them. Cam's reply was short and sweet: Did you get your period?

And so the morning progressed. Not to be too indelicate but my period was coming with a pent-up vengeance and the cramps were bad. Plus I had a raging headache. I took a lunch break and popped a couple aspirin with a diet soda and a pecan torte. And then a lemon torte. I was checking the personal ads just in case someone had found my missing handkerchief when the phone rang.

"Hey. It's me. How're you feeling?" Cam sounded so cheery. It wasn't fair. Did men ever get cramps anywhere other than their legs? Or a raging headache other than when they had been drinking?

"I feel terrible. I need a blood transfusion and I have a headache and cramps and I can't stop eating sugar."

"Should you call the doctor?"

"No, I think it's normal for my stage in life. Where was my bagel this morning?"

"I was in a bad mood so I didn't thaw it. I was being a jerk. You know how it is when we disagree."

"Yeah. We act the same way we did when we were in our early twenties. We haven't developed any more mature coping skills since then."

"Why don't I bring home Chinese for dinner tonight? You probably don't feel like cooking."

"I don't even feel like *living* right now, but yeah, that would be good."

"Why don't you go take a nap or something? That's good for a headache."

"I might. You sure you didn't move Sylvie's handkerchief? It's really driving me nuts that I can't find it."

"I swear. I never touched it after I put it in the drawer. Actually I forgot all about it until you emailed me. Maybe Sylvie is back to haunt the Behrends house."

"If so I hope she can use some of the voodoo on me so I'm back to normal."

"Me too sweetheart. Bye."

Now what was *that* supposed to mean? I felt more emotionally back together and was looking forward to beef and broccoli for dinner but I still had cramps and a headache so I went back to the library and laid down on the couch with the red fleece throw over me. It's times like this I especially like being a writer and not having to venture into an office when I don't feel well. Mycroft was also snoozing on the floor next to me and I could see his legs moving rhythmically like he was chasing something at his usual very slow pace.

What had become of Frankie the stalker? I'd have to find some way to ask Sybil about him. I'd like to fill in the blanks on what kind of personality just followed women around waiting for them to drop something, and then tried to meet them. What had Sybil seen in him? Of course, she'd been very young. It was hard to make good romantic decisions when you were eighteen and hadn't had much life experience.

Uncle Franklin hadn't had much life experience at fifteen. What had happened to change him from an outgoing, creative and imaginative young man to a recluse for the rest of his life? It had to be more than just an incidence of mono. Whatever had plagued Franklin hadn't affected his health as an adult. He was rarely ill. He had never been in the hospital in the twenty-five years that I'd lived here. That's pretty healthy for a man in his eighties. He seemed more emotionally haunted than physically ill. Like Edgar Allan Poe's "The Man of the Crowd," he was alone and haunted by something. But when you are haunted by something in your past does it appear seventy years later and kill you? He didn't go insane by listening to the beating of the Tell Tale Heart. He was stabbed in the neck by someone very real. Someone invaded his home and ended his life.

Why did someone break into our house? Why didn't they take anything? What were they looking for in the library? Mycroft had known someone was here. Mycroft must have seen them because they would have interrupted his evening sleep when they came in the library. I wondered how many times animals are the only witnesses to the truth. Maybe that would make a good book, animal witnesses. I closed my eyes and started thinking about my new book ideas.

I woke to Mycroft's wet, cold nose pressed against my cheek. I reached over and gave his ears some good loving and he returned to his spot in front of the fireplace. I had lost all my enthusiasm for starting my book. The handkerchief was my muse for my new book idea and I was hopelessly unmotivated without it. I struggled to a sitting position, the fleece all entangled in my legs. Mycroft looked at me expectantly, like I was about to do something brilliant. We enjoyed a staring contest for a few long seconds and then he got up and began pacing around the room. He needed to go outside. I decided I could use some fresh air to clear my sleep-groggy brain, so I put on my jacket and headed into the back yard with Mycroft at my heels.

It was overcast and a heavy mist hung in the air, as if the clouds overhead couldn't be bothered to let loose with a decent rain. I pushed my bangs off my forehead, lifted my face to the sky and decided to get a moisturizing treatment. We don't leash Mycroft because everyone in our family, including Claudia, can outrun him. He took care of his important business and then began to amble in the direction of Franklin's cottage. Being in the midst of a serious beauty treatment, I followed after him picturing my skin sucking in all the dew-heavy air and being so much more youthful for it. Keeping my face raised and my eyes closed is not the best way to wander through the woods, and I tripped several times over roots and twigs in my path. I probably looked like I'd had a two-martini lunch, which reminded me that I hadn't eaten a decent lunch at all. I'd be really starving by the time Cam got home with the Chinese, which made me anticipate it even more. I love being extra hungry when I eat a favorite meal. This doesn't happen very often because I'm a dedicated snacker, but being out of the house should help, unless I decided to start eating twigs and dried-up leaves. How filling could they be, anyway? I was thinking about how nutritious insects were supposed to be and remembered when my brother Graham had given me chocolates for my birthday one year and, after I had eaten them all, told me they were chocolate-covered ants. My mom had tried to calm me down by explaining that people in other cultures ate insects and that there was a lot of protein and other valuable vitamins in them. And she had grounded Graham. I had always planned to pay him back sometime but had never found the right culinary vehicle. Another item to add to my list of things I would like to spend time researching if I had the time.

We eventually reached Franklin's cottage and I stood and stared at it while Mycroft sniffed around. It looked really awful. Cam and I had to do something about it, maybe in the spring. It needed paint and some landscaping and probably a new roof. Franklin wouldn't let us make any repairs or improvements while he was living there but now we should take care of these things or the cottage would fall into such a state of disrepair that it would crumble to the ground. If it was fixed up it could be a very pretty little house. Maybe we could rent it out to a college student, one who didn't have wild parties.

I had no intention of going into the cottage but a sudden need to use the bathroom hit and I knew I couldn't make it back to the house. I had no choice but to use the bathroom in the cottage. I went in the side door, into the kitchen. Mycroft ambled in after me and immediately went into Franklin's study and curled up on the rug for a nap. I made a dash for the bathroom. There was no toilet paper left. I fished around in my jacket pockets until I found a napkin that I had jammed in there the last time we went to the movies. It would have to do. The old plumbing in the cottage might not like being attacked by a napkin but I had no choice and didn't really care.

Mycroft was sound asleep. Lacking the heart to wake him, I sat at Franklin's desk and looked out the window at the misty woods. It was the kind of view that let the imagination run and would be a good place for writing. At least Franklin got to see one last fall season through this window where the trees were aflame with color so close to his view that he didn't really miss much by not leaving his house. I knew the deer came right up to his window, never sensing the presence of a human, and there were always squirrels running around for entertainment. This window would be like a rotating art exhibit that changed with the seasons. The only things missing were Dickensian carolers at Christmas. I laughed out loud at the vision of Franklin's reaction if carolers had dared appear on his doorstep. Bah, Humbug!

From among those trees, quickly losing their color and waiting for the first snow to make them pretty again, Ryan and his two friends had spied on Franklin. A seemingly harmless activity but such a violation of a reclusive man's privacy. Ryan had said he had watched Franklin reading and writing every night. I didn't remember ever seeing him writing anything in all the years I'd known him. We hadn't found a journal when we looked through his books. But Ryan hadn't mentioned a journal, just that Franklin was writing at his desk. Interesting. I'd been through these drawers before but I looked inside in case I had missed something, like a ream of paper with instructions on what to do if he were found murdered. There were pens and a pile of blank paper but nothing with any writing on it. Had he been pretending to write? That made no sense. Had he used invisible ink? Dubious. I had been writing children's books for too long. Although invisible ink actually wasn't a bad idea for a future Perry Many Paws book should I decide to continue the series. I have a notebook that I carry with me wherever I go so that if I get a good book idea I can jot it down. Of course, I didn't have it with me now. I pulled out a piece of paper and a pen out of the drawer to jot down my idea. The sheet of paper under the one I picked up looked dingy and as I stared at it, I realized there was something written on the other side that was barely showing through. I pulled it out of the drawer and turned it over. Bingo! The page was covered with small, tight handwriting. I pulled out the rest of the pile of paper from the drawer and rifled through it. Empty. There was just this one page. I put the rest of the paper back in the drawer and huddled over the writing, trying to make it out. Why did he have to write so small? He had plenty of paper.

My brother Alden died December 7, 1941, at Pearl Harbor. My life had been spiraling out of control since April 1, 1938, but Alden's death was my death, too. It hadn't mattered so much that I was damaged because Alden was there to be the Behrends heir, the successful son, the one who would take over when father was gone. He was a buffer for me and made me feel that my failure didn't matter as much because he was there. I was just an extra son. I was safe. I was the understudy and Alden was the star. But all that safety ended when Alden died. The family looked to me to take his place and I was unable to do so. I knew that it would have been better for everyone if I had been the Behrends to die. It should have been me. No one needed me. I was a waste. Everyone needed Alden, most of all me. He should have been the one to live into an old age. I should have died in 1941.

Correction, I should have died in 1938. It would have been fair and just and right. But others are gone and I'm still here and it makes no sense and has been a waste of a life.

I read the paragraph several times, then turned the paper over as if something additional might appear. I went back to the stack of paper in the drawer, piled it on the desk and went through it sheet by sheet, checking both the front and the back. Nothing. It appeared that Franklin was going to write some kind of biography but had never gotten the chance to get more than the introduction done. If only he had started this project last year. I couldn't stand the idea that he had been willing to write it all down and he had died before he got more than a page done. My curiosity was burning a hole in my brain. It was like being in Bing's kitchen and being allowed to smell the baking but never being offered anything to eat. Nothing was going right.

Bob Dylan began singing and for a minute I thought someone was telling me that the answer to Franklin's murder was blowing in the wind. Phone call from Cam.

"Hey, how are you feeling?" he asked. "Did you take a nap?"

"Yes. Then Mycroft needed to go out so I took him and we ended up at the cottage. I just found a single sheet of paper that Franklin wrote about the death of his brother that hints at all kinds of answers to his life but never spells anything out ..."

"... so things aren't going well?"

"Not especially. Why?"

"I just heard on the radio that the Chinese place is closed, seized by the state for not paying back taxes."

"So no Chinese food for us tonight?"

"'Fraid not. I can bring something else ..."

"... but I was looking forward to Chinese," I whined like a five-year-old finding out the zoo was closed. "I really really wanted Chinese. I deserve Chinese."

"I'm sure you do, sweetheart," Cam reassured me, "but there's nothing I can do unless I learn to make Chinese before I get home tonight. I'll bring ribs and corn on the cob instead. And corn muffins. How's that?"

I sighed. Headache. Late period. Cramps. Too much sugar. Missing handkerchiefs. No toilet paper. Only a single page of a tell-all journal. And now no Chinese. How much could one person be expected to endure in one day? "OK. Ribs will be good. Lots of corn muffins, though."

"I promise. Bring that paper that Franklin wrote back to the house, will you? I'd like to see it."

"Sure. Love you. Bye."

I reached down and rubbed Mycroft's ears, waking him up as gently as I could. The overcast sky made it seem later than it was and I was beginning to feel scared in the cottage alone when it looked like night was fast approaching. Mycroft seemed to agree that it was time to go and headed toward the door, his mid-section swaying back and forth. I really should cut down on his food or else make him exercise more. I really should do the same myself. I had almost reached the door when I remembered Franklin's paper and went back in his study to grab it. In my haste I had failed to notice something, something very small yet very significant. In tiny writing at the top right corner of the paper it said, "Page 23."

Chapter Twenty-One

Cam is not as imaginative as I am. That is why he directs a foundation and I'm a writer. It's also why he makes a lot more money than I do and why he wasn't afraid to go back to the cottage after dinner, in the dark, to look for the rest of Franklin's alleged autobiography. He wasn't haunted by imaginary specters floating through the woods or the idea that being in the cottage at night was just asking for something horrible to happen. It's also why he was the one who remembered to bring toilet paper while I was the one carrying the baseball bat.

Cam and I were both surprised when Mycroft indicated that he wanted to come with us. It was so unlike him to venture out at night. Oblivious to our haunted surroundings and the danger that waited us around every tree, Cam chatted on and on about Thanksgiving and Christmas plans and things we could do when Abbey was home. Her Thanksgiving break would be short and she would have her friends with her but she had a long break between semesters at Christmas and so there would be lots of family time. He and Abbey had taken skiing lessons when she was in high school so they were anxious to get in at least one good day of skiing. I liked skiing, too, as long as I could stay by the fireplace at the lodge, drink hot chocolate and read.

Cam held my hand and guided me over the fallen logs, probably the same ones I had stumbled over on my afternoon trip through the woods. "Do you remember that Christmas when Abbey asked my mom for that red sweater that was in the window at Caroline's Boutique?"

"Yes, your mom was so upset because she felt a redhead should not, under any conditions, ever wear red and didn't want to buy it for her."

"I think my mom thought it was an unwritten law."

"But Claudia told us she was going to get it for her so we crossed it off Abbey's wish list. We should have known better."

"Yeah, I'll never forget how excited Abbey was when she opened the package from mom, saw the box was from Caroline's, and pulled it open ..."

"Only to see the exact sweater she wanted only in blue ..."

"She was so disappointed ..."

"I really wanted to slap your mother, Christmas or not."

"Thank God for Sybil."

"She jumped up and said it there must have been a mistake in labeling the packages and that the blue sweater was from her and the package labeled to Abbey from Sybil was really the one from Claudia."

"And in that package was the red sweater. Sybil had bought the perfect gift and saved the day ..."

"And covered Claudia's ass, too."

"That was the true meaning of Christmas, unselfish giving. I think of that every Christmas. And Abbey still has no idea ..."

"Sybil asked us not to tell her. She still wears both those sweaters, too."

We both agreed that Abbey was delightful in every way and reminisced about Christmases past. I couldn't believe that I had thought today was such a "nothing go right" day. I was walking hand in hand with the man I loved and we were talking about how wonderful our daughter was. Sure, my mother-in-law was a clueless witch and my brother was a pompous ass, but the family that really mattered, my husband and our daughter, was perfect for me. They were my anchor and if they were solid, I was solid.

The cottage came up way too soon. It was dark and foreboding and I would have been happy to turn around and go back home. We entered by the kitchen door. It seemed much colder than it had this afternoon and Cam went over to turn up the heat. Grace had told me that when spirits are around the room gets colder. I wondered if Franklin was here and if so, would he be kind enough to indicate where the rest of his autobiography was. At this point I would be happy if he wrote the name of his murderer on the wall in blood. It would only take me about a month of therapy to recover from that and at the rate we were going, there was no way this would be over in a month any other way. Mycroft went back to the rug in Franklin's study and we followed him in. I showed Cam where I had found the paper and he methodically went through the pile of blank paper just the way I had done. He didn't find anything, either. Cam continued to go through Franklin's desk, even going so far as to get down on the floor and shimmy under the desk and thump around.

"Secret drawers?" I asked. "You know, if I lived alone and no one came to see me, ever, I wouldn't feel like I had to hide whatever writing I was doing. I mean, who would he need to hide it from? Why not leave all 23 pages together in the drawer? Why just the most recent page?"

"*If* it was the most recent page. Maybe there are hundreds of pages," Cam's voice echoed from under the desk. "Although most recent makes sense. You're a writer, you would know."

"My books are rarely more than 23 pages, and that's only if the illustrations are really large. But I agree, it seems that the most recent page would be the one in the desk. That would have been what he was working on."

Cam pushed himself out from under the desk and clapped his hands together to clear off the dust. Then he wiped them on his pants. "There are no secret compartments or anything taped under the drawers or behind the desk. The other pages have to be someplace else."

I closed the book I was looking at, a history text book from 1936.

"Do you think the killer took them? Maybe Franklin wrote an expose of the bombing of Pearl Harbor."

"Yeah, his murder really looked like an FBI or CIA assassination. Plus, Franklin had only gotten to Pearl Harbor on page 23, which no one took. It's what happened before Pearl Harbor that someone was interested in if, and that's a big if, he was killed for what he was writing."

"It's the only motive we have so far. Maybe it was a Veterans of WWII assassination," I suggested.

"Yeah. That must be a spritely set of geezers. All they would have to do is wait until Franklin took out his garbage and then run him down with their motorized scooters. A gang hit."

"At least we know Ryan was telling the truth when he said he saw Franklin writing at his desk."

"Let's look in the bedroom."

I hated going into the bedroom. Cam went through all the dresser drawers and looked under the bed. He lifted the mattress, checked behind the curtains and under the rug. He took the drawers out of the nightstand. He kneaded the pillows. He moved all the furniture away from the walls. He knocked on the walls and he got down on his hands and knees and thumped every inch of the floor. Meanwhile, I stood at the door of the closet and tentatively pulled at the arms of the remaining shirts with just the tips of my thumb and my index finger.

"I can't find anything," I reported.

"Did you look in the shoes? Did you check the back of the closet for a secret panel or the floors for an empty space? Did you run your hand all along the top shelf and check in that paper bag up there?

How about the closet door? Is it solid? Could one of the panels open up? Did you check the pockets of all the shirts and pants? Is that dirty laundry on the floor? You should go through that also."

I didn't want to do any of these things. I was a "look through the desk or check out the books" kind of searcher. I couldn't very well complain, though, because now Cam was totally under the bed and poking at the box springs. At least going through the closet didn't require getting on the floor and sticking my head in dark, dusty places.

"I'll keep checking," I assured him. I did wonder about that bag sitting on the shelf of the closet. I tentatively pushed it around and it didn't feel heavy so I pulled it down and set it on the floor. I did my preventive kicking at it so as to give anyone living in there the opportunity to escape. No one took advantage, so I assumed that meant nobody was home and I could safely look inside. The top of the bag was rolled down so it would fit nicely on the shelf. I carefully unrolled it and looked inside.

"Cam!"

I heard a loud clunk and a series of expletives as Cam smacked his head on the box springs and came rolling out from under the bed. "You scared the shit out of me. What?"

I picked up the bag and turned it over, shaking it vigorously. "I think I just found Franklin's bank!"

Money came floating out of the bag and onto the floor. It wasn't taped in nice little bundles but rather all loose and crumpled like it had spent a lot of time stuffed in a pocket. I began to smooth it out. Tens. Twenties. Fifties. We sat on the floor like a couple of kids playing a board game, smoothing out the money and placing it in piles. Once it was laid out it didn't look like the fortune it had originally but it was still a lot of money to keep in a brown grocery bag in your closet with your dirty clothes.

"Rough count, about $850.00," Cam pronounced. "I guess that's not a lot when you consider that he never spent money on anything other than the groceries we brought him."

"He never paid me in crinkled-up money like this. Maybe he ironed it first."

"If this is what the murderer was looking for, he apparently didn't think to look inside this bag."

"Maybe there was more money and that is what the murderer took. You can't expect an old man living out in the woods to have a fortune so he was probably pretty happy if he got half this much, if his motive was robbery."

"Mmm." Cam rocked back on his heels and looked around the room. "I wonder where he kept the money he gave us for groceries." He stood up and opened the closet door all the way. "We need to take all these clothes and things out and have a look."

Cam apparently didn't believe in the thumb and index finger approach and grabbed everything on a hanger and dumped it on the bed. Then he pulled all the shoes and debris on the closet floor out into the middle of the room. He reached into all the shoes and gave me a nod, indicating that I was to do the same with the clothes on the bed. I wished I had my half-price gardening gloves. I sat down and methodically checked a couple of pockets. After nothing awful appeared I settled down and mindlessly checked them all. A big pile of nothing. Cam reported the same thing. I suppose one shouldn't be disappointed in finding a bag full of money but we had hoped to find a murderer.

Chapter Twenty-Two

I t's amazing how little interest a paper bag filled with over $800 of crumbled bills can generate. As soon as we got home last night, Cam called the police. They were mildly interested and said they would be over this morning to pick it up. I hardly slept all night worrying that someone would find out we had a small fortune in our house and would break in, again. I kept the baseball bat next to my side of the bed all night, just in case.

Claudia had been very bored by the whole thing and told Cam that when the police were done looking at the money we could keep it, as she had no interest. As executor of Franklin's will, Cam explained that the money had to go into his estate. Claudia countered that since she was her brother's sole heir, she was giving the money to us and there was no need to give it to her first so she could just turn around and give it to us. We've had mice in our basement that were greeted with more enthusiasm than this bag of money.

Cam stayed home until the police picked up the money because he knew I was uncomfortable being in the house alone with it. Mycroft and I were the only ones who felt the house had been broken into a week ago Tuesday. Even Cam, who had participated in our catch-the-burglars adventure, had chalked it up to "house noises" and post-murder over-sensitivity on both our parts. He refused to discuss the handkerchief, Sylvie's handkerchief, especially now that we couldn't find it. I think he was half-convinced we had imagined it.

It's human nature to want things to be the way we expect them to be, to be the way we are comfortable with, the way we are used to dealing with. I was surprised with myself for being so unsettled over the mystery of Franklin's death. I tend to be a fleer rather than a fighter and I like to keep my head at least a little buried in the sand to buffer life's blows. But now it seemed like everyone else was being an ostrich and I was the only one who couldn't get back to my normal life until I understood what had happened and why. It was as if a blanket of blasé had been thrown over everyone, the police included, and I had been left out. Grace was concerned but only to the point of clearing Ryan. Diane's concerns seemed purely hormonal. Claudia didn't want to be bothered. Syra and Bing were only mildly interested. Cam was involved off and on but didn't seem to be as disturbed and unsettled as I was. I needed a partner to bounce ideas off, someone who was as enmeshed in this mystery as I was.

When I was a child and my friends weren't available to play, I used to sit on my bed and write and draw in my journal. I have dozens of these journals, the first one started when I was six. During my dramatic junior high school years I sincerely believed that my journal was my only friend. During my awkward high school years I truly believed that I would never marry but would live my life through my writing, telling my journal the things I should be able to tell a husband, but knowing that there was no male who would ever listen to me like that leather-bound book.

The current issue was filled with my thoughts on Abbey's departure to college and how my relationship with Cam had changed since she'd been gone. We were identifying with each other as a couple again rather than parents and that took some getting used to. Like an adolescent body, my middle-aged changing body took some getting used to. Some themes carried from book to book—my relationship with and thoughts about my mother-in-law, my struggles with being a good mother, a good wife and good to myself, all at the same time, my concerns about my friends, and rants about my brother. I decided to turn to my journal to help me sort out the mystery of Franklin's death. I had just started to outline the series of events, starting on October 2 when I'd found his body, when I had an overpowering and freakish urge to call Claudia. My friendship with Grace had alerted me to the possibilities of acting on overpowering and freakish urges and, not wanting to ignore the possibility of spiritual guidance, I followed through.

The phone rang several times and I was about to hang up when it was picked up, and I was greeted with a classy British voice. "Claudia Behrends Mack's home. How may I help you?"

"Is this Sybil?" I tentatively asked. I couldn't believe Claudia had actually hired someone to answer her phone.

"Yes it is. Who is calling, please?"

"Sybil. It's Tamsen ..."

"Oh, I thought you were someone else."

"Who?" I couldn't imagine what Claudia and Sybil had going on that required Sybil to answer her phone so formally and with a British accent.

"No matter. Did you want to talk to Claudia?" she asked.

"Yes, is she available?"

"Not really. She's napping. She's hosting the October bridge party here tonight so she needs her rest. She has twelve people coming, including Titus Strickland. He used to be the mayor of Birdsey Falls, you know."

"Yes. I didn't realize he was still ... um ... I didn't realize he lived at Ashland Belle now."

"Oh yes, he's been here for ages. Very good bridge player."

"He's got to be at least hundred …"

"Not quite. He's ninety-five. Still a sharp bridge player, too. And Marilyn Craig will be here. She performed on Broadway for decades and retired to Ashland Belle a couple of years ago."

"I didn't realize there were so many illustrious people living there," I replied

"Oh yes, Ashland Belle is a very popular place for the right kind of people."

Sybil was starting to sound like Claudia now. "What are you doing there, Sybil?"

"I'm baking Claudia's famous chocolate cherry soufflé. She always serves that when she hostesses. It's her signature dish. People expect it."

"But why are you making it?" I asked.

"I always make it. You know Claudia can't cook anything …"

"But then it's *your* famous chocolate cherry soufflé, not Claudia's," I argued.

"No," she answered patiently, "its Claudia's. This is what she is known for at Ashland Belle. It's just that she doesn't know how to make it so I always make it for her. Everyone loves it. Even the chef here has asked for the recipe but she won't give it to him. She hinted that when she passed on she might leave it to him and he always makes sure she gets the best of everything in the dining room in anticipation of it."

"But it's your recipe and you are the one doing the work. I don't understand, Sybil. Why is she taking credit for your recipe and why are you the one making it?"

Sybil sighed a long and tortured sigh. "Because Claudia can't cook. And she doesn't know the recipe. My second mother-in-law, who was an assistant to a baker in Manhattan, gave it to me."

"I still can't understand why you're doing all the work and letting Claudia take credit for it ..."

"Oh for heaven's sake, Tamsen," Sybil replied crossly. "It's a recipe, not the cure for cancer. Who cares who gets the credit? It matters a lot to Claudia and it doesn't matter to me. Now what did you want to talk to Claudia about?"

It had always been hard for me to picture Claudia having even one good friend, much less someone as devoted as Sybil. I let the subject drop and moved ahead. "I wanted to talk to her about Edmund Close but you probably know as much about him as she does."

"I remember him, of course. He was Franklin's best friend. They used to do all those treasure maps and plan all those games together."

"Do you know what happened to Edmund? Did he go to college? Get married? Where did he end up?"

"Oh dear, is it important?"

"Probably not, I was just curious. Because of the photo of you five kids. Do you know what happened to him?" I prodded.

"Well, I know he went to college. I do remember him coming home once in a new car with a bunch of friends for Thanksgiving or something. I was probably around twelve, so the college kids were really intriguing. They seemed so sophisticated. And they were smoking. Claudia and I talked about smoking and decided we would wait until the next year, when we were teenagers, to start."

"Did you?"

"Start smoking at thirteen? I can't remember. I did eventually smoke but I can't remember when I started. Claudia never smoked. She has a delicate system, you know. I'm sure it would make her ill."

Since most things made Claudia ill in one way or another I was sure Sybil was right about the smoking. "Do you remember anything else about Edmund Close? Like what he did after college?"

"You are really hurting my brain, Tamsen. That was a long time ago. If I rub my head too hard, I'm going to ruin my hairdo."

"I understand. Rub your neck. Maybe that will help," I suggested. I didn't want her to give up until I had pulled every memory out of her head. I was sure she would remember more than Claudia, who could probably tell you what party she went to and what she wore forty-five years ago but would not remember actual people other than herself.

"My brain isn't in my neck but I'll try rubbing it in case it works. Let's see." There was a long pause and I was afraid Sybil had fallen asleep. I waited patiently because I didn't have anything else pressing to do. My nails needed filing and I lethargically searched around for a nail file but couldn't find one. I was holding my double jointed thumb up to my ear so I could see if it still cracked like it used to when Sybil's voice jarred me back to the present.

"I got it! I thought of something juicy."

"Go on."

"Edmund wanted to marry a girl after he graduated from college. I was about fourteen or fifteen and I remember it was so romantic."

"Why? Did they have a big wedding?"

"No. There was no wedding. They were star-crossed lovers, like Romeo and Juliet. I remember Mr. and Mrs. Close having dinner with my parents and going on and on about it. The more I listened the more romantic it sounded. I wanted my first romance to be just like that."

"Star-crossed?"

"Of course. What is more romantic than that? Two people who are in love who have no hope of ever being together in this lifetime. It's the stuff that dreams are made of. I'm getting all tingly just thinking about it."

"Why were they star-crossed? Did their parents hate each other? Were they different ethnicities or even … oh jeez, he wasn't in love with another man was he?"

"Of course not! That didn't happen back then. She was a lovely girl. I saw her in the car with him several times. Her father was a doctor in Boston. Very good family. Lots of money. My dad mentioned that more than once."

"So what was the problem?"

"She was Catholic." Sybil pronounced with a tinge of sadness.

"So?"

"*So?* Interfaith marriage was a huge taboo in the 1940s. Her family refused to let her marry outside the Catholic faith and Edmund's family didn't want to let a Catholic into theirs. It was doomed."

"Did Edmund pine for her the rest of his life?"

"He married somebody but I don't know who. I think he was in the army for a while then came home and got married. I think he moved to Chicago or maybe it was Kansas City. Someplace in the Midwest."

"Did he and Franklin keep in touch?"

"No. Franklin didn't keep in touch with anyone, including his own family."

"Do you think Edmund might know why Franklin went into himself that way, why he changed?"

"He might have had some insight but he would be in his 80s now. He's probably dead."

I heard a voice floating in the background. Apparently Claudia was waking up from her beauty sleep. Sybil must have put her hand over the phone because I heard a muffled reply from Sybil and then some more background talk. In another minute Sybil came back on the phone.

"Tamsen? Claudia said that Edmund died about ten years ago."

I was amazed, but not speechless. "How does she know that? She didn't know anything about him when we were talking about his photo a couple weeks ago."

"She said that after seeing the picture she was curious so she called Abbey and asked her to look him up on the Internet."

"Why didn't she tell me she found out he'd died?" Once again I heard Sybil's muffled question to Claudia and the voice floating back.

"She forgot."

***

I was obsessing about Claudia and her forgetfulness, wondering if it was intentional. It would be like her to use my own daughter to get that secret information. But then, she was seventy-four years old. Old people forgot things. Lots of things. Maybe she didn't think it was as important as I did. But if so, why did she take the trouble to contact Abbey and ask her to look it up? Why didn't she ask Cam? Or even me? Why didn't I think of doing it for myself?

I had a partial explanation for that. I write children's books and everything in my books comes out of my head. There is no need for research or accuracy. My main character has six paws. Once you can accept that, you don't spend a lot of time fact checking the other points in the book. Therefore, I'm not on the internet every day.

So, it made sense that Claudia hadn't asked me to look Edmund Close up because she knew I was pretty lame when it came to anything other than word processing. But still, to call Abbey? And then to "forget" to tell me? I stretched out on the couch in the library and posed these questions to Mycroft who lumbered over to place his head on my ribcage and stare at me, soulfully.

"You're the world's most wonderful dog, Mycroft," I crooned to him. "I hope you know how precious you are, you sweet, chubby little boy." I continued to make lip smacking noises and coo chee coo sounds and he nuzzled into my tee shirt and left big wet spots all over it. We had quite a love fest going when the phone rang and I had to abandon the couch in a hurry in to run into the kitchen where I left it.

"Hello ..."

"Tamsen, it's Syra. You need to come over here right away." She sounded serious.

"Syra, what's wrong? Are you okay? Bing? What's the ..."

"I think you know." The line went dead and I stared at my phone like it might offer an explanation. I wasn't sure if she was angry or afraid. I felt the need to hurry. I grabbed my jacket and scribbled "Syra's" on a napkin and left it on the table for Cam. I shouted goodbye to Mycroft and dashed across the street much faster than is practical for a woman in my shape. Soaring blood pressure and a sudden burst of strenuous physical activity, I might give myself a stroke and a heart attack at the same time.

The door was standing open and I ran into the house calling her name. I stood in the living room twirling around trying to figure out where to look first. I heard the door close behind me and turned in that direction. What I saw scared me more than the frantic phone call. Syra stood there staring at me. Staring.

"I'm glad to see that your role as amateur detective hasn't usurped your role as friend. Can I take your coat?" She held out her hand and I stood frozen in place. I could feel a trickle of sweat running down the middle of my back and every nerve in my body told me to flee. This was one of those fight or flee situations and I was a good fleer. Except my feet wouldn't move.

"Suit yourself. Come to the kitchen. We need to talk."

"Maybe we should talk at my house," I suggested as she propelled me into the kitchen.

"That makes no sense."

"Why?"

"Because you're already here. Now sit down. I'll get you some hot chocolate."

I fell into the chair, the same one I had sat in a few days ago when I had interrogated Bing. The trickle down my back felt icy now. I pulled my coat closer across my chest.

"Where's Bing?" I whispered. I didn't mean for it to come out as a whisper but my voice seemed to be fleeing. I wish it would take my feet with it.

"In the basement," she answered as she placed the hot chocolate in front of me. "Do you want something to eat?"

"In the basement?" I croaked. This didn't sound good at all.

"Yes, in the basement. I had to get rid of him so we could talk and you know he won't leave the house," she patiently explained. I wondered if she meant that now he would never leave the house again. Ever.

"What's going on, Syra? You're scaring me."

"Good. Drink your hot chocolate."

By now I realized that the hot chocolate was poisoned, Bing was dead in the basement and Syra was a serial killer. You would think that this would be enough for me and that I would do something daring like throw the hot chocolate in her face or push the table over on her or throw my purse at her head. The woman had recently had a mastectomy and was undergoing radiation. She was weak. She was slow. She was deranged. But I couldn't move. I had to know why. I now understand why curiosity killed the cat.

"Why are you acting like this, Syra? I don't understand what's going on." I pushed the hot chocolate away to let her know that I knew what she was up to and that I wouldn't go down that easily. I had read as many mysteries as she had, probably more.

She leaned back in her chair and smiled at me. "You're going to want to drink that hot, Tamsen. Don't let it get cold."

Was there some kind of poison that got weaker as it got cooler? Or was this reverse psychology and the poison was weaker when it was hot but stronger as it got cold. Maybe she was giving me good advice warning me not to let it get cold. Maybe it worked quicker when it was hot and she was trying, for old times' sake, to save me from an agonizing death. Had Bing drunk his hot chocolate hot? I hoped so. Poor Bing.

"I know you talked to Bing, Tamsen. He told me all about the conversation. Only it really wasn't a conversation in the true sense, was it? More of a grilling to see what Bing would tell you, to find out what he knew. Seems a little underhanded. That's why I wasn't sure if you would come when I called. You seem less like a friend and more like an adversary since Franklin died ..."

"He was murdered, Syra. Murdered in cold blood."

"I'm well aware of that. Why did you need to ask Bing about our parents? Prying into our lives is not going to bring Franklin back. What do you want from us?"

It occurred to me to just tell her emphatically that I had no idea what she was talking about, suggest she check the dosage on her medication and stand up and walk out the front door. And run home. I was determined not to be victimized by this psycho Syra and yet I couldn't leave until I knew what was going on. It was like a book you couldn't put down even though you were going to be late for an appointment. You have to know how it ends.

"Why does Bing think his mother's name was Mary?"

"Because it was."

"Mary Foster?"

"Yes."

"Then who is Hetty Foster?"

"My mother."

So far so good. She seemed like she would answer any question I asked her. Unfortunately nothing she had said made any sense.

"Then you and Bing have different mothers?"

"No."

I pondered that for a few seconds and reached for the hot chocolate. I had it to my lips when I realized what I was doing and hastily put it back down on the table. Some splashed on my hand and I looked at it in horror, expecting it to start eating away at my flesh. It didn't. Syra continued to sip her hot chocolate and stare at me.

"So are you saying Hetty Foster and Mary Foster are the same person?"

"Exactly. My mother's name was Mary Henrietta Foster. She was named after her mother who was also Mary Henrietta. They called my mom Hetty as a child so it would be less confusing. My mom started using her real first name when she was an adult although she never cared for either name." I suppose that actually made some sense.

"Why does Bing think her maiden name was Willard?"

"Because that is what she told him. Us."

"But that is really her father's first name, right?"

"Yes. Her dad was named Willard Foster."

"So why the deception?" I asked. I couldn't believe how easy it was to get her to tell me the truth, assuming it was the truth. It all made sense so far. Sort of.

"I would think it would be obvious. My mom wasn't married to either my father or to Bing's. She made up a story so we wouldn't know ..."

"Then it's true that you and Bing have different fathers?"

"I would think that would be even more obvious. Of course we do."

"But Bing doesn't know it. He thinks your mother was named Mary Willard and she married your father, and his name was Fulton

Foster. But in actuality there wasn't a Fulton Foster but two different men, one your father and one Bing's. Right?"

"Almost. There was a Fulton Foster. He was my mother's brother. She just used his name."

I remembered Claudia telling me Fulton Foster had had polio and had watched the children from his bedroom window. And then he had disappeared. Syra couldn't have killed him too, as she wasn't born yet. Maybe her mother killed him and Syra had inherited the murder gene.

"What happened to him, the real Fulton Foster?" I whispered, clutching the seat of my chair.

"He died," she stated matter of factly. "Does it matter?"

"It probably does to him," I blurted out. "People don't just want to die, you know. We have an innate sense of survival. We are supposed to have a certain amount of time on earth to accomplish the things we are supposed to accomplish and if our time is cut short, we don't get everything done. And that's a problem because we are sent here to get stuff done. So we are supposed to stay. Until our earthly time is over. Only God can decide that, not other people. Other people can't determine ..."

"Why are you rambling on like this?"

"Who killed Fulton?"

"Nobody. He had polio as a child and it left him crippled and eventually caused his lungs to stop working. He died in his sleep when he was ten."

"But ... but he disappeared. Claudia said so."

"Of course he disappeared. They didn't keep him propped up in his window like the dead guy in *Weekend at Bernie's*. He died. They buried him. What's all this disappearance stuff about?

"Claudia made it sound sinister. Like he just disappeared one day ..."

"Well I suppose that to her that is what it seemed like. He was just a couple years older than she so probably her folks glossed over his death, like parents do about anything that might scare a child. Maybe they didn't want her to know that children died. I don't know. Is everyone in your family so dramatic about death?"

"Claudia and I aren't in the same family. At least we aren't related by blood," I affirmed. Somehow distancing myself from Claudia's genes seemed more important than defending my so-called dramatic attitude. "So who was your father?"

"That's the whole point of the secrecy, Tamsen. I don't know who my father was. My mom didn't know who my father was. After Franklin went strange and Edmund went to college my mom was left on her own and she got into trouble at a party one night. She came home drunk and then a couple months later discovered she was pregnant. My mom had a cousin who lived in Syracuse and she let my mom stay there until I was born. My mom never came back to Birdsey Falls. She got a job as a typist in Syracuse and later moved to Binghamton, where she met Bing's dad. She also didn't know his name. After Bing was born she stopped drinking and tried to be a good mother. She did okay. Bing adored her. I want Bing to have happy memories of his childhood. There's no point in knowing all the sordid details."

"But why did you move to Birdsey Falls?"

"Birdsey Falls was part of my mom's fairy tale and Bing wanted to move here. My mom had a great childhood but her parents weren't around much for guidance. All Bing knows of Birdsey Falls is what my mom told him, and it's all happy and adventurous and fun. He misses her. He wants to be here to be close to where she was so happy."

"And I almost ruined it by asking him all those questions ..."

"Exactly. Bing is an innocent. He's vulnerable. I don't know why, but he's always been like that. My mom didn't even want him to leave the house for fear something would happen to him. If you talked to

Grace about it, which I have, she claims Bing is a new soul trying to find his way in a place he hasn't been before. I don't agree with Grace's beliefs or in Spirituality as a religion but I do know there is something fragile and innocent about Bing. I want to protect him. Your nosiness was going to destroy that innocence."

I nodded my head and tried not to look at the basement door. Then I heard it, like the rhythmic thumping of the Tell Tale heart. Why should I be the one hearing the thumping? I didn't kill anyone. I didn't have anything to be guilty about. I glanced at Syra and she didn't react to the thumping, which was growing louder and louder and louder.

The basement door burst open and I screamed. Bing stood there staring at me and began screaming, too.

"What in God's name is wrong with you two?" Syra asked.

I wanted to run over and hug Bing but instead I remained seated. "I think we startled each other," I explained.

"I told you Bing was working in the kitchen in the basement."

"You didn't say he was *working* in the basement, you just said he was *in* the basement," I countered.

"So? What did you think he was doing in the basement?"

I didn't want to say, "lying in repose", so I just shrugged. Bing had recovered the shock of my screaming at him and presented me with a chocolate cake shaped like a cat with a witch's hat on its head. The hat was orange, as were the eyes of the cat.

"Syra said you were coming over this afternoon so I wanted to try this new design out on you. I'm going to make a bunch of them for Halloween. The Birdsey Falls Volunteer Firefighters are having a bake sale and I volunteered to make a dozen cakes. What do you think?"

I stared at the elaborate cake and began to feel as if I had just punked myself. Sure, Syra was angry with me for quizzing Bing about his parents, but she had not been planning to kill me. She obviously hadn't killed Bing. She had even told him she invited me over and then had him make this cake for me to keep him occupied so we could talk. Just talk. Like the friends we were. She wanted to clear the air and warn me to keep Bing's happy memories intact. That's all. And I thought she was going to kill me.

"What do you think, Tamsen? Is it Halloween-like enough?" Bing asked.

I shook myself out of my reverie to tell him how wonderful it looked and to thank him profusely for giving it to me. I was always thrilled to have a chocolate cake in the house. It was security, like having a pile of unread books waiting or a new knitting project. Chocolate cake should be a constant, like toilet paper, in every home.

I gave Bing and Syra each a hug and walked across the street, carrying my black cat cake, feeling like the biggest fool in the world. Would Hormone Replacement Therapy prevent afternoons like this?

Chapter Twenty-Three

I t's hard to imagine my life without Cam, but I was seriously con-
templating it following his reaction to my visit with Syra. I had
been scared to death and, as illogical as it seemed now, the fear at the
time was very real. It had been a raw, primitive feeling, stripped bare
of civility and logic and common sense. Suddenly I was able to understand how someone could grab a letter opener and use it to protect
themselves. Self-preservation is an instinct so deeply imbedded in our
animal nature that it surpasses rational thought, altruism, upbringing
or love. Because I love Syra; she is a long-time friend. I know I can call
her and she will be there in an instant, much as she knows she can do
the same, thus luring me to her house yesterday under false pretences.
I trust Syra. We had shared many confidences that I knew she had
never betrayed. I had left Abbey with her many times when I'd had a
babysitting emergency or when Cam and I spent the night away from
home. You can't trust anyone any more than that. Yet yesterday, when
I felt that I knew she had poisoned Bing and was about to do the same
to me, I was frantically thinking of a way to defend myself. And I
knew, deep down, that I could have grabbed a letter opener and used it
against one of my oldest, dearest friends if it came down to her or me.

The confrontation with Syra had been much more unnerving than
the angry one that took place with Ryan when he caught us snooping

in his room. Syra had been calm. And that cold calm, that feeling that she had thought things through versus being caught off guard, was much more disturbing and threatening than a teenager mouthing off. I tried to explain to Cam that for the first time in forty-seven years I had been afraid for my life. And I had been willing to strike back, to cause harm to another person, a friend, in self-defense.

But Cam hadn't been able to get past the vision of me afraid to drink Syra's hot chocolate, thinking Bing was dead in the basement when in reality he was frosting a cake. He had laughed. I spent the night on the couch in the library telling Mycroft how afraid I had been and what an insensitive jerk Cam was. As always he had listened intently and agreed with everything I said. I should have married Mycroft.

Of course, there was no thawed bagel waiting for me for breakfast. No note from Cam admitting he was the most insensitive, unfeeling, unloving, unevolved man in the world. I grabbed a diet soda and made a peanut butter and jelly sandwich on toast and headed to the library to write. I wanted to channel this anger and this spunky, defiant feeling into a new idea I had for a novel. I hadn't been able to get the story of Sylvie and how she had been abandoned by Roger Behrends out of my mind and I was ready to start outlining my thoughts. I wanted to write an adult novel, taking place in post-Civil War New Orleans. It would feature a Sylvie-type woman who had been rich and a part of New Orleans society until the war had wiped out her family's planta-tion and wealth. Instead of allowing her family to marry her off to the best suitor still available, she was going to rebuild her life on her own terms. She would be a woman ahead of her time, a woman who couldn't be pawned off in marriage by her family, a woman who could live her life without the money or protection of a husband. And I wanted the handkerchief in the story too. She would have a trunk full of these useless embroidered silk handkerchiefs. They would become her trademark as she set out on her survival adventures: the symbol of the frivolity and waste of her former life left as a calling card as she embarked on a life of purpose and meaning. Maybe I would call it The Purpose Driven Handkerchief.

When Cam called a couple hours later I didn't answer. I didn't want to lose my train of thought trying to explain to him why I was angry. I don't know much about post-Civil War New Orleans so I struggled with using the Internet to look up historical dates as well as social history of the time period. That was starting to slow me down so I began just putting x's and highlighting them in places where research was needed so I didn't stop my flow. Later I would go back and fill in the facts.

I was starting to get lightheaded and realized I was starving. It had to be past noon and I was going to crash soon if I didn't make some soup or something. I had just jotted down some ideas of where I wanted to go next when I heard the front door open. Had Cam forgotten to "lock me in" when he left this morning? That was odd. Even when we were fighting he always locked the door when he left the house. It was his way of saying, "Yeah, I'm mad at you but I don't want someone to come in an attack you while I'm gone."

I silently got up, grabbed the fireplace poker and inched toward the bookcase that opened up to the staircase between the library and our bedroom. I motioned to Mycroft to follow me but he just stared. I didn't want to leave him in the library alone but wasn't sure how to get him into the passage if he didn't walk on his own four feet. Plus I had to have the poker ready in case we were attacked.

"Come Mycroft," I whispered. "We're going to play hide and seek. Come on boy ..."

The library door flew open and I screamed. Mycroft jumped to his feet and waddled to the door. "Hey boy. At least someone is here to greet me when I come home from work," Cam crooned as he knelt down to scratch Mycroft's ears. Then he looked up at me, poised by

223

the passage door with the poker raised over my head. "I guess this means you're still mad ..."

"You scared me to death. What are you doing home at this time of day?"

"What do you mean, 'this time of day'? It's six o'clock. It's the same time I come home every day. Remember, dinner, watch the news, read the paper, talk about what we did all day ..."

"It can't be six o'clock. That's impossible," I countered, lowering the poker.

"Why is it impossible?"

"Cause I haven't even had my lunch yet."

"Ah, you must have been writing," he nodded as he stood up and gave Mycroft one last pat. "You always lose track of time when you're writing. Finally got Perry and his friends on the hot air balloon?"

I put the poker back in the stand by the fireplace and went over to my computer to press the save button. "No, I'm working on something different, something that I've had brewing in my head since the night of the break-in and the appearance of the handkerchief."

"Why don't you get to a good stopping place in your writing and I'll make omelets for dinner. If we eat in fifteen minutes will that work?"

"Sure, I can tie up my thoughts by then."

Cam gave me a wave and headed to the kitchen. It wasn't exactly an apology on either of our parts but he had offered to make dinner and I hadn't refused to eat it with him so we were raising the white flags, or at least handkerchiefs, calling for a truce.

The omelet was delicious. Everything Cam cooks tastes so much better than my unenthusiastic attempts in the kitchen. His parents had had a full-time housekeeper when he was growing up and he learned to cook from her. I wish she was still living here. I could really use her help.

"What ever happened to Mrs. Knapp? I'd like to thank her for teaching you to cook."

"She's retired now. She lives at Bugg Hill ..."

"The same retirement village where Diane's parents live."

Cam nodded, poking at the last of the egg on his plate.

"I hope she likes macaroni and cheese." That got a laugh out of him and we smiled at each other. I was starting to hate him less. He reached across the table and grabbed my hand.

"I know you were hurt when I laughed at you last night. I'm sorry. I didn't mean to hurt your feelings but it was hard for me to picture you sitting in Syra and Bing's kitchen sincerely thinking she was trying to poison you ..."

"And that she had killed Bing ..."

"That was even more difficult to imagine. Those two are devoted to each other. Now if Syra thought you were trying to kill Bing I wouldn't be surprised if she poisoned you. That would be totally different. I don't think that man will ever suffer any physical or mental stress as long as Syra is around. She's like the poster girl for the protective older sibling."

"Not something that either of us ever experienced. Graham would have sold me to the gypsies in a second if he knew where to find any that wanted me ..."

"Cassandra didn't even know I was alive. At least you were able to annoy Graham enough that he noticed you."

"You know, I think it was the heat of that protectiveness that made me realize Syra was capable of hurting me. She was so calculating, summoning me over there, convincing Bing to go down to his kitchen in the basement to work. She was just so cold and factual and protective. You had to experience it to know what I mean. Cam, it really was very scary. I think you would have been frightened, too."

"I know. I was thinking today of all the times we felt someone had threatened Abbey and how fiercely protective we were."

"Like the time Ronnie Hicks pushed her down and got her new coat all dirty …"

"I hated that kid!"

"As I recall you wanted him arrested for assault …"

"It was assault."

"He was four!"

"He was a heathen. And what about that Allison something or other who didn't invite Abbey to her roller skating party. She should burn in hell for that. Selfish thoughtless girl," Cam said.

"She's touring with Up With People." I told him as I cleared the dishes and put them in the dishwasher. "You see what we are doing here …"

"Yeah. Yeah," he admitted. "We're turning into nutcases bent on revenge at the mere memory of how people hurt Abbey."

"That's what Syra was like yesterday—a cold, unfriendly nutcase. It was a horrible feeling."

Cam came up behind me and put his arms around me as I closed the dishwasher door. "I'm sorry, sweetheart. I was a clod. If I'd been there, I probably would have felt the same way you did. Hey, I did think of something you could say to Syra next time you think she is going to murder you …"

"Ha ha. Very funny."

"No, really, this is a real conversation stopper. Just call her Syracuse Brinkleberger."

"Why would I do that?"

"Because that was her name for a few years when she was married."

"Syra was married?" I asked. "I never knew that. And that name …"

"Brinkleberger."

"Brinkleberger? How in love with someone do you have to be to take the name Brinkleberger? I wouldn't even date someone with that name just in case I ended up falling in love."

"Well, she must have had a moment of madness because that was her name."

"Why do you know all of this and I don't?"

Cam shrugged and began wiping down the kitchen table. "Bing told me once ..."

"Why wouldn't you tell me that?"

"I never thought about it again until today. Bing felt one of the reasons the marriage didn't last was because Syra insisted that Bing live with them. Apparently Mr. Brinkleberger got tired of the idea. They divorced and Syra took back her maiden name and no one mentioned Brinkleberger again."

"I can see why. What is that, German? Dutch?"

"No idea. If my mom had been a Brinkleberger rather than a Behrends perhaps she wouldn't have been so incredibly proud of the family name." Cam gave me that grin that always melted my heart and gave me a kiss on my neck. "Want to go snuggle on the couch in the library, read the paper and watch Mycroft nap?"

I laid my head on his shoulder and we hugged. "Sounds like the perfect evening."

We had finished reading the paper and were making mild sexual overtures to each other when something popped into my head.

"Oh, my God!" I screamed, bringing Mycroft to his feet and causing Cam to fall to the floor.

"I didn't realize I was such a sexual master ..." Cam began as he got to his feet and rubbed his lower back.

"You're not. I mean you are but you aren't right now ..."

"If you would give me a few more minutes, I mean, we just got started. Of course now my back hurts so that may put a dent in my ..."

"Shush. I'm thinking." I circled the room while Cam settled back on the couch, watching me. He was used to this kind of behavior and knew he just needed to wait me out. He pulled the pillow behind his head and spread out so his legs rested on the arm rest at the other end of the couch. "Very comfy," he whispered to Mycroft, who took that as an invitation to come over and put his head on Cam's chest and have his ears scratched. "She doesn't know what she's missing, does she, boy? Don't worry. Mommy will come to her senses shortly and we will all know what she is talking about."

I twirled around and pointed my finger at Cam. "Syra Brinkleberger. Don't you see? Syra Brinkleberger."

"I don't see," Cam answered bending to look at Mycroft. "Do you understand, boy?" Apparently Mycroft didn't understand either.

"At one time Syra had the initials SB"

"And …"

"SB Cam. Come on. The break-in. The handkerchief …"

"You think it was Syra's handkerchief?"

"Well …"

"But can you even imagine Syra owning a handkerchief? No one our age owns a handkerchief, much less a monogrammed one. And certainly not Syra. She isn't that kind of woman. It doesn't make sense."

"Does it make more sense that the handkerchief belongs to a *ghost*?" I asked.

Cam sat up, rearranging Mycroft's head on his lap, and began to rub his neck. "I don't know …"

"You saw the handkerchief. We both saw it, handled it. It wasn't something we imagined. It was here in this house and it was monogrammed with SB. I love the Sylvie story but even with my imagination I have a hard time believing a ghost left it as a calling card …"

"But what you're saying is that Syra broke into our house to steal who knows what and then left something that I can't imagine her ever owning. In addition, why would she be carrying a handkerchief left over from when she was married? I think that was twenty years ago or longer. It makes no sense ..."

"But you have to admit it makes more sense than Sylvie's ghost leaving it."

"There has to be another explanation."

"And where did the handkerchief disappear to? It's gone. I've looked everywhere."

"I swear I didn't move it."

"I believe you," I assured him. "But it's gone. Someone had to have taken it."

"So now you think Syra came back into the house to get her handkerchief that she left when she broke in. How would she know where it was?"

"There aren't a lot of places to look near the library. She would have eventually opened the table drawer ..."

"And no one saw her."

"We probably weren't home."

"How did she get in? And why did she have a monogrammed handkerchief from a marriage that ended twenty years ago with her when she broke into our house? And how did she get in the first time? The doors are locked ..."

"Cam, the house is huge. It's a monster. There have to be dozens of ways to get into this house that we don't know about."

"That's reassuring."

"Well, it's true. There's no way we can check all the windows on all the floors every night before bed. We'd have to start before dinner and probably fall asleep before we even got to them all. Breaking into this house is probably not very difficult at all."

"Motive?"

"No idea. But it must have to do with Franklin's death."

"So Syra *is* a murderer? We've come full circle from last night's conversation," Cam warned me.

"But this time it's different. We have evidence. Syra was once an SB."

Chapter Twenty-Four

Knowing that your home is a veritable Grand Central Station does not make for a restful night's sleep. I kept hearing suspicious noises all night long and when I woke up from what felt like fifteen minutes of sleep, Cam was already gone to his usual Saturday morning squash game followed by the high school football game. I had a killer headache. I pulled the covers back over my head, thankful that it was Saturday and I had nothing planned.

I awoke again about an hour later and staggered downstairs, dying for a diet soda and something for my headache. Chocolate would be good. My thawed bagel was on the counter with a roughly cut out heart made from a napkin. I smiled even through the excruciating pain. The newspaper was also lying on the counter. Cam knew I loved to read the paper while I ate my breakfast. I settled into my seat and lavishly covered my cranberry bagel with butter. This was the life, minus the headache and sleep deprivation.

I thought of Franklin sitting at his kitchen table. Had he felt this same contentment as he sat at the table and ate his breakfast and read the paper? I hoped so. Maybe the most simply led lives were the most rewarding. No deadlines. No appointments. No expectations. Just a simple day filled with what brought you the most pleasure—eating, reading, writing, sleeping.

But Franklin had never seemed happy when we saw him. Maybe when we weren't interfering with his day, peeking in his window and trying to converse with him, he may have been as happy and content as a human being can be. I was having a nagging thought that there might be something important about Franklin sitting at his kitchen table reading the paper and eating his breakfast when I glanced up at the calendar on my kitchen wall. Oh, my God. My annual appointment with my gynecologist was in thirty minutes!

I leaped up from the table and ran upstairs. How could I have forgotten? I usually obsessed and whined about this appointment for days ahead of time. It was all the doctor's fault for starting Saturday hours. No one planned to go to the doctor on a Saturday. I hadn't taken a shower last night because Cam and I had been up late talking about Syra's initials. And now there wasn't time. I darted into the bathroom and did a cursory cleanup. I grabbed the first clothes I could find and put them on as I raced down the stairs, tripping over my jeans and trying to put my socks on while hopping on one leg. I couldn't find my purse. I couldn't find my keys. There was nothing I could do about the grease stain on the front of my shirt I noticed just as I was running out the door.

I sped out of the driveway and realized I had forgotten my coat. I put the car heater up to high. I frantically pawed around in my purse with my right hand while I steered with my left, trying to find my brush. My purse slipped off the passenger seat and fell to the floor, spilling its contents all over the car. I could see my brush but couldn't reach it unless I bent down and took my eyes off the road for several seconds. Bad idea. I contented myself with a string of curses that would have curled my hair if it had been clean and had any body in it at all. I swerved into the medical building parking lot and almost took out a fire hydrant that someone had placed too close to the road. I parked on the yellow line and bent over to try to grab as many items as

I could reach to stuff back into my purse. The brush still eluded me so I ran my fingers through my hair and tried to puff it up and pretend I was going for the natural look that was so popular among movie stars.

I ran up the sidewalk and banged through the double doors. The elevator was too slow to arrive so I ran up the steps to the second floor where the ob-gyn suite was located. I burst into the waiting room and a dozen pairs of eyes turned and stared. I put my head down and scurried to the check-in window, where I was informed that I was ten minutes late and was to go in immediately; the world of gynecology must have come to a grinding halt in anticipation of my arrival. The nurse led me into the lab room and told me to sit while she took my blood pressure.

"160 over 90," she reported with a frown. "That's very high for someone your age."

I nodded. "I've been running ..."

"Give me a urine sample and we'll retake your blood pressure," she said.

I dutifully went into the bathroom to fulfill my obligation to the little bottle and then spent five minutes washing my hands and cleaning the outside of the bottle before putting it into the little revolving cupboard. Back in the lab room my blood pressure was now down to 140 over 85. I was making progress. The nurse shook her head, still not satisfied, and led me to the scale. I slipped off my shoes but the nurse wouldn't let me remove anything else. "Up six pounds from last year." She duly noted it on my chart.

"I know I'm a little overweight ..." I tried to explain that the stain on my shirt had to weigh something but she ignored me.

She pulled out one of those government weight and height charts and glanced at it. "Yes, you are overweight for your height and build ..."

"But I'm not obese!"

Damn it, she actually had to look at the chart again to make sure I didn't fall into the obese category.

"No, you are not obese. Just about fifteen pounds overweight for your height and build."

Ha. I crossed my arms over my chest and stared at her. I felt like I'd won a couple points because deep down I knew she was dying to tell me I fell into the obese category, which, by the way, I was pretty sure she was well-acquainted with herself. Misery loves company and so does fat. She showed me into the examining room and gave me the standard, "Take off everything and put on the gown; it opens in the front. Get up on the table. The doctor will be in shortly."

Because I was late, I was afraid the doctor would be in before I had time to get modestly settled on the examining table so I hurried to get undressed and clambered onto the table. I spent a lot of time trying to arrange the paper blanket so that it would go around to my back and cover up the expanse of flesh that the short little paper jacket didn't cover. But if I had my rear covered, then my legs were woefully on display in the front and I had planned to shave them in the shower this morning, the shower I didn't have time to take. Hairy legs. Fat butt. Hard to make a decision as to which was more offensive. There was a knock at the door and the doctor and the obese nurse entered the room, startling me and causing me to lose my grip on the blanket, allowing it to flutter to the floor. Hairy legs and fat butt both exposed and both silently acknowledged by obese nurse. The doctor shook my hand and didn't seem to notice my predicament.

He looked over my chart and asked the nurse to take my blood pressure once again. Now it was 130 over 80. He seemed satisfied with that. The nurse left and we chatted about my general health and I asked him about my late period. He assured me it was totally normal and explained perimenopause to me much the same way Diane had. He gave me several pamphlets about perimenopause, bone health, healthy eating and blood pressure. I assumed I wasn't supposed to read those while lying on my back during the exam so tucked them under my back while he examined me.

"You should get a television on your ceiling," I suggested as I lay down and stuck my feet in the stirrups. Cam claims I can't stop talking when I'm nervous.

"Scoot to the end of the table, please."

"Or maybe a computer screen. Then you could show information about birth control or breast self-exams or whatever was most relevant to the person being examined."

"Mmm."

"Or you could ask them what they wanted to see. I'm not going to have any more children but I love seeing pictures of developing embryos."

"Mmm."

"Or maybe you could get permission from your patients to allow their ultrasound pictures to be shown. I'd love to see actual ultrasound pictures. I hear they are so much more detailed now, three-dimensional even. You can actually see the features of the baby."

"Mmm."

"But then you already know how much more advanced they are because you see them every day."

"Mmm."

"Can you believe Abbey is in college now? I still remember being in this office and listening to her heartbeat with you. Do you remember what a beautiful baby she was? I remember you saying how she was such a beautiful baby."

"Mmm."

"Do you remember how nervous Cam was? Cam is my husband. He was more nervous than I was. Of course he could see more of what was going on so that didn't help. He has sort of a delicate system when it comes to blood and stuff."

The doctor got up and put his instruments away. "I'm sorry, were you saying something?" he asked.

"No."

"You look good. We'll call with the results of your Pap in about a week. Stay healthy and I'll see you next year." He shook my hand and left.

***

When I was growing up, all ordeals—piano recitals, doctor visits, dentist appointments, haircuts—were followed by a treat. Cam and I had followed that tradition, too, even if it meant keeping Abbey out of school for another half hour to stop at the Dairy Barn for a milkshake. After the morning I had had, I felt I deserved an awesome treat so headed over to Beaton's Birdsey Café, known locally as BBC, for an early lunch. I ordered their specialty, a chicken salad sandwich on an Asiago bagel and a diet soda and sat back in my booth in the corner to think. I didn't have anything with me to read, having left the breast self-exam pamphlets and other information in my car, so I pulled out a napkin and began to doodle notes about all the loose ends and oddities that were driving me crazy about Uncle Franklin's murder.

First on the list was motive. It could have been a robbery. We were surprised that Franklin had over $800 in a paper bag in his closet. Who knew what else he had of value in his cottage? Just because no one knew about it didn't mean there wasn't something valuable in there. Or was the motive revenge? Did something happen in his youth, something that someone waited until now to repay? Seemed unlikely, but if someone were in prison or didn't know where Franklin was, it could have taken this long to get to him. Or maybe someone was afraid of what he was writing. Ryan and his friends had seen Franklin writing every night at his desk. We had found page 23 of what appeared to be an autobiography. Did someone kill him for pages 1-22? Why? And how about the quote from Edgar Allan Poe I had found in Franklin's boyhood desk? That quote certainly sounded like the words of a man who had something to hide and was tortured by it. For a young boy to copy those words out of a story meant they had a strong meaning for him. It was like he was confessing to something. But what? Did someone from the long-ago indiscretion come back for revenge?

The waitress brought my diet soda in an old-fashioned cola glass with a red and white striped straw. I thanked her and returned to my list.

The second item to consider was means. How did someone get into Franklin's house and kill him? That was pretty easy. He didn't lock his doors. And it appeared that someone had taken the letter opener from his own desk, snuck up on him and shoved it in his neck. He was an old man. It would have been easy.

The third category was the one that kept me awake at night—that coupled with the house sounds that made me think people were pouring into my house like a battalion of carpenter ants. Loose ends. This was a major problem. Too many loose ends and unanswered questions.

"Would you like a refill?" I looked up at the waitress and down at my empty glass. I nodded my head. "Your sandwich should be out soon."

"Thank you."

Loose ends. Loose ends. Too many loose ends. I was making ink dots on my napkin as I counted all the loose ends. I should call this category "things that are driving me nuts." The first one had to be Syra and Bing's mother, Hetty Foster. Or Mary Willard. What was the deal with her? Her life had been less structured than Sybil or Claudia's but she had been from a wealthy family. How did she end up wandering the NYS Thruway hooking up with and having children by men she didn't even know?

Then there was Ryan and the bloody shirt. If I believed his story, then this was resolved. Did I believe him? I wanted to, for Grace's sake. But I didn't really know him. I couldn't cross Ryan and his shirt off the list yet. Then there were the seventy newspapers from April 1, one newspaper each year starting in 1938. Were these a clue or were they just trash, an old man's eccentricity? I had heard about people hoarding old newspapers or magazines but never someone hoarding just one from each year. If I were a graduate psychology student, there might be material for a master's thesis here. A twist on the traditional paper-hoarding psychosis. How much time did we want to spend searching these papers for an answer to his murder? That was difficult to determine.

"Would you like a piece of paper, Hon?" the waitress asked as she slid my sandwich plate onto the table.

"No, thanks. I'll just start numbering the napkins if I need to use more than one."

"Can I get you anything else? I'll keep an eye on your drink for refills."

"Thank you!" This waitress really understood me. I was feeling a good connection between us. I would have to ask for her next time I came in.

After a few minutes devoted to culinary pleasure I returned to my list. I had to pick a chunk of chicken salad off my "motive" paragraph.

Back to the loose ends. The bloody shirt. The newspapers. I wasn't sure if the next thing that popped into my head had to do with the murder but it was something I didn't understand and I needed to. Diane's alleged flirtation with the policeman, Donny something. I'd known Diane a long time, since we were young mothers together. I had never seen her flirt with anyone. I'd talked to this Donny guy and there was nothing wrong with him. He was younger, maybe fifteen years, than we were. He was nice looking. He didn't have red hair or freckles so obviously he couldn't be textbook handsome, but he was passable. I hadn't witnessed Diane flirting with him but I had Grace's take on the situation and had noticed how Diane was dressed more provocatively, fewer twin sets and more V-necks. I tapped the pen against my cheek as an empty glass was whisked off the table and a full one replaced it.

Who had broken into our house and why? I was convinced someone had been in that house even though no one seemed to agree with me. And what was the meaning of the monogrammed handkerchief that suddenly appeared after the break-in. And then disappeared a few days later. I had no idea what kind of follow up I could do to try to figure out who broke into our house and why but I could do a more thorough search for the handkerchief. If Mycroft could open drawers I would suspect him of taking it. Just in case, I would look at all his hidey spots to see if the handkerchief made its way there.

My "suspects" list was rather pitiful. Syra was on there, of course. I wasn't sure if I was convinced she was being secretive solely to protect Bing from learning about his parentage or if there were another motive involved. Syra's mother and Franklin had been friends so maybe there was some old hurt that she finally felt needed righting. Maybe Franklin had been writing unflattering things about Hetty in his autobiography—assuming that is what he was writing. Once again, her motive could have been to protect Bing. Then there was Ryan and his friends. I didn't think there was much of a motive there for premeditated murder. If Ryan had killed Franklin it would have been a spur of the moment thing. A prank gone very bad. Maybe Ryan got caught in Franklin's cottage and panicked. I hoped it didn't happen like that. It would be such a waste of a young life all because of a moment of panic.

Most likely Franklin was killed by someone unknown to me. An old enemy who would probably be in his or her 80s now. Or maybe someone cutting across our property at just the right moment to see Franklin in the cottage counting his money and figured he would be easy to rob. Franklin put up a fight and things went bad. Maybe Franklin recognized the would-be robber and the robber felt he needed to kill to protect himself.

I pushed my empty plate away and stirred the ice in my glass. I had three napkins full of scribbles and no answers. But somehow I felt much better listing everything out. After my confrontation with Syra I felt emboldened and less leery about questioning my friends to get answers. I added one more thing to my to-do list—talk to Policeman Donny. Not about Diane, of course, but about the investigation. Claudia had pawned the police off on Cam. Cam had listened to what they reported but hadn't really questioned them. As a member of the family, didn't I have the right to know what information they had? I would call and make an appointment to talk to Donny. But first I would need to find out his last name.

Chapter Twenty-Five

C am woke up on Sunday morning with the urge to cook. I have never had this urge but I've heard it is a legitimate desire and we need to accept the fact that some people experience it. Cam has a hard time cooking for two, so he suggested we invite his friend John, the one he plays squash with and whose son is the second string quarterback at the high school. Cam had been going with John to the games in case his son played but so far no luck. John is delightful and fun and having dinner with him would be a treat. Unfortunately, if we invited John, good manners dictated that we invite his wife, Jingle. Her maiden name had been Bell and her parents thought that was cute. It had a nice ring to it but personally I would have saved it for my dog's name. Her brother's name was Liberty. The former Jingle Bell was now Jingle Sullivan and the whole thing didn't make sense anymore. Obviously her parents had not been thinking ahead unless they had already picked out someone named Jangle for her to marry. That would have worked nicely.

I'm not overly picky about whom I associate with, but if I'm going to enjoy your company you must at least have a somewhat developed sense of humor. I'm not talking about sharply honed political wit or *New Yorker* cartoon humor. It doesn't need to be real high brow. A good pratfall when you walk into my house is perfectly acceptable. The problem with Jingle was that she had no sense of humor. DOA humor. Nothing. I would think that even if you weren't born with the humor gene or nurtured by parents with a sense of humor, you would have developed some funny coping mechanisms to deal with a name like Jingle Bell. Not even in the most politically correct, mature, sensitive kindergarten class would you not have been made fun of with a name like that. Even the teacher probably made fun of her. Jingle was so literal that I wondered how many years it took her to realize she was not actually a bell but a little girl.

To make matters worse, when Cam called to invite John and Jingle he also invited their son, the wannabe quarterback. His name is John-Winston. There is actually a hyphen. You were expected to call him by both names. John-Winston this and John-Winston that. It's annoying to listen to and more annoying to have to say. But you can't spend the night trying to avoid saying two people's names. I can sail through the evening cleverly avoiding addressing one person by their name but trying to do it with two people is just beyond me. So somewhere in the course of the evening I'm going to have to break down and say John-Winston and Jingle and I'd hate myself for it in the morning.

John-Winston is a handsome kid with manners that make me feel like a cavewoman. He's always been mature beyond his years, is impeccably groomed and never seems to make a false move. If you put him next to Grace's stepson Ryan you wouldn't think you were even looking at two animals of the same species. We had the Sullivans over for a casual cookout last summer and two days later John-Winston sent me a thank you note and flowers. He's sixteen. That's just not normal. He seems a bit unreal, like the *Stepford Wives*.

When the doorbell rang at six o'clock sharp, I had to answer it because Cam was up to his elbows in dinner preparation. I took several deep breaths and reminded myself that this, too, shall pass. It would most likely pass very slowly, but it would pass. Jingle stood tentatively on our front porch until I formally invited her into the house. Her hair was perfectly coiffed and stood out around her head like an auburn halo. Her makeup—and there was a lot of it—was expertly applied. She had a fresh manicure. Her perfume was light and floral. Her slacks were pressed and creased and hung exactly to the top of her shoes, obviously tailored because she was barely five feet tall. She weighed about 100 pounds dripping wet. Maybe less. She was probably close to my age but looked ten years younger. She smiled and handed me a big box of Godiva chocolates. Couldn't fault her for that.

John-Winston followed her in and leaned down to give me a kiss on the cheek. That totally freaked me out. He's not a relative. I barely know him. He's sixteen. Creepy. I dodged it and shook his hand. He was dressed from head to toe—probably socks and underwear too—in J. Crew. I wish Cam dressed like this. I liked it. He was big, like his dad, but had skin like his mother's, soft and pimple-free. Shouldn't all sixteen-year-old boys have pimples? At least one or two? I think John-Winston found the rites of puberty too pedestrian, so skipped them altogether.

Finally John entered and gave me a big bear hug. I like John. He's totally natural. He and Cam had been friends since high school. There were probably a lot of things John understood about Cam better than I did. Cam once told me that if he could have had a brother, it would have been John. If he'd been Cam's brother maybe he would have had better taste in women. Or maybe not. In some ways Jingle reminded me of Claudia. Petite. Perfectly groomed. Perfectly mannered. Perfect pain in the ass.

Cam came rushing out of the kitchen to greet everyone and to pour wine while I passed around shrimp and crab pastries that Cam had made this morning while I was reading the Sunday paper. The guys talked about the high school football game yesterday and how John-Winston almost got to play. Apparently yesterday's game was the closest he's gotten to getting off the bench all season. Jingle crossed her legs at the ankles and folded her hands in her lap, listening intently to every word John-Winston uttered. I sat with my feet up on the ottoman, not the coffee table, and began plotting my New Orleans novel. I was thinking that my heroine might be acquainted with a pirate and maybe create some sexual tension between them. It had to be subtle, though. I wasn't writing a bodice ripper; this was going to be a historical mystery. I never understood the allure of bodice ripping. If I had a beautiful lace and silk bodice and some guy, in the throes of passion, began ripping at it, he'd better be prepared, once his throes had died down, to sew it back together. I reached for another shrimp pastry and noticed that everyone was looking at me expectantly. Uh-oh. Apparently I had the floor but I didn't know what I was supposed to say. Cam came to my rescue.

"I think it should be within the next six months or so, isn't that right, dear?" Behind everyone's back Cam made the motions of opening a book. Someone must have asked me when the next Perry Many Paws book was coming out. I decided to not elaborate in case I was misreading the cues.

"Yes, that's right, sweetheart." Everyone nodded and went back to talking about high school football and John-Winston's plans for college. I heard them mention something about a football scholarship and I wondered how one received a football scholarship when one never actually played in a game. Then I drifted back to my own thoughts.

I planned for my still-unnamed heroine to have a romantic interest in a man who had somehow retained his money after the Civil War and was building a thriving business in New Orleans. He and my heroine had been courting prior to her family losing everything. His family would no longer acknowledge the relationship but there was still some smoldering interest between the two young people. Yet, lingering in the background was the question, how had his family managed to hang on to their money when everyone else lost theirs? Then there would be the French pirate who was totally unsuitable in all ways except that, in his own way, he was an honorable man. I'd also throw in an older wealthy man who was willing to take in the impoverished heroine and her entire family—for a price. Was she willing to pay it to restore her family to its previous status and wealth? She'd definitely toy with the idea. After all, he would be handsome and charming.

Everyone stood up and headed to the dining room so I assumed Cam had announced dinner. I had to pull myself together, or risk winning the "worst hostess ever" award. We didn't have name cards (how gauche) so Jingle spent several minutes trying to arrange the seating so we would be boy-girl. There were only five people so it seemed like it could be resolved easily, except apparently it was proper not only to be boy-girl but also to mix up families for enhanced conversation. Once we were all seated to Jingle's satisfaction Cam served dinner and conversation resumed.

I turned to John-Winston and, since I was looking directly at him, assumed I could ask him a question without addressing him by name. "Do you happen to know Ryan Kelly? He may be a year behind you in school." I saw a flicker of distaste cross John-Winston's face as he set down his utensils and turned to me.

"Yes, Mrs. Mack, I believe I know who you mean."

"Do you have any classes together or spend any time with him? He's the stepson of a friend of mine but I don't know much about him."

John-Winston nodded his head understandingly although what it was he understood was beyond me. "He's a year behind me so we don't have any classes together. I see him in the halls and the cafeteria once in a while, but I don't believe I've ever spoken to him. He's not interested in sports."

"Yes, he doesn't seem like the sports type from what little I've seen of him," I agreed.

"I believe he comes from a broken home," Jingle announced, lightly touching her napkin to her lips.

"He did, but he has two parents now. His home has, I suppose, been glued back together," I clarified, perhaps a tad sarcastically. Jingle shook her head slowly, the professionally applied auburn highlights in her hair catching the light of the chandelier.

"I'm not sure a child ever fully recovers from a broken home, mended or not," she replied. It was just like having Claudia to dinner. I wish Jingle had a sidekick like Sybil to lighten the mood. I guess that was John's job.

Cam wisely changed the subject to funny things he and John had done in high school together. Jingle and John-Winston looked on with distaste. My mind wandered back to yesterday morning when I had been eating my bagel and reading the paper and thinking about Uncle Franklin. Something had come to mind that seemed important at the time. It was just before I looked at the calendar, noticed my doctor appointment and gone into a tailspin of activity. I felt I had lost an important thought. What was it? Something about sitting at the table, eating breakfast, enjoying the morning newspaper.

"… and then there was the time Cam lost his gym shorts while climbing the ropes …"

"I think that's enough of those stories, John," Jingle said stiffly. "Tamsen, did you know that John-Winston was going to work ten hours a week at the *Birdsey Falls Gazette?*"

I shook my head. "I had no idea. What will you be doing?" Jingle probably thought he was going to be the editor.

"I'll be proofing copy and learning about news reporting. I want to be a journalism major when I go to college."

Jingle was beaming. She could smell a Pulitzer. "John-Winston has already taken both the journalism courses offered in the high school and gotten As …"

"Please mom, don't brag ..."

"... and is going to take a course at the college this January. He will already have college credits when he starts school."

I didn't have to look at Cam to know that I was not supposed to try to one-up Jingle by telling her that Abbey had tested out of a foreign language and out of freshman math and English and therefore had two classes *and* the foreign language requirement completed before she ever started college. I just smiled.

"I worked for the *Birdsey Falls Gazette* when I was in high school, but I just delivered newspapers," John added. "You'll be glad you're working in the office when there's five feet of snow, son. Delivering papers in the snow is the worst ..."

Suddenly it hit me. "Newspaper delivery!" I shouted. "That's it. That's what I was trying to remember. Newspaper delivery!"

After that outburst, and my subsequent apology, the evening dragged on. I wanted talk to Cam about my idea but there wasn't an opportunity. We had coffee and dessert in the library and discussed literature. I can hold my own in a literature discussion but my heart wasn't into it, especially when Jingle and John-Winston started talking about how Harry Potter books should be banned for promoting witchcraft and devil worship. John and Cam did argue on Harry's behalf but Jingle and John-Winston were not to be moved. Harry had to go. Good manners dictated that I not call them ignorant psychos to their faces, so I put in a few good words for Harry and then let it go. My mind was on other things.

It was Sunday night, which meant there was a football game on TV. I lived in fear that the three guys would go off to watch the game and leave me alone with Jingle. Luckily Jingle was quite concerned with getting home at a decent hour because John-Winston had school tomorrow. I couldn't get them out of the house fast enough.

When Cam cooked, I always did cleanup. He usually ended up helping me, though, because he felt guilty for making such a mess. He had problems with the clean-as-you-cook method so the kitchen looked like the aftermath of a very enthusiastic food fight. Cam was chatting about how well the evening had gone and I was compliment-ing him on the meal which had been spectacular, as always. Eventually we had worked our way through the mutual niceties and Cam put down his dish towel and leaned against the counter.

"OK. I can't stand the suspense. What was the newspaper delivery explosion about? I think you scared Jingle to death."

"She's probably never lost her cool like that," I admitted. "I hope you weren't too embarrassed."

"Are you kidding? I sent up a prayer thanking God that I married someone who had some passion, albeit oddly timed. Jingle is a living statue. That woman has always given me the willies …"

"Her? What about John hyphen Winston? What's the deal with him? Now that's a creepy kid. They probably won't let him off the bench to play football because they know he doesn't want to muss his hair …"

"Or they may not be able bring themselves to yell his name to go in. With a name like John-Winston he should be playing in a polo match, not a football game."

"You know, I've never understood how you and John can be such good friends …"

"Are you kidding? John's a great guy …"

"No, I think John's wonderful. What I mean is how can you two be so close, have so much in common, and yet he ends up with such a weird family? He's perfectly normal, endearingly so, and his wife and son are from a parallel universe. Sort of a robot mannequin world."

"It's easy to understand John-Winston. He's a mama's boy, the male version of Jingle. She wanted a daughter and got John-Winston instead, so she lavished all her attention on him and barely let John spend any time with him," Cam explained. "The only influence John had on his son was sports. Luckily the kid loves sports."

"Why did John marry Jingle in the first place? He couldn't possibly sincerely like her, could he?"

"Oh, I think he likes her well enough. He married her for the usual reason ..."

"Jesus, Cam. Don't tell me she's great in bed. I won't believe it unless I witness it myself. Really. I have no shame. I would have to see her in bed with John to be convinced she's a sexpot in the sack."

Cam started laughing and rolling his eyes. An observer might think he was having a seizure but I was used to it.

"What's so funny?"

"You. Well, not you. Jingle," he continued snorting and wiping his eyes. "The image of Jingle as a wanton hussy in the sack. It's too much."

"My thoughts exactly. Isn't that what you meant when you said John married her for the usual reason?"

"Absolutely not! Not *that* usual reason. Not great sex ..."

"Then what?"

"He married her because she had a lot of money. Of all the girls he dated she was not only the best looking but also had a lot of money. He decided in high school that he would marry someone with money and he did. Simple as that. Obviously, I was never supposed to tell anyone that ..."

"Believe me, I won't tell her ..."

"Or any of your friends ..."

"I promise. I can't believe you've never told me this before," I chided. "This is really good gossip."

"It just never came up. We don't all get together that often. I try to spare you Jingle—well me, too—as much as I can."

"Bless you for that." We finished drying the pots and pans, turned on the dishwasher, wadded up the dishcloth and several dish towels Cam had used and threw them down the basement stairs where they landed next to the washing machine. Mission accomplished. There was a little wine left over from dinner that Cam and I split before going into the library to relax with Mycroft in front of the fire.

I snuggled under Cam's arm, sipped my wine and stared at the fire. Total contentment. Cam wiggled his nose in my hair. "Your hair is so soft and smells good."

"Mmm. I washed it."

"You have so many beauty secrets."

"We girls without money have to have something to bargain with," I whispered breathlessly.

"I can't believe you have gone this long without bringing up the reason for your excitement about newspaper delivery."

"I'm glad you noticed. I'm working on my impulse control problem. It's dying to come out, though …"

"I'm dying to hear it."

I twisted around so I could face Cam and smashed his nose against my skull in the process.

"Ouch!"

"Sorry. I didn't know you were still sniffing. OK. Listen to this …"

"My nose hurts …"

"Listen with your ears, then. Yesterday morning I had a flashback to Uncle Franklin and how often, when we walked by the cottage in the morning, he would be in that same position, eating breakfast and reading the newspaper. I got all philosophical about life's simple pleasures and how maybe, deep down, he was fully satisfied with his life blah blah blah ..."

"Aren't I the one who's supposed to say 'blah blah blah' when you're talking?"

"Quiet. Anyway, I had a flash of an idea and then noticed I had that stupid doctor's appointment and had to rush back. The idea was lost until tonight when John was talking about delivering newspapers in the snow ..."

"You know. I think it was that experience as a newspaper delivery boy that first made him decide to marry a rich girl. He never wanted to do physically uncomfortable work again."

"Great. Listen. There's a link between me sitting at my table reading the morning paper and Uncle Franklin sitting at his table reading the morning paper."

"OK. What?"

"Delivery! We each had to get our morning papers some way. A paper boy delivers our paper ..."

"And the same newspaper boy delivers Franklin's paper ..."

"And it's Kaleb Kinney."

"Diane's son."

"Right!" I put my hand up for a high-five and Cam sort of flopped his hand at mine. I frowned at him.

"I'm not sure why we are high-fiving," he started.

"So you can't do a good high five until you know?"

"Right. There has to be some authenticity. What are we celebrating?"

"We keep talking about how Ryan and his friends were the only ones who snuck around and spied on Franklin. They were the only ones who might have seen he had money in his cottage or seen him writing or seen him do whatever it was he did that made someone kill him."

"Ah, we totally forgot about the paper boy. He would have seen Franklin every day." Cam's face lit up with understanding.

"And collected money from him. Maybe he even went into the cottage while Franklin got it. Maybe saw where he kept his money. Don't you see? It's been driving me and Grace and everyone else who knows her crazy that Diane has been cozying up to the policeman …"

"Donny something."

"Right. I bet she wants to be sure to steer him away from Kaleb. What makes me mad is that she may have steered him away from her son at the risk of directing him to Grace's stepson."

"But the bloody shirt. That is much more substantial evidence than the fact Kaleb delivered Franklin's newspaper every day," Cam pointed out. "It makes sense for the police to concentrate their efforts on Ryan rather than Kaleb."

"But it can't hurt to have an attractive woman make sure that every time he considers looking at someone other than Ryan you direct his attention back …"

"… to avoid him looking at another person with the means to get to Franklin. Your own son. That seems so ugly."

"We all protect our own, Cam. We would do the same to protect Abbey."

"You would flirt with the policeman to keep him from suspecting Abbey?"

"I'd do what I needed to do. Flirting wouldn't be my first choice. I know I'm really bad at it. But I would want some way to keep up with how the investigation was going to be sure it wasn't swinging in the direction of my own child. I wouldn't just sit around and hope they bypassed her."

"So, what are you planning to do with this revelation?"

"I need to confront Diane. I need to find out if there is a reason she is afraid for Kaleb. He may know something that will solve this. If Diane keeps protecting him we'll never find out."

"So you don't think Kaleb could have killed Uncle Franklin?" Cam asked.

"I'd be surprised if he did. But someone did it and when we find out who, we may be just as surprised."

Chapter Twenty-Six

"**D**iane has three parent-teacher conferences today, at three separate schools." Scott didn't expect her back until late afternoon. As much as I wanted to confront her about Kaleb and find out if my suspicions about her motive behind romancing Donny-Something were true, I knew I couldn't chase her all over town between meetings and try to get her to tell all. I would have to wait and that's something I'm not very good at.

I called Grace to see if she might be able to go out for coffee or lunch but she was too busy. It was five days until Halloween and the store was packed with people entering the guess-what-costumes-the-mannequins-will-be-wearing contest as well as people wanting Halloween books for the kids or scary books for themselves. I felt too guilty to call Syra because I wasn't sure things were right between us. And I was still thinking she was a good suspect for Franklin's murder, although I had no idea what her motive could be other than protecting Bing from the truth about his mother. If that were the case, now I knew the truth, except for the identities of their fathers. Syra claimed not to know. But did she? What if Syra didn't trust me not to tell Bing what I did know? Would she kill me, too? Maybe that hot chocolate debacle had been a run through and she had yet to make the actual attempt. I didn't want to think she was a killer. I thought she probably wasn't. But I wasn't convinced enough to be alone with her under any circumstance. I desperately wanted to talk this all through with somebody but there wasn't anyone left. Except Claudia and Sybil. Such a bad idea ... And getting Sybil alone without Claudia was impossible. I was on my own.

I had been going through the newspapers again with a legal pad at my side, jotting down anything that might possibly be important. I read through the articles about the kidnapping and the lost money again and became intrigued with how that crime might have been solved if it had happened today rather than in 1938. The police have so many more analytical tools at their disposal now that weren't available then. There is something very seductive about unsolved murders and I made a few notes of how to use a variation of this crime in my New Orleans novel. I got curious about Fletcher Ketchum, the brother who had sworn he had taken the ransom to the assigned drop point. What had happened to him? Obviously he was no longer alive; he would have been over a hundred years old now. Did he push the police to keep investigating his brother's murder? He couldn't have been satisfied with the money disappearing and his brother being murdered. I was eating peanut butter toast and some chips for lunch when Cam called.

"Hey, it's me. What're you doing?"

"Eating lunch. You?"

"Eating lunch."

"In your office?"

"No, I'm at Hurley's. I just gave my order ... thank you ... they just brought my water. Guess what?"

"I'm guessing that someone wasn't thinking when he named his restaurant Hurley's," I replied, turning my head away from the phone as I crunched a handful of chips. No sense opening myself up for a lecture on healthy eating.

"What's that crunching sound?"

"I'm eating an apple," I lied.

"Yeah, right. I bet it's chips."

"Maybe …"

"I wanted to let you know that the police called me back about the money we found at the cottage."

"Who called? Was it that Donny guy?"

"Yes."

"Did you find out his last name?"

"No. He said it but I can't remember. I just remember the Sergeant Donald something or other. Anyway, he told me we could pick up the money any time."

"Great. We'll be rich, unless your mom changes her mind about wanting it." I started to think of things I could buy with $850 wrinkled dollars. Maybe I would need to iron it first. Would that be considered money laundering? I didn't want to do anything illegal.

"I don't think she will. She'd take one look at it and pronounce it too ugly to keep. Anyway, what was interesting was that when they looked through the money, they noted that none of the currency was issued later than 1938. That money has been around for a long time …"

"Like seventy years. My God, you don't think it is part of the money from the Ketchum kidnapping, do you?"

"Ketchum kidnapping? Is that the story from Franklin's old newspapers? Money never found. Guy shot. People keep looking for it in the woods? Ah, that looks good, thank you. My chicken Caesar salad just arrived."

"Yes, that kidnapping …"

"But the ransom was much more than $850 …"

"It was $10,000."

"And Uncle Franklin got it how? He was fifteen when that happened. Are you saying he kidnapped this guy and stole the money and then shot him? If so, Ryan could take some prank lessons from him. This is a great salad. They put some kind of spice on the chicken that really adds to the ..."

"I'm not saying Franklin did all those things but the money could be from the ransom. Can you call Donny back and tell him that theory? See what he says."

"Sure. I'll call him as soon as I get back to the office. Gotta go. Bye."

Talk about food for thought. My head was spinning with possibilities now. I tried to picture a one-hundred-and-five-year-old Fletcher Ketchum coming back to town to kill an eighty-five-year-old Franklin, who had stolen the ransom money and killed his brother seventy years ago. Why wait so long to seek revenge? Could a one-hundred-and-five-year-old man manage to walk through the woods to Franklin's cottage? Not likely. Grace had trouble getting out there without having a heart attack. And if there were a younger generation of Ketchums, wouldn't they just go to the police? Why murder an old man? And why not take their money back? Except maybe they did take back all the money but didn't find the last $850 in the paper bag. I needed to think.

I knew that if I went back to my library, I would be tempted to lie on the couch to think and the innate coziness of the room would put me to sleep. So I opted for the solarium, which was filled with a soft autumn sun and bright fabrics. I filled up the red watering can and wandered from plant to plant, giving everyone a drink and an encouraging word, and thinking about the money.

Franklin was fifteen when the kidnapping and murder took place. He was living with his parents, wealthy people. Why would a fifteen-year-old need $10,000? I think cars only cost around $1,000 back then. Did he want to buy a house? Two houses? In 1938, $10,000 would go a long way. Middle-class families didn't make that much in two or three years. I remembered the first line from the Edgar Allan Poe quote: "there are some secrets which do not permit themselves to be told …" Kidnapping and murder certainly would fall into that category.

Lost in thought, I overwatered my Croton and it began leaking all over the floor. Holding the watering can aloft like a lantern I began scurrying around the room looking for a towel. I headed toward the white wicker love seat in the corner, where a big pile of brightly colored cloths were neatly arranged. Funny. I didn't remember those. I set the can down and reached for one and realized the cloths were actually the quilt I had brought down from the attic a week ago Sunday, the day we had Claudia and Sybil over for paella. I had wanted to show Claudia the quilt that night to see if she remembered it and could tell me where it had come from and whether someone in the family had made it. I had totally forgotten because she and Sybil had started telling us about Fulton Foster and his polio and how he disappeared.

Leaking Croton forgotten, I dusted my hands off on my jeans and picked up the quilt. It didn't seem fragile. I really wanted to open it to see what the pattern was. It must be huge because it was heavy.

I decided I would unfold it and lay it out so I could see the full quilt. I couldn't wait to show Cam. I began to carefully unfold it and gently remove the tissue paper that had been placed between each fold. As I unfolded it I became aware of something solid wrapped in the middle of the quilt. Someone had put a book on the quilt and then folded the quilt around it for safe keeping. I kept unwrapping until it was completely open and then just sat on the floor and stared. The quilt hadn't been wrapped around a book after all. It had been wrapped around several brick-size bundles of money. I started counting and got up to $1,280 and was only part of the way through the first brick. There had to be close to $4,000 here. With the $850 from the cottage we were almost halfway to the $10,000 ransom. This couldn't be a coincidence. Especially since this money looked as old as the other. We apparently had old money hidden all over the place.

I tried calling Cam but got his voice mail. I didn't want to leave a message about the money so I hung up. My adrenaline was pumping now and I couldn't sit still and count money or keep calling, hoping Cam would pick up. I needed some action. The attic. Perfect. I would go back to the attic and start looking for other places where money could be hidden and never discovered for seventy years.

I didn't take all my supplies this time, just a cold can of diet soda and a flashlight. I headed back to the area of Franklin's desk where I had found the disturbing quote and the quilt. This must be the right area of the attic for what I was looking for. I revisited Franklin's desk just in case I missed something. The last time I had been up here I hadn't been sure what I was looking for. This time I was. Money. Old money. Knowing what I was looking for made it easier to hone in on possible hiding places. Once again I skirted the perfect pyramid of rolled-up socks that looked like the stash for an old-fashioned snowball fight. I re-examined the box with the foreign coins. The school papers where I had found the Edgar Allan Poe quote were right where I had left them. I was tempted to go through them page by page to see if there were more quotes or maybe some journal-like entries, but I was too focused on finding the money to settle down to the tedious task of paper shuffling. Later.

I squeezed past the trunks and dressers I had examined before and moved deeper into the clutter. I was looking for bags or boxes or even another quilt. I thought I hit pay dirt when I found a paper bag under one of the windows folded down on the top like the one in Franklin's closet. I pulled it open, not even doing my mouse check routine, but it was full of nothing more than *Collier's* magazines. I shook out a few in case there was money hidden inside but there was nothing there. I found some old board games. Cleaned up, these would look good in the library. When Abbey came home for Thanksgiving it would be fun to get her and her friends involved in trying to play them. There were several decks of playing cards and one very fancy set in a cherry box. Very classy. I wandered into a pile of empty boxes and they came tumbling down on me. For a few moments I leaped around and waved my hands battling cobwebs and imagined insects until both the boxes and I settled down. Diet soda break time.

I pulled one of the many available chairs over to the window, rubbed some of the grime away and looked across our backyard as I sipped my drink. It was amazing how quiet it was up here. I wonder what this house was like when Claudia was a child. I couldn't picture her running and screaming from room to room as Abbey had sometimes done when we played hide and seek. Had Claudia ever screamed or laughed or played hide and seek with her parents or her brothers? It was hard to imagine. I could picture Claudia and Sybil having ladylike tea parties in her bedroom with tiny saucers and cups. Probably real bone china, and fancy dolls that were just for show, perched on little chairs around them.

I started laughing to myself, remembering my mother warning me to stop sitting around daydreaming, "collecting cob webs" she called it. Well, I was certainly doing that now, sitting and thinking and literally collecting cobwebs. Maybe she had foreseen this moment in my life.

I decided that in addition to bringing the fancy playing cards and cherry box down with me, I'd bring a couple issues of the *Collier's* and a couple pair of socks just to show Hugh. If they had any value he might want them in his antiques shop. If not, maybe there was someone on eBay who collected such things. On eBay you could find a collector for everything. Probably even these cobwebs. I reached into the bag and pulled out a few *Collier's* and then picked up a couple pair of socks, being careful not to destroy the carefully built pyramid. As I clutched the socks I noticed they made an odd crackling sound. I immediately dropped them on the floor, imagining a fifteen year-old Franklin finding dead mice in the attic and wrapping them up in his old socks, then building them a pyramid like the ancient Egyptians. Mummy mice. That's what all these socks were. Mummy mice built into an eternal pyramid. And I was the grave robber.

I tentatively picked up another sock ball and squeezed it. Crackling. I was literally cracking mice skeletons in my hand. I backed away from the mummy mice pyramid and retreated to the chair by the window. And stared at the pile. Then I stared at the socks on the floor I had removed from the pile. Then back at the pile again. This wasn't accomplishing anything but I needed time to build up my courage to actually open one of those socks. Since right now I didn't dare to even touch them, this was going to be a problem.

What could a mouse skeleton do to me, anyway? If the mice had been dead for seventy years all the ugly parts were long gone. I suppose there might be some fur left. I didn't know how long that took to decompose. But muscles and liquids and anything else squishy would be long gone. I reached for my cell phone to call Cam to ask him how long it took a mouse to decompose in a sock and realized I left it in the solarium. Damn. I should carry that thing around my neck like people do with their reading glasses.

Back to staring at the sock pyramid. I would pretend I was in a game show and I would win a million dollars if I opened a sock and found a mouse skeleton inside. All I had to do was pull the sock open, drop it and run. Not happening. I could hear Cam yelling at me from the audience to do it, to win the million dollars. We could go on an extended European vacation or take a round-the-world cruise. Do it!

Nope. Can't do it. Sorry. Money was a no-go as a lure. There had to be something else. Now the game show host was telling me that Abbey was being kept in a secret room in the studio, tied to a chair that was timed to drop through the floor into a flaming inferno in thirty seconds if I didn't open one of the sock mummies in time. 30, 29, 28, 27, 26, 25, 24, 23 …

Screaming like my hair was on fire I leaped out of the chair and lunged across the room. I grabbed first one sock mummy and then another, pulling them apart and throwing them on the floor until at least a dozen white cotton coffins lay scattered. I looked at my hands in distaste and rubbed them furiously on my jeans. Yuck. A million times yuck. But Abbey was saved!

Suddenly I heard my mother's voice explaining to a neighbor who had been worried that I'd be bored because I had to take a two-day car ride to visit relatives in the Midwest. "You don't ever have to worry about Tamsen. She knows how to entertain herself." I believe I had just become the poster girl for that phrase.

I was about to retreat to my window chair to calm down from my ordeal when I noticed that among the scattered socks on the floor were twenty-dollar bills and not mouse skeletons. I bent over and started picking them up, smoothing out the socks and reaching inside, pulling out more money. I moved over to the now lopsided sock pyramid and began methodically removing the socks and opening them up. How easy this was now whereas five minutes ago I had been terrified—of nothing. It was a parable for life itself. There were a lot of socks here and a lot of money accumulating. First the quilt and now the socks. I was a money magnet today.

Like the brown bag of money, this too was old and wrinkled. I had ripped a few of the twenties during my frenetic display of sock opening while enmeshed in my dramatic thirty-second countdown to save Abbey's life. Once every sock had been opened and thoroughly searched, I had a messy pile of about $2,000. That was twenty-five socks each with four twenty dollar bills wrapped inside. That meant there was a little over $3,000 left to find if we were really dealing with the Ketchum ransom. I had a feeling it must be hidden in the attic somewhere. I was thinking about how the sock pile not only resembled a pyramid but also the head of an arrow. I walked around the destroyed pile and tried to see if the arrow indicated another viable hiding place for money. For instance, if I stood with my back to the window, as far back from the old sock pile as I could get to maintain some perspective, the top of the sock pile would have been pointing across the room to an old metal file cabinet. Good option.

I couldn't imagine where the ugly file cabinet had originally come from. It didn't seem like anything anyone would want in the main part of the house and if it had once been in an office somewhere, why would someone have brought it to the attic? Why not discard it at the office? I gave the drawer a tug but it didn't open. The bottom one was tightly closed, too. Either it was locked or severely stuck. I looked around for something to use to pry it open and remembered that in the room across the hall there had been some tools. I was shifting the rusty old tools around, pulling out a few that might work on beating the cabinet into submission, when I heard the sound of a door closing. It must be true that time flies when you're having fun, or traumatizing yourself, because I could have sworn it was only mid-afternoon. Way too early for Cam to be home. I went over to the window that faced the front of the house and looked out. The driveway was empty. Odd. I checked my watch and saw that it was indeed mid-afternoon: 3:20. Way too early for Cam. So who was in the house?

I walked back to the attic door and opened it quietly. I didn't dare yell down because I didn't want to alert anyone to my whereabouts. If someone wanted to play hide and seek with me in this monstrosity of a house, they had their work cut out for them. I moved slowly down the attic stairs and opened the door that led to the third floor. Everything was silent. I started to relax, assuming I had imagined the sound of a door, when it happened. Something crashed to the floor, probably in the kitchen. This was followed by another crash, then another. My body went into flee response and I headed back to the attic stairs as fast as I could move and still try not to make any noise. The violence of the shattering glass scared me and I was in no mood to confront whoever was down there throwing or dropping things on the floor. There are no locks on the attic doors but I had plenty of chairs to shove under doorknobs. Still trying to be as quiet as possible, I pushed a chair under the knob of the attic door and gave it a good shove. God, I wish I had my cell phone.

There are a lot of rooms in the attic and a lot of doors. I tiptoed through the attic, closing every single door so if someone did make it up here, they would have a lot of places to look to try to find me. I remember hearing that most burglars try to avoid confrontation and aren't really anxious to encounter anyone during the course of their work. If that were true I was making it easy for them to avoid confrontation because I was going to be difficult to find. What frightened me was the breaking glass. It sounded like someone was angry, vengeful. Unless this was the world's clumsiest burglar, this intrusion felt personal. And I was the only other person here.

I began to collect some weapons as I moved further back into the attic. I remember Diane saying once that she didn't think she could hurt another person even if her life were threatened. I would prefer to avoid the intimacy of having to strangle someone but I knew I could swing a hammer at their head if they threatened me. I'm thinking this may not be a very flattering confession, but it's honest. If someone threatened Abbey or Cam I'm sure I could tear them apart with my bare hands. Bare hands conflict was less efficient, so I carried the old hammer and a baseball bat back to where the sock pile and money had been. Somehow it felt comforting, like home. I had been brave in this room.

Whatever the intruder was after, I'm sure they would be happily distracted by the money spread out all over the solarium floor. Maybe they would be satisfied with that and hurry away. I dreaded the idea of them coming through the house, room by room, and hearing them getting closer and closer like I was in a slasher movie.

I laid down on the floor of the attic to see if I could see through the cracks in the floor to the third floor. Nothing. I pivoted around and tried a few more places. Nothing. This was a well-built house. I knew I should sit still to avoid making any creaks or thumps that would alert someone that I was up here. Better that they think they were in the house all alone. I shouldn't ruin their illusion of privacy by moving around and risking a noise. But it was impossible to just sit here and wait. I looked at my watch. 3:43. Time moves slowly when your life is in danger.

I wish I hadn't retreated so soon. I should have stood on the third floor and listened longer. I needed to know what was happening. But I was too afraid to go back out of the attic and check. I started worrying about Mycroft. He wasn't a threat but what if the burglar didn't know that? Would he harm him, thinking he was a watch dog? If so, then it was already done. I prayed that Mycroft continued to slumber in the library and the burglar never saw him.

The attic was gloomy and I didn't dare turn on the flashlight. I didn't want a telltale sliver of light slipping out under the attic door. I sat counting my breaths and listening to my heart beat. It was so quiet. Even if he were in the basement, I felt sure the burglar could still hear my heart beating. It was in my chest, in my ears, in my throat. I was almost wishing for a confrontation, something to end this silent wait-ing, when I heard a scream and a crash and more screaming. There was pounding. Some animal howled. I was sure it wasn't Mycroft. There was more than one person in the house and some kind of creature. My God, what was going on?

I ran to the window, disregarding my plan to tiptoe everywhere. I needed to see something, to know what all this noise was. I pressed myself to the dirty window and stared out at the backyard, trying to find some evidence of what had come into my house. I didn't see anything. I ran across the hall to the opposite window and looked out at the front of the house. Nothing. If only there were a neighbor nearby or someone walking down the street. I wanted to throw all caution to the wind and hang out the window and call for help. I tugged at the window but it was stuck shut. I could break it but it would make too much noise.

And what about Cam? I had to warn him. I couldn't let him come home and into the house when whatever was rampaging down there was still there. I decided to stay in this room where I could see the front of the house and, when Cam drove up, I would break the window and warn him not to come in. Knowing us, a five-minute conversation would ensue discussing the issue. Only in movies did the people actually run when you warned them to run. In my world, you talked about it for a while.

Now it was quiet again. I felt like I was buried alive. I wanted to scratch at the window until my fingers bled. I had to get out of here. I felt the tears running down my cheeks, although I hadn't realized I was crying. I lowered myself to the floor and sat with my arms wrapped around me, making myself as small as possible in this big, cluttered room.

Then I heard it again—smashing, howling and screaming. It was horrible and terrifying and I burst into tears, burying my face in my knees and wrapping my arms over my head as if warding off blows. *Please make it stop.* And it did. I was enveloped in total silence and my sobs sounded loud and primitive, as scary as the howling and screaming downstairs. I put my hand over my mouth to muffle them.

Then the banging started. On the walls, on the ceiling. I could hear them coming up the stairs. It was a muffled pounding, not the sharp crack of wood on wood but more like the sound a human body would make if they were being thrown against the wall. I moved to the door of the room and shoved a chair under the doorknob. I gathered my bat and my hammer and moved away from the window to behind the door. If someone broke in I would hit them as they came through the door. If there were more than one person I wasn't sure what I would do but I planned to do some damage. They would not find me cowering on the floor in tears. Then it stopped. The total silence was back. But this time I knew they were closer. They were on the third floor.

I looked around the room to see what else I could use to protect myself. There was a battered desk next to the door and, not caring about the noise, I dragged it to the door to reinforce the chair. The desk was high and just fit over the door knob. If I leaned against the desk when they tried to get into the room I might be able to keep them out. Of course if they came at me like Jack Nicholson in *The Shining*, I would be in trouble. This door was no match for an ax. But the chair and the desk might give me enough extra weight if it came to a pushing contest. I started to giggle frantically as I imagined that the door opened outward and I had barricaded myself like this only to have the burglar walk up and open the door and stare at me. There was a box of books on the floor so I huffed and puffed and picked them up to put on the desk to add weight. I felt something painful pull on my left side. More. I needed more books. I wasn't going to feel safe until everything in this room was piled up against that door. I tried to lift another box of books and the pain shot through my left side, sharper than before.

Rubbing at my side I walked back to the window, hoping to see a band of burglars and several wild creatures retreating from the house. Nothing. Luckily no Cam, either. Not knowing what was going on, who was here, what the noises were or what the intent was, was making me insane. I would rather be standing on the landing seeing someone I recognized coming up the stairs with a gun pointed at me, explaining all the way why they were here and what they planned to do to me. Then I would run and hide in the attic. 3:57.

I was so barricaded in that it was impossible for me to work my way out of the room and try to see what was going on, even if I dared to do so. I could never hurry back and reconstruct my fort in time if the intruder saw me. Maybe I could get out on the roof. I made sure my barricade was sturdy and walked over to the window to check out the lay of the roof. What I saw out the window stopped me in my tracks.

Cam's car was turning into the driveway. 4:02. Then I remembered that he had a dentist appointment this afternoon at 2:30 and planned to come home afterward. Of all the days. I didn't have much time. I had to warn him. I frantically looked around the room for something to break the window. Why hadn't I done this earlier? I thought I had plenty of time. Now I had seconds. I grabbed the hammer, pulled my t-shirt off and wrapped it around my face to protect my eyes and started slamming the hammer against the glass, one pane after another. I could feel shards of glass sting my chest and tear at my hands but I didn't care. I just kept slamming the hammer against the glass until there was nothing left to break. I pulled the t-shirt away from my face and leaned toward the window screaming Cam's name.

Cam stood in the driveway staring up at the window with a glazed expression on his face.

"Cam! Run away! There's someone in the house. Don't come in. Don't come in," I screamed, waving my arms.

Cam remained frozen in place and continued to stare.

"Run away! Stranger danger! Stranger danger!"

Cam moved back toward the car, looking around and then back at the attic window. "Are you hurt?" he yelled. "Is there someone in the attic with you? Are you OK?"

"I'm fine. I'm locked in. I don't know who it is. Don't come in!" I screamed back. Cam nodded a dozen times and got back in the car. I couldn't see what he was doing but he didn't leave. I wanted him to drive away and be safe but he didn't leave. He just sat in the car. He didn't even have the motor running so he could make a fast escape if the lunatics and wild creatures came running out the front door. Why didn't he leave? I couldn't communicate with him now because he wouldn't have been able to hear me. I would just stand here at the window and make sure he was safe. That's all I could do.

I shook my t-shirt trying to get rid of all the glass and gingerly put it back on, realizing, like slow torture, that there was still glass in the shirt and it was making contact with my skin each time I moved my shirt. I had the shirt halfway on and was about to pull it back off again when I heard the sound of sirens. I yanked my arms into the shirt, scratching my skin from wrist to shoulder and looked out the window as two police cars came into the driveway. Cam leaped out of the car and said something to the first policeman, who motioned him to get back in his car and headed toward the house. A second followed. The other car spilled out two more policemen, who separated and went around the house. I waited.

After a few minutes Cam got out of the car and came across the yard to stand under the window.

"Get back in the car!" I yelled. "It might be dangerous out there."

"Are you all right? Did they hurt you?"

"No. I never even saw them. Just heard them smashing things in the kitchen and coming up the stairs. They didn't hurt me."

"Are you sure?"

"Yes. Yes, I'm fine. Please get back in the car. Please."

Cam hesitated and then returned to the car. I continued to wait. Then I heard a pounding on the attic door.

"Mrs. Mack. It's Officer Donaldson. Let me in." I started to undo my barricade. I had a hard time pushing the desk out of the way because my left side still hurt so I backed into it and shoved it with my butt until I could reach the chair. I yanked it out from under the doorknob, all the while yelling, "I'm coming" so the policeman wouldn't leave. I could hear him knocking at the attic door and calling my name and I continued yelling that I was coming as I emerged from my fort and began to make my way through the attic to the door.

"Mrs. Mack. It's Officer Donaldson. Are you all right? Let me in."

"I'm coming! I'm coming ..."

"Mrs. Mack ..."

"Officer Donaldson ..."

Our voices got louder and louder as I got to the attic door. I frantically tugged and kicked and pushed at the chair under the knob until it came free. The door burst open and I ran into the arms of Officer Donaldson and held on to him for dear life.

Chapter Twenty-Seven

O fficer Donny couldn't peel me off him so he offered to carry me downstairs. That seemed like heaven to me until I remembered that I wasn't the slender young girl I had been when I first came to this house, and politely demurred. I was a little shaky on my feet so Officer Donny held onto my elbow as I went very slowly down three flights of stairs, explaining to him how I was fifteen pounds overweight, which wasn't obese by anyone's standards, even the government chart that they kept in the doctor's office. I told him how much I had weighed when Cam and I were married and how much I gained during my pregnancy. I told him how a woman's weight is redistributed after giving birth and how much easier it is to gain weight during perimenopause, which, in case he didn't know, was the actual name for the period of time, no pun intended, when women went from having regular periods to ceasing to menstruate altogether. By the time we got to the first floor I was feeling more like myself but Officer Donny didn't look so well.

Cam came bursting through the front door and literally swept me off my feet. He was actually crying, which made me start crying and made Officer Donny leave the room. We held each other and cried for several minutes until two women came up to me and explained they were EMTs and needed to check me out. Cam held my hand as we sat in the rarely used living room and they examined my cuts, applying some antibiotic and, in a few cases, a small bandage. They determined that the pain in my side was nothing more serious than a pulled muscle. A police officer stood in the corner of the room, his back to me, apparently waiting to see if I would say anything more enlightening than "ouch", and "oh, that stings". He was disappointed. Cam reluctantly left my side to go upstairs and get me a clean t-shirt and a sweater. The EMTs suggested that I go to the hospital but I didn't think it was really necessary and apparently they didn't either, because they let it drop without an argument. When they left, Officer Donny came into the living room and asked Cam and me to follow him to the kitchen. Suddenly I remembered.

"Mycroft! Oh Cam, did they do anything to Mycroft?"

Cam held me and grinned. "Not unless they gave him a sleeping pill. He's still snoozing in the library ..."

"Are you sure he's alive?"

"Yes. He gave me a signature toot when I went in to check on him. He's very much alive, although something in his intestines definitely isn't." We both laughed, feeling a little giddy and lighthearted until we came to the kitchen door.

Broken dishes and glasses were everywhere—on the floor, on the counters, on the table and in the sink. I didn't even realize how many dishes we had until I saw them smashed on every surface of the room. I looked at the different colored shards and mourned for the new Fiesta Ware dishes Cam and Abbey had gotten me for my birthday. I love those dishes. I started to cry.

"Abbey and I will get more Fiesta Ware. Don't worry. We can fix all this."

I sniffed and held his hand. "It was a gift from you and Abbey. It's so special ..."

"I know, sweetheart. It will still be special. Abbey and I will fix it and we'll ..."

Officer Donny's partner interrupted. "I don't know much about that fiesta stuff but I'd feel worse about the souvenir dishes. Those are more difficult to replace." Cam and Officer Donny gave him a dirty look.

"This is Officer Lumb ..." Officer Donny began. Officer Lumb continued.

"I mean regular dishes you can get in the store but you'd have to go all the way back to Bucky's Bait Shop to get another dish like that. That's awesome how they printed the name of the shop with actual worms. Where is that place, anyway? You guys do a lot of fishing?" Cam and I stared at the mess in the kitchen and Officer Donny stared at us as Officer Lumb continued.

"Look at this ashtray. It looks like someone's butt. I get it. You put your butts out in the butt. Ha! You folks had a lot of great stuff. Look here, a Betty Boop platter. Only it says Betty Boob and she's naked. Nice. You know, you could easily put that back together. It's only in two pieces ..."

Cam and I continued to stare, looking now at individual shards instead of the overall mess.

"It's not our stuff," Cam said tentatively, looking at me. "It's not our stuff, is it?"

"I'm not sure. I mean some of it definitely isn't ours, like all the things Officer Lumb is admiring. Definitely not ours ..."

"And I don't see Fiesta Ware. Those colored dishes aren't Fiesta Ware. Wrong colors ..."

"And they're too fragile. Fiesta Ware is sturdy. Look at that horrible yellow pile of dishes by the sink. Those aren't ours ..."

"And we don't have dachshund dishes. I see lots of pieces of dachshund dishes all over the place!" Cam started pointing and turning me around to look at various odd pieces he didn't recognize. "Those big flower dishes aren't ours. They're ugly. We wouldn't buy something like that ..."

"Excuse me," Officer Donny interrupted. "Do you see anything in this mess that *is* yours? Something that came out of your cupboards? Can you identify anything?"

"No."

Cam and I were told to wait in the library. There were still two officers traipsing around on the second floor looking for signs of disturbance and Officer Donny and his partner were checking doors and windows on the first floor. I curled up under the corduroy throw on the couch and absentmindedly stroke Mycroft's head, which was resting on my knee. Cam got called out a couple of times to look at something and the second time he returned with a diet soda, a pack of lemon wafers, and two aspirin. It was past our usual dinner time so I was starving, not being one of those people for whom stress reduces the appetite.

I was starting to doze when I heard someone arguing in the front hall. I perked up and listened and received what I hoped would be my final shock of the day. Cam was scolding his mother! I wrapped the throw around me and opened the library door so I could hear better.

"... won't have her upset, Mom. She's been through a terrible ordeal so either you are at your most sympathetic or you will just have to leave ..."

"You already said that, Christian, and I don't appreciate your tone ..."

"You know how you are with her, baiting and making jabs ..."

"I most certainly am not. Really, Christian. I realize you are upset but don't take it out on me ..."

"Just be nice to her ..."

"I'm always nice ..."

"No you aren't ..."

This was doing more for my recovery than the combination of diet soda, lemon wafers and aspirin. Unfortunately, all good things have to come to an end and I heard Sybil intercede. Spoil sport.

"All right. We get the point, Cam. Don't badger your poor mother. She is just as upset as you are …"

"Well, I …"

"Now don't interrupt, young man. Your mother came as soon as she heard …"

"How did you hear?"

"I have a police scanner," Sybil replied. I wasn't surprised to hear it. "We would have been here sooner but Claudia was in the Ashland Belle beauty parlor …"

"It takes weeks to get an appointment there," Claudia interjected to show how serious the appointment was.

"… and we couldn't just run right out the door while her hair was still being worked on."

"But you must have heard it on the police scanner more than an hour ago," Cam protested. I wasn't sure why. It's not like we were upset that they took so long to arrive. We would rather they didn't come at all.

"Exactly. It takes several hours to get your hair done, dear. As Sybil said, we rushed over as soon as we heard," Claudia explained.

"It's a good thing the house wasn't on fire," Cam commented.

"I quite agree, dear. A robbery is so much better. Now where is Tamsen?"

I scuttled back to my place on the couch and reached for Mycroft for support. If Cam hadn't been here, I would have fled back to the attic.

The two septuagenarians sailed in. They both came over and kissed my cheeks, mingling Chanel No. 5 and Evening in Paris in my face. I coughed for a good minute until the battling scents dissipated. Mycroft continued to sniff and eye the newcomers suspiciously. Sybil made soothing comments and Claudia looked around the room trying to find something out of place that she could draw to my attention. Cam came in followed by the two police officers, and introductions were made. Cam brought coffee. To his credit, Cam ignored his mother when she asked for tea. I don't think I'd ever seen him be rude to her before. I was thoroughly enjoying it.

Officer Donny asked me to once again go over what had happened that afternoon. When I got to the part about opening the quilt and discovering the bricks of cash, Claudia had to actually put her hand over her mouth to keep from saying something. I toned down the drama that led up to the discovery of the money in the socks but by now Claudia was as wide eyed as a Margaret Keane print and Sybil had gone pale under her layers of makeup. Cam grabbed my hand when I got to the part about the intruder and how scared I was. Claudia nodded in approval at my risking the discovery of my hiding place and my life to warn Cam. All round, the story was well received and I settled back into the couch and pulled my corduroy throw closer around me, spent from recounting the most frightening day of my life.

Officer Donny flipped his notebook back a few pages and scratched at his chin with his uncapped pen, leaving blue squiggles on his face. We all pretended not to notice.

"In summary, this is what we have. A person walks up to your house carrying what must have been a garbage bag full of dishes. He unlocks your front door and drags the bag in, goes into the kitchen, opens his bag and begins smashing things on the floor and against the walls.

"What about the screams?" I asked. I knew there had to be several people and at least one wild creature in the house.

Officer Donny held up his finger.

"Boom box. While he was taking his time smashing things in the kitchen he entertained himself by playing a Halloween CD on his boom box ..."

"... a what on his what?" Claudia interrupted. Officer Donny's finger went up again. Claudia gave him a withering stare. No one gave Claudia the finger, regardless of which one it was.

"... which was filled with screaming and banging and howling noises. Then," Officer Donny held up both hands to stop all the questions from his audience, "... let me finish. Then he heads up the stairs to the second and third floors, banging on the walls with his fists and on the ceiling with a broom, getting closer and closer to the attic door but never opening it. Then he exits out the back door, dropping his boom box behind a hedge, leaving both the front and back doors unlocked and dripping blood on some of the broken dishes ..."

"So you have clues?" Cam interjected.

"Clues? We have fingerprints all over the front and back doors, we have fingerprints on the broken dishes, we have blood, we have the boom box and the CD, all covered with finger prints. We have everything except a calling card."

"What made him leave?" I asked.

"Probably the sound of you breaking the attic window and yelling to your husband," Officer Donny replied.

"But what was the point of all this?" Sybil asked. "It seems crazy."

"Well, ma'am, when you are trying to discover the point of something you need to go right to the end result. What was accomplished?"

"I was scared out of my mind!" I yelled.

Officer Donny nodded his head. "Then most likely, that was the point."

"To scare Tamsen? Why?" Cam grabbed my hand again and began stroking it so vigorously he was exfoliating my skin. I pulled my hand away and patted his leg.

"That makes no sense," Sybil chimed in.

"Do you think it has to do with my brother's murder?"

We all looked at Claudia and then to Officer Donny for enlightenment.

"I don't know. Can you think of some reason it would?" he answered. We all shook our heads slowly. Nothing made sense.

***

Even in a small town, without the benefits of expensive equipment and sophisticated crime scene teams, it doesn't take long to catch a burglar who leaves behind his fingerprints, his blood, and his boom box. Especially when you know he didn't break in but had a key, and when his fingerprints are already on file with the police. Ryan Kelly was arrested before we had gone to bed that night. Officer Donny came calling around ten o'clock that evening to tell us Ryan had confessed to the whole thing. I served decaf coffee in my bathrobe while Cam and I sat on the couch listening to what Officer Donny had to say.

"We brought him into the station a couple hours after we left your house. His parents were with him. He didn't even try to lie about it." He took a sip of his coffee and put the cup down on the table. Mycroft had taken a liking to him so he had his head rested on his knee, and Officer Donny must have been a dog man because he knew just how to scratch his ears to make Mycroft happy. Maybe even in love.

"But why did he do it? And why the odd dishes?" Cam asked. He had been in his pajamas when Officer Donny had arrived but changed into jeans and a t-shirt. I guess men don't sit and chat when one is in his jammies and the other in uniform.

"I've spent hours talking to this kid and I don't think he is really such a bad sort. You can usually tell, even when they're fifteen. Some kids are hardcore nasty at that age and there isn't much you can do. But the majority of them can be put on the right path if they have some help. Kelly is definitely one of those. At least in my opinion."

"Okay. But then why did he terrorize Tamsen like that?" Cam asked.

"First of all, he confessed right away. He knew it was wrong and I believe he was sincerely sorry. He wanted revenge against Mrs. Mack, because he felt it was her fault the bloody shirt had made him a murder suspect."

"But his father would have made him turn himself in, anyway. I wasn't the one to ask that he be questioned," I protested.

"Regardless, he blames you for all his troubles. He was already having problems fitting in at school and the bloody shirt incident didn't help. He knew he had disappointed his father. He needed to lash out. You were his target."

Cam shook his head. "My wife was terrified and was cut by glass trying to warn me. Right now I don't have much pity for the kid."

"I understand. But listen to how this thing went down. The kid uses a spare key that he swipes from his mother so he doesn't have to actually break in. Then, he brings a bunch of dishes he bought at a thrift store rather than smash your actual dishes. He doesn't want to damage your house by breaking in. He doesn't want to damage your dishes by throwing them on the floor ..."

"But he doesn't mind terrorizing my wife. We would gladly substitute the loss of our dishes and the damage to our house if he had just done this prank when she wasn't home. He didn't seem too worried about the damage to her state of mind."

"Look, I'm not trying to make excuses for what he did or say it doesn't matter because there was no physical damage to your belongings. It's just that the way his mind was working makes me think he isn't all bad."

"We don't want him sent to prison or anything," I interjected. After all, this was my best friend's stepson. "But he obviously has some issues, some problems that need attention."

"His parents agree. They were fine with him spending the night in the jail. He's the only prisoner so that shouldn't be too traumatic. Tomorrow we'll need to discuss charges. He's a juvenile so that will make things easier on him. Take tonight and think about how you would like to handle this. Your opinions will be important with the judge."

We sat silently while Officer Donny flipped back through his notebook and took another sip of coffee. "If it's not too late for you folks, I'd like to discuss the money you've been finding." The police had taken away the money from the quilt and the socks when they had left. "The money you found today is the same age as the money from the paper bag, none issued later than 1938. Although it's impossible to know for sure, I think it's safe to say it is part of the ransom money from the Raymond Ketchum kidnapping and murder. Do you know why your uncle would have some of the ransom money?"

Cam shook his head. "Uncle Franklin was fifteen when that happened ..."

"Ryan Kelly is fifteen, Mr. Mack. Look at the mischief he's gotten into."

"That's a far cry from what you are accusing Uncle Franklin of ..."

"I'm not accusing your uncle of anything, Mr. Mack. I'm asking why he might have had the ransom money. Any thoughts?"

"No. It's ridiculous to think of him kidnapping this man and then shooting him in cold blood. He was fifteen!" Cam held up his hand. "Don't tell me all the horrible things fifteen-year-old kids have done. I know. I read the papers. But Franklin wasn't some desperate kid running wild in some gang. He hadn't been exposed to criminal activity.

He wasn't fighting to survive in an adult world. He didn't need the money."

"Ten thousand dollars was a great deal of money in 1938 ..."

"But he didn't need it. Don't you see? His upbringing, his station in life, was such that this type of behavior, this criminal behavior wouldn't be a lure for him," Cam argued. "He had no reason to have done this horrible thing. And how would he have done it? He wasn't criminally sophisticated. This crime is way beyond the nature of a teenage prank." Cam threw up his hands in exasperation. "It really makes no sense. There has to be another explanation."

"You know, something happened in Franklin's life when he was fifteen that put everything off course," I reminded him. "I don't believe he was a murderer but some kind of involvement in this crime would account for why he suddenly changed. It doesn't seem like a mere coincidence that this kidnapping happened around the same time Franklin withdrew from society. Plus there is the money ..." I felt like I was being disloyal to Cam but I couldn't ignore such a strong coincidence.

Cam slumped in his chair and buried his head in his hands. "I just can't believe Uncle Franklin would do something like this. There has to be another explanation."

"What happened to the victim's brother?" I asked Officer Donny.

"Dr. Fletcher Ketchum died about thirty years ago. According to the old police reports, he never changed his story regarding the delivery of the money to the exact ransom drop location. He swore he took it there at the exact time and to the exact place the kidnappers demanded."

"Yet they still killed his brother." Cam shook his head.

"Clean shot to the head," Officer Donny needlessly added.

"There must have been someone else who knew about the ransom drop," I mused.

"Yes, apparently your uncle. He's the one who ended up with the money."

"But how? How would he know? Did he even know the Ketchums?" Cam asked.

"According to the old police report, the Behrends family claimed they didn't know the Ketchums. All the neighbors in this area were questioned, as the murder took place across the street in the woods. No one heard the shot. No one in this neighborhood knew the Ketchums."

"Was Franklin questioned?" I asked.

"No. Only his parents. Other than hoping someone heard the shot or saw someone in that area of the woods, I doubt the police felt there was much information to pick up from the wealthy residents of this neighborhood. The questioning looks pretty superficial." Officer Donny looked up from his notes. "With your permission, we would like to search your attic for the rest of the money and the murder weapon."

Cam stared at him in disbelief. "And without our permission you will get a search warrant and do it anyway, right?"

"Yes."

"Then you have my permission. That attic is huge ..."

"Perhaps Mrs. Mack can show us the area where she found the quilt and the socks. We'll start from there and branch out."

"You can use my map," I offered.

Chapter Twenty Eight

The police found the remainder of the money in the attic, rolled up in empty tennis ball containers. We had the $850 found in the bag in Franklin's cottage, $4,000 found in the quilt, $2,000 found in the socks and $3,150 found in the tennis containers. Total: $10,000, the exact amount of the ransom. I had fallen asleep on the couch in the library but woke up when I heard Cam letting the police out the front door. He was arguing that Uncle Franklin would not murder someone for the ransom and then never use a penny of it.

Cam offered to carry me up to bed but we both knew it was an empty gesture. I dragged myself upstairs, threw my bathrobe on the floor and hopped into bed without washing my face or brushing my teeth.

As so often happens when you fall into bed utterly exhausted, I couldn't sleep. Cam was holding me so tightly that I also couldn't breathe so had to wiggle out of his grasp to gasp for air. I remember holding Abbey the same way and her hearing her little voice plead, "Mommy, you're snufficating me." It felt good to be "snufficated" with love but, being human, I did eventually have to take a breath.

"Do you think it's possible that all those kids in the picture had something to do with the kidnapping?" I asked as I readjusted myself on Cam's chest and gave him a hug.

"My mom and Sybil were six ..." he protested.

"I know. Not them. The three older kids—Franklin, Edmund and Hetty. Do you think they were involved somehow?"

"It's hard to believe. How is your side? Does it still hurt?"

"A little. The aspirin helped, though."

"How about all the cuts?"

"They're stingy but fine."

"You should go to the doctor tomorrow."

"We'll see." We both knew that meant I wouldn't go. "How do you think Franklin got the money without being involved?"

"No idea. But there has to be another explanation. I think we can be pretty sure that he knew where the money came from."

I raised my head to look at him. That really hurt my left side so I lay back down with a thump on his chest. "You mean because of the collection of newspapers?"

"Right. Whether he kidnapped anyone or not, he had to have known where the money came from. He collected all the newspapers for every year after that, over seventy years. I think that proves he knew the story, was watching to see how it developed and then kept track of it for the rest of his life."

"Guilt?"

"Maybe. Or curiosity. Or fear that someone would reopen the case and look for the money. The story was mentioned in each April 1 edition and summarized so everyone knew how the case stood. He would have known if the police were out searching again for the money or the killer. My arm is getting numb."

I shifted over to my side of the bed so Cam could stretch and shake his arm back to life. "Do you think your mom or Sybil know anything? They're the only ones left to ask. Franklin, Hetty and Edmund are all dead."

"No. My mom never even read a newspaper until she married my dad. Her father didn't think she should be exposed to all the nastiness going on outside the sanctuary of their home. I imagine Sybil was brought up the same way."

"The police will probably question your mother ..."

"I wish them luck."

"Yeah, they'll have to fight their way past Sybil to get to her."

"Not worth the effort. She won't know anything. Although I can't think of what anyone was hoping to accomplish, this money and this kidnapping and murder are the only motives that have come up for Franklin's death." Cam reached out for my hand and pulled it to his chest. "I was so afraid for you tonight ..."

"Me, too. I was ready to drop a brick on the head of anyone who tried to hurt you."

"It's scary to think we have these violent emotions inside us. Humans can be unpredictable when they're protecting the ones they love."

"I was willing to unwrap mouse mummies to save Abbey."

"Huh?"

"Never mind." I reached back and fluffed up my pillows. Cam laid his arm across my stomach. "Why would someone kill Franklin now, after all these years, if it was about the money and the kidnapping?"

"Maybe he stirred up the pot somehow. Made someone nervous."

"How? He didn't talk to anyone or go anywhere."

"That we know of. He may have talked to people. Who knows what he was doing all day," Cam pointed out.

"Maybe he knew who the Ketchum killer was and threatened to expose him."

"After seventy years? And if we don't think Franklin could have been the killer because he was only fifteen then, how old could the killer have been and still be alive now?"

"I suppose if I were a hundred and someone threatened to expose me for a murder I committed seventy years ago, I wouldn't care at this point …"

"Certainly not enough to hike out to the cottage and stab someone."

"But what about a relative, someone younger. Someone out for revenge or for the money? That could happen," I suggested, moving Cam's arm. "Too hot."

"Sorry. The police have been checking into all that and haven't found anyone."

"Maybe it's someone obscure, like the victim's grandson's ex-wife's ex-con cousin."

"That's certainly obscure enough. Officer Donny said they had reopened the Ketchum case. With the technology they have now they can recheck the ropes, the bullet and other forensic clues, run them through a database of known criminals and old cases to see if they get any matches."

"I don't think that will tell us who killed Franklin …"

"If they know who killed Ketchum they may be able to find his grandson's ex-wife's ex-con cousin. And that might be Franklin's killer."

"I just want it all over before Abbey and her friends come home for Thanksgiving," I sighed. Cam took so long to reply that I thought he had fallen asleep. I closed my eyes and pulled the blankets up around my neck. I felt Cam kiss my cheek and whisper in my ear, "It will be."

***

It was Tuesday again. I ate my breakfast that morning wondering if I should cancel WOACA that afternoon. I didn't feel great but mostly I didn't want to embarrass Grace. Everyone would know Ryan had been arrested for terrorizing me and smashing thrift store dishes all over my kitchen. I hadn't spoken to Grace yet and meeting her for the first time after the incident in front of all our friends could prove awkward. I tried to call her a few times but no one answered. They still had a land line and no caller ID, so I didn't work myself up to a snit thinking she was trying to avoid me. Although I wouldn't blame her if she were. Poor Grace. Among my calls to Grace, I received a call from Syra saying Bing was making crème brulee for the meeting. Crème brulee is one of my favorites so I decided that was a message from somewhere telling me the meeting should take place.

In light of everything that had happened recently, Cam planned to hover around the house in case one of my friends went berserk and tried to kill me. He settled in the living room with a backlog of *National Geographic*s and today's paper. He left Mycroft with me in case one of my friends needed something sniffed. I still hadn't been able to reach Grace and wasn't surprised when she didn't show up for the meeting. She had enough to deal with at home and there wasn't much solace anyone in the group could give her under the circumstances.

"Do you think we should do something for Grace?" Diane asked, wiggling her spoon under the crunchy sugar of the crème brulee to scoop out the custard underneath. "Mmm. Yummy, Bing."

"Do you think she'll still have her Halloween party at the book-store?" Bing asked. It seemed like an odd question since he had never gone. "There's enough for everyone to have two desserts or to take the other home if you want."

I had a sliver of the braised sugar on my spoon and was licking it like a lollipop. "I tried calling her all day but didn't get her. She must know we all support her and we're here if she needs us. She'll let us know when she's ready."

"What about the party?" Bing repeated. "It would be awful if she didn't have the party."

I shrugged. "I don't know. The invitations are all out. It's only three days away. My guess is it will still take place, but who knows." I glanced over at Syra and noticed she wasn't eating. Her head had fallen back against the couch cushion and her eyes were closed. "Are you OK, Syra? You look beat."

She opened one eye, rubbed her hands on her face and sat up. "This is the week the radiation treatments started to make me tired. The exhaustion comes around the middle of the series of treatments. I don't feel bad, just tired."

I don't know what possessed me but I just blurted it out. "Do you have an embroidered linen handkerchief left over from when you were married?" Not surprisingly, she stared at me like I was nuts.

"No, but I do have a tissue in my purse if you need one."

"Me, too!" Bing reached into his pocket and pulled out a travel pack of tissues and handed it to me. "Is this okay or do you have to have linen? Do you have an allergy to paper or something?"

"No, it's just that I found a linen handkerchief with 'SB' embroidered on it and I thought maybe it was Syra's …" I knew I sounded stupid but I had to get this out in the open.

"Why would Syra have 'SB' on her handkerchief when her last name is Foster?" Diane asked. "And does anyone still have monogrammed linen handkerchiefs anymore? I think my great-grandmother had some but she was born before the turn of the century. The last century, not the one that just turned."

"1800s," Bing clarified.

"Right. So why would you think Syra would have an antique handkerchief like that monogrammed with the wrong last initial?" Diane asked me. Little did she know that once I cleared up this handkerchief mystery I was going to focus on her relationship with Officer Donny and see if my suspicions were right.

"When I was married, ages ago, my initials were 'SB'," Syra wearily admitted. "I went back to my maiden name when I got divorced. So I was 'SB' for a period of time, a long time ago. No monogrammed handkerchiefs, though, Tamsen. Sorry."

Of course she would hardly admit it. And I thought it was strange she didn't even ask me why I wanted to know. Was it because she knew why? Or was she just too tired to care. No one else seemed to care, either. Surely they weren't all guilty of breaking into my house. I was getting paranoid. Bing and Diane had started a side conversation and Diane was writing down the crème brulee recipe. Syra and Mycroft were dozing, enveloped in the heat of the fire. I really missed Grace. I politely waited until Diane had put the recipe in her purse before attacking her.

"Did your whole flirtation thing with Officer Donny stem from your need to keep him from suspecting Kaleb?" That effectively killed the side conversation and woke up both Syra and Mycroft. Grace would have been proud.

"Huh?" Bing said staring at me. Diane played around with her purse and refused to look in my direction, as if there was more than one person who had flirted with Officer Donny and had a son named Kaleb. I intrepidly forged ahead.

"When it dawned on me that Kaleb was Franklin's newspaper delivery boy as well as mine, it occurred to me that he might be suspected of killing Franklin. Not many people go to that cottage on a regular basis. Kaleb was there every day. He had more opportunity than anyone ..."

"Stop it! Kaleb wouldn't hurt anyone. You know that, Tamsen. You've known him all his life. Why are you saying these things?" Diane burst into tears and Bing was finally able to give someone his little tissue packet. She ferociously pulled out several tissues and handed it back. "Why are you being so nasty? I would never accuse Abbey of murdering anyone."

"I'm not accusing Kaleb, Diane. I'm just putting two and two together and wondering if your flirtation with …"

"I am not flirting with him. Why do all of you keep saying that?"

"Because you are," Syra stated. "We're not judging you, but we couldn't help but notice it. It was so out of character."

"There's no point in denying it, Diane. We did all notice. Are you really attracted to him or does it have to do with keeping his attention away from Kaleb? That's all I'm asking," I said more gently.

"He started it," she said defiantly. "I mean, I was scared for Kaleb. It was awful …"

Bing wiggled over next to Diane and put his arms around her. I could picture Hetty comforting him the same way, rocking him back and forth and saying meaningless comforting things to him.

"Tell us about it," Syra urged.

Diane sniffed and blew her nose. Bing moved back to his portion of the couch to give her some space while she composed herself.

"Right after you found Franklin, the police kept questioning us. You probably don't remember, Tamsen, because you were in some kind of a daze …"

"Shock. She was in shock," Syra said.

"OK. You were in shock. But those of us not in shock were scared, scared there was a killer loose in the neighborhood and then scared of saying something that would make us look suspicious. I mean, I've never been questioned by the police before …"

"So your natural inclination was to flirt with him?" Syra interrupted. "That wasn't mine."

"Mine, either," whispered Bing.

"Of course not! But when he first interviewed me I got the distinct impression that Officer Donaldson, the one you call Officer Donny, was attracted to me. It was weird. I haven't felt that for a long time. I'm the mother of five; I've been a full-time mother so long that I sort of forgot I was also a woman. His interest made me feel, well, pretty again. And young. Come on, you remember what it felt like in high school when you thought someone found you attractive ..."

"No ..." Bing shook his head.

"... and it made you look at him in a different light? He made me feel good about myself. It's like some long-buried flirty feelings were dredged up and dusted off. Still, I didn't plan to do anything about it, just enjoy his attention but then ..."

"You fell in love?" Bing asked, his eyes wide with anticipation. Diane reached over and patted his leg, the same way I pat Mycroft when he attempts to follow me up the stairs but can't get his leg up to the first step.

"No, I didn't fall in love. I just sort of savored the feeling."

"So what happened to put you in major flirtation mode and buy those low-cut sweaters?"

"They weren't that low cut, Syra. Just regular sweaters ..."

"But not something you usually wear. Those sweaters were definitely out of character," I pointed out. "Come on, Diane. We've known you forever and you never wear suggestive clothing, ever."

"I know. I know. It's just that the police began to question Kaleb. He's the newspaper boy. He makes his deliveries before school so he was there early in the morning ..."

"Oh, my God. He must have found Franklin that day before I did. He would have been there way before I went out to check on him." I realized. "Why didn't he say some ...?"

"That's the problem! Don't you see? Kaleb did see him when he took him the newspaper ..."

"But he didn't say anything?" Bing asked. "That seems strange."

"Yes. Yes. It seemed strange to the police, too. So they kept questioning him and questioning him and I was so scared, not that Kaleb would have murdered Franklin, but that it looked suspicious ..."

"But why didn't he report it?" I asked. "Why run away?"

"Because he was scared! He was scared the killer might still be there. He was scared that the killer might have seen him and go after him, too. He was scared he would be late for his eight o'clock math test. He's just a kid. He ran away. People don't find murder victims every day, you know."

"I never have," Bing offered.

"But the police thought his behavior was suspicious and Donny kept coming to the house to talk to Kaleb and to Scott and me. I got caught up in the flirtation because it felt good and it gave me a chance to stay close to the investigation and to plead Kaleb's innocence. It just sort of snowballed, the flirty feelings, the protective feelings, the fear. I just wasn't myself. But it's different now."

"What do you mean?" Syra asked. "How's it different?"

Diane ran her hands up into her jungle of hair, sending it shooting off her head like an electrical charge. "Scott noticed. He saw how Donny treated me and how I responded. But the worse thing is he noticed one of my home pregnancy kits missing ..."

"Oh, no! That's totally my fault," I cried.

"I mentioned a while ago that I was down to just one and we were joking around about having to take a weekend trip out of town to stock up again. I kept it right in the linen closet and when he went in there to get soap he noticed it was gone. He thought Donny and I had ..."

"Had you?" Syra asked.

"No! Of course not. Donny never even touched me except maybe to take my hand to comfort me or to touch my arm or something. Nothing sexual. Ever. But it took a while to convince Scott. He almost called you, Tamsen."

"I wish he had. I'm so sorry he misunderstood."

"It's good, actually. It got everything out in the open. I realized I had been making a fool of myself. Scott and I realized we needed more couple time. Lots of good came out of it. Most importantly, Donny finally believed Kaleb was guilty of nothing more than immature judgment. It all turned out all right."

"So you and Scott are good? Because I can talk to him if you think I should," I offered.

"No, thanks, we're good. Everything is settled," Diane assured us. "Even Kaleb seems to have put it behind him."

"Are you pregnant, Tamsen?" Bing asked. "It would be fun if you had a baby!"

"Fun for whom, Bing? No, thankfully I'm not pregnant. Just starting the 'change'." Bing had been to enough WOACA meetings that he needed no further explanation about the 'change'. He looked disappointed about my baby news.

"I guess that solves the Diane and Donny mystery," Syra sighed, resting her head on the back of the chair and closing her eyes.

"Not quite," I said. "Is Donny's real name Donald Donaldson?"

"No, worse," Diane smiled.

"What could be worse?" I asked.

"Milton. Milton Donaldson. That's why he's always gone by Donny." We all agreed that he'd made a good choice.

Cam's phone had rung several times while we had been in the library and I hoped I hadn't missed a call from Abbey. Bing was about to take another crème brulee to Cam in the living room when he strolled into the library.

"Finally decided to join WOACA?" Diane asked. "We can always use the input of a man— no offense Bing."

"None taken."

"Hey, we discovered that Officer Donny's real first name is Milton," I announced proudly.

"Great. I just discovered whose DNA was right next to the body of Raymond Fletcher!"

Chapter Twenty-Nine

Four pair of eyes stared at Cam and he soaked in our astonishment and admiration.

"The missing money story?" Bing asked.

"Yes. The ransom was paid, Raymond Ketchum was killed and a note was left in his pocket saying something like, 'this is what happens when you don't pay the ransom.' But his brother swore he paid it and the mystery was never solved ..."

"Except you, sitting in our living room eating crème brulee and reading your backlog of *National Geographics*, have solved it." I said.

"And we only solved the mystery of Officer Donny's first name. I feel so inadequate," Syra laughed.

"There wasn't much to solve about Donny's name. I told you!" Diane reminded us.

"Well, actually Officer Donny told me who left DNA all over the crime scene too. I didn't *personally* solve it," Cam admitted.

"Tell us about the crime scene. After seventy years, how did they finally find something?" I asked. I was assuming it wasn't Uncle Franklin's DNA because Cam seemed too relaxed and was enjoying himself too much. If his uncle had been a teenaged criminal I'm sure he wouldn't be announcing it to the WOACA members with such pride. Cam settled into a chair and tented his fingers in front of his chest.

"Well, as you recall …"

Oh jeez. This was going to take a while.

"… Raymond Ketchum disappeared the evening of March 30. The following day his brother received a ransom note and was told to deliver $10,000 to a specific place in Camden Woods, behind the house where Bing and Syra live now. The police thought it was an odd coincidence that the ransom was $10,000 because that was the exact amount Dr. Fletcher Ketchum kept in the safe in his house and only …"

"Oh yeah, I remember that part. The police thought maybe Raymond was in on the kidnapping and was trying to get money from his brother. We read that in the old newspapers," Bing interrupted. "Imagine, he was killed in the woods behind our house and right across the street from you and Tamsen …"

"Only none of us were born at the time," Syra pointed out.

"But what if we *had* been. We might have seen something," Bing continued.

"But we *weren't*, Bing. Let Cam continue," Syra admonished.

"Sorry."

"That's OK. You're right though, Bing. It all took place across the street from this house. Anyway, according to Dr. Ketchum, he got the money out of his safe, put it in a bag, and took it to a specific tree in the woods. Then he went back home and waited for his brother to be released …"

"Only he didn't and …" Bing started but stopped when Syra gave him a stern look.

"Right, Raymond never came home. The next day, a man named Ernest Whitcomb was walking his dog early in the morning and discovered the body propped up against the ransom drop tree and there was that note in the pocket …"

"… and the money was gone!" Bing finished dramatically. "Never to be found again. "Well, until you and Tamsen found it in your house …" Bing trailed off.

"True. In 1938 they didn't have the forensic equipment we do now or the databases of known criminals, MOs of crimes, fingerprints, DNA and all that other stuff. The police were pretty isolated and had to rely on questioning people, checking the body and the surrounding areas for clues. They didn't come up with much. They had the rope that bound Raymond Ketchum's hands and feet and a bunch of cigarettes—some common brand back then. They could have been anyone's …"

"How do you know about cigarettes? That wasn't in the paper. Or the rope?" I asked.

"Officer Donny told me. They closed the case after a couple of years but they still have to keep all the evidence, reports, crime scene photos and things …"

"Like on the TV show, 'Cold Case'," Diane informed us. "Tamsen, you should write about all this and submit it to the show. It would be a perfect story."

"Am I the only one who is dying to know whose DNA was at the crime scene? Get on with it, Cam!" I pleaded.

"OK. When the money started turning up and it became pretty obvious it was the ransom money, the police reopened the Ketchum case. They got out all the evidence and started running forensic test results through the various criminal databases. They got a hit." Cam's pause was so pregnant that if Diane had one of her pregnancy kits here it would have exploded with positive results.

"And …," I prompted.

"The DNA matched that of a serial criminal who has been in and out of prisons all over the country since the early 50s." Pregnant pause number two. Apparently Cam was expecting twins.

"Who?" Syra and I yelled.

"None other than Ernest Whitcomb."

"You mean the dog walker? The guy who discovered the body?" Bing asked.

"Yup. Apparently he was somehow involved in the kidnapping and murder and it must have started a life of crime. He never actually served time until the 1950s but he was suspected of numerous home break-ins, gas station holdups and, in 1953, the robbery of a bank in Florida. He was caught, finally found guilty of something, and went to prison. That's why his fingerprints and DNA are on file."

"But we all know he was at the crime scene. He found the body. It doesn't seem strange that his DNA would be there," I argued. "I don't see how that implicates him in the actual crime."

"There were five cigarettes, Tamsen. Five. Can you imagine walking through the woods with Mycroft, discovering a man with a bullet hole through his head and then settling down to smoke five cigarettes before you mosey off and call the police?" Cam countered. "He had to have been at the crime scene for a while. Maybe he was the one waiting for the ransom to be delivered. Maybe he was the killer. But he certainly had more to do with the crime than just discovering the body. He died in prison fourteen years ago. No one will ever know."

Those have to be five of the most frustrating words in the English language.

***

I couldn't sleep that night. Something was wiggling around in the back of my mind and it was driving me crazy, like an itch in the middle of your back.

I couldn't stop thinking about pregnancy. I felt bad about Scott's misunderstanding of Diane's missing pregnancy kit. And then there was Bing's innocent enthusiasm about me being pregnant. And Cam's pregnant pauses. Was this a spiritual enlightening and maybe I was pregnant after all? I hoped it didn't mean Abbey was pregnant. No, she had too much sense. But accidents happened. Claudia had made it pretty clear that Cam was an accident. If Claudia could get pregnant by mistake, anyone could. Except Abbey, of course. Cam had convinced himself that Abbey would not even be thinking about sex until she was at least forty. I was more realistic and pegged it closer to thirty. Either way, at eighteen she had at least ten or more years of virginity ahead of her.

So what had me thinking about pregnancy? I put my hand on Cam's shoulder and gently shook him.

"Cam, are you awake?" Nothing. The man sleeps like a fossil. I rubbed my leg up and down his. He smiled. Great. Now I had probably provoked some sex dream. How can he feel me but not hear me?

"Cam! Are you awake?" I lay on my back and started bouncing up and down on the bed. This usually worked when he was snoring. He kept that stupid smile on his face and just rocked around like he was sleeping in a canoe. Hopeless.

***

The sun was pouring in the room. I reached out for Cam but he was gone. My bagel was sitting out on the counter, nicely thawed. I made myself a tasty little breakfast, high on carbs and calories and low on nutrition, and sat down to read the morning paper. That made me think of Kaleb, which reminded me of WOACA last night and made my head start to ache with whatever it was that was up there and needed to get out. I was scanning the TV listings for no particular reason, as Cam and I rarely watched TV. I guess it makes me feel good to look at all the things I won't be watching that night. There is a local fishing show named "Clive Cubby's Fishing Journal." Love that name. I turned the page. Wait. I turned back to the TV listings and stared at Clive's listing. Journal. Clive had a fishing journal. I had a daily journal. If I was trying to remember something, maybe if I went through my journal, day by day since the murder, I would trigger some kind of memory.

I set my dirty dishes in the sink and headed back to the bedroom. I keep my journal on my nightstand in sight of God and everyone. I completely trust Cam not to read it and, as far as I knew, he has never even opened it. Ever. Besides, there isn't much in there that Cam doesn't know unless he doesn't listen to me when I talk. I puffed up my pillows and settled back into bed to read. I hadn't written much the week following Franklin's murder except to note the day of his funeral, October 6. I had started making longer entries on October 11 when we had gone out to the cottage to clean.

Blah blah blah newspapers. That wasn't it. Old books. Kitchen utensils. Photo of kids. Nope, not that day.

The next entry was for October 12, a Sunday. Bad day. I'd gone to Ashland Belle to show Claudia and Sybil the photo of the kids and Grace had found the bloody shirt in Ryan's closet. Grace spent the night with us. I skimmed through the next couple of days, going back to the cottage with Syra, blah blah blah big fight at WOACA meeting and then the first break-in. I'd entered a lot of details about the night of the break-in and the handkerchief and even part of the Sylvie story but none of that was triggering a memory.

Ah, Wednesday. Here was the pregnancy-related stuff. I read and reread my fears about being pregnant and getting the pregnancy kit from Diane. Diane and I had been to Bugg Hill to visit her parents. Gourmet macaroni and cheese. Talked about Franklin as a child. Other people in the dining room with us. A woman with green hair and the hair conditioner scare. Then there was the woman who had gotten stuck in the bathtub and needed the EMTs to get her out. My head was pounding now. The woman who got stuck in the tub. It was so close.

I grabbed my cell phone and dialed Diane's number.

"Diane. It's Tamsen. Do your parents tell the same stories over and over?"

"Yeah, about as often as you find stashes of old money in your attic."

"Do you remember a story about a woman stuck in the bathtub?"

"… and the EMTs had to get her out. Sure. That's a cornerstone of the repertoire. Why?"

"Hard to say. There's something about that story that I think is important. Is there more to the story?"

"Not really. She's very large. Friendly, nice …"

"Something else …"

"Jeez. Her name is Muriel Wilson. Her sister Maxine lived with her but died right before my parents moved in. She talks about her all the time. And she had an uncle who discovered a body one time. She talks about that a lot …"

"That's it! That's it! Your parents were telling me about her getting stuck in the tub and then something about an uncle finding a dead body. Ernie. I know your parents said his name was Ernie. I think it was Ernest Whitcomb and she's talking about Raymond Ketchum's body."

"That seems like a leap but I suppose it could be true. But why …?"

"She may know something or have heard something that would tell us why Uncle Franklin ended up with the ransom money. I need to know."

"Why? Obviously Ernest Whitcomb couldn't have come after Franklin after all these years to get the money. What difference to Franklin could it make now?"

"I can't stand not knowing if he was a criminal or a victim or, especially, if this money had something to do with his murder. I need to talk to Muriel."

"Well, she's real friendly. I'm sure if you dropped over there around lunch time you'd find her."

Chapter Thirty

S ometimes I operate on impulse and don't think things through. Actually that happens a lot. I think it comes from being a writer and sometimes getting confused with what is reality and what is fiction. After talking to Diane I headed out to Bugg Hill in hopes of striking up a conversation with Muriel. Should I just walk up to her and say, "Hey. I heard you got stuck in the bathtub once. How did that feel?" Or maybe I could start talking about dogs and finding bodies and see if the entire uncle story would come out. I've noticed with Diane's parents that you can trigger a specific story if you give the right cues.

There weren't many people still in the dining room when I arrived but luckily I spotted someone who fit Muriel's description right away. There were two other ladies seated at her table chatting so I skulked around outside the dining room door waiting for a chance to get her alone. Several people asked if they could help me and I politely demurred. After about ten minutes, the two ladies grabbed their walkers and headed out. One didn't make it any farther than the sitting area outside the door, collapsed on the couch and immediately went to sleep. The other headed for the elevator.

Muriel smiled as I approached her table. I introduced myself as a friend of Ted and Thelma's and she asked me to sit and join her. She waved to the waiter and he brought me a glass of tea. I hate tea. Hot tea, cold tea, presweetened tea, it doesn't matter. Apparently it was the drink of choice so I thanked him and poured in four packets of sugar hoping that would help kill the taste so I could at least politely sip while I pumped the poor woman for information.

One of the many endearing things about elderly people is that they don't need a formal introduction to strike up a conversation. She seemed glad to have someone to talk to and didn't need a lengthy made-up explanation as to why I was there. She told me about her sister Maxine and how she had died, leaving her all alone in their apartment. Maxine had a cat that Muriel was taking care of and she was worried that when the cat died—it was twelve years old—she would have nothing left of Maxine. I noticed that her eyes were puddling up. I reached over to squeeze her wrist and was reminded of how warm and chubby Abbey's thighs were when she was a baby. I squeezed again, and my eyes began to puddle up, also.

"You're a very sympathetic girl," she told me. Actually I was being empathetic but why quibble with semantics.

"Thelma told me that you had an interesting story about an uncle who found a body in the woods. Is that true?" I gave her my wide-eyed wonder look. Cam says it makes me look like I have Grave's disease but I think it lends an aura of innocence to my questions.

"Yes. Absolutely true. Well, not absolutely true because he wasn't really my uncle."

Oh great. This was going to be a big nothing. She probably made the whole thing up. "Who was it?"

"It was Maxine's uncle."

"But Maxine was your sister, so it would be your uncle, too," I gently clarified. She was obviously confused.

"No, Maxine and I weren't really sisters. People just thought we were because of our names, Maxine and Muriel, and because we lived our whole lives together. I grew up in Maxine's house. But we weren't sisters. It was just easier to let people think we were. Do you see what I'm saying?" Muriel tilted her head and several chins cascaded toward her shoulder.

"Um, yes. I guess I see what you're saying," I replied. I wasn't sure how to respond. Was she telling me they were lovers?

"Are you a little bit shocked?"

"Um, do you want me to be shocked?"

"Yes, a little," she smiled.

"OK then, I'm a little bit shocked."

She nodded. "That's why we always told people we were sisters. I hate shocking people. It's so unladylike."

"Yes, I suppose it is. But there was really an uncle who found a dead man?"

"Oh yes, Maxine's Uncle Ernie. It happened in 1938. Did you know the Lindbergh baby was kidnapped in March 1932?"

The Lindbergh baby? What did any of this have to do with the Lindbergh baby? Did Uncle Ernie kidnap him too? I could be fairly sure that Uncle Franklin hadn't been involved in the Lindbergh kidnapping. He would have been only seven years old, and no one is that criminally precocious.

"Maxine and I were fascinated with the Lindbergh baby. He was the same age we were so we were always watching for him to turn up in school or other places around town. He never did, of course. He died you know."

"Yes, I had heard that. Terrible tragedy. Did the Lindbergh baby have something to do with Uncle Ernie and the body he found?"

"The Lindbergh baby had a lot to do with the dead man. But it's a long story and, well, Maxine and ... Maxine and her mother and I agreed never to tell it."

"I understand. I don't want to make you do something you aren't comfortable with but I'd be very interested in hearing the whole story. Maybe now that Maxine and her mother are gone …"

"Do you have stories you aren't supposed to tell anyone?"

Oh dear. I felt like I was at a slumber party and we were playing truth or dare. This was obviously an "I'll tell you if you'll tell me" proposition. This woman was going to be a tough negotiator and I didn't have much to negotiate with. I didn't want to sic Officer Donny on her and she would probably be less likely to tell him than to gossip with me. But what could I negotiate with?

"Listen Muriel, I'd very very much like to hear the story of Uncle Ernie and the dead body, but I'm not sure what I could tell you in exchange. Maybe we could …"

"OK. I'll tell you. But I'd feel better if I had some ice cream. Want some?"

I shook my head. She signaled to the waiter, who immediately brought her four Dixie cups and a flat wooden spoon. She pulled the top off all four of them and began eating a little from each of the four containers—chocolate, vanilla, strawberry and lemon. I waited patiently.

"It was March 1938 and the sixth anniversary of the Lindbergh baby kidnapping. The papers were full of all kinds of theories even though the kidnapper had been caught and executed. The trouble all started on March 16. It was my birthday and Maxine's mother had made me a cake, had friends over and given me a really great party …"

"Why didn't your parents give you a party at your house?"

"Because they didn't know it was my birthday."

"How could they not know …?"

"They were drunks and there were nine kids in my family. Maxine's mother took me in a couple years earlier and they hadn't even noticed I was missing. Maxine and her mother were my family. And Uncle Ernie."

"Uncle Ernie lived with Maxine?"

"Yes, he was the younger brother of her mother. Tall, dark and handsome—attractive, if you like that sort."

"Everyone likes tall, dark and handsome."

"No, I meant men. If you like men. Anyway, Ernie came home the night of my birthday and he was angry. He had been fired from Clancy's Hardware, where he unloaded trucks and stocked shelves and stuff. Maxine's mother took in people's laundry but that didn't pay much so we relied on Ernie's income. He and Maxine's mother fought about it all night. He was mad that she had spent all that money on a birthday party for me, someone who wasn't even part of the family. She had insisted I was part of the family and I remember how good that made me feel." Muriel eyes filled with tears and I handed her a napkin to blot them up. She attacked the four containers of ice cream and continued.

"Ernie started coming up with all kinds of ideas on how to get money. I asked him once why he didn't just find another job and he said it was because he would probably just get fired again. One of the ideas he had was to go over to my dad's and demand that he start paying Ernie something for keeping me at their house. He came back with a black eye and a cut on his arm from a broken whiskey bottle. He never went over to see my dad again. He did do some yard work for the big houses across from Camden Woods.

"Did he ever do work at the Behrends house?"

"Is that the one that looks like it should be in a Boris Karloff movie?"

"Yes."

"Yeah. He did a lot of work there. They had a huge yard and no one who lived there knew how to do anything. By the end of the month things were getting very tense. Maxine's mother and Ernie fought every night after Maxine and I went to bed. She wanted him to get a steady job and he wanted something that would give him a lot of money at once. He wanted to go to the race tracks but she wouldn't give him enough money to do that. That's where the Lindbergh baby came in and caused all the trouble. You know, my bottom is getting numb from this chair. Let's move into the sitting room. The furniture is real comfortable out there."

I helped launch Muriel out of her chair and took her elbow and propelled her to the couch that did not have the sleeping grandma on it. I sat in a wing chair next to the couch so we could talk without being overheard. There were only three of us in the room and one was snoring so it was fairly private.

"You know, it's nice of you to come and talk to me. This place is full of people with stories but not enough people to listen. We each get to say a few sentences of our story and then someone interrupts with a few sentences of their story and so it goes. I think my story is more interesting than Vivian Nothnagel's account of her trip to Albany to see a quilt show but she keeps telling it over and over and I never get a word in edgewise. Maxine was the only one who ever listened to me."

"I'm very interested in your story, Muriel. I think you were up to the part about Ernie doing yard work but wanting to make some quick money. And the Lindbergh baby was about to get involved ..."

"Oh, yes, the Lindbergh baby. You know, the ransom was paid—$50,000—but Bruno Hauptmann still killed him. That seems so wrong. It's not like the baby could identify him or anything. He wasn't even two years old. His body was found in 1932 but people still claim to be him, even now. Maxine and I read everything we could about the poor Lindbergh baby. So sad."

"Yes, it's terrible. I may be kind of dense but I'm having a difficult time figuring out how the poor little Lindbergh baby factors into the Uncle Ernie story ..."

"That's because I haven't gotten to that part yet."

"Could you?"

"All right. Everything is a rush with you young people. Well, Ernie hadn't been eating dinner with us much since he lost his job but this one night he was. Maxine and I were talking about the Lindbergh baby, which is all we had been talking about all month. Maxine's mother tuned us out but Ernie listened as we recounted the entire crime and told him all the theories and how we were still checking out the boys our age in case he showed up. He said that if he were going to kidnap someone, he would grab them off the street and not try to sneak them out of their house in the middle of the night. Ernie also said he thought it was stupid to take someone famous because everyone all over the world would know about it. Ernie was usually pretty stupid but he had a point there."

"It was a couple nights later that Maxine and I heard all the commotion downstairs. We could hear Ernie's voice and someone else coming in the back door making all kinds of banging noises. We were pretty sure Ernie was drunk and was bringing a girl home. Maxine's mother never allowed him to do that because of Maxine and me. She told him it would be a bad influence. We heard Maxine's mother go downstairs and then lots of yelling. We kept watching out our bedroom door because we wanted to see what the girl looked like, but only Maxine's mother came back upstairs. The next morning she looked awful. Her eyes were all red and puffy and she barely talked at all. She gave us a few slices of toast and sent us to school an hour early. We decided that she had seen some kind of man-woman thing going on between Ernie and the girl and it had made her sick. But it was that night that was the very worst."

"What happened?"

"Ernie wasn't there for dinner and we didn't see him all evening. Then, late at night, we heard him come slamming in the back door and cursing something wicked. Maxine's mother went down to talk to him and he yelled and banged the walls and ran around like some kind of tornado. Maxine and I were so scared we crawled under the bed to hide. But we could still hear everything."

"What was he saying?"

"Mostly a bunch of curses. But there were two things he said over and over again—'where did the fucking money go' and 'your brother doesn't care if you die'. Maxine and I loved saying, 'where did the fucking money go?' over and over. Even as adults we used to say it whenever we misplaced our purses. Where did the fucking money go? Funny how those phrases stick with you all those years ..." Her voice trailed off and she stared at the ceiling.

"Muriel..." I prompted.

"What? Oh, yes. Ernie and Maxine's mom and the yelling. Well, they always fought about money so that didn't seem strange. Maxine's mother must have lost some money or something. But we couldn't understand why he kept telling her that her brother didn't care if she died. *He* was her brother. We were afraid it meant he was planning to kill her. We knew we should do something to protect her but we didn't know what to do. We were just little girls. We fell asleep under the bed and when we woke up early in the morning things were calmer. At first we were afraid to go downstairs in case Ernie had killed Maxine's mother, but then we heard her voice and we jumped up and down and hugged each other. Things were still weird, though. We heard a dog in the kitchen and we didn't have a dog. We raced down to see if maybe they had gotten a dog for us but everyone was still angry. Ernie said he was taking care of the dog for a friend. Maxine's mother just sat at the kitchen table and cried. That was the morning Ernie found the dead body in the woods."

"April 1?"

"Right. When he told us we thought it was an April Fool's joke, but then his name was in the paper and everything. We thought he would be excited about that. Regular people like us never got their names in the paper. But he just sat in his room all the time and then, a couple weeks later, he left."

"Where did he go?"

"I don't know. Maxine's mother said he was too upset by all the problems in the world and he had to leave because he couldn't be happy in Birdsey Falls anymore. I never saw him again."

"Did Maxine's mother talk about him?"

"No. She wouldn't answer our questions when we asked about him so we eventually stopped. End of story." Muriel leaned back and closed her eyes. I reached out and touched her hand.

"Thank you for telling me the whole story. It was a long time ago but you really should tell the police. I can give you the name of someone …"

"Why?"

"Muriel, it wasn't a girl Ernie was trying to hide in the basement. And he wasn't mad about Maxine's mother losing money. He wasn't the brother who didn't care if his sibling lived or died. I think your Uncle Ernie was involved in the kidnapping of Raymond Ketchum," I explained.

"It was so long ago. Everyone is dead."

"The case has been reopened. They know Ernie was in the woods for longer than it took him to discover the body. Your story will help tie up some loose ends."

"But why would they reopen the case after seventy years?"

"Because the ransom money was found in my attic."

"So *that's* where the fucking money went."

***

It didn't take much to convince Muriel to tell her story to the police— I just promised her that they would not interrupt her and she would not have to compete with the Albany quilt show. By ten o'clock the next morning Diane let me know that her parents had called her to tell her the police were at Bugg Hill, talking to Muriel. I explained that Muriel's uncle was Ernest Whitcomb and Muriel had hearsay evidence that he had kidnapped and killed Raymond Ketchum. It was Cam who pointed out that, when the story broke, the part about the ransom money being found in the cottage and in our attic would also be out. Claudia would have a fit if her family was implicated in any way, even peripherally, in a kidnapping/murder. But facts were facts and there wasn't much we could do to cover it up. We would have to live with the consequences.

We still had no idea how Franklin factored into the crime. We were all tired of hearing ourselves say, 'He was *only* fifteen'. We accepted that Ernie Whitcomb had made Franklin's acquaintance while doing yard work at the house that spring. What their relationship had been after that no one could guess. Still, who, after seventy years, would kill Franklin? There was no one left.

It was the day before Halloween and I knew Grace would be busy preparing for her big party and announcing the winners of the "Guess the Mannequins' Costumes" contest. We had too much to say to each other to try to cram it into a hurried phone call. What a blessing friendship was. Muriel and Maxine had made it through a rough childhood together. They had shared their family secrets and yet not been damaged by what they knew. They had been able to share the burden. Franklin, on the other hand, had taken the burden of guilt on himself. It had festered inside him and poisoned his life. Ernie had gone on to live his life, dishonest as it was. Franklin had locked himself up, both emotionally and physically, and withered away. He had paid a far higher price than Ernie for the debacle in Camden Woods.

I fished around on my desk and found the Edgar Allan Poe quote from the attic. Now I understood why it had appealed to Franklin and why he had written it down.

There are some secrets which do not permit themselves to be told ... mysteries which will not suffer themselves to be revealed. Now and then, alas, the conscience of man takes up a burden so heavy in horror that it can be thrown down only into the grave.

Franklin had taken up a burden so heavy in horror that only his death would release him from its hold. I could understand why Franklin might kill himself. I couldn't understand why someone would kill him.

While I was looking for the quote I also ran across the notes I had made on a napkin last Saturday at the diner. Most of the loose ends I had listed were now tied up, but we still didn't know who broke into our house and left the "SB" monogrammed handkerchief. The police suspected Ryan of the first break-in based on the fact he had admitted to the second break-in. Both times a key had been used. Both times nothing had been taken. Ryan insisted he had only broken in that one time, to scare me. The police were convinced he was lying. He was currently under house arrest and then would probably need to perform some community service. Cam and I were satisfied with that. The community service would help him to be a little less self-absorbed and more aware of other people and their problems. He was so full of self-pity right now that he couldn't see outside himself.

The appearance and disappearance of the handkerchief was eating away at me. It seemed insignificant in the scheme of all that had happened but it was unexplained and things like that drive me nuts. And then there were pages 1-22 of what Franklin had been writing in his cottage. Page 23 appeared to be part of an autobiography and started with the death of his brother Alden at Pearl Harbor. But what we really needed to know was what had happened prior to 1941 and that was the part that had disappeared. I was convinced it was important and that the murderer had taken it, maybe even killed Franklin for it. But what could he have said that we hadn't already pieced together and who would kill him to keep it a secret? The people with the most to lose were Ernie Whitcomb's family members and they were all dead. Muriel certainly was willing to tell the story. Who would be trying to protect Ernie now?

Arresting Ryan and knowing who killed Raymond Ketchum answered none of these questions. I was willing to keep blundering around and doing the police's job for them but I had no idea where to blunder off to now. It was like staring at a blank computer screen with no idea what to write. I'd run out of ideas.

Luckily I was overflowing with thoughts about my new book, so I attacked my blank computer screen and worked steadily for several hours. I still hadn't thought of an appropriate name for my heroine but I had decided that she would operate on the fringes of society, not being afraid to take a little pleasure while trying to get information from her high society suspects. Her motto would be: *There's more than one way to question a handsome, charming gentleman.* But it was not going to be a bodice ripper. She would be the aggressor, and no one would take advantage of her. She was the one in control. New Orleans post Civil War society would find her terribly offensive; twenty-first-century women would find her incredibly inspiring.

Chapter Thirty- One

It was our first Halloween in eighteen years without a child at home. Granted, the first couple of years Abbey had no idea what was going on but we dressed her up and took her out just to show her off. She stopped trick or treating when she was thirteen but she would still dress up and answer the door, handing out candy. Then, once the evening had quieted down, we would all head to Trenary Booksellers for the Halloween party. The store was closed for business, but Grace took advantage of the space and all the wonderful spooky decorations to host a party for her friends. You can imagine what a great setting a dimly lit bookstore with ghosts and witches hanging out among the books can be.

Hugh had urged Grace to go ahead and have the traditional Halloween party. Apparently they were almost euphoric that they were raising a juvenile delinquent rather than a murderer. This year, in the aftermath of the break-ins, we weren't sure we wanted to leave the house. Officer Donny came to our rescue by offering to have a patrol car parked in our driveway, by the front door, to scare off anyone who might be tempted to pay us another visit.

Cam loves Halloween and putting together a costume. He starts planning in August and spends a lot of time thinking of a theme for us and making arrangements for wigs and clothes and other accessories that we will need, like rubber weapons or fake blood. As long as I am covered from head to toe and there is no suggestive skin showing, I'm happy go to along. This year I was going as Guinevere. I did have to insert a lacy camisole under the dress as apparently some costume designer was under the impression that ladies in the middle ages showed an extreme amount of cleavage. But the dress was beautiful, midnight blue, and not too heavy to walk around in, and I loved the little headpiece with the lace that flowed down my back. I didn't have to worry about my hair; just hastily put it up in a sloppy bun and put the headpiece and train on. I looked very elegant and maybe even just the slightest bit thinner.

Cam chose to portray Lancelot in full armor, as if he were off to a jousting match. He did have sort of a chain mail opening on his elbows and knees so he could bend but he still had a Frankenstein walk. Getting him into the car was a huge project and I had to gather my skirts up to my chin to drive. Since he wasn't able to sit comfortably and still close the passenger door, we had to lay him flat on his back in the back seat with his knees up in the air. Luckily it was a short drive to the bookstore.

Hiram, dressed in his usual Ichabod Crane outfit, helped me pull Cam out of the car. We had to park a couple blocks away so the three of us strolled down the street making small talk about the weather and the brilliance of holding meetings at a round table versus a rectangular one. Once we reached the door and were safely inside, Hiram scampered back to his cubicle after grabbing a plateful of pumpkin bread and candy corn. He rarely made much of an appearance during the party, preferring to watch from the safety of his work area.

Grace's assistant Jenny, dressed as a French parlor maid, flapped her feather duster at us and ooed and aahed over our costumes. Cam, in turn, silently ooed and aahed over her costume while she and I talked about who was there and what they were wearing. Jenny seductively flounced off and I smacked Cam on his helmet as he stared after her.

"What?" he asked, stiffly turning his head to look at me.

"You're oogling Jenny."

"No I'm not. I was just thinking that she must be really really cold."

"Yeah, right." I would have smacked him again for good measure but I was distracted by the arrival of Santa and Mrs. Claus. "Grace!" I threw my arms around her and we hugged, communicating the way old friends can. Her hug told me how sorry she was about what Ryan put me through and my hug told her I didn't hold her responsible and that I was fine. Hugh and Cam, on the other hand, shook hands and had to use actual words—however few.

"Sorry about …"

"Not your faul …"

"Still …"

"Forget about it."

We moved further into the store, greeting Diane and Scott (a nun and a priest), Syra (Abraham Lincoln), Diane's parents Ted (Frankenstein) and Thelma (unclear), Sybil (Mother Goose) and …

"Oh my God, Cam. What is your mother?"

"Tamsen, let's not start on that now. We're at a party …"

"No. No, I'm not trying to get you to say 'selfish mean-spirited soulless witch'; I mean her costume. What is that costume?" I put my hands on his arms and physically turned him so he could see his mother, who was standing talking to Reverend Sibley (cowboy) and his wife (cowgirl).

"Good Lord! That is … Jesus, I don't know what that is …"

"Try creepy," I suggested.

"I want to go home." Cam tried to turn toward the door. I grabbed his arm.

"Now you know how I feel when I see your mother."

"Not funny. Seriously, I don't feel well. We need to go home." Cam tried to pull his arm away and turn at the same time, which started a *Wizard of Oz* Tin man-like dance that brought applause from Ted and Thelma and directed his mother's attention our way.

"We can't go until I've had candy corn and orange-frosted cupcakes ..." I insisted.

"We'll stop for some on the way ..."

"Cam, she's coming over. You can't run away. Or keep your eyes closed. Man up!"

Claudia approached us doing the seventy-four-year-old's version of a skip. She was dressed in a short blue dress with a white pinafore wearing a long blonde wig and carrying a giant lollipop.

"Please make it go away." Cam was muttering with his eyes closed. I slapped my hand against his metal back, almost knocking him to the floor.

"Claudia!" I greeted my mother-in-law.

"Tamsen, dear ..." She lowered her lollipop and peered at my dress. "It's a shame they don't provide a bosom with the dress. I'm sure whoever you are trying to portray would have had a healthy bosom. Once you put something on, dear, it totally loses all sense of eroticism. Have you ever noticed that? Now, Jenny's costume is perfect for her."

"Mother! What are you?" Cam pulled up his visor to have a better look and then quickly put it down again.

"Obviously, I'm Alice in Wonderland. Heavens, Christian, did we waste all those years with that nanny person who read you all those children's books? What was that woman's name? She wasn't with us long ..."

"Nancy," Cam mumbled. "And she was my nanny until I was ten ..."

"Was it really that long? I never saw her much ..."

"That's because she was always with me."

"Ah, that explains it. This Nanny Nancy should have read you all the classics. I'm sure I told her to do that."

Cam stiffly shook his head. "I'm familiar with the character, Mother. I just never expected to see you dressed like her. I mean, isn't that costume a little bit ... um ..."

"Yes, it *is* amazing someone my age could look this great. My legs are still good and, when you are petite like me"—she glanced my way—"you can carry this off." She began to slowly twirl around, showing off her costume and kicking her legs up a few feet off the floor to make sure we saw them, too.

"Mother, please stop. Really. I'm begging."

Claudia smoothed down her pinafore and smiled. "Why is Syra dressed as Abraham Lincoln? Is she gay?"

"Why would you think that?" I asked, immediately wishing I hadn't.

"Because she is dressed like a man. I thought maybe now that she was missing her breasts she had turned gay or something."

"Claudia, just because a woman doesn't have breasts it doesn't mean she is gay ..."

"Oh yes, dear. I should have known that," she responded, staring at my chest. "Silly me." And off she flounced.

I turned to Cam and opened his visor, leaning my face close to his. "I. Really. Hate. Your. Mother." I slammed the visor back and headed toward the orange-frosted cupcakes.

I passed by the nun and priest, who were canoodling in the children's books section. Apparently all was well in the Kinney home, thank God. Diane better restock her supply of home pregnancy kits. I gave them a wave but they didn't notice me. I grabbed an orange-frosted cupcake, a cup of mulled cider, two snicker doodle cookies and handful of candy corn and made my way to the mystery section to hang out in Sherlock

Holmes' study. Next to the children's area, this was my favorite place in the store. If I could get my New Orleans mystery published I knew Grace would give the book a place of honor in this section.

"You dropped some candy corn."

I looked up from my musing to see Harry Potter pointing his wand toward the floor. I bent down to pick up the candy that had slipped off my plate.

"Who are you supposed to be?" Harry asked.

"If you're a wizard, shouldn't you know that?" I replied. Harry's face broke into an affable smile.

"Hogwarts hasn't offered that course yet."

"Ah, that explains it. I'm Guinevere. Do you know who that is?"

"Of course. You must be with the guy in the armor over there. He looks like he needs help eating."

I took the last bite of my cupcake and brushed my hands off on my napkin. "He won't starve. Maybe the underdressed French maid can help him get some food."

"That's my girlfriend," Harry informed me. "Who's the weird old broad in the little girl costume?"

"That's my mother-in-law." We looked at each other and burst out laughing. Just then Jenny wiggled in and sat on Harry's lap. Her little skirt flounced up and I could see her black silk underpants. I wondered if they came with the costume or if she wore that kind of underwear every day.

"Hey, Mrs. Mack. You met my boyfriend, Chip?"

"Sort of," Harry-Chip acknowledged, reaching out his hand to shake mine. "Chip Carson. Nice to meet you, Mrs. Mack.

"Chip is going to the police academy in Dover. He'll be done in May and then he'll be a real policeman," Jenny informed me proudly.

"Great. Are you planning to stay in this …?"

The Death of Perry Many Paws

We were interrupted by Santa Claus asking Jenny and Chip if they could help him bring more cider in from the storeroom. They excused themselves and left and I returned to thinking about my new book and then to the current Perry Many Paws book. My editor had loved the hot-air balloon idea. Now he was talking about expanding the locations of the Perry stories; oddly, now that I had him thinking the way I wanted him to, I wasn't sure I wanted to continue with the series. Now that Abbey was an adult it might be time to put Perry to sleep, well not *that* kind of put to sleep, but to let him rest while I took on a new literary venture.

"You're not being very sociable, Tamsen. Are you all right?" I looked up into the empathetic eyes of the overly made up Mother Goose and smiled.

"I'm just thinking about my latest book, Sybil. Have a seat." I waved her into Dr. Watson's chair, having appropriated Sherlock's for myself. "You're looking very ... um ... colorful." The pancake makeup was smudged in a few places and the red lipstick was getting a little lopsided from eating and drinking. Her bonnet was sitting a little jauntily and I noticed her hips and tummy fighting against the material of her dress. She didn't look comfortable, maybe even less comfortable than Cam.

"My feet are killing me. These flimsy little slipper things don't give you any arch support at all. I should have worn my support hose. And this dress. And it must have shrunk. I'll complain to the costume shop. This is my size but it's a little tight. Are you going to eat those cookies?"

I passed her my plate with the two snicker doodles and she laid it on her stomach and began eating. "I miss Abbey. Remember last year when she came to the party as Raggedy Ann? She was perfect."

I nodded. Abbey was the quintessential Raggedy Ann, with her red hair and light sprinkling of freckles across her nose.

"Children are so innocent. It's a shame they have to grow up," she mused.

I put my hand on hers. "I know this isn't any of my business, Sybil, but it seems like you would have been such a great mother. Did you not want children or …"

She gave me a sad smile. "I always planned to have children some-day but was never in a marriage that felt strong enough. I made some bad choices. My first husband was charming but infantile …"

"You mean Frankie Bowe?

Sybil jerked her head up and stared at me. "How do you know about Frankie Bowe? Surely Claudia didn't …"

"No. No. Claudia never talks about your personal life with me. It's just that when I was looking through Franklin's newspapers …"

"You mean that pile with just the April 1 issues?"

"Yes. Your marriage announcement was in one of them …"

"Ah yes, April 1. Such a stupid wedding date, but it was romantic to me because we had met the previous year on April 1 when Frankie found my necklace in the Fox Theater. Silly how such a little thing leads to marriage and then …well. It was a bad marriage. He was a bit of a nut. I was just eighteen so it took me a couple of years to realize it."

"What happened to Frankie?"

"I'm not sure. When we divorced I moved to New York to try the theater. I had a few parts, you know."

"Yes, I know," I tried to cut her off so she wouldn't expound on her theater career, which I had heard about too many times to count.

"While I was doing some theater I married one of my fellow ac-tors, Godfrey Bane. He was an understudy and so was I so we had a lot of free time off stage. Of course his name wasn't really Godfrey Bane that was just his stage name. His real name was James Button, Jimmy Button. Not a very good stage name, is it?"

"Doesn't have the right ring to it, I guess …"

"So I was Sybil Button for a while. He was legally still Button. I would rather have been Sybil Bane. I love the sound of it."

"That does sound classy," I agree. "What happened to Jimmy, or, er, Godfrey?"

"The usual. He got tired of me and took up with a new young understudy. We weren't even married a year. Like I told you, I didn't have good luck with men. Oh, and don't tell Claudia. I never told her about Jimmy. It's embarrassing when you're twenty-one and your husband leaves you for a younger woman after 7 months of marriage. I have my pride."

Sybil wiggled until she was comfortable in her chair and stared at the fake fireplace. I stood up and looked out at the party. Cam was at the refreshment table and Hugh was trying to help him get something into his open visor. Hiram was hiding in his cubicle. Jenny and Chip were dancing to "The Monster Mash." Claudia had Syra cornered by the sci-fi section and I was glad I couldn't hear that conversation. I glanced back at Sybil and decided to stay where I was. I did wish I had those snicker doodles back, though.

"No, I didn't have good luck with men," Sybil continued as if she hadn't stopped talking five minutes ago. "After a couple of years in New York I came back to Birdsey Falls. Claudia had married Edward Mack and had Cassandra. I was curious about Edward because Claudia had always planned to marry someone important. Someone who would have lavish parties and introduce her to other important people. But she married Edward instead."

"Why? Claudia doesn't seem like the type to settle for less than what she wants."

"Her father picked out Edward for her. Edward was easygoing and very handsome. He came from a middle class family so didn't have any family money to fall back on. She and her father really thought he would change his name to Behrends in exchange for Claudia and the Behrends money. He adored Claudia but he wouldn't do that."

"I can't blame him."

"She tried to convince him on their honeymoon. Apparently he made some remark indicating that he would have thought Claudia would have been glad to get rid of such an undignified name—Bare Ends, get it?"

I murmured that I did.

"And she was so angry that she didn't speak to him for the rest of the honeymoon and for a good month after they got home. She probably would have never spoken to him again for insulting the Behrends name but she discovered she was pregnant with Cassandra and things softened up between them."

"Did you ever fall in love again?"

"Oh, yes. Just saying you don't want to ever fall in love isn't enough to keep it from happening. And I am a tenderhearted person. I eventually married Roscoe Beatty. We were fairly happy but then he died ..."

"I'm sorry. What happened?"

"We were on vacation in Chicago. He bought us some sausages from a street vendor and was attacked by a dog ..."

"He was killed by a dog?"

"Oh no. The dog jumped on him and stole the sausages so Roscoe chased the dog, which ran out in front of a taxi. The dog got hit by the taxi and went flying over the roof of the car. It landed right in front of one of those quaint horse-drawn carriages they have for the tourists. Roscoe went running behind the car to get the dog ..."

"Why?"

"To get the sausages back, of course. The horse reared up when the dog hit him ..."

"Roscoe was killed by the horse?"

"No. The horse started trampling the dog and Roscoe reached under the carriage to get the sausages …"

"And the carriage ran over him?"

"No. The carriage was rocking back and forth but Roscoe was able to crawl under to retrieve the sausages. He rolled out from under the carriage clutching the sausages and climbed onto the curb. Of course all the traffic was stopped now and quite a crowd had gathered …"

"Naturally …"

"Roscoe turned around to see all the commotion in the street and, unfortunately, so did the person in the apartment several floors above him. They were trying to put a huge fan in their window, and when all the commotion started they lost focus and …"

"He got hit by the fan falling out the window."

"No. The fan fell out the window and crashed on the pavement just inches from Roscoe's feet. He was recovering from his near escape when he saw a dozen police running down the street blowing whistles and trying to get things organized. They were coming right at him."

"And?"

"Well, they scared him to death. He dropped dead right next to the smashed fan."

"After all he went though it was the sight of the police that killed him?"

"Yes. You see, Roscoe had a bit of a problem with the police as a young man and had spent some time in jail. When he saw a dozen police coming straight at him, blowing those whistles, it literally scared him to death. Heart attack."

"Good Lord."

"At least I didn't have to divorce him." Sybil pulled herself painfully to her feet. "I could use some more cider. Don't hide in here too long or you'll miss all the fun!"

She had a point. It was a party. I should be out there socializing and looking for more refreshments. I wandered out of the Sherlock Holmes room making a resolution: Since death was inevitable, when I went, I wanted to go in a humorous way that would bring people a good laugh for generations to come. It's the least I could do for those left behind. I didn't want a painful death, but I would happily embrace a silly one.

Cam caught my eye and came over, holding an overflowing plate and a cup. "I'm really getting the hang of this costume now. Look, I can feed myself."

"I'm proud of you," I said while stroking the visor on his face.

"If you had this on you would be happy to be able to even move. I don't know what I'll do if I have to go to the bathroom."

"Maybe Santa can help you."

"I'm sure he'd love that. Where've you been?" he asked, flicking his tongue at his plate and securing one piece of chex mix. I reached for his cup.

"Try two hands. I was in the Sherlock Holmes room where I had an interesting conversation with Sybil. We got all the way up to husband number three."

"You're right. It is easier to eat with your hands than your tongue."

"I'm going to go check on the snicker doodles. Sybil ate all mine. Can you manage on your own?"

"I'm fine," he assured me. "I need to find Scott. Oh, and while you were talking to Sybil, John and Jingle arrived. Guess what they are?"

"I don't know. What does the costume for man-who-married-a-dingbat look like?"

"Very funny. I'll give you a hint. They look great standing next to Santa and Mrs. Claus."

Cam gave his visor a flip and went to find Scott. I looked around and finally spotted John and Jingle, dressed as elves. Jingle had long green pointed shoes with bells at the end. She tinkled whenever she walked. Good. That would help me to avoid her.

I grabbed a handful of snicker doodles and chatted briefly with Ted and Thelma, still unable to determine what she was dressed as. I caught Hiram sneaking out for more cider and told him how I had gotten the idea for my next Perry book from the hot-air balloons on the bookcase outside his cubicle. He stared at me and then scurried away. I snuck past John and Jingle, who were having a serious discussion with Hugh's assistant, Toby (guy from "RENT") and his partner, Tyler (other guy from "RENT"). John and Jingle bought a lot of antiques so Toby was probably combining business with pleasure. Tyler was listening politely. I noticed Cam collapsed in a bean bag chair in the Children's Section. It would take a tow truck to get him out of that. He and Scott were having an animated discussion about something; Scott was animated, Cam was sort of stiffly rocking around in the chair. It was a good party despite all that had happened in October and I was feeling a sense of contentment for the first time in weeks. This was followed by a sense of needing to use the bathroom after three cups of mulled cider so I proceeded to the back of the store where Grace maintained a lovely powder room for her customers which was always cleaner than my bathroom at home.

If you are wearing layers of clothing, it takes a while to get yourself settled in the bathroom. Once I was comfortable I didn't want to cope with rearranging my dress again so soon, so I reached for one of the dog-eared coffee-table books Grace keeps stacked on a white wicker table across from the toilet. These are books that have been thumbed through too often to sell, so she puts them in the powder room for customers to enjoy. I'd looked at the one about European castles a dozen times, so I picked up the book about famous Hollywood beauties and flipped through the pages.

Growing up I had never been able to decide if I wanted to look like Natalie Wood or Elizabeth Taylor. I decided that this was a good time to decide once and for all. As I was reading the list of Elizabeth Taylor's husbands, I was trying to imagine her in a situation where she was required to list all of her names on a form and what she would do when she ran out of room. I'd have to ask Sybil if that had ever happened to her. Can you fit Sybil Bright Bowe Button Beatty Bright all on one line? If she had anything monogrammed from her single days she would have been able to keep it forever. She had always been an "SB."

My heart started pounding and I slowly replaced the book on the table. While struggling with my dress I thought about the era when Sybil had grown up, the 1930s and 40s. Women had monogrammed handkerchiefs then. Sylvie Behrends and Syra former name Brinkleberger were the only other "SB"s I knew. And of the three, it seemed more likely that Sybil would have a monogrammed handkerchief. It was something that Syra wouldn't have and, let's face it, Sylvie was dead and the handkerchief had been very real. It wasn't a ghostly apparition.

I opened the bathroom door, remembering all the times Claudia had whipped out her handkerchief to wipe imaginary smudges off Abbey's face. I was certain Sybil had carried a handkerchief also. I just didn't remember if it was monogrammed or not. I wandered out of the powder room in a daze, trying to remember the chronology of the handkerchief's appearance and disappearance. It had appeared the night of the break-in. Cam had shoved it in the drawer of the table by the stairs. Cam told me Sylvie's story. We had forgotten about it. Then I decided to write my New Orleans mystery, inspired by Sylvie's story, and I wanted the handkerchief as a muse. I had gone to look for it and it was gone. That was the day after we had Claudia and Sybil over for paella. The handkerchief had disappeared between the night of the break-in and the night Sybil had eaten dinner at our house.

A dark figure loomed in front of me and I jumped and grabbed the powder room door to keep my balance. It was Ichabod Crane, staring at me like he could read my thoughts and found them very distasteful.

"What do you want?" I squeaked.

"Um, well, if you are through in there I'd like to, um, use the, um, lavatory," he answered, turning a bright shade of pink.

I straightened out and smoothed down my dress and adjusted my hair. "Yes, of course, please go ahead." There was no reason for me to be so jumpy and certainly no reason to be afraid of Hiram. Or anyone. I was seriously beginning to think I hadn't been "quite right" since I'd found Franklin's body. Murdered bodies may be strewn about willy-nilly in books but in real life, most people never stumbled on one in their entire lives. I had reason to still be affected by it.

"Your mother-in-law thinks I'm gay."

Once again I jumped and grabbed the powder room door. It flew open and Hiram was exposed washing his hands at the sink. He screamed like a girl and scrambled to shut the door, pushing me out of the room quite violently. I stumbled forward into Syra's arms and she caught me before I hit the floor. Claudia came around the corner and took one look at us, sniffed and turned away. Hiram came out of the bathroom.

"What is *wrong* with you?" he asked, staring at me down his long nose.

"Sorry, the door wasn't locked ..."

"So you just barge in when a gentleman is in the lavatory? You knew I was in there."

"I fell against the door and it opened. You were just washing your hands, Hiram. You weren't undressed ..."

331

"I was in the *bathroom*!"

"I'm sorry. I didn't do it on purpose ..."

"I trust that this incident will go no further and will remain among the three of us," he warned us.

Syra and I nodded.

He stared at me, his face a couple inches from mine. "I am relying on your good word and delicacy as a gentlewoman and," he turned to Syra, "a former president." He stalked off.

"Do you really think he believes we wanted to see him in the bathroom?" Syra asked.

"I have no idea, but that is probably the most intimate thing that has happened to him in decades, so I guess he was profoundly affected," I replied, once again trying to smooth down my dress and adjust the veil on my head. It seemed to slip back and forth very easily and at any given moment was never straight. "Oh, and sorry about Claudia ..."

"That's OK. You have no control over her. I'm going to find Diane. See you later." Syra popped her stovepipe hat back on her head and returned to the party. I heard the tingling of bells so darted behind the book shelves and hid until I heard the powder room door close. The coast was clear so I darted back out into the main room and began to mingle my way to the snicker doodles.

"Can you help me with something, dear?" Sybil interrupted my snicker doodle raid with a gentle touch on my back. "I need something from my car."

I turned to her and noticed that her face was flushed, like she had just climbed the stairs or was embarrassed. "Do you want me to go get it?" I asked, wondering what she could need in the middle of a Halloween party that she had forgotten to bring in in the first place. Claudia was scatterbrained but Sybil was usually more organized.

"I need to get it myself but I would like you to walk outside with me. It's dark and the sidewalk can be bumpy …"

"Is it something I can just find for you so you don't need to go all the way to your car? What is it?"

Sybil leaned in closer and whispered in my ear. "Incontinence."

"Oh. Well, I have some pads in my purse if that would save you a trip to the car," I offered. Since my flirtation with perimenopause I had started bringing pads with me everywhere because apparently I no longer would know when I would or wouldn't get my period.

"Those don't work as well. I have special ones in the car but they are too large to put in my purse. I thought I was all set but then the lure of the mulled cider made me lose my usual self-discipline with liquid intake and now I have a problem. I'd ask Cam but I don't really want to explain it to him and he can't seem to walk very well in that costume. Do you mind?"

I brushed off my snicker doodle covered hands and took a last sip of cider. Getting away from the refreshment table was probably a good idea. Sybil's incontinence was a godsend. Maybe when we got back the snicker doodles and candy corn would be gone. "Of course I don't mind. Let me get my coat."

"Can we go out the back so no one sees us? I don't want people to ask where we're going."

I nodded and headed to the back of the bookstore where the coats had been hung. We passed the powder room door and heard singing. It was Cam. For some inexplicable reason he always sings when he washes his hands. He doesn't sing in the shower, just when he washes his hands. It's one of those habits that are cute when you are first married but after twenty-five years has you looking for duct tape. Sybil and I both recognized his voice and rolled our eyes.

"Claudia doesn't do that, does she?" I asked.

"Good heavens no. I don't believe Claudia has ever sung in her life."

That sounded about right to me. Every time I saw a trait in Cam that did not resemble his mother I should be thankful rather than critical. I resolved to learn to love his hand-washing solos in the future.

It was cold outside but the sky was clear. The night was beautiful and perfect for a walk if you were bundled up enough. Some Halloweens were too rainy to really enjoy being outside and many times we had had snow. This was a textbook fall evening and I felt glad for all those parents and their little trick or treaters wandering the streets in pursuit of sugar. Now that we were outside Sybil had become quite goal-oriented and was practically pushing me along the alley in the back of the bookstore. I've never seen anyone so desperate for adult diapers. If the commercials captured some of this emotion, we'd all be out frantically buying them. Sybil once again had a viselike grip on my arm and was propelling me down the street at a speed both dangerous and ridiculous, considering how we were dressed. We finally reached her car and I leaned against it, out of breath.

"Sybil, you really need to see a doctor about this. I think there are pills or something."

"I know. I know. But it's too embarrassing to talk about." She handed me her keys and pointed to the trunk. They're in there. Better grab two. You can hide one under your dress."

I opened the trunk and leaned inside. There was more stuff in here than under Abbey's bed. I pushed a bag of empty soda cans to the side and ran into a plastic bag filled with plastic bags. Then came the magazines, books, three unmatched gloves, an orange silk scarf, an unopened package of press-on nails, a tiger print beach towel, a piece of firewood, a red plaid metal lunch box, several containers of gas, a salt shaker, four combs, one yellow espadrille, a coloring book, a bunch of paper and, finally, a plastic bag labeled "Confidence, Women's Size X- Large."

"Got them!" I pulled out two and handed them to Sybil who had caught her breath and come around to the back of the car to help me look.

"Thank you. I can't make it back to the party. I'm going to run into the coffee shop across the street and change. Come with me. I'll buy you a hot chocolate." Sybil started across the street and I reached up to close the trunk and follow her. I gave the Buick junkyard one last look and my eyes fell on the pieces of paper. They were spread out all over the floor of the trunk and a "Page 22" caught my eye. I moved them around and saw the words "Camden Woods" and "kidnapping." My hands froze and slowly I straightened up and looked over at Sybil. She was halfway across the street and turned to see why I wasn't coming. She froze.

I was rooted to the spot, my hand still on the lid of the trunk. She began to walk back across the street, staring at me. I couldn't move. I couldn't speak. She came right up to me and slammed down the trunk.

"Get in the car, Tamsen."

"I don't want …"

"Get in the car. We need to talk."

She grabbed my arm and pulled me to the side of the car, yanked open the passenger side door and pushed me in. I landed sideways on the seat and she had to stuff my dress and my legs in before slamming the door and getting in on the driver's side. I was still trying to untangle myself from my skirts when we went squealing out of the parking space like Jeff Gordon after a pit stop.

Chapter Thirty-Two

By the time I was able to sit up, we were heading out of Birdsey Falls. Every time I started to ask a question Sybil would eyeball me into silence. I felt like I had with Syra when I thought she was poisoning me with hot chocolate. Once again, I was being overly dramatic. I wasn't even sure that was Franklin's manuscript in the trunk. It could have been something Sybil wrote. The page 22 could be a coincidence. She could have pages 23-50 back there, too, for all I knew. There was lots of stuff back there. I probably hadn't seen half of it. As to why she was acting like this, there could be a lot of reasonable explanations. By now she had probably wet her pants so she wanted to go home to change, although we were going in the opposite direction of Ashland Belle. Maybe we were going to my house to change. It was the right direction for that. She probably didn't want to talk to me because she was embarrassed. Next Halloween we would be laughing about the whole thing. I just needed to stay calm and not overreact or do anything to make her think I suspected her of anything more serious than a weak bladder.

"Are those Franklin's papers in your trunk?"

Sybil never took her eyes off the road but her hands clenched on the steering wheel. "Why would you ask that?"

"Because I saw a bunch of pages including a page 22 in your trunk. I found page 23 of something he was writing in his desk but the rest were gone. Those are his papers, aren't they? How did you get them?"

"He gave them to me."

"Why? What are they?"

"Just an old man's ramblings about his life. He wanted me to put his thoughts in some kind of order for him. He had trouble concentrating."

"I didn't know you went out to the cottage to see him."

"I rarely did. Claudia didn't like to go because it made her too sad to see him like that so I went once in a while to check on him, bring him something, talk to him a little. He wasn't much of a conversation-alist. The last time I went he gave me the papers."

"Oh. You know, you have a lot of junk in your trunk. Were those full gas cans you had back there? Those are dangerous to store in your car."

"I know. I just got them today. I keep running out of gas. Something is wrong with my gauge. Once I get it fixed, I'll get rid of the cans."

"Where are we going in such a rush? We're driving around in circles. We just passed my house."

"I need to talk to you about the ransom money you found. We needed to get away from the party and all the people."

I glanced around at the woods and the blackness of the road ahead. "Aren't we far enough away now?"

"I suppose so." Sybil pulled the car to the side of the road and turned off the engine. "There are some things you need to know about that money. What I'm going to tell you, you are free to tell the police now that Franklin is gone. Then you need to let the whole thing rest and get on with your life. Let Claudia move on. Do you swear you will?"

"I'm not sure what I'm swearing to. But yes, I would like to get on with my life. Tell me the story first and then I'll swear if I can."

"It's pretty simple, really. Ernie Whitcomb worked at the Behrends house doing yard work. He got to talking one day with Franklin about the games we were all playing under his direction. Franklin told him about the maps and how we had to go out and look for things, our versions of treasures. Apparently Ernie thought that was pretty interesting and asked Franklin to make him a map to a place in Camden Woods, a tree with a deep hole under it. He said he was going to show it to a friend of his and see if he could follow it. It was sort of a challenge, Ernie implying that no one other than kids could follow one of Franklin's maps. Franklin took a lot of care with it, going back and forth to the tree several times and mapping it out in great detail. He said Ernie thought the map was great and even gave him a dollar for it. In 1938, a dollar was a lot of money, especially for someone in Ernie's position. Franklin was surprised he was willing to part with that much money …"

"Because he had no idea that Ernie was expecting to use that map to get $10,000."

"Right. So that was the end of it until the morning when they found Raymond Ketchum's body and everyone started talking about the missing ransom. I was totally oblivious to all this at the time. Remember I was only six. I never heard this story until ten or eleven years later …"

"Franklin told you?"

"Yes. Within a few days, reading the newspapers and watching the police in the woods, Franklin realized the part he had inadvertently played in the whole crime. Once things had calmed down Franklin went to the tree that Ernie had asked him to make the map to. Sure enough, the ransom money was there."

"How? How could they miss it? Did the brother take it there after Raymond had been shot? Why?"

"No, that idiot Ernie Whitcomb had shown Franklin the tree he wanted him to make a map to but had gone to the *wrong* tree to pick up the ransom. Ernie had given the map to Fletcher Ketchum and then, without a map for himself, gone to the wrong tree. The man was incompetent."

"So he killed Raymond Ketchum and the ransom money was there all the time, only in another location?"

"Yes. Franklin realized Ernie had made a mistake. He didn't know what to do but he felt guilty about making a map for a crime that ended in murder, so he took the ransom and hid it in his house."

"Why not tell the police? He didn't do anything wrong."

"He was fifteen. He made a map telling a man where to make a ransom drop and the whole thing had ended in murder. He was scared to death and wasn't sure if he had committed a crime or not. He didn't dare tell anyone; he just hid the money …"

"And spent the rest of his life tortured by it."

"Yes."

"That's horrible. And he was writing about it in those papers he asked you to look at?"

"Yes. I guess he finally needed to let the whole story out."

Sybil and I sat and stared at the dark road ahead. This is what Franklin's future must have looked like to him after he found the ransom money. I remember reading an article many years ago about the human brain and how it doesn't finish developing until our twenties. It pointed out that teenagers make a lot of stupid decisions because of this lack of development. They just don't think things through the same way an adult does.

"Sybil, who do you think killed Franklin?"

"I don't know. At least they don't think it's Grace's step-son anymore. If the police can't figure it out, I doubt we will."

"That's not a satisfactory answer."

Sybil reached over and held my hand. "I know it's not. You're still young and need to know all the answers. When you get to my age you realize that you can wait for a while because you don't have a long time until all the answers will be known to you. Have patience, dear." Sybil turned sideways, looking directly in my face and continued to hold my hand. "Remember earlier tonight when you asked me about having children?"

"Yes, of course."

"I've always felt that Claudia allowed me to share motherhood with her and that Cassandra and Cam were almost like my own children. Then you came along and I had another child. If I had had a daughter I would have liked her to be just like you."

I could feel tears welling up as I reached over and hugged Sybil, suddenly so appropriate in her Mother Goose outfit. "I've always wished you were my mother-in-law, Sybil ..."

"Don't sell Claudia short ..."

"I'm not. I've always given her the benefit of the doubt but she has consistently been mean-spirited and selfish and self-centered ..."

"She is who she was brought up to be, Tamsen. Maybe with different parents and a different society and time she would have been more like you want her to be. But she was a success in everyone's eyes. I was the failure making one disastrous marriage after another and going on the stage ..."

"I like you better."

"Thank you dear. I hope you like me enough that when I'm gone you'll be kind to Claudia and protect her from the ugly things in life."

Sybil was so sincere that I didn't want to tell her that Claudia *was* one of the ugly things in life and I was the one who needed protection. She obviously saw a side of her that I'd never seen, which maybe didn't even exist. But she meant well.

"I'll try," I promised.

"Good. Thank you. Now it's time to stop all this crying and sentimentality and get going. I really do need to take care of the personal hygiene issue we started to take care of a while ago. Can you reach into the backseat and get one of those pads for me?"

"Of course." I leaned over the seat and grabbed one off the seat where Sybil had thrown it when we made a quick and dramatic getaway from town.

"And, if you don't mind, would you just step out of the car for a few minutes so I can change? I know it's cold but I promise to be fast. Please? An old lady needs every shred of dignity that she can get."

"Sure."

Once again she reached over and gently squeezed my hand. I scrambled out of the car in my long skirts and moved to the side of the shoulder to give her some privacy. She started the car, probably to get the heat going again. I looked up at the stars. The night was unbelievably clear. I felt like I was at a planetarium and shortly different constellations would light up and a voice would explain to me what they were. I entertained myself describing the beauty of the autumn night sky and the constellations that were visible in all their glory at this time of the year. Suddenly I heard the gears shift in Sybil's car and she spun its wheels, spraying dirt at me as she drove down the shoulder and bounced back onto the blacktop, tail lights racing away.

I was still standing there, dumbfounded, when I heard a terrifying crash and a loud explosion, and the woods burst into flames. Fire shot toward the sky like some kind of macabre fireworks display. I hitched up my skirts and began running toward the fire, screaming

Sybil's name. If Grace had been there I know she would have serenely closed her eyes and felt the presence of Sybil's spirit as it rose above the flames and shed all its worldly worries and pain. My spirituality is not as finely tuned as Grace's, so I ran around screaming, heading toward the fire and then backing up as the heat rushed out to me like some poisonous snake flicking its tongue in warning. Finally I moved away, praying that the crash had killed her instantly and she had been gone before the car exploded and burned.

"Oh God, Sybil. What have you done?" My voice sounded hoarse and foreign. I kept backing away and stumbled to the side of the road, where I collapsed on the ground and cried. I heard the sirens and automatically scooted back from the road to the edge of the woods as the fire truck and two police cars wailed past me. I could still feel the heat of the fire but I was shivering all over.

Several more cars had joined the firefighters and the police. People in various states of odd attire were wandering aimlessly, watching the firefighters and wondering what had happened. I moved further back among the trees, too exhausted and too stunned to do any more than watch.

The sound of someone calling my name pulled me out of the fog and, like Perry Many Paws emerging from his cave after a winter of hibernation, I lethargically crawled to the edge of the road to see what was going on. Creatures—witches, fairies, pirates, gypsies, a box of oatmeal and lots of the most authentic fireman costumes I've ever seen.

"Tamsen! Tamsen! Oh God, where are you? Someone do something! Hiram saw her get into Sybil's car. She must be here ... Why isn't anyone doing anything? Get her out of there! Do something, you idiots ..."

I watched, fascinated, as two men dressed as policemen grabbed a Tin Man and pulled him away from the fire. The Tin Man kept screaming and fighting but the two policemen were too much for him, encumbered as he was by his outfit. I started laughing hysterically as one of the policemen actually punched the Tin Man, and he lumbered to the ground like a pile of cans falling off the kitchen table. Well, that should shut him up for a while. There was enough noise and confusion without that hysterical tin can disturbing everyone while they were trying to work. Some people had no consideration.

I was cold. The long dress was keeping my legs warm but the rest of me was cold and I couldn't stop shivering. Even my feet were jumping around uncontrollably and the only way to get them to hold still was to actually grab them with my hands. This wasn't easy to do. After a couple of half-hearted attempts to get hold of them, I made a concerted lunge and felt a sharp pain surge down my thigh.

"Awwwww. Son of a bitch, that hurts!" My scream jolted the Tin Man to a sitting position and he started pivoting in a circle while trying to bring himself to his feet.

"Tamsen! Where are you? Dammit. Where are you?"

Cam! How did he get here? I grabbed the nearest tree and pulled myself to my feet. Ouch! Another pain shot through my thigh. "Cam! Over here. I can't walk …"

"Hold on, sweetheart. I'm coming to you." I heard the clanking of tin coming closer. "Don't try to move," he said huffing and puffing. "You may be seriously …"

"I'm fine, but I can't walk …"

"You will walk. I promise. I'll make sure you walk again …"

All we needed was some dramatic music to make this 1940s Hollywood scene complete. I started to giggle, remembered Sybil and burst into tears.

"Oh God. You're crying. You never cry. You must be in pain."

I leaned against the tree and stretched out my arms as Cam came clobbering toward me. His helmet was gone and his red hair was covered with ash. There were streaks of soot on his face, streaks that I would swear were tears. And his jaw was rapidly swelling and beginning to distort his mouth so he now resembled the Phantom of the Opera emerging from a can of soup. His face lit up like a Christmas tree when he saw me and we fell into each other's arms laughing and crying and, in my case, swearing because of the pain in my thigh.

Bear hugs. Whispered endearments. Happy tears. Sooty kisses. Sir Lancelot in tarnished armor carrying a bedraggled Guinevere out of the woods, yelling for an ambulance. The EMTs gathered around us, delighted to finally have someone to care for, and I was whisked into the back of the ambulance. The doors were slammed on Cam as he shouted instructions to the EMTs and encouraging words to me on his devotion regardless of my ability to ever walk again. I blew him a kiss and then was rushed away, siren wailing and people making way.

The EMT began to examine me and when he put pressure on my thigh I screamed. "We have leg damage, possibly vertebrae damage," he yelled to the driver. "Call it in."

I shook my head. "I don't think there is any ..."

"How did you survive that crash, ma'am? If you come away alive, regardless of the damage to your leg, you are the luckiest woman I know."

"I wasn't in the car when it ..."

"Ah. You jumped out! What incredible reflexes and fast thinking. You may have broken your leg or your back. You still have feeling in your leg. That's a positive sign that you will be able to walk again ..."

"It's amazing what surgery and rehab can do now. Be positive!" yelled the driver.

It was obvious that I wasn't going to be able to get a word in so I just leaned back and closed my eyes. Both men were so proud of me and so encouraging that I didn't have the heart to tell them I that my only injury was a pulled a muscle in my leg, the result of trying to touch my toes.

Chapter Thirty-Three

I spent the night in the hospital. It didn't take long for them to determine I wasn't seriously injured but there was some concern about my confused state of mind. They gave me a mild sedative and I slept well. In the morning I talked to a psychologist who pronounced me normal enough, considering the shock I had had. They prescribed some sleeping pills and sent me on my way.

Cam took me home and I looked forward to continuing the ride on the wave of affection that had overwhelmed us last night in the woods. I imagined a day spent recovering on the couch, in front of the fire, with Cam running around waiting on me and telling me how his life would have been destroyed if I had been in the car when it crashed. My friends would drop by, one at a time, and I would feign loss of memory when pressed for details of the event. I wasn't sure what I was going to tell people yet. I wasn't even completely sure just what had happened or why. But I knew I could put it off for a day or two until I had time to think it through. I was recovering from an ordeal. Certain latitude was granted in tragic situations such as this.

Therefore, I was dumbstruck when I headed into the library for my day of repose. I didn't expect to see a tragic figure in a peach silk peignoir languishing on my library couch, propped up with a dozen pillows, a cup of tea and a plate of cookies within easy reach. Cam came up behind me and put his arm around my waist.

"After leaving you last night I went to break the news to my mom. I didn't think she should spend the night alone so I brought her home to stay with us until she comes to grips with Sybil's death," he whispered in my ear.

"I hate whispering …"

"I know," he continued to whisper, "but I don't want to disturb her."

My hair smelled like smoke. I was coughing from smoke inhalation. I was limping. My eyes were red and puffy. I had horrible visions floating through my head and a million unanswered questions. Meanwhile Claudia was lounging on my couch, perfectly made up and perfumed, dressed in layers of peach silk that flowed around her diminutive form like a pastel pastry confection. If she had been crying there was no sign of it. It would be easier to feel sorry for her if she looked as bad as I did. Claudia raised a limp hand in our direction.

"Tamsen, dear, are you all right? Cam and I were so worried about you." The delicate white hand fluttered back to her side like a swan floating across the water. I felt like an ugly, filthy, smelly blob. Slowly I walked into the room and went to the couch. I had a sudden vision of Claudia raising that swan hand at my face and making me kiss her ring.

"Yes Claudia, I'm fine. I'll be coughing for a few days and my eyes hurt and …"

"That's good, dear. We don't want this tragedy compounded by losing someone else." Sigh.

"Mom, you should be resting. This has been a huge shock. Maybe Tamsen and I should leave you alone so you can sleep. Or I can help you back upstairs to your room."

Her room? Claudia had an actual room now? How long was she going to be here? Why couldn't she just sleep on the couch and then go home? Did she actually need a room of her own? I headed toward my favorite leather chair and started to sit.

"Wait, dear. You don't want to do that. Don't you think you should shower and change before you sit on the furniture?"

I glanced at Cam and he shrugged.

"Fine. I'll go shower. And change. Then maybe I can bake some pies and make a full Thanksgiving dinner for all of us."

"Thank you, dear, but please don't bother. Thanksgiving is three weeks away so there is no sense in going to all that trouble now. It would spoil our anticipation of the actual event. But we'll need something hearty for dinner after what we've been through. A pot roast, maybe?"

***

The shower and clean clothes felt good. The pot roast, made by Cam, tasted wonderful and did a lot to improve my spirits. The four-hour nap, alone in my room and far away from Claudia, was incredibly restorative. I was beginning to feel like my old self as the three of us sat around the fireplace munching on German chocolate cake, a donation from Bing, and drinking after-dinner coffee and diet soda. Mycroft was seated at my feet. The room was cozy with a gentle light from the flames and a few lamps softly lit around the room. I felt at peace. I knew that either Cam or Claudia would ruin it. It was just a matter of time. Cam won.

"I can't believe you left the party and didn't tell me where you were going."

"I was just going to the car with Sybil and …"

"But you left town! That isn't quite the same as …"

"I didn't know I was going to leave town, Cam. I was just planning to go to the car with Sybil to get something …"

"But you drove away …"

"But I didn't *know* I was going to drive away, so how could I tell you something I didn't know!"

"Please don't yell, children. I don't want to get a headache."

Silence followed while Claudia sipped her coffee and daintily wiped her mouth with her napkin. We had to get out the cloth napkins because she felt paper was vulgar. I felt like blowing my nose in my cloth napkin just to show her what vulgar really was but I decided to keep it clean in case I needed to wad it up and stuff it down Cam's throat the next time he opened his mouth.

"I don't know what I'll do without Sybil," Claudia sighed.

Yeah, you'll need to learn to make your own famous chocolate cherry soufflé. I wonder what the people at Ashland Belle will think when you don't make the soufflé anymore. You will probably tell them you are retiring the recipe in honor of Sybil.

"She was like a sister to me. We've been friends our whole lives. I can't believe she's gone. Why was she so careless?"

"I don't think she died just to inconvenience you," I said. Cam gave me a look that would have earned him a kick in the shins if he had been closer.

"Well, whether she meant it or not, what she did is completely disrupting my life."

"I'm sure you don't mean that the way it sounds, mother …"

"Really? I don't usually misspeak but maybe I'm overwrought. You could hardly expect less under the circumstances."

Cam nodded, totally oblivious to the tension in the air. Cam's love for me might be blind but his love for his mother was deaf, dumb, blind and imbecilic.

"Why would she do something so careless as carry several containers of gasoline in her trunk?" he asked. "She must have realized how dangerous that was."

"She said her gas gauge wasn't working and she kept running out of ..." I began to explain.

Claudia gently shook her head. "Nonsense. I've driven her car several times recently and the gas gauge worked just fine. I don't know why she drove that old Buick. It's such an old ladies' car."

"She was seventy-something, Claudia," I reminded her.

"Exactly my point. She shouldn't have been driving an old ladies' car. I tried to get her to buy a lovely Cadillac like mine. If she had listened to me she would still be alive." Cam began to soothe his mother so she wouldn't feel that she was in any way responsible for Sybil's death by being unable to convince her to buy a Cadillac. I began to try to think about all the reasons I loved Cam in spite of his mother. My mind quickly wandered back to Sybil and our fateful drive away from the Halloween party. All I could see was her speeding away from me. The explosion. The fire. The heat. The horrible heat.

"I don't feel very well. I'm going to bed."

Cam jumped to his feet and offered to go up with me. I waved him away. I needed to be alone.

I was sure I wouldn't be able to sleep after my long nap this afternoon. My mind was racing with questions and I would never be able to relax until I knew what had happened, what had been going through Sybil's mind. I propped myself up in bed and prepared to think it through from the moment Sybil approached me at the party until she drove away. Franklin's manuscript in the trunk. The containers of gas. The drive out of town. The crash. My good fortune to not be in the car. It all swirled around in my head and I immediately fell asleep, more confused than ever.

I awoke to the pop of a soda can and the smell of cinnamon. Someone was rubbing my back. I snuggled more deeply into the blankets, wishing I could drink the soda and eat the cinnamon thing without having to sit up or open my eyes. Basic human needs won out and I crawled out of bed and headed for the bathroom. Cam ushered me back into bed and set the breakfast tray on my lap.

"Cinnamon rolls compliments of Bing. He and Syra send their love. Grace called. Diane called. Officer Donny called." I stopped eating and dropped my cinnamon bun back on the plate.

"What did Officer Donny want?"

"You have frosting on your cheek. No, left cheek. Got it."

"Officer Donny?"

"Oh, yeah. Just routine follow-up after an accident. He's stopping by in a while to talk to you …"

"How long?"

Cam glanced at his watch. "About forty minutes. Relax and eat. You have plenty of time."

"Is your mother still here?" I tried to sound nonchalant but I know it sounded accusatory. Cam reached out and patted my leg.

"Yes. And I'm sorry. I want to devote my full attention to you but I can't forget about her entirely. Someone has to be there for her …"

"I know. I just wish it wasn't you. We've been lucky having Sybil all these years to take care of her and now …" I realized I sounded like Claudia, viewing Sybil's absence as an inconvenience to me. That was disturbing.

"She'll settle back into her own routine soon."

"And what if she doesn't? What if she can't stand to live at Ashland Belle without Sybil?"

"You mean, what if she wants to move back here?" Cam actually blanched at the idea. There was hope for him yet.

I was showered and dressed when Officer Donny arrived. Part of me dreaded talking to him and part of me couldn't wait. Maybe he would have the definitive answers to what had happened the prior night.

Claudia had taken to her bed, or rather, taken to our guest bed, and was not to be disturbed. Having her stay here would be relatively painless if she could remain in her bed with a "do not disturb" sign on her door. If I didn't have to see her or talk to her, I could easily work around her. It was up to Cam to make sure she was fed regularly.

Bing had kindly supplied us with a dozen cinnamon buns so we were able to be hospitable to Officer Donny and his partner, Officer Lumb, as we gathered in the solarium. Officer Lumb was struggling with sticky fingers, his pen and his notebook while Officer Donny did the talking.

"How was Ms. Bright's state of mind last night at the party? Did she seem her normal self?"

"Yes. She was socializing as usual. She and I talked for a while in the Sherlock Holmes room ..."

"Huh?" Officer Lumb licked the frosting off the end of his pen and stared at me.

"The Sherlock Holmes room. That's the room where all the mystery books are. Grace has it set up to look like Sherlock Holmes' study." Officer Lumb continued to stare at me. "You *have* heard of Sherlock Holmes ...?"

"Yeah. Guy with a cape and pipe. Did drugs and no one arrested him. He admitted it. Even put it in writing and no one arrested him. Not right."

"You *do* realize he was a fictional character."

Officer Lumb flicked crumbs off his notebook and flipped the pages. "No excuse. Should've been arrested."

"Can we get back on track, please? Officer Lumb, are you writing this all down?"

"Kinda sticky," Officer Lumb mumbled. "Yeah, I'm writing this down."

"Good. Please proceed Mrs. Mack. You said you and Ms. Bright were talking in the Sherlock Holmes room at the bookstore. What were you talking about?"

"She was telling me about her former husbands."

"Did that upset her?"

"No, not at all. It was just chit chat. She was in good spirits."

"And during this conversation she asked you to leave with her?"

"No. We each went back to the party for a while and then she asked me to go to her car with her."

"Why? Why did she want to leave the party?"

Officer Lumb coughed. "Can I have another one of those buns?" Cam passed him the plate. "Did you make these? They're really good."

"No, Bing Foster made them." I answered. "He lives across the street."

"Never heard of him."

"He doesn't get out much."

"Is he Syra Foster's husband?"

"No, her brother."

"Good cook."

"Lumb!"

"What, sir?"

"Can you finish your snack so we get back to the questioning?"

"Sure."

"Thank you. Now, where were we?"

"Well, sir, Mrs. Mack said, 'She was telling me about her former husbands' And then you said, 'Did that upset her?' And then Mrs. Mack replied, 'No, not at all. It was just chit chat. She was in good spirits' Then you said, 'And during this conversation she asked you to leave with her?' to which Mrs. Mack replied, 'No. We each went back to the party for a while and then she asked me to go to her car with her.'

You then asked, 'Why? Why did she want to leave the party?' It was at this point that I asked for another bun."

Good Lord, he did the entire recitation without reference to his notes. Officer Lumb was an idiot savant.

"Thank you, Officer Lumb. Now, Mrs. Mack, why did Ms. Bright ask you to leave the party with her?"

Officer Lumb was licking frosting off his fingers like he didn't have a care in the world. Officer Donny had to repeat his question before I was able to divert my attention back to him.

"Um, yes. Leaving the party. Sybil wanted me to go with her to her car to get an item she needed. She didn't want to go alone in the dark."

"What happened after she asked you to go to the car?"

"Well, we walked to the car and she asked me to get something out of her trunk ...'

"What?"

I didn't want to embarrass her but on the other hand there needed to be a legitimate reason for taking a drive in the middle of a party. I decided to keep as close to the truth as possible and assume that Officer Donny was as squeamish about "women's issues" as most men were.

"It's kind of personal ..."

"This is an investigation into a woman's death. I need the facts."

"Well, Sybil was an elderly woman and um, sometimes things don't work like they used to. She had a problem with incontinence. She needed to change."

"But you said she asked you to go to her car with her to pick up an item, not change her clothes."

"Yes, well, it started out that she needed to pick up an item, an undergarment ..."

355

"Adult diaper?" Lumb asked, eyeing the remaining cinnamon bun.

"Well, yes. You could call it that."

"So once you got to the car she changed her mind?" Officer Donny prodded. Suddenly a cohesive story came to me.

"Yes, yes, that's it. At first she just needed to pick up a fresh undergarment to take back to the party. But when we got to the car she discovered there was a more complicated issue."

"She wet her pants." Lumb announced, reaching for the cinnamon bun and taking a big bite.

"Well, the situation was that she needed to change a few items ..."

"So you got in the car to go home with her?"

"Yes. She didn't want to go alone so we headed off together to repair the damage and then planned to head back to the party. It wouldn't have taken long ..."

"But Ms. Bright lived in the other direction. Why did she head out of town the wrong way?"

Now that was a stumper. I suspected why Sybil had headed to the woods, but I really needed more time to work this through. Unfortunately, I wasn't going to get it. I was a professional writer. I should be able to do this.

"She seemed to be headed toward your house rather than hers," Officer Lumb suggested.

"Yes, that was it. She inadvertently headed toward my house rather than hers."

"Old people can be absent minded," Lumb offered.

"Exactly. She was embarrassed and got confused and went the wrong way."

"And kept going the wrong way, even past the turn off to your street?" Officer Donny asked. He sounded a little dubious.

"That does seem odd," Cam added.

"It *was* odd," I agreed. "But remember, it was very dark and Sybil wasn't used to driving after dark. And we were talking and distracted by the situation …" I trailed off, not sure where I was going with this. Why was I floundering around? I just needed to change the facts a little to make this turn out right. I desperately wanted to protect Sybil's memory.

"Let's see. She planned to go to her house and change her clothes. But she went off in the wrong direction to go to your house and change? Change into what? What would you have at your house?"

"I'm not sure what she was planning to change into …"

"But then she drove right by your street and continued on out of town. What was the plan at that point? Something doesn't add up, Mrs. Mack."

I took a long drink and frantically scrambled for something to say that would tie this whole thing up and send the officers home. It was like writer's block. For the love of God, someone give me an idea. Now.

"There were no skid marks. That's very curious," Officer Donny informed us. "There should have been very definite skid marks where Ms. Bright tried to stop herself from driving into the woods. When you lose control of your car it's natural to violently apply the brakes." Officer Donny paused and waited for my explanation. I was still waiting for the spirits to enlighten me so I just stared at him. "And why weren't you in the car? Why, right before the accident, did you get out of the car?"

She headed at top speed toward the trees with a trunk of gas cans and never applied her brakes. After she made me get out of the car. It was so obvious what had happened. I needed to fix this. I rubbed my face with my hands. Once, twice, three times. I knew what had happened. I knew what the story had to be. I knew what Sybil wanted the story to be. I could, I would, do that for her.

"Mrs. Mack?"

Cam reached over and grabbed my hand. "Are you all right, sweetheart? You look pale. Maybe you need to lie …"

"No. No, I'm fine. It's just hard to think about what happened. To talk about it …"

"We need your statement."

"I understand. I just needed a minute. OK. Sybil planned to go home to change. She went the wrong way. We headed to my house instead but she missed the turn. She realized she was headed farther into the woods, away from town, and she planned to turn around. But then I needed to get out. I'd had several glasses of cider. You understand …"

"You had to pee," Officer Lumb contributed. Thank you, Officer Lumb.

"Yes. Exactly. It was dark and no one was there and I wasn't sure I could make it home, especially if Sybil kept wandering around missing turns and going in the wrong direction, so I asked if I could get out for a minute. She, of course, understood and let me out while she went to turn the car around and come back and get me …"

Officer Donny looked at me sternly. "But there were no skid marks. She lost control and headed toward the trees and never put on her brakes. That suggests …"

"Yes, I know what it suggests. Unfortunately, it's a common story among elderly drivers. Sybil started to lose control of her car and slammed her foot on the accelerator rather than the brakes."

"And just happened to have three containers of gasoline in her trunk so when she hit the trees the car exploded," Officer Donny concluded somewhat suspiciously.

"Yes, that's what happened."

"Oh God," Cam moaned. "Poor Sybil."

No one said anything. I offered up a prayer of thanks to the spirits. Cam shook his head and looked on the verge of tears. Officer Donny continued to stare at me suspiciously. It was finally Officer Lumb who broke the uncomfortable silence.

"So, in conclusion, one woman died because she peed her pants and another woman lived because she didn't."

Chapter Thirty-Four

The front page of the newspaper was filled with the final story of Raymond Ketchum's murder. With Muriel's help, the police had all the details they needed. Sybil's violent death took a back seat to the discovery of the ransom money and the solution to the kidnapping/murder of 1938.

The paper had wanted to interview Claudia about her brother and the money but she had refused. Cam, assuming his professional MBA persona, had talked to them, explaining that Claudia had been six years old and there was no one left who had been around on that fateful night. The paper had printed a three-day series on the Ketchum kidnapping and murder and now everyone knew the part Franklin had played, why he had become a recluse and why there had been $10,000 hidden all over my house. There was no theory about his murder.

Public opinion seemed to sway toward Franklin being an innocent bystander who had panicked when he discovered he had inadvertently played a part in the kidnapping/murder, and had hidden the evidence. Since he was a member of Birdsey Falls' most prominent family and never spent any of the ransom money, people were quick to forgive him. He was just fifteen.

Meanwhile I was now haunted by what had happened Halloween night along that star-lit road in addition to not knowing who killed

Franklin. I didn't know what had made Sybil do what she had done but deep down I knew her crash had been deliberate. I was seriously considering asking Grace to hold a séance in her bookstore so we could attempt to contact Sybil and ask her to explain.

Fortunately for me, the police weren't as mystified by Sybil's actions as I was. They were quick to believe both that a middle-aged woman would have incontinence issues and that a seventy plus woman would mistake an accelerator for a gas pedal. That story was my next-to-last gift to Sybil.

By the second week in November, things appeared to be back to normal in Birdsey Falls. People were preparing for Thanksgiving and arguing over when was the appropriate time to start decorating for Christmas. Abbey had done well on her midterms and was looking forward to finals and the end of her first semester at college. Cam and Bing were busy planning the Thanksgiving menu despite the fact that it was always the same. Claudia had accepted the fact that we would never know who killed Franklin and seemed relieved that the whole town was no longer talking about it. Ryan was doing his community service as a volunteer at Bugg Hill, alternating between bussing tables and doing yard work. He was still being blamed for both the break-ins at our house although he would admit to only one. Syra was relieved that Bing had been protected from finding out the truth about his mother's past and still believed her to be the happy housewife he remembered. Diane was back to flirting only with her husband. Grace, Hugh and Ryan had tentatively settled into a more comfortable, although not problem-free, family life. By Thanksgiving Day it appeared that everyone was moving on.

Except for me. The police had it wrong. The paper had it wrong. I was the only one who knew what really happened and, like Franklin,

I was cursed with the burden that could only be released upon death. Not my death. Someone else's.

***

The day of Sybil's funeral, Claudia had given me a small package wrapped in *Hello Kitty* paper. Sybil had left all her worldly goods to Claudia but had asked Claudia to give this to me. I put it in my purse, reluctant to look at what she had left for me, and it wasn't until later that night, after Cam had gone to sleep, that I remembered it. I had put on my robe and slippers and crept downstairs to get the package out of my purse. It was small and lightly taped but my fingers fumbled with the brightly colored paper and my eyes filled with tears, picturing Sybil sitting on the side of her bed, wrapping this and knowing she would be gone when I opened it. I eased myself into a chair and slowly pulled the paper apart. Inside was a second package wrapped in tissue paper with a brief note attached.

Franklin loved the works of Edgar Allan Poe.

I contemplated that thought for a few seconds and then opened the tissue paper. Inside was a lovely white linen handkerchief with an 'SB' monogram. If it wasn't the exact handkerchief we had found after the break-in it was certainly its twin. Sybil's handkerchief. I clutched at the handkerchief and wandered into the library, plopping down on the couch in a daze. Mycroft grunted to acknowledge my presence.

So it was Sybil who had broken into our house the first time. Actually, she didn't need to break in because Claudia had a key. She walked in. Why would she do it in the middle of the night? Maybe because she and Claudia were inseparable and that was the only time she was alone. She could hardly leave in the middle of the day and tell Claudia, "I'm going to break into Tamsen and Cam's house. I'll be back in time for dinner." Plus, I was frequently in the house during the day. If it were in the middle of the day I would notice someone coming in my front door and rummaging around. But if we were asleep upstairs, anyone with a key could move in and out of the house at will as long as they didn't make any noise.

"But why, Mycroft? Why would Sybil need to sneak into our house? What did she need?" Mycroft rolled onto his side and his feet began jerking wildly. He was obviously in hot pursuit of a squirrel and not listening to me.

I closed my eyes and must have drifted off. I was jerked awake by the hugest brown eyes in the world. Mycroft obviously was puzzled as to why I was in his "bedroom" in the middle of the night but he was completely accepting and non-judgmental and I didn't feel I needed to explain myself. I was his human and no matter how foolishly I acted he would love and accept me. I reached over and scratched his ears. "I love you," I whispered. Mycroft circled his rug several times and then flopped back down and went to sleep.

I neatly folded up the Hello Kitty wrapping paper and the tissue paper and placed them on top of the note. I would keep them all together until I could figure out what it meant. Maybe it didn't mean anything. Not everything in life was a mystery waiting to be solved. Unless you counted this October. That had been one mystery after another. But now it was over. I bent over to pat Mycroft one last time and for some inexplicable reason thought of "The Purloined Letter." It was a short story by Edgar Allan Poe. In the story a stolen letter is hidden in plain sight, but no one can find it because they are looking in elaborate hiding places. Why was I thinking about Edgar Allan Poe? Because Sybil had wanted me to.

Franklin loved the works of Edgar Allan Poe.

I realized that, after the break-in, nothing had been missing because Sybil hadn't taken anything. She had left something: her monogrammed handkerchief by mistake and something else on purpose. Something that she was directing me to with her final note.

We had two complete collections of Edgar Allan Poe's works. Cam's father had bought a matched leather-bound set thirty years ago and Franklin had had an entire set in his cottage. They were now on the library shelves next to the newer leather-bound set. I ran my fingers along the bindings until I found a collection of short stories containing "The Purloined Letter." I didn't even need to open it up and shake it to see the envelope wedged behind the front cover. It was addressed to me.

The first time I read it I was perched tensely on the edge of the couch, my breath coming faster and faster until I reached the end. The second time I read it I was lying next to Mycroft, reading it quietly to him. The third time I read it I never made it to the end because tears were coming too fast to wipe away and I couldn't go on. I pushed it under the couch and laid down next to Mycroft, snuggling into this warm body and crying into his fur coat.

***

Thanksgiving was a huge success. Bing, Cam and I were an awesome team in the kitchen and everything came out perfect. Abbey's friend from New Zealand was the most charming, intelligent, handsome young man she had ever brought home for us to meet. It was quickly evident that they were not, nor would they ever be, a couple. Too bad. I would have had the most beautiful grandchildren in Birdsey Falls. Maybe that wasn't as grandiose as having the Behrends last name but it was certainly something.

Bing didn't have to talk to anyone he didn't know. Syra was getting her appetite back and even asked for seconds. Grace, Hugh and Ryan were obviously trying hard to be a family and Ryan even entertained us with some elderly antics from Bugg Hill. Diane, Scott and family weren't here. At the last minute they decided to take a family trip for the long Thanksgiving weekend and were at a ski lodge in Vermont. Claudia seemed her usual self and with a couple of people around the table who hadn't known Sybil, it somehow made her absence easier to accept.

The day after Thanksgiving, Abbey and her friends were up early to participate in Black Friday sales. They had been gracious enough to invite Cam and me to join them. Cam had eagerly accepted but I pleaded post-Thanksgiving fatigue and stayed home. I had one more important thing to do.

The envelope from Sybil needed to be hidden, well hidden. I had kept it nearby for several weeks and read it over and over but now it was time to find a resting place for it. It was time to move on. I was home alone but still sought the privacy of the secret stairwell leading from our bedroom to the library in which to sit and read the letter one last time.

Dear Tamsen,

If all has gone well, no one will ever read this letter. But since Franklin's death I have known that it is unlikely. It's important that someone know the complete truth to the kidnapping/murder of Raymond Ketchum as well as the solution to Franklin Behrends' murder. I tell only you, Tamsen. Truth is only beauty when it doesn't destroy someone's life. We cannot protect the dead at the cost of those still living. I trust you to honor this.

If you are reading this it is because I have already told you what I want to be the official version of the Camden Woods murder. Much of what I told you about the ransom incident was correct. Ernie Whitcomb was fascinated with Franklin's treasure maps and he did ask him to make a map of the ransom drop in Camden Woods. Franklin had no idea why or what it meant; he was just flattered that an adult respected his map-making skills. Franklin had no part in the planning or the execution of the kidnapping. All he did was innocently make a map for the guy who did the yard work.

Unfortunately for all of us, it was the night of the ransom drop that Franklin told the four of us about the map he made for Ernie and made us a replica. Franklin, Edmund and Hetty were quite keen on trying to discover what Ernie needed the map for. There was much speculation that he was hiding cigarettes or whiskey in the woods. Maybe naughty magazines. Maybe meeting a lover. When you're fifteen, the idea that you might catch a man and a woman making love was pretty exciting stuff. I remember Hetty hoping he hid cigarettes because she had no interest in seeing Ernie Whitcomb naked. Claudia and I thought the whole thing was funny. We were six and nothing short of a treasure chest of jewels would have satisfied us. It never occurred to us that a man like Ernie Whitcomb would be unlikely to possess a treasure chest of priceless jewels. Like I said, we were only six and still believed in Santa and the Tooth Fairy and becoming princesses when we grew up.

Franklin, Edmund and Hetty never went into Camden Woods the night of the ransom drop. Mr. Behrends had taken them to see Errol Flynn in "The Adventures of Robin Hood". *Franklin told me once that that night, at that movie, was the last time he had been happy. I saw the movie many years later and after that could never picture Robin Hood as anyone other than Franklin. If he had lived the life he was meant to live I believe he would have been an adventurer and a humanitarian. Such a waste.*

As I did many times, I spent the night at Claudia's. Neither of us had a sister and we were inseparable. The Behrends' had some friends over and they were playing cards in the solarium. I think there was a lot of drinking going on too. They were oblivious to two little girls who were supposed to be upstairs with Claudia's nanny. But the nanny was asleep and Claudia and I were wide awake and decided to go to Camden Woods and find that treasure chest with all the jewels. We took a flashlight and Franklin's sled because we knew we wouldn't be able to carry all the treasure in our arms. We had the replica of the map Franklin had made for Ernie and had very little trouble finding the spot. You can imagine how disappointed we were when there was no treasure chest but only a leather bag pushed into a hole at the base of a tree. Between the two of us we pulled it out and rolled it onto the sled and headed home, still convinced that there would be something good inside.

On the way to find the treasure I had pulled Claudia on the sled because she didn't want to walk in the dark. She wanted to ride back on the sled with the treasure on the way home and was put out when I couldn't pull both her and the treasure. We both had to harness ourselves to the rope of the sled to get it back to the house. We pulled that sled for what seemed like hours, falling and getting dirty and tired. Claudia complained all the way back and wanted to abandon it, but I insisted we get it back to the house to show Franklin what we had found by following his map. As usual, Claudia won and we abandoned our treasure in the bushes on the edge of the property right after we dragged it across the road. We did unzip the bag and felt inside, still hoping to find some jewels to take back up to the house with us. We couldn't identify what was inside but were incredibly disappointed to find only a bunch of paper. My dad was a businessman and no one in our family was allowed in his study because of all the important papers in there. So I knew papers were important and I wanted to take the bag back and put it in the hole. I think this is the first and last time Claudia and I had a fight. We were both tired and dirty and bruised from lugging the bag this far and she refused to help me take it back. I argued that someone was expecting to find these papers and it was wrong for us to take them. I knew how angry my father would be if *his important papers were missing. Claudia announced she didn't care about anyone's stupid papers or what happened to them and ran back to the house. I tried by myself to take the bag back but was only able to drag the sled across the street again and then no further. I couldn't do it alone. I abandoned the canvas bag, covering it up with branches and leaves, and went back to Claudia's house. I've been haunted ever since by the decision we made. Claudia never gave it another thought.*

I couldn't sleep all night and around four in the morning I went into Franklin's room to wake him up and tell him what we'd done. I told him that there were important papers in that bag and where I had hidden it and asked him to take it back to the hole so no one would be mad. He was surprised we had actually found something by following his map and was curious. Besides, I was crying hysterically and the only way to calm me down was to go and put that bag back. So he sent me back to bed and went to get it.

That was the end of the whole thing as far as I was concerned. By morning Claudia and I had made up and I didn't want to start fighting all over again by talking about the bag. Her mom took us shopping for new dresses that day because she said there was much too much confusion out in the woods and she wanted to get away from the house. I didn't see Franklin but knew he was reliable so assumed all was well with those stupid papers. Never once that day, or for years to come, did I connect the kidnapping and murder with that leather bag. The innocence of childhood.

I know Franklin changed drastically after that day. Franklin being sick just became a part of who he was and I never thought anything of it other than to miss the adventures he was always creating and telling us about. Hetty and Edmund drifted off into their own lives. Claudia and I were totally absorbed in our own world.

When I was seventeen I was completely obsessed with the romantic poets—Yeats, Shelley, and especially Lord Byron. I used to imagine that I too could "walk in beauty like the night" and inspire great poetry in handsome men. Franklin became a Byronic figure to me. He had a tortured and unattainable quality about him and he was very handsome although devoid of all the vigor and enthusiasm he had at fifteen. He was twenty-six but not really a man of the world as he never left his house. Whenever I was there with Claudia, he just wandered around with a book in his hand, his hair flopping over one eye, oblivious to everyone. Suddenly, at seventeen, that seemed the most romantic and sad thing in the world and I was determined to walk in beauty and bring him out of his malaise, no doubt caused by being too sensitive to survive in an everyday world.

One afternoon when I knew Franklin was home alone and I could see him reading in the solarium, I went over to see if my love and beauty could rouse him from his melancholy. I entered the solarium and he was so absorbed in what he was reading that he never knew I was there until I was close enough to touch him. I didn't dare be quite that bold so I coughed and he looked up at me as if trying to remember who I was. I was imagining how the sun was catching my hair like a halo around my face. I knew my dress was very flattering to my womanly figure and that the color accented my eyes and made my skin glow. I stood there in expectation that suddenly I would see the light come into his eyes and that he would reach out his hand to me and draw me close, realizing that I was everything he had been waiting for. I was the lifeline he needed to return to the person he had been. I remember thinking that this was probably the most important moment of my life and I stood there, drinking it in.

"Claudia must never know!" he yelled at me. I took a couple steps away from him. He wanted a secret romance? Of course, they were the best kind. But what about when we got married, wouldn't she have to know then? I was confused. "No matter what it takes or what you have to do, she must never know."

"Never?" I whispered.

"Never. You and I must take this to our graves. As long as Claudia is alive she can never know. There are secrets that do not permit themselves to be told. We must take up this burden, heavy in horror, and carry it with us to the grave."

I thought his poetic way of stating things was romantic but I was fairly sure that a burden heavy with horror was not the romance I had pictured. I was afraid. "Burden?"

"Claudia's childish selfishness killed a man. She must never know. The horror of it, the burden, it would ruin her life. We can't let that happen. Swear to me." Then he reached out and grabbed my hand, holding it so hard I was afraid the bones would break. "Swear to me!"

"Yes, yes, I swear," I told him, the tears running down my face. "I swear she'll never know."

He abruptly released my hand and turned away from me. "I took the money back but it was too late. Ketchum was already dead, lying there soaked in blood by the hole where the money was supposed to be. I just stood there and stared at him. His eyes were open and he stared back, asking me why he had to die. I kept telling him I was sorry. I explained to him that Claudia was a little girl and she was too tired to bring the money back. He didn't understand. He didn't forgive me. Now that we had all handled the bag I was afraid there might be clues on it that would make the police think I killed him, so I took the money back home. It was too late for it to help him now. Claudia must never know. We must protect her. It would ruin her life."

I stood there a while longer but Franklin never turned around, never looked at me again. I quietly left.

If Claudia had let us take the money back right away Raymond Ketchum wouldn't have died. And that is what really happened in Camden Woods. Franklin and I kept the secret for seventy years. And

371

then, for some reason, he decided to write all about it. He had made me swear and now he was going to tell people. I couldn't let him do that to Claudia. I've always protected her. I couldn't let Franklin stop me now. So I killed him and took the papers, his important papers, to keep the secret we had sworn to keep. In the end, I know he was grateful.

Once again sobbing with pity for the brave and valiant boy who had devoted his life to saving his sister's peace of mind, and for the beautiful young girl who had dedicated her life to protecting her best friend, I gently folded up the letter for the last time and slipped it under the carpeting on the stairs. Then I slowly closed the door to the bedroom and, alone on the stairs of the secret passage, with no one in the house but me, I screamed and berated the selfish little girl who had refused to take the ransom back into the woods and who had spent her whole life being protected by everyone around her, even at the cost of their own happiness and peace of mind. And as much as I wanted her to know, as much as I wanted to hurt her with the truth I knew, for the sake of Franklin and Sybil and all they had sacrificed, I would carry this burden, heavy in horror to my grave.

Chapter Thirty-Five

"Happy anniversary to you. Happy anniversary to you. Happy anniversary, dear WOACA. Happy anniversary to you." Bing gingerly set the three-tiered chocolate wedding-style cake on the wicker table, beaming like a proud papa. "Okay everyone, blow out the candles and make a wish! WOACA is four years old today!"

We gathered around the table, arms around each other, and blew out the four candles. "A groom and four brides?" I asked. "We seem to be celebrating an anniversary, a birthday and a wedding all at the same time."

"I've never made a wedding cake. I wanted to try something new. I couldn't find any cake toppers of just regular men and women so I had to settle for the groom and four brides," he answered.

"They're cute. Where did you get them?" Grace asked plucking one of the brides off the cake and licking the frosting off her feet.

"Online, of course," Bing laughed. "Even if I ever left the house to go shopping I wouldn't have the nerve to buy one groom and four brides. People would think I was some kind of polygamist."

The first Tuesday in May meeting of WOACA is always special. It's our anniversary meeting. We were meeting in the solarium on a glorious spring day. The tulips were in full bloom and the view out the solarium windows exploded with color. It was impossible to be anything but happy and content, surrounded by beauty, special friends and a three-tiered chocolate wedding cake.

If someone took a picture of the five of us gathered around the cake it would look like a poster for friendship. Five friends, each unique, yet each bound together by common threads. A moment frozen in time. Yet over the past eight months we had all suffered through personal problems as well as doubts about each other.

We all were still struggling. Diane's family wanted to take a four-week trip out west; Diane wanted time to be alone. Syra had desperately wanted to enter the Boston Marathon; her stamina gave out after a mile. Grace wanted a quiet, loving home life; Ryan wanted nothing to do with her. I was worried that the secret I carried would come between Cam and me; I had made Sybil a promise.

"Let's make a toast to the publication of the latest Perry Many Paws book!" Grace announced. "Now Tamsen can focus full time on her New Orleans novel.

"The bodice ripper?" Syra asked.

"It isn't a bodice ripper! It's a historical adventure slash mystery. No bodice ripping," I replied.

"But there are sex scenes, right?" Grace asked. "From what you've told me, your heroine isn't above taking a handsome man to bed to woo secrets out of him."

"Too much information," Bing announced covering his ears.

"The book is full of the social history of New Orleans post-Civil War. There are murders connected with the carpetbaggers bleeding the defeated South of its riches. And yes, the heroine is beautiful, full of life, not concerned with convention. She is in favor of equality between the sexes and that includes in the bedroom …"

"So there are sex scenes!" Diane said.

"Yes. But not too graphic." I reached over and pulled Bing's hands away from his ears. "No graphic sex scenes."

"Quite a departure from Perry Many Paws," Syra pointed out.

"True. You can only take so much Perry Many Paws and then you're ready to move on to the next stage of your life. This New Orleans series, if I can get it published and continue to write it as a series, is the next stage of my writing career."

"Is *Perry Many Paws and the Balloon Adventure* your last Perry book?" Bing asked. "I really love the Perry books."

"It's my last one for now. Maybe I'll take him up again in the future, but for right now I want to concentrate on my new book."

"Did you finally think of a name for your lusty bed-hopping heroine? I know you've been struggling with it." Grace asked.

"Yes. I'm calling her Fanny Behrends ..."

"Fanny Bare Ends?" Bing asked. "That sounds kind of graphic."

"Not Bare Ends. Behrends. B.E.H.R.E.N.D.S."

"Oh, God. Does Claudia know?" Grace laughed. "You know how she treasures the sanctity of the Behrends name."

"No, she doesn't know. I don't ever want Claudia to know I'm writing this series ..."

"How can she not know once it's published?" Diane asked. "Your name will be on the book and Grace will have it in her front window for Willoughby and the rest of the mannequins to read."

"My agent and I both agreed that my name is so synonymous with the Perry Many Paws series that I should use another name for this book. We wouldn't want kids to think this was a gigantic Perry Many Paws book and start reading it."

"So what'll be your pen name?" Syra asked.

"Sybil Bane. The night of the Halloween party Sybil told me that she liked the name Sybil Bane ..."

"Honoring Sybil with the exact kind of book she would relish. I love it," Grace laughed. "Perfect."

"No one in Birdsey Falls, with the exception of the five of us, Cam and Abbey, will know that I'm Sybil Bane. So, even if Claudia heard about or read the book she would have no idea that I was the one who used the Behrends name so outrageously."

"Payback?" Syra asked.

"Without a doubt. I'm not sure how Cam will take it, though." I said. "It could be a bit of a problem. But I won't change my mind. I *need* to call her Fanny Behrends. Nothing else will work for me."

"Maybe he'll understand," Grace said. "Having no one know the real identity of Sybil Bane will be a great mystery. Even if Claudia tortures me to find out who used the Behrends name so cavalierly, I'll never tell." She had settled into the room's most comfortable chair and was savoring her slice of cake. "Life in Birdsey Falls needs more mystery."

Bing cut another slice of cake and the heady scent of coffee filled the air. Between the rich layers of chocolate cake was an intense coffee mousse with ground-up chocolate-covered coffee beans. I don't drink coffee but I love the smell and the taste. I practically stuck my nose into the cake to savor the scent. Heavenly. The first bite deserved my full attention. But while my taste buds were totally absorbed in their task, my mind meandered back to Sybil.

I thought of her final letter to me and the part Claudia had played in the whole sad tragedy. I had learned that some secrets do become burdens so heavy in horror that they must be taken to the grave. For the sake of Franklin, Sybil and Cam, I was willing to carry this secret to the grave. But no one can blame a girl if she needs to lighten her burden from time to time. Fanny Behrends would be a big help in lightening mine.

Sneak Preview of the second book in the Women of a Certain Age Series, 'Death of a Hot Flasher".

Death Of A Hot Flasher

"Do you think they've lost Ambrosia? We've been waiting forever."

My mother-in-law didn't respond. She was staring intently at a row of urns as if some street performer had placed a shell under one and her life depended on picking the right one.

"Claudia." I nudged her elbow. "Do you think …?"

"I heard you. I'm wondering if Edward would prefer to be in that metallic blue urn rather than that flowery one I picked out."

I stared at her while she remained transfixed by the urns. "Edward's been dead for over twenty five years …"

"I'm well aware of how long my husband has been dead. I just thought …"

"But you would have to dig him up to change urns …"

"*I* wouldn't have to dig him up. They have people for that."

I couldn't help it. I started to giggle. The vision of this seventy-something-year-old woman with her impeccable makeup, perfectly coiffed hair and three hundred dollar shoes digging up a cemetery was too much for me. I giggle when I'm stressed. We'd been sitting for almost forty-five minutes in the tastefully decorated parlor of the Musgrave Funeral Home, waiting for someone to bring us the cremains of Ambrosia Fox. Ambrosia was a dear friend of Claudia's former housekeeper. She was the last of her biological family and we were doing a favor for the people who had been Ambrosia's extended family for the past fifteen years, the Bugg Hill Senior Home residents. My daughter, Abbey, was working at Bugg Hill this summer and we were having lunch there with her today. It only seemed right to volunteer to pick Ambrosia up on our way over.

My mother-in-law squeezed my arm with a fierce strength alarming in a seventy-plus- year-old woman who barely weighed 100 pounds.

"Behave. You're embarrassing me."

"How? There's no one here. That's the problem. I think they lost Ambrosia." I glanced out the window and watched a man play tag with his daughter while he waited for his outdoor grill to burn down. At least someone was going to get some lunch today. As I stared at the grill a gruesome thought occurred.

"If they lose someone's ashes you don't think they, um, substitute different ashes in their place, do you?"

Claudia gave me her 'I can't believe anyone could be so stupid' look. "Don't talk like an imbecile. It embarrasses me. I hear someone coming."

I didn't hear a thing but sure enough the woman who had ushered us in here almost an hour ago appeared with a tasteful velvet bag and some papers for us to sign. She talked in a soft whisper as she handed us Ambrosia, never referring to the long wait, and smoothly ushered us out the door. As I unlocked the car door I handed the velvet bag to Claudia who would have nothing to do with it.

"I am not riding across town clutching a complete stranger's remains. Put her in the trunk."

"I knew and liked Ambrosia. I can't put her in the trunk."

"I'm not holding her." Claudia flounced into the front seat and firmly closed her door. I put Ambrosia in the back seat, seat belt pulled snuggly across her velvet bag, whispering, "This is what I have to deal with Ambrosia. Sometimes it's not easy still being alive."

Claudia and I were headed to Bugg Hill Senior Home, the mid-scale senior living center where the middle class sought community living once their homes had become too much to handle. Claudia, of course, lived at Ashland Belle, the upscale senior living estate where the upper class sought refined living once their house staff found their homes too much to handle. My daughter, Abbey, had just completed her freshman year at Boston University and was working as kitchen helper and general factotum at Bugg Hill. She had invited Claudia and me to have lunch there today as her guests. It never occurred to me that Claudia would actually accept the invitation as the residents 'weren't really her type' but here she was, over-dressed and over-jeweled, looking like she had just come from a royal wedding.

Although Claudia barely tolerated me throughout my twenty-five year marriage to her son, she couldn't seem to get enough of me now that Sybil was gone. Her devoted friend of seventy years had died this past October. My husband, Cam, and I had assumed she would fill the void Sybil left with all her other friends at Ashland Belle, but it turns out that all the friends that clustered around my mother-in-law, had been more Sybil's friends than Claudia's. This was perfectly understandable. Sybil was a warm, loving, generous, free spirited woman. Claudia was the spawn of Satan dripping in pearls and sarcasm.

The entrance to Bugg Hill, a hand painted sign with an arrow, was underwhelming, as was the building itself. It was built to provide a comfortable residence for seniors who needed a simpler and safer lifestyle. Claudia surveyed the rambling box-like structure with distaste.

"It certainly lacks any architectural aesthetic. It's totally devoid of personality. Why would someone live here?" she questioned.

I went to open the passenger door. She would have sat in the car all day if I didn't. "They live here because they can afford it. Not everyone can pay $5000 a month for an apartment, Claudia."

"Really? How odd."

I'd been to Bugg Hill numerous times. My friend Diane's parents and Claudia's former housekeeper, Millie live here as does a woman, Muriel, whom I met last fall. Now with Abbey working here, Bugg Hill was becoming a home away from home—which is why I stopped short when we came in the door. I immediately noticed a new reception desk in the middle of the large lounge right inside the door. I was dumbfounded. Claudia stood there waiting to be greeted.

An elderly woman with a hawk-like face wearing a great deal of make-up sat behind the desk dressed in what appeared to be a vintage suit from maybe the 1930's or 40's. Perched on her head was matching hat with an elaborate hatpin. A gold nameplate on the desk said "Miss Maude Bellamy". The woman looked up and cleared her throat. Seven times.

"I don't believe you have an appointment. You can't see Mr. Trotter without an appointment. I'm surprised you would think you could." She reeked disapproval. I thought my mother-in-law was the only one who could do that. Claudia confidently approached the desk.

"Rest assured, Miss Bellamy, that we do not wish to see this Mr. Trotter. We are here to have lunch with my granddaughter and to deliver the cremains of Ambrosia …"

"Oh, dear." Miss Bellamy pulled a lacy handkerchief from her sleeve and dabbed her eyes.

"I'm sorry," I apologized. "Was she a good friend of yours?"

"Not really. But no one should die before their time," she replied giving her eyes one last furious dab and returning her handkerchief to her sleeve. "I'm the only one who understands." She straightened up and stared at us. "Can I help you?"

"Well, yes. We need to leave Ambrosia's, uh, urn with someone ..."

Miss Bellamy's arm flew up and she pointed down the hall. "There." She resumed writing. Claudia gave her a head jerk and a sniff to let her know what she thought of her manners and we headed to the dining room. "As my mother would have said, *that* woman has a face that would benefit greatly by darkness. Come along Tamsen."

We unceremoniously left Ambrosia and her velvet bag on the desk of Chaplain Rose and headed to the dining room to meet Abbey. Claudia was disappointed that she couldn't have shrimp cocktail on demand, had to use paper rather than cloth napkins, had to sit on a card table chair rather than a padded Windsor chair, and that if you wanted wine you had to bring your own.

"It's different than Ashland Belle, Grandma, but still a wonderful place to live," Abbey assured her. "I love working here. Everyone is so appreciative and they ..."

"Is that dreadful Kelly boy still working here? I think I see him sneaking around," Claudia interrupted. Sure enough, Ryan Kelly, the step-son of my best friend, Grace, was refilling water glasses and glancing furtively our way. Ryan and I weren't on very friendly terms since an incident last fall when he broke into my house and nearly scared me to death. He had been given probation and community service at Bugg Hill Senior Home. He must have some redeeming qualities because Bugg Hill offered him a part-time job when his community service was over.

Abbey nodded her head, her long curls catching the light. Although she looked like me, she had her father's beautiful red curly hair and freckles. Claudia had considered Cam quite an aberration when he had been born a red head. She was more accepting of Abbey.

"Ryan's not really dreadful, grandma, just sort of odd. The residents here seem to like him."

Before Claudia could launch into a tirade against Ryan, I changed the subject. "I don't see Muriel here today. She's not ill is she?"

"It's Wednesday, Mom. The last few Wednesdays she and the other ladies in the knitting group have skipped lunch. I'm not sure why."

That was a real oddity. If Maude Bellamy had a face that could benefit greatly by darkness then Muriel Wilson had a body that could benefit greatly by a decade of skipped lunches. I couldn't imagine what would keep Muriel away from her lunch. I love to knit but not at the cost of a good meal and I was a third Muriel's size.

"What *is* this?" Claudia demanded, timidly poking at her entre.

"Macaroni and cheese," Abbey answered. "It's pretty much a staple here. The most popular dish they serve …"

"I don't know about this …"

"Try it grandma, it's good." Abbey turned to me and I expected her to roll her eyes, but then remembered that she adored her grandmother. Abbey and Cam both seemed totally oblivious to how frustrating and annoying Claudia could be. Luckily, I was aware enough for the three of us. "I know you like a mystery, mom. This whole absent-every-Wednesday-lunch by the knitting group is just weird. They used to meet and knit right outside the door every Wednesday so they could be the first ones into the dining room. Now they don't show up at all."

"Did you ask any of them about it?"

"Yes. I asked Ivy Davis and she just gave me this Mona Lisa smile. Same with Trudy Mills and Agatha Whitney. When I asked Muriel she just made this grimace and said, "There's no accounting for tastes." The other three seemed sort of spacey and Muriel seemed disgusted. It's very weird."

Claudia pushed her macaroni and cheese around on her plate but I don't think she ever ate any before she pushed the plate away. "Maybe they don't like the food."

"I don't think that's it, grandma. At the risk of being unkind, all the ladies in the knitting group cannot get on the elevator at the same time or it exceeds the weight limit ..."

"You mean four of them weigh over 1500 pounds?"

"No, seven of them do. In addition to the four I mentioned there's also Enid Doyle, Thelma Harrington ..."

"Diane's mother ..." I interrupted.

"And Millie Knapp, your old housekeeper, Grandma."

Claudia daintily patted her lips. "Mrs. Knapp? Really? This isn't Ashland Belle but I can't imagine how Mrs. Knapp can afford to live here. She was just a housekeeper. And she didn't have any family."

Abbey glanced over at me. I shrugged. "Dad pays her bills."

"Since when?" Claudia asked with great indignation. "Tamsen, did you know Cam was paying her bills? Why would he do that? She was just a housekeeper when he was growing up. I'm surprised he even noticed her. This is very disturbing."

"Why is it disturbing, Grandma?"

Claudia reached out and patted Abbey's hand. "You don't know what you are talking about dear. You're too young to understand what is appropriate and what isn't ..."

"That's not true, Grandma. I'm almost nineteen years old ..."

"Quiet dear. You're too young to understand what you don't understand." Claudia smiled indulgently at Abbey then turned to me with a cold stony glare. Jekyll and Hyde. "Explain Tamsen."

I was longing to tell her that rather than being oblivious of Mrs. Knapp slaving away in the kitchen of Claudia's enormous monstrosity of a house, Cam had considered Mrs. Knapp a surrogate mother.

Claudia had tired of the whole mothering experience by the time Cam was born six years after his sister Cassandra. Claudia had taken one look at him with his red hair and very un-Behrends like features and emotionally shooed him away. If it weren't for the attention of his father, now deceased, and Mrs. Knapp, Cam would have been a much neglected child. Mrs. Knapp taught him to cook, made sure he had his homework done, proofread his papers, kept track of doctor appointments and made sure his father attended every baseball game and track meet. She even helped Cam fill out his college applications. While Cam loved his mother, he felt a deep and abiding affection for Mrs. Knapp. When her savings ran out Cam stepped in and took over her daily finances. He even paid for her sister, which apparently Claudia had no idea existed, to come to Birdsey Falls twice a year to visit her. But I didn't want to go into all of that with Claudia right now. Or ever.

"There's nothing to explain, Claudia. Cam and I can do what we please with our money. We choose to help out Mrs. Knapp as she is a long time friend of the family ..."

"She was the *housekeeper*. It's not as if I didn't pay her. Are you going to support the postman and the newspaper delivery boy for the rest of their lives also? How about that homely checkout girl at the grocery store? Or that boy with all the jewelry stuck to his face at the gas station?"

We were saved from the rest of Claudia's rant by the arrival of Ted Harrington, my friend Diane's father and current resident of Bugg Hill. I've never met a plainer, more non-descript man than Ted Harrington. He literally blends into his surroundings. He would have made a great spy. Ted was outgoing and happy, especially on macaroni and cheese days, but today he wandered to our table and, after giving us a distracted greeting, just stared at the wall. I could tell Claudia was deeply offended. She expected to be fawned over especially as she was not a regular at Bugg Hill. I reached over and squeezed Ted's wrinkled hand.

"What's wrong? You're not eating your mac and cheese. Do you feel all right?"

Ted gave me a weak smile and patted my hand. "I'm worried about Thelma. Something strange is going on. She and her knitting friends are up to something. And she won't tell me what it is. We've never had secrets before. Yup. Something strange."

"They stopped eating lunch on Wednesdays. Maybe they're working on a special project," Abbey offered. "I'm sure it's nothing to worry about."

"Thelma's been acting strange …"

"In what way?" I asked. Ted's face got red and he glanced uneasily at Abbey and Claudia. "Well …"

"Go on. You'll feel better if you talk about it," I said.

"It's just that lately, um, well, lately she's been, you know."

Abbey and I looked at each other and shrugged. I glanced at Claudia. She was staring intently at her hand, waving it back and forth to watch the sun reflect off her diamond. Ted leaned in closer to Abbey and me and cleared his throat.

"She's been frisky."

"Frisky?" I wasn't sure he and I were thinking the same thing. Did he mean she just had more energy?

"I don't mind, you know, her being frisky and all. But sometimes she gets frisky after seven o'clock and I just can't handle those late nights. I'm in my 70's you know. I don't understand how knitting through lunch on Wednesday afternoons makes a lady frisky that evening. But it happens every Wednesday. And, for the last two weeks she hasn't even taken her knitting with her. Something's going on."

"I think you're right." I said. "Someone needs to infiltrate the Wednesday knitting group."

33312201R00237

Made in the USA
Lexington, KY
23 June 2014